UNDER
THE
MOON

UNDER
THE
MOON

Suzanne Stewart

ARCHWAY
PUBLISHING

This is a work of fiction. All of the characters, names, incidents, organizations, and dialogue in this novel are either the products of the author's imagination or are used fictitiously.

Archway Publishing books may be ordered through booksellers or by contacting:

Archway Publishing
1663 Liberty Drive
Bloomington, IN 47403
www.archwaypublishing.com
844-669-3957

ISBN: 978-1-6657-3817-0 (sc)
ISBN: 978-1-6657-3818-7 (hc)
ISBN: 978-1-6657-3819-4 (e)

Library of Congress Control Number: 2023901860

Book Cover - Suzanne Stewart, Rachel Sten
Book Design - Rachel Sten
Illustrations - Suzanne Stewart

Print information available on the last page.

Archway Publishing rev. date: 03/31/2023

Preface

This story is written in honor of my two daughters who are half-Japanese and half-Caucasian. While they were growing up, there were few Asian stories and very little written about Japanese immigration to Hawaii. This novel describes a little section of the very rich cultural life and the changing times of the people from that period.

Set in two different countries, Japan and Hawaii, the story begins in Japan—Nippon, the Japanese name—at the end of the 1800s during the Meiji era. This was a tumultuous time in Japan's history, when the country went from an agrarian feudal system to an industrial economy that rivaled any in the West in less than fifty years. It was at this time, because of economic upheavals, weather-related droughts, and new unbalanced tax levies, that so many Japanese emigrated to Hawaii and the West Coast.

The main character is of two different classes in Japan to show the convolution of the class system during the Meiji period and to create a semblance of life at that time. At the beginning of the Meiji era, class structure was very rigid. Merchants were the lowest class, just above the untouchables, because they dealt with money, which was considered lowly by the Confucian values on which Japanese society was based. Above the merchant was the farmer class; farmers were more valuable because they provided food, an essential item. Above the farmers came the samurai, the soldier/philosopher class, who were supported monetarily by the local lords. At the top were the members of the court and the royal family.

Due to extreme competition with western powers, Japan changed its economic and cultural structures to align more with those of the West. At this time, the lowly merchant class rose to the top because of their economic power, while many samurais were floating in a sort of no-man's-land, with no longer any formal place in society or means of income. Some samurai were part of the newly created government, but many were not. Those samurai families who looked ahead made alliances with the merchant class, such as we see in Ueme's fictional family.

A note about the use of the word *modern* in the story. Please remember that every person thinks that their time is "modern." But what we consider modern today is much more advanced than what was modern for a Meiji woman.

For My Daughters

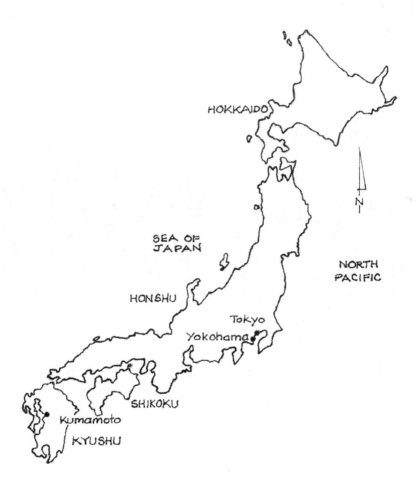

FOUR MAJOR ISLANDS OF NIPPON

Village of Five Bridges

Kumamoto Prefecture

Island of Kyushu

Nippon or Nihon

(Japan)

late 1890's

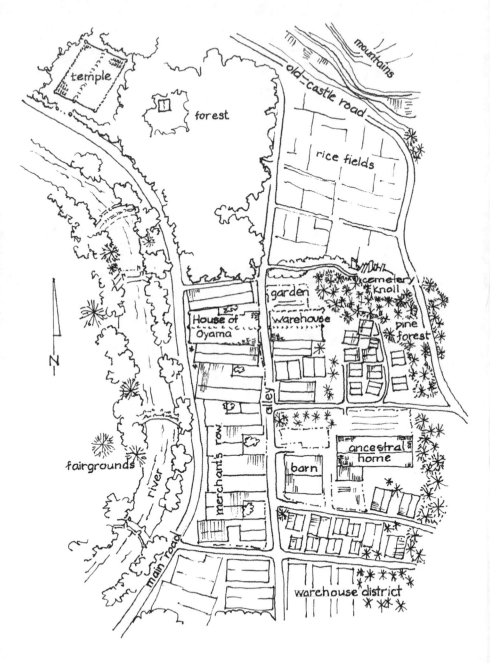

Village of Five Bridges

Chapter 1

HOME

September 1899, Cemetery Knoll, Village of Five Bridges, Kumamoto Prefecture, Japan

It is dawn. A young woman is on a knoll overlooking a vast expanse of farmland stretched out beyond her. She is talking to the land. "How can 'paradise' be any more beautiful than you, my valley?"

Leaning against a large granite gravestone, she places some fruit and rice balls on its ledge. She knows they are waiting for her. The chests are packed and on the carriage. Why is it all so rushed? The pain of leaving. The pain of not understanding anything entirely yet having to keep moving because life kept moving. She longed for childhood days when months were counted in hours and the ends were unseen. How can she remember all this? She can hardly breathe for the sorrow choking her throat. Why does she have to leave her home?

Bowing to the stone and then turning toward the fields below, the rice appearing as green waves blown by the soft winds of early morning, she whispers, "Goodbye."

May 1898, Cemetery Knoll, Village of Five
Bridges, Kumamoto Prefecture, Japan

The rain had stopped. There I was, thinking about my life, me, Ueme, seventeen, just graduated from high school, contemplating my place in the universe.

My arms were getting wet through my cotton hakata, as I was leaning on the damp memorial stone in our family cemetery, sleepily gazing out at the valley below. Steam was rising off the rice fields as the sun warmed the earth. The young rice shoots poking out of the water gave the valley a gentle blue-green color. Here and there, water in the irrigation streams sparkled with reflected sunlight. A flock of geese flew north towards the distant mountains that were visible above a horizontal cloud of mist. The squawking of those birds interrupted the quiet of the early morning and my daydreaming.

I loved this spot, so private, so old. To the east, on my right, was the Castle Road. The samurais had marched up this road every year coming from the southern regions on their way to pay homage to the daimyo, ruler of the province. The road stretched north alongside the valley towards the foothills and then curved at the end of the valley, making its way for many more miles west toward the castle that lay far beyond view, past the forest that is the western edge of our valley.

My grandfather had loved to come to this spot to bring gifts to honor our ancestors. He'd often brought me here to tell me stories from his youth. It was here the past came to life. One could imagine the samurais on horses, in armor and helmets, their attendants carrying the banners representing each village, the colors flowing in the breeze. In those days, the valley was mostly meadow, where deer and rabbits and the occasional mountain cat roamed. The skies were so full of birds that, during spring migration, the elders say, they darkened the whole sky, moving as giant flapping undulations toward the majestic heights of the mountains. No wonder it was believed the ancestors lived there on top of everything.

Beyond the fir trees behind me, the town had grown south, and the rice fields had expanded north past the edge of the valley jumping over the old road, climbing the foothills. The castle road was not used much, because our main road now ran alongside the river to the west beyond the forest. The daimyo was now an elected official with less power, no military, and now called governor. There were no more samurai processions.

My obachan, my grandmother, was pleased for that. She would often repeat the story of my uncle returning from the Satsuma Rebellion of the samurai in the early days of the Meiji reign. As a young boy infatuated by the glamor of war, Uncle had run off to join it, against his parent's wishes, to be a water boy for the warriors. From this spot here on the gravesite knoll, my grandmother had watched the defeated samurais returning home. Seeing her son's body draped over a horse's back, she'd run screaming across the valley to him. He bore the wound to this day, as he walked with a slight limp from field to field checking on his rice crop.

The sun, having risen higher now, was warming my arms and shoulders. My eyes had started to close when I heard the sorrowful moaning tune of the shakuhachi coming from the forest. Ah, the flute player was awake. I was reminded of why I was there, to put offerings on top of the monuments for the ancestors, especially for Grandfather, on the anniversary of his death two years ago. I bent down and removed the rice sweets and fruit from the folded silk furoshiki bundle I had brought with me.

Finished with my task, I stood and turned west to start down the path back to the alley. A cooling breeze from the ocean miles away blew the hair from my face. I had a full day ahead of me with household chores. Ah, my reward for rudely "spying" on the flute player with my friends yesterday, but really just the chores every woman had to get out of the way to have a life. I was feeling a bit resentful that, no matter what infractions my brother would make, he would not get rewarded with more chores.

At the end of the cemetery path, I walked through our vegetable patch, shooing some rabbits out. The noise from the alley caught my attention. When I had left the house at dawn, all had been deliciously quiet. Now the alley, being the epicenter of morning village life, was in full action. Kitchen boys were scurrying up the alley carrying the night soil away from the houses, saying, "Sumimasen" (So sorry, please excuse), trying to avoid bumping into anyone with their smelly load.

Peddlers of all sorts, selling vegetables, tofu, fish, and even knife sharpening, wandered down the alley knocking on the kitchen doors. "Ohayo gozaimasu" (Good morning), in many different voices, a rhythm sounded the morning chorus.

Sitting on the bench in the alley outside our kitchen were my two schoolmates, Ito and Saiko, waiting for me. At my approach, their faces lit up.

"Hi there, Ueme. Your mother said we could wait for you here." Ito smiled at me, moving over on the bench to make room for me.

Saiko leaned out to see me as I sat and questioned, "Where have you been so early already?"

"We have come to talk about our futures, maybe our future husbands?" Ito laughed.

"Ah, well, I am afraid I will have no time for frivolous talk today—though I would just love to escape by listening to Saiko recount one of her romantic magazine stories!" I sighed.

"Oh, why?" Ito asked.

"My parents were upset that we were rude in sneaking up on the flute player yesterday. Apparently, he is an old friend of the family."

Ito straightened her shoulders and, with surprise, said, "You are being punished because of that? My father explained to me how disrespectful we had been, how the old must be revered, but I am not being punished! Oh, such a shame that this would be the end result of our little excursion into the woods yesterday. We just wanted to have some childish fun spying on people as we used to do. Just a kind of graduation prank before our adult lives come crashing down on us!"

Saiko, a little more sheepishly, added, "My parents hardly spoke of it. But their silence has been overwhelming. I asked what I could do to make amends, and they spoke as if a grave crime had occurred, and nothing was to be done. Mother will forget it shortly, but Father is not as forgiving."

"Oh, you samurai families! You take everything too seriously. Yes, we were giggling and laughing while trying to peek through the bamboo at him. But he had kicked his dirty foot at my head. I had no idea he could see us. You have to admit he is strange, living off in the woods by himself and waving that bamboo stick around, dancing in his field." Ito frowned.

"He was practicing kendo, samurai swordplay. They use bamboo sticks instead of steel swords like that for practice. My brother used to play that with me before he became too sophisticated to play with a girl."

"Oh, I am sorry you are being punished for my giggles. But here, let's not forget that we graduated with honors all three of us just two days ago! My parents have given all three of us presents. Take this and open it later. You will love it!"

Ito's merchant family sold beautiful trinkets, heirloom jewelry, and quality gift items. My package, wrapped in colorful rice paper, was sure to be lovely. I placed it in the fold of my hakata sleeve to look at later.

Ito leaned over and pulled a small bag from her sleeve. "I almost forgot. Here's a few coins that you earned for the combs we decorated last week. People loved them. We sold them all. Let's plan a time to decorate more combs. My father says they are a real hit with the schoolgirls."

I grabbed the bag and put it also in my sleeve and leaned in to my friends. "Shh, I don't want my parents to know. They say I have no need for money, but they do give my brother his allotment of coins each week."

"Ah, that's the samurai influence in your family, I am sure. My parents applaud my efforts to make money for myself." Ito sat straight up on the bench with pride.

Madam Iwata, our kitchen maid, was at the door. "Ueme, your obachan will be here in a short amount of time. You need to prepare the *onagaishi*" (the present) "to bring with you. Right now, your father has a guest who needs attending to. You have much to do. Come inside."

Saiko and Ito leaned over and looked at me questioningly.

"I am to apologize in person." I grimaced and bowed my head slightly.

"Owoowh," came as a whisper from the two of them as they quietly slipped off the bench to go up the alley to their respective homes.

Madam now had her hands on her hips, her sleeves pushed up in a stance that meant hurry up.

Inside, the kitchen was cool. Madam was there with a dishpan of water. "Ueme, how you love the dirt! Sandals are for wearing, not carrying. You are so like my youngest! But she turned out fine, as you will. She is married with two children and one on the way. I no longer worry! Wash your hands and those feet. This may be a dirt floor, but it is clean! The tray is ready, but you need to change your yukata first. There is a freshly washed one in the laundry. Go change there. But do not worry, not one of our favorites."

The tone in Madam's voice told me that Otasan was ready to get rid of this particular customer. Tea time!

As I changed into a different yukata, I thought about my changing role as a young woman. I hoped the customer with Otasan would appreciate my gracefulness when I brought the tea. I wanted the people of this town to notice that I was no longer a child. I had my high school certificate, I had responsibilities, and I was a gracious hostess. Bolstering my ego, I kept thinking about who I was and my place in the world.

Mother had reminded me often, "You have the best of both worlds with samurai and merchant heritage. Merchant women run businesses and are able to speak more freely than samurai women. Samurai women are perceived to have status and elegance. You can have both." I had the best of both worlds. This aligned with the modern view of women, as my friends and I had often discussed. However, I thought often that I would prefer to be the one having tea with the customers than the one in the back counting up the accounts as mother had to do.

My obachan, being the samurai woman she was, did not agree. She lamented that manners were being ignored. She had grown up under the rule of the shogunate,when samurai had noble positions and carried swords in the street! Imagine, they were allowed to chop off anybody's head if they felt somehow displeased! I was happy samurais did not roam the streets with their swords anymore. As I washed my feet, I kept thinking about the roles of women.

My friends and I read the newspapers from Tokyo. We saw the fashions that were advertised, and sometimes Mother asked our opinions on the styles. Women were gaining some respect. Mother said that women had long had respect in the merchant class, her class. However, the whole class was considered lowly. So, that made us respected as top of the bottom of the pile? It was confusing. Ito, of merchant class; Saiko, of samurai class; and I discussed these issues. It affected our generation of women. We hoped things were changing for the better for us.

Having changed my yukata, I was back in the kitchen, and I looked around. Morning chores were done. The dirt floor was swept. Breakfast had been cleared away. Madam Iwata and mother were sitting on a bench in the alley cleaning vegetables and discussing the dinner meal. Father had a customer in the shop. Poking my head out the door, I said I would be taking the tray in to father now.

Mother spoke up. "Your father is not with a customer but, rather, the village headman talking about town business. He will be anxious to get rid of the gossipy little man." Then she turned her head toward Madam, and they both laughed.

The black lacquer tea tray was laid out with some rice crackers and some sweets. I poured the steaming water into the bronze teapot. I chose two small teacups with blue raku designs covering the insides of the cups. Father preferred these simple cups to the delicate Chinese porcelain cups. My otasan had the simple taste of samurai Zen philosophy.

Father's samurai training placed highest value on learning and the arts, such as poetry and brush painting. However, I noticed that this artistry demanded that samurai women served them. Women's role was not so lofty. This was confusing to me. How did these roles affect me as a modern woman? Saiko, Ito, and I wanted to be fully conscious of our lives and to have some control over our destinies. We did not want to be like our obachans! My thoughts kept running away with concern over my future role. I must put my attention on my tasks today.

Walking silently and steadily through our inner chambers, I bowed at the entry to the shop. "Otasan, please excuse my interruption." This was necessary to say, even though Father had requested that I bring the tea to him. Politeness! "Perhaps you desire some tea?"

I placed the tray on a small low table, away from the fabrics. I was always conscious that Mother did not trust customers to be graceful. More often than not, they would somehow get stains on any fabric in the room, no matter how far away. But Otasan, Father, was more trusting and calmer about food and bolts of fabric in the same room.

"Domo arigato, Ueme, thank you, and please say hello to our town headsman, Bufuku-san."

I turned my bow specifically to the man. "Ohayo gozai mashto, Bufuku-san. This is a lovely day filled with the joy of spring. May you and my otasan enjoy this tea together."

I backed out of the room bowing just slightly. Father was very strict about our bows. Mr. Bufuku was actually below us, but we must be polite. Thus, this was a "one-degree bow." Mother had named the bows according to angles and degrees. She was the mathematician in our family. She also, being of merchant class, found the strictness of Father's samurai bow categories a bit funny.

Now, on to cleaning the formal inner room! I polished the wood of the tokonoma shelf whose purpose was to display artful pottery. Admiring the sheen of the wood, I stood back to admire the summer scene in the scroll above it. Always, the scroll would be a poem or scene of the opposite season, to remind us of the days to come. In winter, there would be a scene of summer to warm our hearts. Similarly, in summer, the scene would be one of snow to cool our brows. I dared not touch the scroll. It was an old one, much favored, but the edges were now getting a bit torn. Soon, though it was spring, we would put up a fall scene.

Enough gazing. With another clean rag, I started to wipe down the tatami mats that covered the whole floor. They were very thick woven straw mats with silk brocade edges that helped with maintaining the warmth of the house in winter and also made the floor easier to kneel on. Our family crest, a simplified silhouette of a peony symbolizing prosperity, was woven into the brocade. No one ever wore outside sandals on this floor. Even so, they required regular cleaning to keep dust from being matted between the smooth fibers.

To keep my energy up, I kept reminding myself that doing chores kept one's body smooth and lithe and beautiful. Saiko's magazines always reminded us of how to keep our inner and our outer beauty and how all the feminine chores helped us do this. Ito scoffed at this and said it was propaganda. Smiling to myself, I was grateful for the fun companionship of my friends.

Chapter 2

THE FLUTE PLAYER

Lunch was over. I had washed and changed into my spring flowered yukata for the visit. Light was streaming into our kitchen through the alley door onto the herbs in pots at the windows. I walked to the bench that had the prepared rice sweets, a container of pickles, and a small bag full of rice grains that would be my gift to the shakuhachi player. Madam Iwata surveyed me up and down to make sure my hakata and hairstyle were appropriate for the visit.

She smiled. "Wonderful, Ueme. You look very pretty. Now, please pick out a silk kerchief of a design you prefer for wrapping the gift. You will find your mother has a number of beautiful ones folded in that cupboard over in the office by her desk. Then come here and show me that you know how to fold the furoshiki so the gifts can be carried properly."

Madam Iwata was being quite formal with me today, but her slight smile gave away her tenderness. I welcomed that small smile. My graduation week had turned from joy and celebration to a somber list of chores. I should be grateful when this day was done.

I was sitting on the bench waiting for Obachan with my furoshiki properly tied and balanced on my lap. Soon, I saw her appear at the top of the alley road, walking from her house and carrying a basket full of vegetables.

"There you are and all ready to go. I must thank Madam Iwata for getting you in shape! Are you ready for our visit?" Obachan was actually in a good mood, unexpectedly. "You know, Ueme, I am glad that you girls did such a silly thing yesterday. It has given me a chance to go visit Katsuo. I am sure Katsuo has not been so offended by your silliness. And now we have a glorious visit to make." Obachan surprised me with her cheeriness.

Our house was the next to last at the end where the alley turned into a narrow dirt road entering the valley. In a few steps, we were on the old road next to the forest that Ito and Saiko had taken with me just yesterday afternoon.

The sun was strong, and I was glad Grandmother had insisted we wear our farming hats of bamboo with the broad brims. Soon, we turned into the old path that went into the woods.

There were only patches of sunlight now as the trees became denser. Oaks and maples now became more prominent over the furry branches of the hemlock. Then we came to the beginnings of the bamboo grove, called a chikurin. Someone long ago had cut a path through it, quite overgrown. The change in vegetation created a different mood with different sounds, different bird tweets and frog chirps. I was lost in my own thoughts about the many moods of the forest as Obachan and I walked side by side silently.

Chop, chop, chop. Sounds of a woodcutter rang out.

Obachan yelled, "Katsuo! You have visitors. I am Shihoki, daughter of Tamako. Do you remember me?"

The cutting stopped. There was a crashing through the bamboo leaves. Suddenly, a very stout and very wrinkled personage was upon us, giving Obachan a big hug. Obachan's cheeks turned bright red from embarrassment at this familiarity.

The wrinkled person responded, "Awoeeow! Never feel shame! We are humans, and we need love. I give you love that I feel for my dear departed friend Tamako."

"Katsuo, I want to introduce my granddaughter to you. This is Ueme."

I bowed and tried not to stare. I was curious. This person always

11

seemed to be a man and was wearing men's clothes but now talked like a woman.

"Ueme wanted to know why you live so far away from everyone and why you always played your flute so sadly." My grandmother gave me away.

"Ayeeahhgh! Time enough for that later. Come, we will have tea and mochi rice sweets."

We followed Katsuo to a clearing in the wood, where her thatched roof hut sat at the far corner in the sunlight. To one side were the logs of wood to be chopped, and at the other side, quarter pieces were laid up for winter. There was a covered veranda on one side, with two tatami mats laid out under it.

We removed our footwear and kneeled on the tatami while Katsuo brought out the brazier and the tea things. Obachan presented her gift of vegetables to Katsuo. I presented her with my silk bundle. She bowed very low, exclaiming how beautiful the gifts were and how kind of us as she left to put them inside her house. She returned with some quite lovely bowls and other tea things. I marveled at how this unkempt creature was preparing a formal tea ceremony for us in this perfect rustic environment.

Obachan said, "Pardon me, Madam Katsuo, may I compliment you on this beautiful bowl that you have placed before us?" Appreciation was one of the first rules of politeness. Obachan looked at me. It was my turn.

What to say? My mind was reeling, trying to think of a polite word to say. I chose one. "And how cooling it is to be here on your veranda." (This was not quite a veranda, but Katsuo wasn't quite dressed in a kimono!) Obachan beamed at me.

"Ah, if it were only so. My apologies. Please be patient while I heat up the water." Katsuo was busy lighting the fire but took the time to look at us and to bow as she spoke.

Soon, the water was boiling, and Katsuo placed a tray of sweets before us. She took the bowl from in front of Obachan and proceeded to wipe it with a clean cloth she produced from out of her sleeve. I feared the dust from her clothing would fall into our tea. This worry occupied my mind for such a long time that I failed to notice that Obachan was now passing the tea bowl to me. Suddenly, I was awakened out of my muddy imaginings by Obachan's shoulder poking into mine.

I took the bowl and turned it ever so slowly and admiringly until it was time to drink. Peering into the tea as the bowl tipped to my mouth, I was relieved to see no evidence of mud or dust, just delightful tea, thick and green.

Katsuo pushed the tray of sweets toward me. I studied them carefully and took one mochi, which was wrapped carefully in a large maple leaf.

We sat in silence for quite a while. I was never really good at long silences.

"Obachan, may we ask Katsuo about her story?"

Obachan was taken aback. "Oooh, I am not sure if this is the time."

"My story? Of course, you are curious." The old woman looked intently at me. "I must apologize before starting on my history. I had no idea about the world and people. I was raised to obey and not to look. And I had fanciful ideas. If only I had been more observant beyond the glamour that so entrances young people. Learning from observing, I would then have discerned the inner values, the inner character of people around me. But in the end, life forces one to be strong and, after finding that inner strength, to stand up for oneself. Yes, I think you could benefit from my story." She looked into my eyes so fiercely I blinked and turned away.

Then she began. "More looking, yes, but that is life, isn't it? Full of mistakes. But one can wonder if there are any real mistakes?"

That was the start of her tale. By the time it was finished, I had eaten all the sweets on the tray.

"It happened in the time of planting. I was visiting my uncle and cousins to help out with the planting of the rice. I had grown up in another prefecture. The daimyo had sent his nephews out to observe and lend a hand with my uncle's rice planting. He wanted the young men to understand the land.

"There were three of them, all brother, all samurai. The youngest, Ayumo, was especially eager to join in the planting. He had been trained in swordplay and horsemanship. His muscles were strong. We young girls were all impressed and excited, since samurai never associated with us farmers. He talked to us at lunch when the other two went elsewhere to eat. We shared our food with him. He came day after day. We never saw the other two after the first day.

"The youngest son and I became very fond of each other, having spent so much time together. Seeing us together displeased my uncle. My uncle would scold both of us for becoming friendly and always sent the young samurai back to his uncle's house whenever he saw us together.

"I had become entranced with the young man. Ayumo had filled my head with funny stories to entertain me. I felt proud that a young samurai was showing interest in me. Every day, we laughed during any break we had from the planting, taking every opportunity to spend time together. After a while, Ayumo also began talking about us having a future together.

"There had been a festival at the end of planting, with food and music and dancing. The young samurai and I spent the whole festival together. Auntie and Uncle were furious with me. 'He is trouble,' they had said. I had tried to defend him, but they had insisted that it was improper and that this young man was only out to ruin me. I was to return to my village after the festival.

"During the festival, Ayumo explained to me that he had no prospects, as he was the youngest of three sons. No position or property was to come to him. He needed to know how to be a farmer. I could teach him. I explained that I did not know much about farming, that it was my uncle's farm, and that my father was a craftsman with a trade that didn't pay much. The young samurai talked about his feelings and his hopes with me. No one had ever talked to me so openly and sweetly before. We decided to sneak away the night before my departure home to my parents. Thus, we rode by horseback to a Buddhist temple in the hills. We were married by a priest and proceeded to make a life together.

"My uncle felt he was responsible for this huge mistake and so let us rent a piece of land from him in a remote parcel. We were supposed to feel shame at what we had done, but we did not. We were very happy. We struggled to plant our first crop of rice and some vegetables for trading. The summer was unusually hot and dry that year. We had trouble irrigating the field. And an interesting thing happened. I noticed that, though he was strong, my new husband did not seem to have stamina. He would start a task but never have the energy to finish.

"During all this time, I was working while carrying our child. The baby was born in the winter. We did not have much wood stored up for heating and cooking. That winter was very hard. Somehow, all three of us made it through, and we rejoiced in the spring air and sunlight. It was time to plant again. I could only do so much with taking care of the baby. My husband made a great show of going off each morning to plant, but I noticed that not much was being done.

"In midsummer, the baby was to have his six-month birthday. We wanted to celebrate. I wanted to invite my cousins and aunt and uncle to our little house to show them our appreciation for all they had done for us. But my husband insisted we needed to make a journey to see his family first. This was a big journey, and I was not sure how we could do that. My husband insisted that we make the effort. He wanted to make amends with his family.

"We were to be on the road for several nights. We thought we would camp out, as we had no funds for an inn. The weather was mild, and we traveled with the one horse a good distance that first day. We made it through the first night and decided we needed to replenish our water supply the next day. We found a farmhouse alongside the road at the end of the day. The family was very generous with water and some other supplies. They invited us to stay the night to make it easier on the baby. However, my husband was insistent that we not stop for the night but that we keep on traveling a while longer.

"The next part of the road was dark, with many overhanging trees. The woods encroached on each side. I wanted to stop and settle in for the night. But Ayumo said no. We were taking turns on the horse.

"I remember having just settled myself on the horse. Ayumo was about to hand me the baby when bandits on horses rushed out of the woods at us. I was knocked off the horse and beaten. The marauders kept yelling, 'Give us your money.'

"We yelled back, 'We have none.'

"Ayumo was on the ground wrestling.

"I screamed for the baby. 'Where's my baby?' Then I was knocked out and dragged into the woods.

"When I came to, local townspeople were giving me water to drink and asking if I was all right. They told me it looked like there had been a robbery. They wanted to know where my husband was. I said, 'They must have knocked him out also. Please go look for him.' Then I wailed, 'My baby. Where is my baby?'

"The local farmer's wife then arrived and tried to comfort me. 'You must be calm. A grave event has happened here tonight. I am afraid your baby might have been stolen.'

"'But what about Ayumo?' I questioned. 'Has no one found him? Is he alive?'

"The strange answer came, 'We can find no trace of him.'

"I was eventually taken back to my uncle's house. I was so overwrought with grief that I could remember nothing of the trip for months. My relatives did not speak of it. I cried for my baby. My breasts became infected, and my aunt had to put hot compresses on me to relieve the swelling.

"My sad outbursts disturbed my family. Thus, I decided to move back to the house that my husband and I had shared. Uncle and Aunt tried to prevent this. They hired the village wise woman to counsel me. She came to visit me every day for many weeks. She prepared special foods that were supposed to relieve the grief. She made me walk in the sun for an hour each day.

"She would talk to me. 'A great wrong has been done to you. But you are also guilty. You disobeyed your elders, who always know what is right for you. You must make a decision. You can be strong and live your life, or you can become an invalid and be a burden to others.'

"It was as if I had been slapped in the face. 'Now I am to blame? I was a good wife and a good mother. I worked the land harder than my husband—'

"'Aeeyah!' I was interrupted. The wise woman actually slapped my hand. 'So did you not recognize who your husband really was?' She seemed disgusted by my lack of intelligence.

"'He was samurai,' I replied.

"'Correct. And you are not. Recognize the order of things!' The woman was talking so loud at me that I had to cover my ears.

"Auntie came to talk to me. 'We have inquired of the daimyo what has happened to your son. He is upset but will not talk to us. However, one of his ministers has set a meeting with uncle for tomorrow.'

"Uncle came back from the meeting and told me, 'Ayumo planned everything with his parents. No one will say it outright, but this is what the minister implied. You will never be allowed to see your baby again. The daimyo feels remorse and is prepared to give money.'

"'I do not want his yen!' I replied. I could not believe my ears. Money in place of my child?

"'Be smart. You have nothing. No one will marry you. You need money.' Uncle spoke quietly and sadly.

"From that day forward, I decided to flaunt convention. I would take a man's name, a strong one; wear men's clothing; become my own farmer; be my own master; dance in the sun and sing to the moon. I would have to find my love in nature. And in honor of my baby boy, I celebrated his birthday every year with a flying carp. I always kept track of my boy through people traveling to that area. My baby grew up, became samurai. But you know, I never got to see him. He died many years ago in the rebellion over by the castle." Katsuo pointed to a ragged wind sock in shape of a faded carp blowing in the wind.

Obachan had left halfway through the story to walk into the rice field and pull some weeds. I could not move. Katsuo's grief had become my grief.

I started to moan very quietly.

Katsuo empathized. "There, there. It happened so long ago. I sometimes think it happened to someone else, not me!" She continued, "See that deer at the edge of the clearing? She is my pet. I have many animal friends here, and townspeople come to me for advice on the medicinal use of herbs and pay me with gifts like this beautiful tea bowl."

Then Katsuo looked at me, "Ueme, you must come to visit me sometime and bring your screaming friends!"

My eyes opened wide. Of course she recognized me as one of the very impolite, nosy girls.

Katsuo smiled generously. "Oh, I see you girls, you know, crouching down staring at me. The four of us will have tea one day, yes?"

I felt color rising in my face and looked down to hide my shame.

"Oh, never mind. All is in fun, eh? Don't you worry about me." Katsuo patted my hand, and I could feel her farmer's calloused skin.

Obachan finished her weeding and returned to the house. Katsuo gave her some little bags of herbs with instructions for use. We bowed, and Katsuo bowed. As we found our way back through the bamboo grove, Katsuo's somber notes on the shakuhachi followed us.

That night as I lay on my comfortable futon stuffed with soft cotton, in my beautiful two-story home with my bedroom window that let the moonlight stream in, I thought about what I had heard today—how different things were now. The samurai life was over. We were a modern world now. It was the Meiji era, the era of enlightenment. Yes, we young women must listen to our elders, but life was not as severe now if one made a mistake in class status.

Look at my family. My mother, a merchant, married my father, a second son from a samurai family. We had blended the two classes. My grandfather was very astute and stayed abreast of the times. He'd explained to me many times about my heritage, how samurai status no longer guaranteed an income, how he had been quick to procure rice lands for income for his first son and for his second son to marry into the wealth of a merchant family. And me, with my two friends; we were women with high school diplomas, the first women in our families with formal education equal to a man's. The emperor said we young women with diplomas were an integral part of the new Nihon, the new Japan.

I let go of Katsuo's tale. What did it have to do with me when life was so different now? I fell asleep enjoying happy thoughts about my own future life.

Chapter 3

THE DINNER

The sun warmed the back of my hands. I was kneeling in the dark soil pushing the seeds into the ground. I had to keep reminding myself to pay attention to my rows.

Grandmother's voice was insistent. "Listen to your obachan. Order will gain you all the riches of this world. Pay attention to the details in life, and you will never go wrong. It is just as important to make your rows of bean seeds straight as it is for your father to keep his accounts in order."

"But, Obachan, Mother is the one who keeps the accounts in order."

"Yes, yes, that is not important. Look at your row. It is angling toward the last one. Do it over." Obachan then angled her body away from my part of the garden and leaned over her rows of daikon, the white radishes that were shaped like carrots. She pulled out the little weeds in between the beautiful green leafy tops.

Obachan stood up. "Well, I have done enough helping with your garden. Time for me to return home to take care of my own chores. Be sure to let your parents know the work I have done here."

With that, Obachan chose her footsteps carefully between the plants to reach the alley. I watched her sturdy shape walk determinedly up our alley to the ancestral home at the other end, too far to see from my vantage point.

I noted her strong body, as well as her strong intentions. "May

I be as strong as my obachan," I whispered to the mountains in the distance. "But let me be more gracious," I added, referring to her habitual insistence that we have obligations to her for any type of help she gave my family.

I would not say anything to Mother about Obachan's work in the garden. As Mother says, "We will always be indebted to her because I married her son." Obachan should be indebted to *Mother* for marrying *him*. "After all, samurais without merchants are poor ineffectual businessmen," says mother. Then Mother would smile at me and laugh, saying, "But how we love our poor samurai!"

Once Obachan had left me, I relapsed into daydreaming. Looking across the rice fields to the mountains, a hazy blue in the distance, I thought of all the ancestors who came before us and worked these fields, had families, and laughed in the sun here. This was the most beautiful place on earth.

A distant voice pulled me back. "Ueme, come in from the garden. Those tatami mats are waiting to be wiped down." Madam Iwata called me from the kitchen door.

Brushing the dirt from my hands, I stood up and carefully placed my feet on the soil so as not to hurt the baby plants. The straight rows just completed were worthy of some pride. I was grateful to Obachan for her discipline. Picking up my sandals at the edge of the garden, I ran barefoot through the alley to the back door. The next chore was cleaning the front sales room to get ready for our spring customers.

Inside, as usual, I had to wash up and change clothes so as not to bring the garden dirt into the house. In the laundry room, I remembered my gift from Ito hidden behind some things on the shelf and also my bag of change that I had hidden in a pot under some gravel in the corner of the garden. I first checked the pot in the garden—still there. My pot of change still did not hold much, but I had hopes. Too early to even plan about such a small sum.

Then back to the shelf inside. I took out my present and

unwrapped it. There in my hand was a black lacquered box with a bird painted in gold and a silken red tassel attached. Opening the box, I saw it was filled with perfume. I took my finger and rubbed it on the soft wax. It smelled of sweet jasmine. I dabbed some on my wrist. Just the release of the fragrance transformed me into an elegant lady of the court sitting near the dais of the emperor.

I was so easily distracted. I put the box into the ample fold of my sleeve and proceeded on to my chores.

Entering the sales room, I saw a tea tray on the floor and stooped to pick it up. Surveying all the unkempt bolts of cloth and dust everywhere, I realized that cleaning this room might take all day. I decided to ask mother for a lunch break so I could enjoy some time with my friends.

After delivering the tray to the kitchen, I walked over to mother's desk in the far corner of the office.

Mother was flicking the beads of the abacus, *click, click*. I listened for a second to the constant rhythm, *chk, chk, chk*. The abacus was made of ebony and the beads of ivory, a present from a very distinguished client many years ago when my mother's parents ran the business.

I interrupted her. "Mother, I am presently cleaning the sales room. The bolts are all disheveled, and there is a lot of dust. It will take the whole day. May I take a lunch break to spend time with my friends? After all, we have just graduated and have things to talk about."

Mother looked up and smiled, "Of course you may. Also, your father has made folded paper origami envelopes with yen inside for you to give the girls as a present. You can give them their presents at that time."

Saiko, Ito, and I decided to have a picnic at the fairgrounds across the river. Sitting on a large cloth, we shared our rice balls and pickled fish and fresh cucumber slices. Our tin cups were filled with cold tea, and Saiko brought out some rice candies.

"Look, my auntie gave me these candies as part of my graduation present. Aren't they pretty?" Saiko laid them out on a silk kerchief.

"Mmmm, arigato" (thank you), Ito said as she daintily pushed one into her mouth.

"Shall we talk about our futures?" Ito seemed anxious to delve into this subject. She brought it up all the time.

"I am worried about my future. I do not want to talk about it!" Saiko seemed angry.

"Well, I know someone whose future is pretty well set!" Ito looked into my eyes expectantly.

"Why are you looking at me?" I felt heat coming into my cheeks, as Ito was about to divulge my secret hope out loud.

"Because you know who you are going to marry." Ito spoke with a knowing eye, looking at Saiko.

At this, Saiko perked up. "Why, is it arranged already? Tell us how it happened."

"No, no. Ito is exaggerating. I think the silk merchant's son favors me. That is all."

"Your father is Bushi. That would be an advantage for a merchant's son," Saiko insisted. Then she continued, reciting from her latest read, "Oh, to have a love where the young hero caresses the cheek of his betrothed, to lock arms in heartfelt embrace—far from their families, who disapprove of their love. Determinedly, they have run away to a new, beautiful land, rich with possibilities. Their hearts beat together as they lay side by side naked in the sunlight."

"Oh, Saiko, that is quite romantic! You will have to lend me that story to read," Ito said.

"So, you think life is really like that?" I asked. "It seems my parents only talk about the practicalities of marriage."

"When one is truly in love, the practicalities will fall into place. It is important that there be true feeling between the man and the woman," Saiko continued. "That is what all the magazine articles say."

Ito agreed, "Look at our headmistress at the school. She is married to a very handsome man. True, they are quite elderly, but I am sure they are in love, with their hearts beating together. He brings lunch to her every day, and they eat together. I am sure that will happen for you, Ueme."

"Well, I do not know what will happen between us. He is going to university next year." I was imagining how hearts could beat together.

"Well, then something will be decided soon before he goes," Ito said.

I felt ashamed for having ever said anything. Perhaps I had incurred bad luck by my presumptions.

Saiko started to pack up the lunch things. "Let's start to walk back, and then I will tell the two of you about my dilemma."

We all got up. The sun was high in the sky, but it was spring, and the sun sent a gentle warmth to us.

Saiko continued, "I am nervous. My otosan has been talking about money a lot lately—and in front of me. This is not like him. You know we are all girls in my family. There is no one to carry on the family name. My otosan has been talking with my obachan about the value of our family name. I am afraid he will trade our name for a suitor for me!" Saiko was near tears.

I tried to calm her. "Well, that is no shame. Many families do that. It is an old custom."

"Ueme, please. You know what goes with that custom?" Saiko's tears were glistening on her high cheekbones now. Her classic high-cheekbone beauty held a frustration that seemed to have finally broken through. "Shame."

I looked at Ito, who was bewildered. Saiko was the only person of Samurai class who Ito had ever had as a friend. Ito shrugged her shoulders and nodded her head violently at me as if to say, *Do something*. Saiko's tears were making her very uncomfortable.

I was trying to think of what to say, so silence reigned. We had walked to the edge of the river where the path split. We had a choice of which bridge to walk over, since we were in between two of the famous "Five Bridges" for which our town was named.

There were sounds of birds fluttering in the tree branches above our heads, and some leaves trickled down to land in our hair. A decision had to be made.

"Which shall it be? Ito stood with her arms pointing in each direction. She pointed to the right. "Will it be the Bridge of Loving Kindness or the Bridge of Noble Truth?" She ended with a nod to the left. The truth of the world was much on our minds these days as we searched for our places in the world.

We conferred and chose the bridge to the left. There was a reason for that choice. As Madam told me often, 'There is a sound reason behind every choice. There are no random choices. Even when you think you have made your own choice, it most likely has been chosen for you, and you just do not know it.'

Knowing these dictates of fate, we young modern women had made ourselves conscious of our decisions and the reasons behind them. We had a reason for each of our decisions. So, lately we had been looking into some "rules" for decisions. Confucius seemed to favor right over left. Confucius favored men over women. So, perhaps, as women, we should choose the left.

We started walking toward the Bridge of Noble Truth.

So many stories were floating in my head from yesterday's visit, Saiko's magazine stories, and now this possible future of hers. Three days ago, everything had seemed so much simpler. I continued our conversation. "Saiko, I really do not know of another custom. What do you mean?" I really was puzzled.

"Oh, Ueme, it is only second sons who marry thus. They have to

25

take on someone else's family name. My husband will have to take on my family name!"

"Of course, that is why the money is paid to his parents!" I felt clearer.

"The shame, Ueme, the shame," Ito pleaded.

"But, Saiko, there is no shame for your family. The transaction for money is private. Sometimes, it is actually a very small sum between families who know one another. It can be a gift to your family so the name carries on."

Now Saiko was angry. "The shame is not for my family. The shame is for my husband, who loses his own name, purely because he is second son! My new family will be started with shame."

"Oh, do the men really feel shame in that? Then why do your families do it?" asked Ito.

"I have heard merchant families do this also," I said quickly to Ito. Sometimes, Ito was too proud of her family's fortune in yen, as well as the rising status of merchants under the current emperor. And these unpleasant aspects of marriage were purposely not told to girls, so they would not fear marriage. We had so much to learn.

A happy thought occurred to me. "But what if the son really likes you and falls in love with you? Then wouldn't the shame then turn into a badge of honor for his beloved?" I was surprised at my own brilliance.

"Yes, Saiko, you are so beautiful and graceful and smart. Your husband is going to be just silly over you. How can it be otherwise? He is actually getting a real bargain." Ito lapsed into merchant talk.

"Do you think that is possible? Maybe he will be a good man," Saiko said, looking wistfully at the sky.

"Have you met him yet?"

"No, but I do think it will be sometime this year."

Ito perked up with an idea. "Oh, this could be one of those romantic stories, where the girl has no idea and hears just awful things about her intended. She becomes frightened and runs away, only to find out in the end that he was a wonderful man and actually loved her. But she loses her chance because he ends up not waiting for her return and marries another." Ito was caught up in her own tale.

"Eeeyahh! Ito, that is not helping!" I said.

Then Ito said, "You know, no matter our married situations, we also must consider our occupations. We are educated women. It is important that we continue to think about using our minds. We do not want to just be obedient wives."

"I feel like I may have no time to even consider that." Saiko's tone was depressing.

"Maybe things are happening very quickly, but I think Ito is right. We cannot forget who we are. I know that, in the business world, there are many new developments they teach in the universities that help businesses prosper. There is more to learn." I was remembering a conversation mother had with someone in the alley yesterday.

"Oh, yes, my father has been reading up on new accounting methods. He actually asked me to see about taking a course in it," Ito said.

Saiko sighed. "I am more interested in reading novels than anything else. What skill do I have?"

Ito laughed. "Isn't that the best kind of person to be a teacher of young minds?

"Actually, you are a great teacher, Saiko. You have helped me with many a haiku ever since we were little."

"I never thought of that. I do like to explain things."

"Yes, you do."

In silence, we crossed the main road and walked up a side street, arriving at the top of the alley near my obachan's house.

Ito left to go to her house, and Saiko soon was at her own kitchen door. Walking the rest of the way to my house, I contemplated which bolts of cloth to put back in the warehouse and which to store upstairs. If I was organized about it, I could finish that sales room well before the afternoon was over.

Seeing Jun, our Korean kitchen boy, in the alley, I realized I could garner some help with this chore.

"Jun, sumimasen, I need to have some bolts of fabric put away in the warehouse. They are in the sales room. They need to be wrapped in rice paper and tagged. Can you help me?"

Jun, ever the obliging one, nodded affirmatively. Ah, now I could finish more quickly. Just knowing there was an end to this task gave me more energy.

Jun and I wrapped the bolts and delivered them to their respective storage places. Mother had placed the bolts for the new spring line in the middle room, waiting to be displayed in the front room. After that, Jun left. Usually, he only worked mornings for us but would welcome any extra chore for more money.

I spent another few hours scrubbing the brocade edges of the tatami mats with wet cloth and soap. It was an impressive floor, with our family crest woven into the edges of all the mats. Anyone entering to buy fabric would see the crest as they knelt down to sit on the mats, a gentle reminder they were in an establishment of high status. The House of Oyama was known for its quality fabrics. People did not come to our establishment to buy just their indigo cotton for everyday wear but also their silks for fine kimonos. We were known for unusual silks with artistic designs.

Finally, everything had been dusted, and the sitting pillows had been shaken and beaten to get dust off them. They had been sitting in the sun on the meditation rock, waiting to be placed back in the room. I placed the new bolts in the room, tore off the rice coverings, and replaced the mats and little tables that father used for business. I carefully replaced father's log and price books with his pen back on his table. I closed the windows and surveyed my work. It was a proper place of business now. I sighed with pleasure at my work and with relief that I still had a few free moments left in the afternoon.

Bending forward and backward to relieve the kinks in my posture, I realized how dirty and sweaty I was. Wanting to catch my breath and relax a bit, I sneaked into the formal garden and sat down on the meditation rock.

I started daydreaming about the silk merchant's son. I thought of how qualified I would be as a merchant's wife. Remembering that the high school now offered an evening course in business, I decided to ask my parents if I could take it in the fall.

I wondered if he really cared for me. And had he mentioned it to his parents? Dare I think of him this way? I was imagining his dark eyes looking sweetly at me and saying vows of love. I imagined the scene. I was wearing the kinsha silk and had real spring blossoms stuck in my beautifully coiffed hair.

"Ueme, pardon me. Your father told me to come to look for you."

Startled, I shook myself out of my daydream to see the merchant's actual son opening the front gate of the garden and about to step in. I stood up immediately and regretted how I looked. I was hot, tired, and dirty from my chores. I was not wearing the kinsha silk. Oh, oh. My life was ruined. There were so many rules about behavior and dress code. I was never to see anyone outside the family in my work attire. It must always look as if we had more servants than we actually had.

And Haru was dressed very formally. How handsome he was with his family crest emblazoned on each side of his chest on his black silk kimono. Why was he dressed so? Of what event was I not aware? I began to think back to events of the past week. Had anyone mentioned some gathering I had forgotten?

"Konnichiwa" (Good afternoon), "Haru!" I bowed thirty degrees. After all, I was not even dressed properly. Nothing was proper here.

"Konnichiwa! May I enter the garden?"

"Of course, be my guest. However, I am not dressed to receive company! It is so rude of me to receive you so. Forgive me. I had no notice of your visit."

"Oh, my apologies. It is not your fault. How gracious that you have time for me." Haru was bowing as he kept walking toward me.

My horror at the situation increased as I was now seeing my dirty hands. A merchant's status was often precarious, and appearances were most important to maintain a business of the high order that our family had.

Haru and I often got together after our fathers had met and closed some transactions about the new silks Haru's father would bring to our store. The two of us were very informal in those visits, but I was always clean and dressed.

Haru continued in a most formal manner. "Please let me explain. My honorable father changed his merchandise route at the last minute this morning. I thought it would be most favorable to ask his permission to come here today, rather than wait for next month. I expressed my intention to him. I was most desiring to come along so I could see you."

Not getting any reaction from me, Haru searched for more words. There was no reaction from me because I was stunned, and I was also counting the number and degrees of Haru's bows. Parental teaching could not be ignored!

Haru composed himself with a most serious face, saying, "For two people to get to know one another, more visits are desirable. Last month, we hardly had time to talk. It is hard to get to know one another when we only see each other once a month. Of course, I am not to presume that you wanted to see me also. However, I really enjoyed hearing you sing to me with the samisen last time. And I thought you said you had fun also?"

I was still silent. *Think, Ueme, think. You are looking stunned and not at all elegant and worldly.* I was talking to myself to help my brain wake up. Haru looked uncomfortable now.

Then his face brightened. "Of course, I found our excursion to catch the frogs to write haikus about them very instructive."

I wondered, Was he making fun or did he truly appreciate my education in the classics?

Haru bowed again. "Would you honor me with a visit? Do you think we could take a walk outside today? It is very pleasant. But I do not want to interrupt you."

Due to all Haru's bowing, I had a hard time hearing his long speech and was focusing so much on his words that I had completely forgotten I was not in the kinsha silk!

I shook myself out of my stupor. Perhaps because I was looking so disheveled, I felt the only way to save face was to speak formally. After all, Haru was being strangely formal himself.

I carefully chose my words, "Sir, please do me the honor of waiting for me to change into a more pleasing appearance." Then I bowed.

I walked very politely out of the garden, choosing each step with my feet toed in. Finally, inside the main room, reaching the stairs, I ran up, grateful I was finally out of view. Madam Iwata was upstairs folding some cloth.

Huffing and puffing more out of surprise than because of the running, I pleaded, "Oh, Madam, please, may you help me? I need to clean up and change clothes. The merchant's son is here! Haru is here. And he is formally dressed!"

"Aeeow! You mean the handsome one with the charming smile? Oh, how unfortunate to see you thus! I will go get the bucket of water." Madam walked quickly toward the stairs.

I started to fix my hair, and Mother entered the room. My mind was such a jumble. Why doesn't life wait for our thoughts to catch up?

"Ueme, I think we will be having dinner tonight with the silk merchant and his wife and son. We must hurry. We have much to do."

"Mother, he has asked me to walk with him. I am cleaning up my appearance." I was combing the knots from my hair and wincing.

"Oh, this is more serious than I thought!" Mother grabbed the hairbrush and oil for my hair.

Madam Iwata entered with the bucket and cloths to wash me. In just over ten minutes, the three of us performed a task that usually took an hour. At that moment, we three women were all of like mind, accomplishing the production of female beauty only known to our sex. A bond, common to only we women, it was an almost professional alliance but full of familial devotion and love.

I was about to start down the stairs when I remembered my graduation gift. I ran back into my room and grabbed the dirty hakata rolled into a ball on the floor. Searching the fabric, I found the shape of the perfume box. Pulling it from the sleeve, I showed Mother and Madam Iwata my prize. Quickly, I opened it and dabbed the perfume on the back of my neck and on my wrists. Mother and Madam smiled knowingly at each other. Madam Iwata leaned over my shoulder and adjusted my kimono, pulling the neckline back to expose the nape, considered the most provocative exposure as it reveals blushing. Mother smiled approvingly. For the first time, I realized I had entered a new phase of my female life.

Full of the confidence poured into me from my elders, who were holding their breaths at the top of the stairs, I walked down quietly in my kinsha silk kimono. My hair was coiffed with decorative flower blossoms fastened to my stylish bun just like for our mercantile shows. Arriving at the veranda, I stepped down into the garden, where the patient young man sat staring into the garden.

"Oh, there you are," Haru said as he raised his head from inspecting the pond. From his expression, he was impressed with my new appearance. Clearly delighted, he said, "Oh, oh, oh. Ah, many compliments to you! I thought you looked very fine before. Now I cannot even express words to describe your beauty."

"Hai! Yes, no more talk. Let us take that walk!" Taking charge, as I was the mistress of the house, I lifted my arm up to point to the rear gate. This was a purposeful move of pride to allow Haru to see the beauty of the silk design in my long kimono sleeve, just as I would for my father's customers.

Immediately, I was seized by the conflicting emotion of shame at showing off my elegant attire, but I squashed it in favor of thinking that this was for his delight. I was acting out a part in one of Saiko's stories!

We walked to the cemetery knoll and talked of our families' respected gravesites, each of us complimenting the other, being quite polite. Then silence fell.

And just as it became uncomfortable, Haru coughed. "Do you think we would make a good couple, Ueme?" He was looking at me, carefully searching my eyes.

"Hai, we are good together. You make me smile. That is good. I know my figures and am good with the abacus. And I can entertain customers with my samisen."

"Oh, yes, you mean in business? Certainly. But, you know, one-to-one personally—that is what we should think about. Don't you agree? For my part, I know you would be good for me! And I want to know if you think I will be good for you?" He smiled.

"Yes, you seem to walk very well. You are healthy, and you are smart." I said this rather in fun as I stood back and looked him over, trying to redirect the conversation to something lighter. I was not prepared for a serious talk. These issues between men and women needed some thought, and I felt I needed more time.

Haru laughed again. "Ha, you see! I think we will have a good and fun time together. When we are done with business at the end of the day, we will smile together. I want that. My parents do not smile together. What about your parents?"

"Hmm, my parents are quite happy together. They sing together. Sometimes, they sit together and look at the moon from our garden rock." I was thinking about his question. Tilting my head thoughtfully, I said, "Yes, I want to be able to smile with my husband."

Haru took both my hands in his. I could feel his warm skin and his fingers circling my palms. We were standing close now, face-to-face. I could feel his warm breath.

Haru pulled my hands to his chest. "Ueme, with my heart, I am asking you to marry me and live happily with me."

I was silent for a while. This was serious, and I had known this moment would come eventually but was somehow unprepared. I wished this could be a school assignment, and I could take it home to think about. But if I did not give my assurance today, it would be taken as a rejection. There might not be another opportunity. His parents were here and expected an answer. It might even affect business. I liked Haru better than any other boy, and he was a merchant of high status as we were.

I decided to make the leap. "Yes, Haru. I do like you, and I do think we have fun together. I accept your proposal."

Then Haru, very seriously, slowly lowered our hands and leaned toward me, speaking very softly as he turned us around to face the path back down the hill. "Now, we must tell our parents. I told my father this was an important day. Let's go back to your house."

Thoughts were flying in and out of my head. My heart was pounding. I sensed something great but unknowable was happening. Images came and went. My limbs seemed to lose all strength. Yet, somehow, I managed to walk with Haru down the hill back to the alley.

So, this was how it was done. So quickly, was this it? We were now betrothed? My mind scrambled to think back to how the day had started out. Surely, there had to have been some sign of its importance earlier. I searched my memory for any sign I might have missed. I felt sweat forming on my forehead. Oh dear, Haru must not see sweat. I started to casually lift my arm to brush away the beads of sweat but realized, *I am in the kinsha and must not ruin it!* My distress was at a fever pitch as we approached the rear garden gate.

Saying nothing, we were both letting the seriousness of the task before us settle in to our hearts.

Lifting the latch to the gate, Haru stopped and explained, "My mother came with us today. We are all eating the evening meal together in honor of this occasion. If you had not agreed, we would just have said this was a dinner celebrating the twenty years of fruitful business our parents have enjoyed together."

Haru looked at me and smiled. "But now we can celebrate us."

Haru continued a little more slowly, holding my hand and rubbing his fingers gently back and forth over it. His touch was creating so many emotions within me. I was breathing too heavily. I slowed my breath down and started counting ten breaths in, ten breaths out. I was remembering Brother's samurai training.

Haru noticed my breathing and stopped walking. He looked at me with comfort in his eyes. "It will not be scary." He continued, "Father has brought some very expensive sake for the occasion. Ueme, I am sorry this seems so rushed. Father wants me to be engaged when I start my education at the university. I insisted that we see you. We will not be married until I finish my first year at the university." Haru took a deep breath, sighed, looked away, and then smiled at me. I could see this had not been an easy task for him.

This was great information. How is it that I accepted without even asking questions about the timing and all of that? Where was my brain?

I could have many months to prepare myself for the new role.

I was able to breathe more slowly.

As we arrived at the center of the garden, we could see the interior room beyond the veranda. The shoji doors between the inner rooms had been opened to allow for a longer low table to be set for the two families. My obachan was already kneeling at one end, being the head of our family. All my family were dressed in their best kimonos. My father and brother were in their formal black silk kimonos with our family crest on their shoulders. Their hair was fastened in the samurai topknots. Mother looked elegant in her peach silk with pine branches cascading down the side.

Mother and Madam were bringing in plates of food. As we stepped up to the veranda, Haru's father walked forward and leaned in to speak to Haru. They whispered. His father stepped back and smiled.

Haru and I slipped off our sandals and were guided to our places opposite from one another at the table. Brother was very solemn and did not look my way at all. Mother and Father were keeping their heads bowed. I appraised the beautiful table setting. It gave me a bit of pride that we were able to welcome Haru's family in such style.

Grandmother opened the meal with a prayer to the ancestors and to Buddha. Then Mother started to serve the men and Obachan. I noticed that Madam had filled our special red and black lacquer bowl with the rice and smaller gold and black ones with the pickled vegetables. The fish soup filled the enormous Chinese porcelain bowl that my father's father had received as a gift from the last daimyo. There were multiple small centerpieces of spring blossoms of plum and cherry in simple arrangements down the center of the long table. The men picked up their hashi. Their chopsticks were special ones made of mother of pearl. My father took a bite of rice, a signal for rest of the men to eat. The women watched. Satisfied the men had been served, the women then relaxed and picked up their hashi.

It was not until the end of the meal that our betrothal was mentioned. The two bottles of sake were opened, and the conversation became much louder. Many toasts were made in our honor. The two fathers seemed to toast each other excessively and seemed to be the happiest people at the table. I was complimented over and over for my beauty. I was increasingly conscious of sweat beads forming at my hairline.

Haru was complimented over and over for his strength. He sat very tall with his shoulders straight and just a hint of a smile on his lips. When he looked across at me, his eyes were dancing smiles at me. Returning his smiles, I thought back to him practicing kendo with my brother years ago. I realized that was when I was first attracted to him, his gentle energy, his easy skill with the kendo moves, never needing correction, unlike Brother.

That night, I lay a long time listening to the night sounds, the cry of the hoot owl that lives in the tree next to our warehouse across the alley, the clinking of an empty bucket being carried down the alley. I kept going over what had happened today.

The wedding would be after next spring, perhaps at the beginning of summer. Then I would move to the city and live in an apartment with him, paid for by his father. Both families would invest in a business for us when he was finished with his studies. It had all been planned out tonight.

I wondered whether it would be proper for me to take some courses at the university, since I would be there. Could women study at the university? My thoughts went back to the kitchen. Mother, Madam, and I had been cleaning up after the banquet. Mother and Madam were discussing what the wedding banquet should be like. Then the discussion turned to the timing of the events.

"Well," I had said, "it won't be until next spring, after his first year at the university."

Mother then said thoughtfully, "You know, if you and Haru are living near the university, perhaps you could take a course there. I think they let women take some of the courses."

What an idea, so many possibilities. Mother had put that thought into my head as we were taking dishes into the kitchen. Of course, she, being the head of our school board, was always interested in formal education for women.

I had many questions. I wondered why my parents had acted so calmly, as if they had known about the betrothal. Like a bud slowly turning into blossom, I finally realized it. This was an arranged marriage. It just happened that the two people already knew and liked each other. Fool I was that I thought I determined my own fate.

Chapter 4

HAIKU

First, the roosters crowed, then I heard the banging of the bamboo water buckets up and down the alley. I had to get up. It was cooler today. I didn't want to leave the warm quilt that was wrapped around me. Sewn from many patches of calico, it was colorful and thick and warm and reminded me of my grammy, my mother's mother, a very kindly woman who had died years ago.

Thinking of her, I rose, rinsed, washed, and put on my working yukata. Mother said that nothing had changed. I was to do all my chores and think of nothing that had occurred with the silk merchant's family. That was to be my mental challenge for the day. However, my whole being was on high alert regarding this upcoming change in my life. As girls, we were always taught that a proposal of marriage was the ultimate goal of our teenage years. I should feel exceedingly calm now that my future was secure. I was not calm on the inside.

As I came down the stairs, the fragrant scent of rice steaming in the central pot over the fire comforted me with its regularity, the standard routine of the morning. Mother had been up for a while. Jun, the kitchen boy, was busy taking out the trash and night soil. He looked up at my entrance and smiled his hello. The sun was rising over the rice fields; soon, the kitchen would be fully lit with it. The double doors were open to the alley, and fresh air and birdsong filled the house. I went back to the interior room to make my morning prayers to Buddha and to the ancestors. There, on a small shelf, were small scrolls with the names of my two grandfathers and grandmother brushed in artful black strokes.

Mother was sitting in the formal garden meditating. I could hear her chants off and on, peaceful, calming sounds. While I waited for Mother, I started to peel some daikon roots. I had already eaten my bowl of rice with pickled fish and sipped my cup of hot tea. Feeling full and happy, I continued on with my chores. The wood floor of the kitchen, the elevated part, felt smooth beneath my knees. I wondered to myself, How many women before me had knelt here peeling daikon?

I started to grate the daikon, taking my direction from Madam Iwata. Mother's prayers were extra long today. She prayed for our neighbors down the street, who had just moved away due to a fire in their warehouse two weeks ago. Also, she prayed for my good fortune. She was thanking Buddha.

I was remembering the fire. It had been a terrible night. I was dwelling on those thoughts, rather than on my future. Such commotion. Everyone had tried to save as many goods from the house as possible. "All praises to Buddha," as Madam Iwata would say. No one had been hurt, but the family had lost too much to continue living in our village. The fire had started in their warehouse. As purveyors of paper goods, the warehouse had been just fuel for the fire. With the family now gone, both Brother and I had lost two of our childhood friends. Mother had lost a fellow school committee member, one of the few education advocates for young women in our small village. The woman had also been a dear companion with whom mother had long talks comparing notes about raising children and about modernizing our community.

Father's response to the whole event had been to call in contractors and "modernize" our house and warehouse with the latest fireproofing methods. They had worked on the house all last week. Father had been studying documents, teaching himself the modern methods for preventing fires, giving orders, and checking that each task was performed correctly. He also had talks with my brother and me, serious talks about the dangers of fire, detailing each new fire safety item to us. I was not sure we could remember all the details, but we did surely remember his somberness. Father was deeply grateful to the ancestors that it had not been his warehouse. He kept saying, "That could have been this warehouse. It could have been this house. Everything about this establishment is just food for the flames. Fire would just love to eat all this up. Oh, I cannot imagine anything worse. What would we do? We have no relatives to help us out of this. My brother borrows money for his taxes from me! Oh, what would we do?"

Mother's response to this was, "Your father gets overly emotional. He feels for that family as if it were his own. He gave them five bolts of cloth to take. Imagine, five bolts of our finest silks! Three would have been excessive. He gave one for each member of the family. We cannot afford such charity often. But it was necessary to calm your father down." Mother always justified father's poor business sense.

"When Grandfather died, he helped your father bathe and dress your grandfather. Your uncle had been too distraught to help with that filial task, which had been his duty as firstborn. The paper merchant had been a very good friend to your father. It was a very kind deed, more than neighborly. To care for one's father's body is the men's job, but some men's tears can be as strong as a woman's. Your father and uncle take after their father. Certainly, Obachan, their mother, has more control of her emotions. I have never seen her bat an eye!"

We learned much about our own family when other families had trials!

This week, the warehouse was being upgraded with plaster lined walls, and new bells installed. Father had also hired full-time warehouse guards, who were trained fire workers. Still, we had many paper-lined doors and walls that would be fuel for a fire, so Father had us doing fire drills.

Two nights ago, he rang the bell until we all had trundled down and out to the alley. He surprised everyone! He also surprised the night watchmen who he had hired and who he had forgotten to inform of the drill. The night watchman had summoned help and started flinging buckets of water from the number of ready-filled ones onto the walls of the warehouse. He was about to fling water at the kitchen door just as we were exiting into the alley. Mother said it would have served father right if he had gotten a bucket of water in his face.

So, today, we must finish cleaning the upstairs storage room, one of the last few rooms still full of plaster dust from last week's renovations, more cleaning for the women.

Now, mother had finished her meditation, had entered the kitchen, and was directing Jun in his chores. The garden was now empty. I quickly entered, wanting to get my chores over with as soon as possible. Having grabbed a broom, I began sweeping the pine needles from our formal garden. It was our "Moon Garden." Father and Mother often sat together on its rock and looked at the moon from here.

The goal with maintaining this garden was to look as if our pine trees did not shed needles, as if this garden was a perfect part of heaven. The gravel was to look like waves circling a grouping of small and large rocks resembling islands with clumps of iris and grass. Above all was the carefully crooked, naturally looking, kurumatsu pine. It was the centerpiece of the garden, with horizontal branches full of fluffy pine needles representing clouds. Our garden was a poem, and I, not a poet, was in charge of keeping it poetic! Father came in every so often and corrected things, so I was not worried about offending the ancestors. Mother sat in it more than anyone. This was her little heaven.

Brother and I used to collect the needles each morning. Where was Brother now? Somehow, he escaped all household duties. He was busy with other interests. Yesterday, he gave me his latest haiku:

Pine needles fall
Water surface breaks
Ending beginning

At first, I thought it was for my new situation. However, I had since thought he was making all these haikus for some "intended." I must remember to ask my friend Ito. Ito would know everything that happened between all our friends on this end of town. Her father's store carried so many everyday items there was a constant stream of villagers in and out of the store and, thus, a constant stream of gossip.

The needles fell faster than I could sweep. Finally, I raked the gravel. It was not perfect. I bowed to the gravel as I exited backwards, surveying all the needles still on the ground. I was not equal to this task, and I accepted that it was beyond me. The Taoist thought was what I needed now, ten thousand things, ten thousand needles. I bowed to "it." Then a thought unbidden entered my mind. *"The event" was here in this garden yesterday afternoon.* I had to stop thinking about it!

But how could I? I was going to have to leave my home. I would be living too far away for regular visits. Sadness, along with a weird excitement, crept around the edges of my mind.

Coming down the alley, Madam Iwata was approaching singing:

Sakura, Sakura
Ya Yo I no so raw a
Mo wa tosu giri
ksumi ka kamoka
Ni oi zo I zu ru
I za ya
I za ya
Mi no
Yu ka n

I joined in singing my brother's and my favorite cherry blossom song from our childhood winters, waiting for the spring to come.

As she entered our doors, Madam beamed at me. We were comrades in music. She was basically in charge of the kitchen, as mother was heavily involved with the store. Songs filled our kitchen even as sweat poured down Madam's brow while doing the more strenuous tasks. I had learned to roll sushi with her, to cut sashimi just so, and more. Mother would start to teach me some of my kitchen skills but would soon be interrupted by Father, who needed her complete attention with the fabric or the accounting books. So, today in the middle of slicing the fish at an angle just so, Mother had to hand over the knife to Madam Iwata to finish out the lesson with me.

I had passed some threshold. Things were not the same. Today, some memories were coming to me from a few years ago. Childhood memories were swirling in my head. I was remembering a typical morning when the fishmonger came, as he did most mornings to sell fish at inflated prices to my mother. He was a wily one, always trying to sell us his day-old fish, but Mother never let him get away with it. Their daily discourse was full of banter and one-upmanship. It was entertaining. Madame Iwata would listen at the sidelines, winking at me every so often as mother matched him wit for wit. She was a master bargainer. It was in her blood, generations of prosperous merchants. And I think the fishmonger delighted in this daily challenge. He always left smiling!

It was still early morning. I was seventeen and had graduated with honors. Mine had been the first class in our village that had attended school from the very first grade through all of secondary years. We were touted as the new guardians of the new age of Nihon! I felt like I must experience all my present life with more energy, more attention. But here I was, already feeling nostalgia for my childhood.

I looked out the door to the alley. Ushio was there with the honorable calligrapher making signage for the store. It was time for the spring sale and new signs were needed. Pushing down my feelings of jealousy, I was curious as to the design of the signs and walked out to watch. Brother looked up. "Ueme, what do you think of my haiku that I put near your futon yesterday?"

"Good morning, Brother and honorable Katakana-san. The paint strokes are beautiful. Do you think I could try to make a sign?"

Mr. Katakana looked up from his work and shook his head. "Oh, no, this is not women's work. We are almost done anyway. You would not enjoy this. You must hold the brush just so." He then looked down and continued on with his black brushstrokes."

I thought, *As if I cannot hold a brush!* He was an old man with old ideas.

"I think you could make the strokes in colored ink so it would seem more like spring!" I loved to upset the stodgy calligrapher, an old man who seemed to have no imagination beyond the same black stroke signs year after year. However, he never looked up. I was gone as far as he was concerned.

Brother looked up at me and laughed. "Go back inside or you will put him in a bad mood, and then I will pay for your remarks!" Was Brother not ever going to say anything about my betrothal? Was he not going to acknowledge my new position?

I had studied calligraphy with my brother for a number of years when I was younger. I'd even had my own brush and ink stone. Now, I pushed down my jealousy at working at kitchen things when I would have preferred to be about large things like signs being made outside in the sun. That was all well and good. I played the samisen with grandmother two days a week for her teas, and Brother had never been invited to those events.

I decided to answer my brother's earlier question. "Well, who are all these haikus for anyway? You seem to be writing many of them. Some are terrible. But yesterday's was not so bad. I am not a good judge. I don't know the rules for the exact rhythm of the words."

"Oh, yes, I love your false modesty, Ueme. Anyway, it is not the rhythm I care about. It's the meaning!" Brother was actually sounding more serious than usual.

"Oh, well, I guess it does say something about pine needles!"

"No, no, the beauty of water sliced by needles."

"No, I did not get a sense of beauty from it. Beauty in pine needles? I would choose something else for a vision of beauty. But then, I have swept too many needles to feel their beauty." I laughed and left my brother bent over his strokes of black paint creating words saying, "Beauty of Spring Sale," "Prices Slashed by a Sword," and so on.

Mother was at the alley door. "Ueme, we have some important customers coming this morning. Father is preparing his poems to read. He must recite a different poem for each person. Every customer must feel his experience in the shop is unique. You know those old samurai families! Madam is preparing multiple tea trays."

Mother continued, "I have asked the warehouse supervisor to bring over the specific bolts, one for a girl's first kimono, one for a son's graduation, one for a new tea kimono, and then the 'ready-made wares' for the men's Western business attire. Our head seamstress is arriving at eleven this morning." She then looked as if she had forgotten what she wanted to say to me.

Suddenly she brightened. "Oh, yes, I want you to model the three new spring kimono fabrics. The messenger brought them over last night from the seamstresses. We have a blue background shantung with pale cherry blossoms trailing down the side of the front, a yellow background with green leaves and I'm not sure which color flowers—it is not my favorite—and then the peach kinsha with the spray of blossoms on the back, just peeking out over the front sleeves, very enchanting!"

Her instructions continued. "Do the yellow first, get it out of the way and then the blue and pink—really, shantung is a bit heavy for a spring kimono. Finish with the kinsha silk; with the lightness of the fabric and the subtle design, it will be our most popular. Madam is almost finished with the tea trays, so she will be able to help you. I am sorry to rush you, but I am behind with arranging the prices. I had to dress father appropriately."

She continued, "The details are so important. If I do not get things right, I will surely hear from your obachan, and I do not have time for that." She disappeared into the house, and I followed. That was the way with a merchant family—busy, busy, busy. As if nothing had changed!

Upstairs, the kimonos mother had mentioned were laid out carefully in our "preparation" room. The second floor was where we had our sleeping quarters and also some business rooms. One was for dressing models, the preparation room. Usually I was the only model, but sometimes I would be able to invite my friends. Now that we were older, we could exhibit the adult kimonos. It was fun being able to be fashion models!

Another room was for storing some fabrics. Father did not want to have to run across the alley to the warehouse in the middle of a transaction. And another was a sewing room where some machines were set up for making some of the ready-made clothing, mother's new venture. She even had some items such as lace for edges of blouses under the kimono and calico cotton for quilting. My obachan was not allowed in this room, on mother's orders. It had modern things that people wore now that copied some Western ideas. These ideas were very far from the old, very spare philosophy of the Bushi. Mother said Obachan would only create a needless fuss if she were to ever see these things. I liked that mother was a modern woman. Sometimes, I would boast about my mother's sophistication to my friends.

First, I needed to put my hair up into a formal style. I really needed help with this. I had applied some fragrant hair oil and smoothed out my hair with a very fine-toothed comb. I tried to hold it up to pin it into the stylish buns, one at top of my head, one just below the first. Madam Iwata rushed in and took hold of the mass of hair and rescued me.

"Don't worry, I've got it. Hold still. Ah, Ueme, you have beautiful, thick hair. So nice to be young! I believe you had a very eventful night yesterday. I am very happy for you. She patted my cheek. But didn't we all know it was coming?"

I thought to myself, *I didn't really know. Now that it has happened, it seems too soon. At least the wedding is far away.*

Madam was very skilled at arranging hair. She'd raised three daughters and a son, and mostly by herself. Her husband had died quite young. She'd had ample practice fixing hair for stylish young ladies. Her husband was samurai class, but, alas, the Bushi received no money under the Meiji rule. She'd scraped and saved to be able to get good matches for her daughters. Wearing the proper hairstyle was very important. Madam had told me many tales of their adventures finding her daughters' present husbands. Listening to her now was more fun than our chores in the kitchen as Madam regaled me with the fun stories about her own daughters while she helped me dress. The dainty flower pins she put in my hair seemed to wiggle outside my head on their own. Powdering my face and neck, she then arranged the kimono with the obi sash just so. When she was done, I felt like I was about to be presented before the court of the emperor himself.

I stepped as lightly as I could in my tabi socks and sandals coming down the stairs. The shoji door to the store was partly open, and I knelt down next to it and listened for my cue to enter. Madam was right behind me with the tea trays. I heard father reciting his poems from his favorite poets, Basho, Buson, and the modern Koseki. I could see him kneeling near the front by the store windows. Screens had been placed to obscure the street view and created a feeling of serenity, far from the bustling crowd.

When father bowed at his finish, that was the cue for Madam and I to enter. Madam entered and offered the tea and cakes. I stood waiting as I heard mother introduce the line of new fabrics. After her introduction, I walked as gracefully as I could with many small steps. I walked to the front of the showroom and then turned and stood before the screens. A very mellow light was suffused through the screens, creating an aura of enchantment. Meanwhile, Mother described the quality of the silk and the poetic emphasis of the design. Then I turned very slowly to give the customers a long look at the fabric and how it could be made into a fashionable kimono.

This was mother's genius. She would direct the seamstress to use the pattern in the silk to the best effect in the kimono. Most people would not have the eye to imagine the way to best place the flow of the cherry blossom branch or the falling autumn leaves so the eye would always be wishing for more. Father always said to Brother and me, "In this way, your mother is the true haiku poet!"

However, Mother was very certain that Father's samurai standing and his elegant manners were the prime reason for our clientele. And these clients could be demanding.

This afternoon the sky threatened rain. Customers were gone, and accounts needed to be updated. Mother called to Father, "I need help with the accounting for this quarter's taxes."

Father answered, "The front garden is calling, Yuki. I must prepare for the sale tomorrow. The garden must be perfect." Father would always rather garden or do anything other than accounts. I knew I would be called to help mother so I quickly followed Father out to the front, where he had sculpted a very narrow formal garden. There was a large rock, a peach-colored azalea in full bloom, and a small pine that Father was grooming to be as beautiful as the one in our inner garden.

"Otasan, may I help you with this garden?" I wanted to be part of this garden now. I'd never cared before. But now, with my future here so truncated, it seemed important. I started to pick up some trash that had blown in from the street.

"You know, Ueme, I think now is a good time for you to help me. Young people need to have practice in the fine art of gardening."

49

He looked up from cutting his azalea and smiled at me. Perhaps my otasan was feeling nostalgic, too.

Otasan continued, "Yes, great idea for you to help right now. I see that I must put some oil down on the street here or the dust will be tracked into the store tomorrow. Here, take these shears and trim the azalea; it has started to overreach the pine." Father then left to go back to the warehouse to bring out a drum of oil.

So, I began to trim the azalea. My hands were shaking. I could not believe he would let me touch his plant. I cut off a tiny blossom here, a leaf there. I did not dare trim a limb. Then I saw that I could pull some weeds that had grown up alongside the large rock, a task not so dangerous. Father had a name for the rock, Tora, which means tiger. Father saw a tiger in its shape. I saw the Moon Princess's earth father, the bamboo cutter, because there were many craggy wrinkles on one side, like an old face. Some moss grew in the crags, very fortuitous. I stooped to pick up the fallen blossoms and then heard the familiar sounds of a funeral procession. A light rain began to fall and completed the somber mood.

A family was bringing the ashes of their loved one up the hill to the Buddhist temple to be blessed by the priest. There were several vehicles, one for the formal mourners, one for the ashes, and one for the closest family members and many walking beside and behind the carriages. I stayed stooped as if in a respectful bow.

Father had just brought out the barrel in a hand truck and was rather noisy with unloading it. Then he saw the carriages. The horses were all decked out as well as the vehicles. Father stood up tall and did a formal seventy-degree bow.

As soon as they passed, he said to me, "Fortunately, tomorrow there is scheduled to be a much larger funeral procession from a very prosperous family. We shall feature the lighter colored rinzu silks, as well as the spring collection of kinsha silks, very light weight for the warmer weather! Where was Brother with the signs? We must get them up now." Father was beaming at his good fortune.

Father picked up his garden shears and started trimming, "Ueme, you did a fine job on this azalea, very fine. I see I can trust you with these shears again in the future."

I felt a small glow of pride that I had done that task well for him.

Father was crouching by the tiger rock and trimming a very low azalea branch. "Ueme, do you realize that our ancestors surely smiled on this property? We acquired a place on the street that is on the way to the most beautiful Buddhist temple in this domain. We must be forever grateful and live up to the potential of this property!"

He started to rake the ground and continued his thoughts. "We always have people who can afford our most expensive fabrics coming by here and viewing our displays. Yes, it is sad to have funeral processions, but always in life, there is the opposite. Here fortune and misfortune are side by side." He waited until the procession was past and then started to spray the oil onto the dirt roadbed.

I went inside to help Mother with the accounts. I had felt a bit ashamed of deserting her to spend time in the garden. When I am a merchant wife, I want my husband to share in the billing tasks. Perhaps this is a conversation I need to have with Haru. The *click, click, click* of the abacus announced the work being done as Mother's fingers flew over the beads adding up the accounts. Mother was bent over the low desk that was in the far corner of the first inner room. There were shelves filled with papers and a locked cabinet for records. An oil lamp gave light over her desk, as that corner could be dark in the afternoon.

"Mother, can I help you with the accounts or shall I go into the kitchen?" I knelt near her to take over some of the sums.

"Oh, no, I am fine. Please see if you can help Madam Iwata finish up. We are having a cold evening meal with some leftovers because I want her to go home as soon as possible. It threatens to be a big storm tonight." Mother smiled at me and put her hand out to cover mine.

Stroking my hand softly, she said, "Ueme, I am sorry we are so busy when you have just had such a big event happen. We haven't even had time to invite friends over to tell the news or to just slow down a bit to take tea and biscuits. Father and I are very pleased with your choice. And we want to have a grand meal in the ancestral home with Uncle's family to tell the news. But for now, we will keep it quiet. We have so much time." She kissed my cheek.

I smiled at her and then rose and turned toward the door to the kitchen. Oh, but was it my choice? I had been thinking about this. Now that the marriage was set, I had more worries than before.

Mother spoke again. "Oh, and can you please find Brother? The warehouse needs to be battened down for the wind. The warehouse attendant had to leave early, and we do not have someone out there until midnight tonight. Your father said this to him already, but Madam Iwata said she has not seen him since midday." Mother's brow was wrinkled with worry.

I entered the kitchen and stepped down to the dirt floor to help with some washing. I had forgotten to look for Brother. Madam had hung up some towels to dry inside and was busy taking laundry in from the drying yard. In the yard, the laundry was blowing wildly in the wind. I grabbed a length of fabric and brought it inside. Madam Iwata told me to go into the alley to see about the warehouse doors.

In the alley, I saw Brother, who had just arrived and was taking care of the doors. Looking up the alley, I saw someone running towards us with her hakata blowing wildly.

"Ueme, Ueme, you must come with me." It was Ito and she was crying. "Come quickly. I have news about our dear friend Saiko. Her mother asked me to come get you."

I was confused and frightened by this news. "What is it?"

Ito grabbed me by the sleeve. "Come before the rain. Saiko can tell you herself. Her mother called on me because she thinks Saiko's friends can help her through this time."

"Well, I do not see the need for mystery. Let me tell Madam Iwata where I am going." I ran inside to let Madam know that I was needed down the alley at Saiko's house and that she was to tell Mother I would probably miss the evening meal.

Ito and I walked arm in arm against the wind to Saiko's house. Saiko's kitchen maid let us in the door. She was busy, similarly to our Madam, with bringing in the laundry. Saiko's mother heard us and came to the kitchen to beckon us to the second floor, where Saiko had wrapped herself tightly in a thick quilt and was rocking herself back and forth on the tatami mats. Her face was wet with tears.

Her mother was kneeling beside her, saying over and over, "Sumimasen. Sumimasen" (I am sorry. I am sorry.) "It was not up to me. Your father's mother insisted on this, and your father agreed out of fear. We do not mean to hurt you."

Ito boldly turned to Saiko's mother and said, "Madam, please excuse us, but I think we can help Saiko better if you leave the room. You truly want us to help her? She will not talk to us while you are here. Please leave just for a while. Onegaishi masu, please." And she bowed her head toward Saiko's mother. We were kneeling around our patient.

Saiko's mother slowly rose to her feet. She looked truly defeated and sad. Whatever had happened seemed to not have been according to her wishes either.

When she had left the room and walked down the stairs, Saiko sat up and threw off the quilt. She got up and closed the shoji doors. She motioned for us to huddle together, sitting on the floor. She remained quiet while she calmed herself.

Then she started to explain. "They have done it. Today I was formally betrothed to a man who is fifteen years older than me. He and his family came today, and the deed was done. I was not even warned. Mother dressed me in a new kimono and lied that we were going to have tea with some important people for father's business connections, someone who might hire him at the university. Well, I guess it wasn't really a lie! I was exchanged for a job. I was bartered off! It really was business." She started weeping again.

There was a cotton towel on the floor, all crinkled from her earlier cry. I picked it up, smoothed it off, folded it squarely, and offered it to Saiko as a new cloth. She buried her face in it. Her white face makeup was smearing off into the towel. She grabbed a fold of the cloth and pushed it into her cheek and pulled down. With all the tears, the makeup was now running. and she pulled that cloth down her face, strip of skin after strip of skin. until she was back to her own color, blotchy now with emotion.

It was too quiet. I spoke. "Did you get to meet him?"

Ito and I waited. Finally, we heard, "Hai, yes."

Another silence. Ito asked, "Is he handsome?"

No answer. I asked, "Is he bald? So many men are. Many look much older than they really are due to the lack of hair. Perhaps he is younger."

Saiko looked up at us and straightened her shoulders. "No, he is not bald. I do not know if he is handsome. I cannot tell."

"Didn't you look at him?" Ito was incredulous. I knew her thoughts, *After all, if this is your future, one better get a good look!*

"I was so nervous. When he told me his age, I just went to pieces. He is almost my father's age! I just couldn't see clearly after that. Truly, when I looked at him, his face seemed to change shape and color. His nose seemed to wander around."

We sat and looked at her. We just did not know what to say. In these situations, sometimes people lose their minds. Poor Saiko.

"My mother always told me we were a modern family, and we would always have our daughters' best interests in mind. She said they would never do something against my wishes. Mother has always said she was happily married, and she wants all of us to be." Saiko burst into tears again and leaned in to the floor. "Why, oh why, was I born a girl?"

My mother had always explained to us that, though we as women shouldered a burden with all our household chores, boys did not have it easy either, as they could be called upon to fight in some old man's war. She wanted me to understand that life carried its difficulties for everyone. Thinking of this poor man who had not managed to find a wife when he was younger and, from Saiko's description, may also be ugly, I felt I just had to say, "Well, it doesn't look like the boys do that much better in this situation!"

Ito gave me a very mean look.

I continued, "I mean, perhaps this man is also having to follow his parents' wishes. But maybe with both of you in this arrangement, maybe you can find common ground." I was searching for good where there seemed to be none.

Ito spoke up, "Saiko, since this is happening, you must now take control. Your parents, I am sure, feel very badly. I can see your mother does. Now, make some demands, like, um, such as, ah ..." Ito was searching for words, and the silence extended uncomfortably.

I interrupted the silence. "I have an idea. Ask to have a private meeting with him to get to know him. And ask for information about him. What does he like? What are his talents? If he is so old, he must have talents. Find out his history. Ask your family to investigate. Tell them that this is owed to you as the oldest daughter."

With a quiet voice, Saiko asked, "Is anything owed to me as first daughter?"

Ito picked up this train of thought. "Absolutely, just as first son! Just stick up for yourself. The empress has said a lot of things women should be doing. Your parents have no way of knowing all the empress says. Make it up as something coming from the court as part of our great modernization. Your parents won't bother to check. Make many demands. Tell them they can pick two of them, and you will be satisfied."

I was a bit shocked at this idea. I was sure Ito got her boldness from her weird uncle who sold the chickens. But what an idea! With boldness, many new things had been thrust onto the people of Nihon. We had often heard the older generation complaining about all the new edicts demanding everyone accept new ideas, all for the benefit of the nation. We had only lived with the new ideas, so we did not mourn the old ways.

Saiko just sat there trying to take Ito's words into her head. Ito and I looked hopefully at her. Could she be brave and stick up for herself in some way in this new turn of events?

"I haven't told you the worst part. They want the marriage to take place in three months' time."

"Will you be seventeen then?" I asked.

"Yes, just." Saiko started to fold up her quilt into a very neat, very square bundle.

I thought about what we did in my household when the women wanted to talk. We would go to the kitchen, where the water could be boiled and we could relax informally with cups of tea. "Saiko, may we go downstairs to the kitchen and sit there to have tea?" I asked.

"Mother will probably let us. Kitchen maid has gone now to her house. But it is raining hard. You should both go home."

We walked to the kitchen together. Saiko's parents had secluded themselves behind the shoji doors. We could see their shadows on the paper walls, cast from their oil lamp. Seiko loaned us each an oiled umbrella to keep our heads dry on our journeys home.

Outside in the alley, with our umbrellas opened over our heads, Ito said, "We shall talk tomorrow. Things can change so suddenly."

"Sayonara," I said, knowing that neither of my friends had heard my own news of betrothal. Knowing that I would keep it from them a while yet created a strange feeling of deceit in me. However, Mother and Father said there was no need to talk of it yet. With Saiko's news, by autumn, there would not be three of us anymore.

Chapter 5

SPRING CLEANING

Ding, ding.

The bell that hung from our alley door rang. Someone had used it to make two rings.

"Very important civic meeting! Ha!" Madam laughed.

There was a small sign beside our alley door. It said, "One ring— normal business. Two rings—important civic business." Three rings in groups following one another equaled *emergency.*

Madam Iwata said, "Yes, very 'civic' business," and did nothing but continued on with her kitchen chores.

I ran to tell my father, "Otasan, two rings at back door!"

"I know. I was expecting it. Most likely, it is Madam Kumodo's messenger. She wants a meeting before noon, I am sure."

Mother was right behind me. "Ueme, we need to prepare the formal room. Please help me with the tokonoma."

We dusted and oiled the wooden shelf. Mother asked me to go find the autumn-colored raku bowl. I crossed the alley to the warehouse. Our tokonoma vases, bowls, and scrolls were stored up on the second floor.

As I passed Madam in the kitchen, I sighed. "Always we have to do such work for this visitor!"

As I climbed the outside steps, Madam Iwata called up to me, "Ueme, your mother says to get the autumn scrolls also. Bring three so we can pick the most appropriate."

I climbed the exterior stairs of the warehouse a little reluctantly. I did not like thinking of autumn when now it was just spring, my favorite time of year. It brought knowledge that summer was coming soon. Who wants autumn that heralds the beginning of winter?! Just then the second-floor door opened, and Brother stepped out with the meanest girl from our secondary school.

"Hello, Ueme, I was just showing Akeme some of our raku bowl collection. Her father is also a great connoisseur of glazed ware." Brother started to help the "darling Akeme" down the stairs.

Ever the coy one, Akeme smiled at me before looking down at the steps. I could see the back of her neck peeking out from her kimono, and it was very red. I was thinking, *Ooh, your father taught you anything about pottery? Oh, please, you are just after the most eligible boy in town.*

Staring at them, I wondered, *How can he be attracted to her?* She cheated on all her mathematics exams. She had no friends, and her parents were not friends with my parents. She was pretty, though. Surely Brother was not so shallow that he didn't see her true inner qualities?

Madam Iwata saw the whole thing and quickly returned inside the kitchen door. She did not want to know.

"I thought you were so busy with your calligraphy signs, Ushio!" I yelled after him.

He didn't bother to turn around to answer me.

Inside the storeroom, I went over to unlatch a solid wooden window to let in some light and air. A shaft of light cut across aisles of shelving. I crossed over to the last aisle and chose a large beautiful bowl. It was mostly gray but had a slash of burnt orange inside the bowl from the bottom up to one side. The slash seemed to cross over to part of the outside, just a hint of it. It made you want to look inside the bowl. The artist was leading you. This was my thought as I remembered father's explanation. Leaving the bowl where it was, I went down the aisle to the scrolls.

I picked up three scrolls that were all rolled up in rice paper and tucked them into the sleeves of my yukata. Then I went back and carefully picked up the bowl. I thought how Madam Kumodo would be impressed with this piece by a famous potter, known across all of Kumamoto, as I navigated the steps down to the alley.

Mother and I arranged the formal room, the middle room just behind the front store display room. Madam Iwata was directing Jun to clean the koi pond, while she was raking the gravel in our formal garden just across from the interior rooms. The light was beautiful today, and I wished we had time to just sit on the veranda and gaze at the fish.

Mother had the scrolls unwound and laid out on the tatami mats. She called out, "Madam Iwata, would you please come here and help me?"

Madam Iwata laid her rake down and stepped up to the veranda. "Yes, how can I help?"

"Oh, I am not sure if Madame Kumodo has seen these scrolls before. Her visits are quite regular. I do not want to be embarrassed. She already thinks I am not worthy of Mr. Oyama."

"Madam, the scroll laid out to the far left is of Chinese origin. She will like that. You know what a Chinese scholar she is." Madam Iwata spoke with simple authority.

Before Madam Iwata came to work for us, she had been married to a man of samurai heritage, a man of great scholarly learning, knowledge which he had shared generously with his wife. Scholars did not make much money. Thus, he had nothing to provide for his family during his long illness and after his death. It was then that Madam Iwata had applied for the position as kitchen maid with us to provide for her young children.

Our family has benefitted from Madam's great knowledge on many occasions. Thus, in gratitude, mother had given Madam many bolts of silk over the years.

We hung up the Chinese scroll and took down the summer scene scroll. Oh, I just hated to see that happy scroll get rolled up. I asked mother if we could hang it upstairs somewhere for now.

"Wait and see," was her answer.

I noticed she rolled it up rather quickly, as if that was my answer.

"Ueme, Madam Kumodo has always liked to hear the samisen and your voice. Have you got a piece you can play?" Mother had a pleading look on her face.

"Well, may we ask Obachan to come and help me? Jun could bring her koto on one of the carts. There's enough time if we do it now." Desperation was in my voice. I did not want to do this alone. Madam Kumodo had never been gracious to me. She scolded me for tiny infractions of manners whenever she visited, as if she were my own obachan and had the right.

"Jun, go with Ueme up the alley to the ancestral home. Take the small cart with you. Ueme has an errand for you." My mother was on this suggestion immediately.

Madam Kumodo was easier to take with Obachan around. My obachan did not know a Chinese scroll from a Korean pot, but she knew her music, and she also knew everyone's place. Where do you think my father got his training for his mathematical bows? My obachan would be adding more samurai class to the event.

The alley had a lot more stones than I ever knew. I heard the scraping of every one of them as Jun dragged the cart over each one. Was he purposefully aiming the wheels for each stone? I turned around to look at him and saw his mischievous eyes and smile.

Jun was very smart. When he did not enjoy a task, he would let you know it. He was about my age. In a few years, he would be married, and this job would not be suitable. I did not look forward to that because we would have to get someone new. I actually liked Jun. Sometimes, he and I would both conspire against Mother and Madam Iwata to avoid certain reprehensible tasks. One of them was to be sent to one of the other merchants down the alley to purchase some goods. We would have to deal with the merchants' wives at the back doors. Some of them were not pleasant.

An incident with the printer's wife last month came to mind. A woman of low integrity, she would not listen to my directions for some leaflets for the school that Mother had prepared. She kept interrupting me and asking about my brother and what was he doing and so on. She had always hoped her daughter would capture Ushio's eye.

While we waited for her to take our order, she insisted that Jun not sit on her alley bench. She yelled at him to not get it dirty, implying he was not clean. Some people treated Koreans poorly, as if they were untouchables. Then she actually demanded that he draw some water for her from her well, as if he was her servant. Luckily, I heard her demand and pulled Jun away down the alley, pretending not to hear her.

We both decided she was a person not worthy of even a one-degree bow. And, no surprise, she did not follow my directions on the printing. When Mother complained to her about the bad printing, the woman blamed me for her mistakes.

We arrived at the entrance to Grandmother's garden. She was in the garden on her knees pulling weeds and humming a tune. The garden gate was partially open, and Jun knocked loudly on it. Grandmother looked up squinting into the sun.

"Ueme, Jun, ohayo gozai mashto. What a lovely morning! Ayee, you look so serious! What is happening? I would expect beams of joy on your face at least, Ueme!" Obachan was referring to the betrothal dinner a few nights ago.

"Obachan, I have no right to ask you, but I am so distraught. Your skills are needed to save me from disaster. I throw myself at your feet." I was exaggerating my circumstance for effect.

"Oh, my, what disaster is befalling the House of Oyama? Can we avert the storm? Tell me what lifesaving measures need to be done!" Grandmother mocked my emotions.

"Will you please play the koto with me? Madam Kumodo is coming for a visit." I bowed ninety degrees.

"Oh, really, Ueme, do not use that bow on me!" Obachan scoffed.

Then she smiled. "Ahh, so! It is the advertisements for the new spring fabrics! She is so predictable. She does this for a free tea. Ah, so pompous in her 'Zen frugality.'" Obachan was full of her "ah, so's" as she leaned down to pull another lanky weed out from between the peonies.

"Obachan, we need to bring your koto back to our house this morning. We do not have much time."

Obachan straightened up. "My koto?"

She looked at Jun and the rickety cart. "I am not sure. The koto belonged to my mother. It came from a talented koto maker in Kyoto. We must wrap the koto box so it will not get damaged. Let me see. Mmm." She was silent as her thoughts wandered.

"Ueme, come with me. We need to get a large futon. Jun, please look in the barn for some rope."

Obachan slid open some closet doors. "Ah, this will do. It is old, nearing time to be a rag. It was made by my mother-in-law." She pulled out a carefully folded futon quilt. It was made of darkly colored cloth and stuffed with cotton. It was somber, not the cheery colors like my quilt at home. Then, I realized, my father's grandmother had made the quilt, someone who I had never met or heard of much.

"Obachan, what a lovely quilt. Great-Grandmother must have worked hard on this quilt. We should be very careful with it, don't you think?" I was questioning the judgment of my obachan.

"Oh? No, I do not think so. She was not a nice woman. She locked me in the closet, you know!" Obachan frowned at this memory.

"What?" I was rather surprised at such a mean act.

"Never mind, just mother-in-law stuff. Just be wary of mothers-in-law!" Obachan was very businesslike in her manner.

"But, Obachan, you are my mother's mother-in-law! Are we wary of you?" I wanted to understand more. After all, I would soon have a mother-in-law.

"Yes, and I live here in an addition at the rear of your uncle's house. which is very good for your mother and your auntie! It is also good for me. Not good to have more than one house mistress in a family! And believe me, dear Ueme, this quilt is perfect for our use."

Back down the alley, Jun and I carried the wrapped koto into the kitchen. Sweets were already on trays with little vases of flower buds. The tea was steaming in the pots. I ran upstairs to change. Madam Iwata was there already with oil and combs for my hair.

"Well, we shall make a great presentation for the woman. This should help your father get through his meeting with her. Your mother said you should come down later. She will let you know." Madam Iwata was shaking her head in disapproval of our impending visit. She had never held her tongue regarding the pompous woman.

"You know it is important for your parents to impress this visitor. Your mother has been worried about the drop in local silk sales. All the small villages have not seen prosperity for a while. Most of the samurai families and farmers have been clutching their yen tight inside their yukatas—in part because of the poor rice crop and also the tax system that favors cities over the countryside."

"Oh, I know. My friend Saiko's family is having some issues. I did not know it was widespread."

"What? Her father is not very delicate. Saiko should not have to worry about his problems!"

"I need to learn about things like this if I am to be a merchant's wife. Thank you for telling me."

"That is precisely why I have decided to talk to you more openly." Madam Iwata smiled at me.

I then looked at Madam and asked, "And so we must please the dragon lady because she has connections to the governor's establishment in Kumamoto city? Her son is a magistrate. They all need silk kimonos for work?"

Madam Iwata laughed. "Yes, Ueme. Keep your eyes open, and you will do well in this life."

Dressed for my musician's role and carrying my samisen, I leaned over the top steps to hear the conversation. I stepped quietly down the stairs. Madame Kumodo seemed a little excited. She was brimming with gossipy news of her son's hopes of being appointed as one of the ministers to the emperor.

Father and Madam Kumodo were both kneeling facing a small table. Father had just finished reciting his frog haiku. She was giving small tittering laughs. I thought it was a good sign. I overheard the last part of the conversation.

"But the signs and the brightly colored clothing and cloth are being so crudely displayed. You know, I do mention your establishment to my son's friends," Madam Kumodo complained.

"Madame Kumodo, this is merchandizing, selling. It is necessary." Father spoke very sternly, ignoring her thinly veiled threat. But the threat was real. Those government officials gave us the profits through the silk sales. Our cotton business was the bulk of sales but not the bulk of profits.

"Oh, your father would be so ashamed. This is not the Bushi way. I give you a large order on every new year for satins, brocades, and silk. That should be enough." Madam Kumodo sounded very distressed.

"Dear Madam, your orders are much appreciated, so much appreciated. Please accept my heartfelt thanks for your order. I accept them as gifts from your heart in honor of my father. However, you must remember, my father chose this position for me. He arranged it. And it is good."

My otasan continued, "Madam Oyama and I have a very prosperous establishment. I am proud of it, and I am sure my ancestors are smiling on us. After all, my family's good fortune

comes from this establishment. You know this is true, Kumodo-san."
Father bowed, his head almost touching his knees.

He continued, "As for the need for signs and sales to bring in
business, I need an income for the whole year. I have a family to
support and employees to pay. You appreciate the new fire watch
crew that patrols the alley, don't you? And the new superintendent
at the girl's high school? Your granddaughter attends that school, I
believe."

Madam Kumodo retorted, "Oh, but those are civic jobs paid by
the civic committee funds."

"Madam Kumodo, only 50 percent is paid by the committee."

Madam Kumodo readjusted herself and bowed just slightly.
"Oh? I must apologize. I had no idea."

"Our business with dignitaries is due, in large part, to my
friendship with your son. We only want to honor all with our trade.
Perhaps, one day, your son can bring you to one of my mother's
concerts?"

Madame Kumodo smiled and bowed. Father had cleverly
pointed out her rudeness in never attending Obachan's music events.

I heard the other shoji door slide open. Mother and Grandmother
were entering with tea from the other side. I slid my door open and
entered. Grandmother's koto was set up in front of the Tokonoma.
Everyone was seated. I bowed and addressed Madam Kumodo,
"Konnichiwa, Madam Kumodo."

Then Father bowed slightly to Madam Kumodo and suggested
it was most appropriate that we have a small concert to honor the
advent of spring. My obachan sat very still and looked very elegant
in her gold and light blue kimono. After a few moments, she leaned
forward and began to pluck the silk strings of the koto. The notes
came slowly and singularly and promoted a meditative mood. Her
solo ended, and she nodded at me.

Now Obachan began a new tune with quick notes that I
accompanied with my samisen. Another nod, and we both started

singing the folk tunes we had practiced ever since I was small child. When Grandmother and I sang together and my fingers were pulling the notes from the samisen strings, I would be transported to a place beyond the present. My mind would wander, but somehow, the notes would flow rhythmically from my fingers and my throat. This was my talent.

Obachan and I sang three tunes. I could feel the sentiment in the room lighten with our songs. This was the reward. We were all traveling on the music together. Then, at Obachan's nod, she and I played the classical piece we had been practicing. It was full of slow notes and exact timing, with no words. The mood became meditative again, and then silence encompassed our small group.

After the perfect amount of time, Mother rose to her feet. Madam Iwata entered again with the sweets. More tea was offered. After many compliments on the tea and the Chinese scroll, the visit was over. Madame Kumodo took her cue and bowed. She was ushered to the garden, and Father led her to the alley through our garden gate.

I think we had all been hunching our shoulders and holding our breath. Now, all tension was released with one common sigh.

Father came back from the garden and bowed to all of us. "Good job. She is happy until next season! You know, her son used to be a schoolmate of mine. I want to keep the peace. Things have changed so much for that generation. We must be kind."

Grandmother's face changed shape. "Harumph! Yes, it is business. But heaven's sake, when do things not change? I was born samurai, and my mother was attendant at the daimyo court, but I do not go making fusses all over town about people misbehaving. So, six bolts of cloth, and she supports a whole establishment? She has no clue about money. She must know people laugh behind her back! I am embarrassed for her."

I noticed my mother and Madam had disappeared into the kitchen and were already preparing our evening meal. Father and

Grandmother were deep into talk over their matters, and I escaped through the garden out to the alley.

I breathed in the cool late afternoon air. Looking toward the mountains, the rice fields below and our vegetable garden nearby appeared so lush and green. I went back through our courtyard and upstairs to change into work clothes so I could spend time in the vegetable garden adjacent to the rice fields. After this event, I just wanted some relaxation, something positive and not full of tension—time in the garden with my hands in the soft dirt.

Having slipped out the rear garden gate, I walked toward the end of the alley. I looked back and saw Jun wheeling the cart in the opposite direction toward Obachan's house with the carefully wrapped koto in it. Beside him walked my obachan, who seemed to be instructing him in something very serious.

In the garden, I slipped off my sandals and felt the soft dirt under my toes. Then I knelt between the rows of vegetables and sang while pulling weeds. There were cucumber flowers ready to put out fruit and carrot tops growing bright green and feathery. The rice workers had all gone home for the day. It was quiet without the noise of all the hoes click-clacking. They would be back early before the sun was up. But for now, I had the great expanse to myself. Clouds hung over the distant mountains. A cooling breeze came from the sea in the west, from the other side of Kumamoto city. Gratitude for my beautiful life overcame me. I was blessed.

I thought about the silk wholesaler's son. What would our lives be like? Would we have a vegetable garden and a view of the mountains? Did my intended know how to grow vegetables? As my thoughts kept rambling, I realized I knew so very little about the man with whom I would spend my life. We had never spent more than a few hours together. He was from the other side of Kumamoto city. I had never been there. It was quite far from here. What was his family house like? I would be living in the busy city after the wedding.

Think, Ueme. I smiled to myself. He was so handsome. His hair had a slight wave, which gave it a beautiful shape on his head. His forehead was broad, supposedly good for a successful life. He had a nicely shaped nose, not too broad at the base but not a sharp, ugly pointed one. His neck was strong and neither too narrow or too short. *Stop!* I told my dreaming self. Those were only superficial qualities. They meant nothing.

A new thought—shouldn't he be writing to me considering our new state? I had received no letters. It had been three days. I could have received a letter by now. A slow worry started to grow like a weed among the flowers, just a sprout today and, by tomorrow, choking out the good plants.

A rabbit had come close, and when I moved, he jumped over the row of carrot tops and shook me out of my thoughts. Seeing how rabbits had munched many of our seedling tops, I shouted at him, "Shoo!"

It was time to go back and help with the kitchen chores. Enough thinking—I was getting overwrought with it. *Stay in the moment, Ueme.* Life required much discipline.

That evening, brother showed up just in time for food. Father asked him about his progress on sweeping the warehouse and setting the mousetraps. Brother shrugged. Father calmly asked him to do it for certain on the next day. I was watching this and wondering how he could get away with his attitude. Mother and Madam Iwata were constantly scolding me for my "attitude." As Father and Brother were served, Mother and I could now kneel at the table and eat.

Staring at my rice bowl, I was transfixed by new worries. Noticing that Brother and Father had finished, I jumped up and took their empty dishes to the kitchen. The tea tray had been prepared by Madam Iwata, who had left earlier for her own home.

I looked at the kitchen as if for the first time. I saw things I had never noticed before. Madam Iwata had some little pots lined up on the windowsill with mint and green onions growing in them. There was a basket in the corner. It was filled with some calico squares and some folded-up sewing. Who was working on that? I wondered. Was it Madam Iwata's or Mother's? How little did I notice these every day details.

A loneliness started to creep over me. This would no longer be "my" kitchen. I knelt on the raised wood floor that bordered the kitchen on one side, a foot above the smoothed dirt floor. I had been clutching one of the work towels. I looked down at my lap and unfolded the thin cloth, stretching it out before me. I had not ever really appreciated the various designs in blue indigo on these common cloths. I put it softly to my cheek, realizing it came from one of our Oyama bolts of tenugui cotton.

Mother came into the kitchen. "Is the tea water hot? Father is waiting for his cup of tea, Ueme."

"Oh, so sorry. I have just been looking at the kitchen, at the floor, at the ceiling, at all the tubs and baskets. It really is such a lovely room. Don't you think so, Mother?"

My mother looked at me impatiently. "Oh, Ueme, really! Let us bring in the tea. You can look at the kitchen later when we clean up."

Later, upstairs, I was lying inside my futon breathing in and out. Father said this is important, big deep breaths. However, I should be standing like he does. He stood with his legs spread a bit and his back straight. He did this usually out in the garden, with his arms stretching out and coming straight into a soft clap, stretching out the arms as the breath came in. Suddenly, I saw Father doing this exercise and heard him exhorting me to join him in the healthy act. Oh, I would not be seeing him in the mornings after next spring. That was not so far away.

Finally, my mind was made up! I was not ready to leave my home so soon. In this modern era, girls were not always married so early. I needed to talk to Mother about this. She and Father had adopted all the modern practices for the store. We had ready-made, already sewn clothing to sell for the men's Western suits, and we had ready-made Western-style blouses and dresses for the women.

Mother received the fashion magazines for women from Tokyo to show the latest kimono and obi styles. She was always ready to take an unusual order to be sewn for a customer. Also, Mother and Father were very involved with the new schooling edicts from the emperor and empress. Father supported secondary schooling for the girls as well as the boys, though many families did not send their girls. My parents were very modern. I was finally able to fall asleep, realizing I could just talk to everyone about my idea for delaying the marriage. It would all work out.

Chapter 6

SAIKO'S PARTY

Saiko's marriage was coming soon. I had prevailed upon Obachan and my parents to have a celebration before the actual wedding, to be given by her neighborhood friends, Ito and me.

Saiko was nervous. Ito and I were nervous for her also. She had met the man once more after the betrothal. She had been emboldened by Ito's suggestions and had asked permission to have another visit with him. The parents had all consented to this. Saiko had had tea with the man and had asked him many questions. It seemed he'd been engaged before but the engagement had fallen through. Saiko could not pry the reason out of him. She imagined all sorts of scenarios, and this didn't help with her mood about the marriage. She was trying very hard to be positive.

In the past summer, I finally admitted to my friends that I, too, was betrothed. My desire to talk my parents out of the timeline of the marriage had come to nothing. My wedding would be next spring or early summer. The time seemed to be flying by for all of us. My parents had to tell me, with a bit of sadness to disappoint me, that the timeline was because of Haru's schedule and his parent's desire that he be married while at university.

These marriages went against all our childhood hopes and desires. My friends and I were going to do things differently from our parents, but it seemed tradition was a river that didn't stop or change its course for us.

Saiko had said to Ito and me that it was fine. She was confident her betrothed was a good man. She was happy. Saiko was pure samurai. Her family did not give her any power, but neither did they train her to wield a sword or knife, as would have happened in the past for a samurai woman.

Obachan and mother had been organizing the party at our ancestral home, Uncle's house. The house had been the family home for many generations. The main timber in the ceiling was a trunk of a huge pine and ran down the length of the house. It had been blackened by years of indoor cooking that had taken place under it before the new kitchen had been added as a separate room. The large, blackened log seemed weighed down by our long family history that included much happiness, as well as much sadness. I preferred our flat, lightly colored wood ceiling in our first floor to the giant openness of the old home.

We would have the tea ceremony and the banquet here. Then later, we would celebrate with the music of koto, samisen, shakuhachi, and taiko drums. Obachan had prevailed upon friends for the music. It would be all women. Our feast would include many delicious foods—special sushi with green tea soba, cucumbers, shiitake, kombu and pickled *takuan*, and sweetened red bean *aduki* paste. Auntie and Mother had been coordinating the treats.

Obachan had asked me to come early to hunt for the best tiny maple leaves and pine needles to garnish the treats. She mentioned that the chrysanthemums were blooming in her vegetable garden and could also be used.

When mother and I arrived, one long, continuous low table was set. The interior shoji doors had been opened to make one very large room. The side doors were opened for a view of the moss and rock garden. Auntie stood at the entrance to the kitchen and beckoned Mother to carry her basket of goods in her direction.

I recognized some of my younger schoolmates, who had been

hired to help with the serving. They sneaked knowing glances at me but kept their heads low in deference to my obachan's strict orders.

I wore my most famous light green silk kimono and purple brocade obi with orange silk braid tie. My kimono had a very spare design of scattered, tiny white flowers. My hair had been done perfectly by Madam with some chrysanthemums placed artfully within the coiffed strands. I felt very grown-up, sophisticated. Conscious of my elegance in front of my schoolmates, I went outside to look for the proper leaves and needles for garnishes in the old garden in back of Obachan's quarters.

As I entered the garden gate, I was surprised to hear my dear friend crying in the corner.

"Why, Saiko, what is happening? Have you a problem with your kimono? Can I help you fix your obi?" I asked my friend.

"No, no. I am just realizing the tremendous meaning of today." Saiko was dressed in a pale peach silk with delicate blossoms falling from the neckline to its hem. Mother had supervised the design.

"Oh?" I sensed my job now was to cheer up Saiko. The garnishes would have to wait.

"I am going away." She paused, and I waited. "You know." She looked at me with her dark eyes intent on mine. "In a few days, after the ceremony at the temple. My cases and trunks are all packed. This is the end of my life here."

"And the beginning of a new life," I felt obligated to say, my mother's words echoing in my head.

"It may just be that. One never knows what it will be like. I am to serve his mother, you know. I am the bride but really a servant. Here I am, all dressed up. Fancy kimonos and new yukatas have been sewn. Poems have been written and read in my family's honor. Oh, great happenings."

I was silent. I did not know where this conversation was going.

Saiko continued, "But me, me! Will I be allowed to be me? These people do not know me. My marriage is really a business transaction. That is what it is. Surely. I am guaranteed not to be poor with this family, but will I be allowed to use the money? My mother-in-law will dictate everything, from what I wear to when I wear it. I will be cleaning and dusting and folding and maybe even weeding the garden. Who is my husband? I do not know. They say you can learn to love anyone. But what if he doesn't like to keep himself clean? What if he smells bad like, like …"

She stopped and turned to look at me with a gleam in her eye. "What if he smells like bird poop?"

A big guffaw escaped from my mouth, and I quickly covered it with my hand. The mood had changed rapidly. I looked to see if anyone heard my outburst. The three of us as young girls had decided very early in our childhood what some of the worst smells in the world were. We had chosen bird poop. It did smell bad. But what about mice or rats or? No, bird poop was the worst; because birds were beautiful and sang pretty songs, the contrast made it particularly noxious. And when a bird pooped on your head, it was the worst insult of all!

We both were leaning carefully, to protect our silk kimonos, on the bamboo fence at the end of the garden. We rocked back and forth with laughter, buoyed up by sadness at the forthcoming departure.

"Ito says I should run away, that I should not allow myself to be used this way. So where will I run? Ito's idea is unrealistic. There is a structure to our lives in Nihon. Everyone fits into her place perfectly. Mother tells me all the time, 'Wait until you have children. Then, you will see how perfect it is.'" Saiko sighed.

"Ito is full of talk. She obeys her parents just like we do. Don't worry about what she says. She hasn't said what she is doing with her future! It is just talk." I wondered for the first time about who Ito would marry.

Saiko was smoothing out the long sleeves of her kimono and holding out the long fabric as if she was seeing it for the first time.

Sleeves of an unmarried woman were especially long, indicating her marriageable status. It was an impractical style, and Saiko would probably be the only one wearing it today, though many of us are marriageable.

"Your kimono is very grand and shows off your complexion beautifully." I felt a compliment was in order.

I moved away from the fence, having seen some fallen maple leaves that could be picked. Then I progressed to the chrysanthemum blossoms. I should have brought a knife. They were not so easy to snap off. I spied a garden tool carelessly left out by Obachan's garden boy and used it for the blossoms. Saiko let go of her sleeve and started to collect more leaves to contribute to my basket. There was a paved path through the garden that we followed in an effort to keep our kimonos in proper order.

"It's the last time I can wear this style, you know. It really is rather a difficult style anyway. I keep tripping on the sleeves when I go up any steps." Saiko lifted her sleeves again.

"Yes, but it really is a fortuitous kimono for this occasion. Everyone will be admiring you." It was comforting to talk about trivial things when the plight of our lives weighed heavily upon us.

My basket was full, and we started back toward the house.

"Saiko, you have not told me very much about your betrothed? How do you find him?" I asked, hoping to hear good news about him.

"He makes jokes. We laugh a lot. He writes to me. I think that's good. Don't you?" Saiko said, looking to me hopefully.

"Oh, most definitely. That is a very good sign. By the way, where is Ito?" I noticed that she normally would have found us and joined in our conversation by now.

"Let's go inside and see what is happening."

Saiko and I walked out of the vegetable garden and stepped up onto the veranda.

Mother appeared at the other end of the veranda. "Where are the leaf garnishes? Hurry, hurry. The tables are finished being set in the large room. We will have the tea ceremony in a few minutes for just our small group in the formal garden. But where are Ito and her mother? The tea waits for them and the two of you." Mother was practically breathless in her explanations.

The tea ceremony was quiet, somber. We dutifully admired nature and all its unruliness in the garden and in the misshapen teacups that were passed around with the thick green tea inside. Purified after twenty minutes of sipping and breathing, we retired to the main room where the rest of the guests had gathered. Some of the older women had already partaken of some of the sake. There was much talking going on and, as Obachan would say, much gossip. Our tea companions had all taken their places at the long table, and we joined in the party.

Saiko, Ito, and I sat through many pleasantries, answering the questions put to us from the older generation. The serving girls started taking items from the table in an effort to clean up and return to their own homes to help preparations for their own families' dinners. The big event was coming to a close, and Saiko's departure was that much closer.

The sun was getting low in the sky. I said, "Listen, Saiko, Ito, this will be our last sunset together and our last walk down our alley. Let's go now and not miss the moment when the stars first shine on our good fortunes."

Leaving the group busy with their long goodbyes, we walked to end of the alley. The moon was rising over the rice fields. The mountains appeared misty in the distance. We could feel the fine breeze on our cheeks.

Ito spoke. "I do not think we will be as happy as we are here ever again. Yes, we will have happy moments. But things will happen in our lives—who knows what? Our lives here are the backdrop for our future happiness. Even tonight is tinged with a bit of sadness that our dear Saiko is leaving our village forever."

I responded, "My, how dismal! First Saiko, and now you, Ito!

Life is good and full of promise. We know more than our mothers did. It is a new world with each generation. We shall steer life more than our mothers or grandmothers ever did."

Ito spoke again. "Yes, it is good for us to look at positives. But remember this. Whoever controls the money controls the family decisions. And who inherits? Hardly ever a woman! So, she doesn't come into money from her ancestors either. Who runs the businesses? And who collects the payments? We do all that and hand it over to our fathers and husbands."

I responded, "Ahh, such a merchant woman, always looking where the money is! Let us forget money and material things. Remember the tea ceremony and Buddha's exhortations. We need nothing material for true happiness." I wanted this afternoon to end happily.

"Ueme, we live on earth, on this dirt!" Ito picked up a clod of mud and threatened to throw it at me.

She continued, "May I remind you that, as a woman, you will not be given anything by anyone. You must give to yourself. Grab your own chances. And grab whatever should be yours. And that may save you one day from starvation."

I laughed. "How serious is this conversation! What do you think of this, Saiko?"

Saiko shrugged her shoulders. "You both have dealt a lot more with money than I have. I am hoping my husband is good with money. Then he can teach me."

"Oh, Saiko, if you want to learn, teach yourself! And you laugh, Ueme! Think of all that work you do at your parents' business. It belongs, in the end, to your brother." Ito released the clod of mud to the ground and tried unsuccessfully to clean her hand with a leaf.

"Hah, my brother cannot even work the abacus. And he could care less for the business. My father knows how important it is to me." I really did not like this conversation.

"And will that change the inheritance laws? Have you heard

about our new constitution that was supposed to change life for us? Hah!" Ito looked me in the eye.

Saiko, the bride, interrupted our arguments. "No one is trying to steal anything from us. It is just the natural order of things today. I am to be married and be part of another family."

"And may it be good!" Ito and I chimed in.

The half-moon rose in the sky over the mountains. We turned around to go back to our alley that had darkened considerably in our absence.

I walked all the way back to Obachan's to help Mother bring items back to our house. We tied up some boxes and baskets. Jun was there with the cart. Jun and I left through Grandmother's back garden gate, feeling the drops of the evening rain on our hands and sleeves.

Mother had stayed behind. She was deep in conversation with another merchant wife. Mother, ever the businesswoman, was discussing strategies on how to overcome the low cash flow this fall in the village. I heard something about how the price of indigo dye had risen and about a marketing strategy of ordering more of the lower quality, thinner cloths such as tenugui with lower prices to entice buyers.

I thought about that conversation. Mother always talking business strategies. Father talked of poetry and kendo. But it really was the two of them together that made our business a success. Father had a way with people, and Mother had a way with the abacus.

With my future looming in front of me, I was now paying attention to conversations that I had always ignored before. Perhaps that was why I'd never noticed when Mother was worried before.

Chapter 7

FULL MOON

The maple leaves were the most brilliant we had ever seen. At the height of color, Father and Mother planned a family picnic at their favorite spot on the mountain. We traveled by rented cart to Mt. Aso and climbed a colorful slope, stopping at a rock outcropping to spread out our little feast. Obachan insisted on coming, declaring she wasn't dead yet and deserved to see the view from the mountain again before she died. That phrase would allow her any wish. Brother had been forced to break his plans with his dojo buddies for some sword game nonevent that he claimed was going to change his life.

"Here it is," said father as he spread his arms wide toward a sloping expanse of red and gold reaching to the valley below. The air was cool and crisp, a welcome change from the summer's humidity.

"It has grown lovelier, Masumo, than it was on *our day!*" Mother said cheerfully as she gazed admiringly at the beauty before us.

Brother, Obachan, and I stood looking at the view worthy of a scholar's paintbrush.

"Soo, what is this about 'your day,' eh?" cooed Obachan. "Not your wedding day? That was in the winter." Grandmother looked to her son for the explanation.

"Aah, my children." Mother sighed as she reached for Brother's and my hands. "This is where your father declared his love for me!"

"Well, I am confused—if this is not your wedding day!" Brother seemed annoyed at the sentimentality.

"Our marriage was arranged, of course." Father looked at Obachan with a certain gleam in his eye.

"Aughmph, not that again." Obachan was preparing to defend her parental authority.

"No, no. You know how happy I am that you chose Yuki-san, mother!" Father looked at Obachan, who was pursing her lips.

"Oh, well at first, I put up quite a fuss, I know. I wasn't happy with being pushed around as second son. But one year after living with your choice, I discovered I had fallen in love against my will and was happier than I ever thought I could be."

Father then took Mother's hands and, looking at her and she back at him, said, "We wanted our children to know how our lives started out and how unexpected turns in life can be better than you ever think."

"So true, Masumo-san, so true." Mother's words were strong and clear as she looked straight into her husband's eyes. "We had never told anyone about our love declaration day. Yes, I too, had fallen in love with your father. It was a match made in the heavens. And now that you are both coming of age, we felt it was important for you to know that marriage can be full of love, as well as being practical, even if it is an arranged marriage."

My stomach sank. Was this a message to me? Or Brother? Yes, he was older, but I thought he was going to study at the university before marriage. Mother quickly came over to me.

"No, no. I can see you are misunderstanding this picnic. We just wanted to share this with you both and with Obachan. We have more time yet before the marriages happen and our little family is dispersed!"

"Ueme, you always take things too much to heart. Why don't you and Obachan play us a cheerful song on the samisens, eh? Autumn is a time of appreciation. See how the wind blows the leaves off the branches. They fall on the ground and nourish the next year's growth." Father unwrapped the samisens from the protective cloth and handed one to me and one to his mother.

We sang songs of falling leaves and blue skies.

We stayed until the sun passed behind the clouds permanently and the sky darkened. The wind picked up strength, seeming to say, "Get going, eh?"

Droplets started hitting our kimonos and our noses. Rushing to get everything back into the cart, father asked the driver to hurry us down the mountainside before we became drenched with the rain. The driver indicated he liked the idea, and we were off. It felt like we were tumbling down the mountain. Grandmother held onto the edge of the cart with her strong, tiny hands. Mother and Father were laughing, while Brother and I expressed our childish displeasure at being so squished in between everyone, with us taking all the bumps.

By the time we reached our street, the water had reached through our clothes and into our skin. Cold and damp, we unloaded the cart while father paid the driver and offered him to come have some hot tea before setting out to his depot. The driver explained he was anxious to get his cart back to the barn, and he bowed deeply before setting off.

Inside, we quickly changed into dry kimonos. Mother and I hung the wet things out in the back of the kitchen. The kitchen boy had returned and made up the kitchen fires. At mother's instructions, he brought two hibachis into the middle room to place under the low table. Then she gave him some of our leftover sweets from the picnic, some plum jellies and bean cakes. She lent him our lacquered umbrella and told him to hurry home.

As Obachan was busy fixing our tea and rice crackers, I carried the tray with the cups and kettle into the middle room. Brother and Father had assembled the quilts all around the table. After I placed the tea things on the table, I joined everyone, shivering under the quilts with our knees near the warm hibachis. After a while, our shivering stopped, and Grandmother started telling us the latest news about our cousins up the hill at the ancestral home where she lived.

Our cousin, Hachi, was doing well in his position in the

Ministry of Transportation. The ministry was paying for him to take engineering classes at the local college. He was happy and saving money. He was assured of a permanent position in two years. Grandmother was beaming. She loved the practical. I thought this was so because she fought against her own "flighty love" of music. And of course, he was the first son of her first son. He would carry on the family name and honor, if not the fortune.

As for the girls, my cousins Meme and Miki, had been apprenticed to work at the governor's mansion, to learn the proper arts as upper-class young ladies. As Obachan talked, it was clear she was not happy with her son's and daughter-in-law's choices for them. These positions seemed frivolous and meant only for procuring husbands of high status. These granddaughters, she feared, had not been taught any survival skills.

Obachan explained that, whenever she had invited them to help in her garden, they had declined. Whenever Obachan was pickling her vegetables, their mother would stick up her nose and say that her daughters had better things to learn. They never accompanied her into the woods to pick mushrooms, lichen, or bamboo shoots. As Grandmother recited all their "failures," she shook her head. "Prosperity is always followed by despair. We must always be ready for it."

At that, Father threw his head back in laughter. "Mother, we have had a perfectly lovely day. Let us not let the rain bring sour thoughts upon it!"

As a daughter of samurai, Obachan had practiced swordplay and learned how to wield a knife to protect herself. She had muscles; she had stamina and knowledge of plants, food preparation, and herbal healing methods. These were all things one needed when trials came. The daughters of the first son were learning how to be weak. That was how Obachan was viewing it.

I, on the other hand, had thought they were having a grand adventure. To be at the governor's mansion and to be invited to parties—that seemed like a very fortunate experience to me. And they both knew how to play instruments. Meme was good at the koto. Miki played the samisen.

No. Obachan shook her head in disagreement. Neither had the feeling for music. You and I, she pointed to me, we have the feeling and the touch. It was true. I thought about music while doing everything. That rock over there, what tone was it? How to express that rock in a music phrase, or that stalk of rice blowing in the wind? Notes took geometrical shapes in my mind.

Father looked at Obachan as she finished up her news of his brother's family. "Mother, Jintaro built you an addition onto the main house so you could be independent of the household, and now you seem to wish that you had had more influence. We cannot have everything both ways. Perhaps this was best for the girls. Surely they will learn something at the governor's complex besides how to bat their eyelashes. I hear there are some high-level cabinet meetings held there that allow the young people to attend. Perhaps their interest in these things will be piqued."

"Ah, we all have different ideas on how to raise our children with these changing times," Mother replied to the discussion. "Jintaro's girls are lovely and smart. They will benefit somehow from this experience."

The next day it rained. One rainy day was followed by another and another. It was an early beginning of the winter rains. The water no longer seeped into the ground but made rivulets everywhere. The streets became impassable with all the ruts and holes created by the gushing water. We kept fires burning in the kitchen and in the braziers. We even put braziers in the warehouse to prevent mold from ruining the fabrics. Father was wild with worry over the possibility of fire. He was not worried about us causing it but, rather, about ignorant townspeople who did not have the proper fear of rogue ashes flying through the air. He had his best watchmen on the premises in shifts throughout the day and night. Some patrolled the alley looking for troubling smoke or flames; others kept watch over the braziers in the warehouse, inside and out; and another extra person helped with the household braziers.

It was a lot of work. Mother delegated the accounts over solely to me. Brother was to help Father with customers at the front of the house in the store and lend a hand when needed for maintenance of the warehouse and alley. Mother and Madam stayed in the kitchen preparing food for all the extra workers. The kitchen boy was unable to come very often, as he was needed at his own home.

It had become unseasonably cold along with the damp. There was no sun during the day. And at night, with all the cloud cover, there was no moon. The pounding water had beaten off all the leaves on the trees. The surfaces of the street and the alley were slippery with the wet leaves.

We had all come down with coughs and colds. Father said it was because of the mold. The rain had finally stopped, and the sun peaked out for few brief minutes at a time and then disappeared again. There was continuous cloud cover. We all longed for a full day of sun and a night when we could see the moon.

Mother had taken to praying and meditating for long periods in the meditation garden. It needed cleaning up from all the mud and wet leaves, but she insisted it was her best holy place.

The rain had stopped, but the fog lingered. And still there was not much sun, and never a moon.

People began to establish the regular routine again. The fishmonger and the tofu woman arrived at their regular times. The kitchen boy was back. Mother and I resumed our morning cleanup routine. Scrubbing the floors with the wet brush, I had the opportunity to look directly into Mother's face. There was a gray tinge to it.

"Mother, you should get out into the sunshine. You are looking pale!"

"Don't we all look pale after this season of constant rain?" she answered.

I wished I had paid more attention. However, what could be done when fate intervened?

Uncle made a surprise visit to our house. I only said that because we usually went to his house for important occasions. He rarely came down the hill to our alley. He and Father talked for a very long time in the store after hours. Mother and I supplied them with tea and then whiskey. When Uncle left, my father asked my mother to take a walk outside with him.

When they came back from their walk, they asked Brother and me to join them for a cup of tea. Brother was already half-asleep in his alcove. Mother explained that they had discussed an issue and decided it was important we knew about it. Uncle was moving his political group to our upstairs storage room. It was no longer safe for the group to meet in his barn. Some people were not happy with the new constitution. The government had asked for input and then seemingly ignored input from the outer provinces. I was so wrapped up in my own dilemmas that I could not really understand the fuss. Mother and Father had talked before about Uncle's political skirmishes with the establishment. So now he was going to involve my parents.

Father would move some bolts of cloth downstairs to make room. Brother and I were not to notice anything, and if anyone asked us about it, we were to say nothing and look blank. We were to give nothing away. Brother lightened up with this knowledge of intrigue. Father looked at him sternly. "This is serious. People's lives are at stake. Your uncle's life, perhaps more, if you give information to the wrong people."

Mother interrupted the stern lecture. "This is why I insist that you both be told, so you can understand the seriousness. Your silence and your nonaction will be very valuable. No matter what you see, you must remain calm and just disappear. You understand, yes?" Mother seemed to be agitated by it all.

I heard her say to Father, "Masumo, why should we take such risks? I wish you could deny Jintaro's request. He wastes his time with this political intrigue. And now he demands we make space in our house for his pastimes. He would do better to take care of his farming business, in which he seems not as interested."

Father had replied, "He is elder brother. I cannot."

"Jintaro worries so much about his own rights and ignores the economic depression that sits heavily over the village. I doubt his version of the constitution will be any more favorable to the village or to women." Mother shook her head.

Two nights later, the group convened. Mr. Satsuo, Mr. Yasui, Mr. Oto, Mr. Nabuki, and some others who I did not know, all wearing their dark indigo jackets and pants, came in through the alley entrance one at a time. I noticed that Mother was not required to interrupt them with tea. After two hours, Father crept downstairs and entered the tokonoma room that was our sitting room.

I heard him tell Mother that he was annoyed at the constant disagreements within the group. It seemed they spent more time disagreeing about every little point, rather than accomplishing their goal.

Otasan said, "I have no patience for this type of thing. Jintaro makes a very good moderator. He has more patience than I for their unending arguments."

"Ah, it is always easier to see others' foolishness than our own," replied Mother with a little laugh and smile.

"Oh, you and your Confucian sayings!" Otasan laughed.

"That's not Confucius; that's my grandmother! Do not go back up. Let them finish without you," Mother advised.

"Mr. Oto is constantly requiring that every proposition is written and spoken correctly, even before there is a discussion of the idea." Otasan picked up the newspaper to read.

"Oh, I have never cared for that man. He is a lazy one and takes no care for his wife, though she is an invalid," Mother whispered back to Father.

"Satsuo says his wife wants more rights for the women. Mr. Yatsui seemed to be the one to really grasp the issue of unfair taxes. But no one picked up on his points. Nabuki stood up and gave the same speech he gives every week. 'We must have peace, peace above all else.' He is so afraid of another rebellion."

I was straining to hear my parent's voices; they were speaking so softly.

"Oh, and then Satsuo says, 'Precisely that, how can we have peace if our women are unhappy?'"

"I am surprised that any of them care whether their wives are happy," said Mother.

"Oto then slings his arms wide and says, 'Why must you keep bringing up unsubstantial things?'"

Mother said, "I never liked that little man."

The men started to come down the stairs to leave. Mr. Nabuki poked his head into the room and said, "Perhaps we are not able to make a better constitution than the officials. We criticize, but are we any better?" He shook his head.

Looking around the room, he saw me and bowed in my direction. Then he bowed in Mother's direction and left.

Brother and I were not much impressed with all the old men, with their comings and goings. How could any of them be dangerous? We paid no attention to them.

As the rain had stopped, the soil took some weeks to dry. And now, in the dead of winter, the air chilled, and the cold was upon us.

Now we needed the braziers for the cold that numbed our fingertips. I spent as much time as allowed in the kitchen helping

Madam. Mother stayed up late working the accounts. Due to her late nights, she was waking up later in the morning. I was feeling guilty about enjoying the warmth in the kitchen. I found as many chores to do as possible there.

One morning, the fishmonger, after his regular price haggling with mother, scolded her. "Madam, what has happened? I miss our arguments. No one can trounce me as well as you. You have been letting me charge you too much. This is not fun. This has to stop! Here, I won't take this coin from you. Today, you get the fish for free, for all the extra charges you have been paying!"

Mother looked at him and smiled. She said nothing in reply but bowed to him.

The fishmonger shook his head and looked at me as he left. "There is some '*thing*,' something. What is wrong with your mother?"

After he left, I looked at my mother with fresh eyes. "Mother, what is wrong?"

Mother looked at me in the queerest way, and then she sank to her knees on the polished floor. "I am very sorry. Sumimasen. I lack energy today. I need some rest. Ueme, help your father today in the store. I will rest a bit. Madam, I trust you can decide on the evening meal."

For two weeks, Mother lay in bed. Father suspended the meetings of the old men. He said he was not able to do what Jintaro could do. These men needed a leader, someone more like his brother. He also said he did not want to disturb his wife with their nonsense. The house had become very quiet. Rather than something welcome, the quiet settled over us as heavy as fog. It appeared we all were moving slower, with a heaviness to our limbs.

Father needed help. Conferring with brother and me, Father agreed we needed Obachan to come and stay with us and take care of Mother. It was comforting to have Obachan's presence in the house, to hear once again someone ordering Jun to do his chores efficiently and to hear her voice taking over the kitchen chores with Madam.

The doctor came several times, but the herbs and poultices did nothing. Madam made soft mochi rice and chicken broth. Madam had changed her routine and stayed later and came in earlier.

Our neighbor brought a Chinese acupuncturist to our house. Father was open to any suggestions. A rather imperious man, the acupuncturist demanded herbs to be brewed while he worked on Mother. We sent Jun out with a list to purchase the packets of medicine. Madam steeped the herbs on the days of his visits. The musty smells filled the air, adding to its heaviness. The Chinese man barked out unintelligible orders to Madam and me, making us frantic with our lack of understanding. Obachan spent her time with father in the shop avoiding "the awful man."

The acupuncturist traced what he called meridian lines all over Mother's body and kept shaking his head. "You should have called me sooner."

His visit and the doctor visits alarmed us, as no improvements came from them. Grandmother had moved Father's sleeping place away from Mother's room, which disturbed him greatly. He would get up and roam around at night, unable to sleep calmly, not being able to be beside my mother. Sometimes, he would wake me and ask me to make him a cup of tea. It was just an excuse for him to have someone with whom to talk.

It was during these nighttime talks with Otasan that I learned stories of the samurai childhood he and Uncle had had. We often sat in the accounts office downstairs. We knelt under the light from the oil lamp, by a low table with sweets provided by Madam, sweets that always remained untouched.

Otasan's stories were from the days of the old regime, when the shogun ruled and samurai were noblemen. Otasan said his father still carried a sword when he was very young. Carrying swords was outlawed when the young emperor was installed in the seat of power. There were those who had seen that our old ways needed to be changed for the sake of Nihon's independence. Many new laws affected our family status and that of other samurais. The stipends for samurai military services disappeared, and samurai needed to find ways to earn money for the first time in centuries.

Luckily, Grandfather was someone who had been able to change with the times. Many found it hard to wrap their minds around new ways. Grandfather knew that things were changing and did whatever he could to purchase more and more land to rent out as rice fields. Grandfather became a modest-sized landholder. In this way, the family had an income. But each year, the taxes levied on the rice harvests had grown higher.

Looking to find other ways of making money, he'd made the acquaintance of my mother's father, a merchant. This alliance between them was monetary, as well as political. Grandfather could get things done for the merchant with his samurai connections, and the merchant helped Grandfather make commercial investments. It was only with the help of the merchant family that we were able to keep the ancestral home. Many samurai had to sell all their property. And of course, one of the deals was my parents' marriage.

I brought tea and rice to Mother for her meals. Sometimes, she was able to eat, but most times, she could not. I wanted to talk with her. I wanted her to sing songs with me. I thought this would all pass. But the ominous air in our house grew thicker. Grandmother had us all praying to the ancestors, morning and evening. Father took Brother and me to the Shinto shrine. There, we waved our hands over the smoking incense before entering the temple yard. The priest took Father's money offering. He blessed our family, praying for our ancestors and lighting special papers for Mother's recovery, which, he assured us, would definitely help our mother.

Neighbors came to visit and brought soups filled with the vegetables Mother loved, but she hardly ate and became thinner every day. I had even stopped thinking of my betrothal or of Haru. I had trouble even remembering that momentous day at all. I asked Father once about the silk merchant's visits. Had he come to the store lately? Father was so distracted, I dared not ask again.

One morning, the sickness broke. Mother rose up off her futon. She made tea and rice and served us all breakfast together. Obachan had risen earlier and had stayed away in the meditation garden saying her prayers.

Father was beaming, as well as Brother. I cleaned up the breakfast things alongside my mother just as we always had. The air was soft, and a nice breeze came through the kitchen's double doors.

In the kitchen, as the weather was unusually warm, the doors were wide open with a view to the fields. Mother and I knelt side by side on the wood floor, looking out the back to the rice fields and beyond our vegetable patch to Uncle's fields.

Mother started to talk. "What a grand life we have. Look how beautiful the weather is today. This is the kind of day my mother loved, a sunny day with a light breeze, a blue sky and all my family around me." Mother looked sweetly at me.

Mother continued, "She used to say that, you know. Your grandmother would start the day early and thank all the ancestors. She had more ancestors to thank than we do. Being modern, I only keep our immediate ancestors on our shrine. I do not have the time for all those prayers. And I want you to do the same. When you have your children, you do not need to keep my mother and father at the shrine. I want you to remember that. Do not burden yourself."

Looking up, Mother said, "Oh, how my mother would love a blue sky, a promising field, a prosperous business, healthy children. We must be grateful."

"Mother, I am grateful you are feeling better today." I hugged her, and she held me close.

She touched my hands with hers. "One never knows each day from the next."

She sighed. "I wish you had known my mother. She was strict, yet kind and very beautiful. Her father had money and educated her. She read novels and wrote poems. She was trained in the art of tea. Merchants are not supposed to do these cultured things, but who can prevent you if you have the money?

"And she was smart, she kept the accounts for the store, just as you and I do. She had a mind for the abacus. My how her fingers would fly! And her sums were never wrong. No merchant or customer dared to question her accounts." Mother was speaking with pride.

She asked me, "Would you please have Brother come here and look at the sky with me?"

I left her in the kitchen and went to find Brother. The light breeze blew clean air into the house, carrying birdsong that echoed off the warehouse walls to our door. I felt my shoulders relax and realized it had been a long time since I had felt this relaxed. Walking upstairs to the storage room, I heard Madam singing in the kitchen.

Mother and Brother talked together for a little while. They walked out to the alley for a bit, and then Brother left mother's side happily to get Father in the shop.

Mother and Father sat on their rock in the garden and stayed there until the air cooled and Mother started to shiver. Father had been draping his arm over her back, holding her gently all afternoon. Madam brought tea out to them.

Mother took hold of Madam's arm and raised herself up off the rock. She said, "Madam, I think I shall go lay down now."

Father rose with her and helped her to the stairs, where she gently touched his arm and motioned him to let go of her arm. She walked up the stairs by herself.

She looked back at Madam and Father saying, "I will be all right. Sumi-masen. I am so tired from sitting up all day."

I had been kneeling at the door of the tokonoma room watching all this. I searched for Obachan to tell her how Mother had recovered. Grandmother had been busy straightening up the shop. She looked at me as I entered the room.

"The shop is not in good order, Ueme. Your father has not been able to roll up the fabrics correctly. There are tally sheets and receipts piled in this corner in no particular order. Ueme, you need to spend more time in the shop. You have been doing well with the accounts, but the shop is in disarray." Obachan was all business.

"Obachan, did you know Mother has been up today and talking with all of us? Come, see for yourself. She will want to talk to you before she takes her nap."

Grandmother looked up from the pile of fabrics and told me to make tea and warm up the soup for our dinner. Then she walked slowly up the stairs.

That evening, we all sat down to eat our soup, but no one could touch a thing. Mother had lain down and silently died. When Grandmother entered the room, she had already gone to the ancestors.

I was crying hysterically. Obachan and Father were shushing me to be quiet. Brother sat at the table for only a minute and then disappeared.

Obachan looked at me. "The neighbors will be coming over soon to help with the body and to help your father. You must compose yourself, or you disgrace yourself and the family."

Grandmother was sterner than I had ever experienced. My comportment was more important than Mother's death. *How stupid,* I thought angrily. *I have a right to cry, to scream if I want.*

Disgrace the family? What family? We had just lost the most important member! How I hated the silence that was our way. "Nobleness is seen in the quiet composed man even whilst he suffers with gaping wound." Those words from one of Saiko's dramatic magazine stories came to mind.

But I bit my lip and went to the bathhouse to wash my face with cool water. I walked into the alley and looked out at the fields that Mother and I had looked at only hours before. There they were. Did they know their admirer was gone away forever? Were the rice stalks bending in sadness or to the breeze? Or was the breeze blowing in sadness?

And then I looked up. There it was, surrounded by the dark sky with long, slow, narrow, winding streaks of wispy white clouds, like rivers in the dark, sometimes touching but never covering, the great round beaming full moon.

Chapter 8

WHITE SILK

It would not be a stranger's procession but ours that would go up the road past our store to the shrine and then to the family plot for the burial. Father and Brother were taking down all the flags and signs advertising the latest silks and cottons from the front of the store. They would be replaced with drapings of white material, honoring Mother.

All the family would be clothed in white kimonos. The silk merchant sent his gift of the finest white silk, enough bolts to clothe the whole family, as soon as he heard the news. He had always been fond of my mother. He had said she was the most refined cloth merchant he knew, fair as the petal of the plum blossom.

Mother's seamstresses had been busy making all the kimonos, for Father, Brother, Grandmother, my cousins, Auntie, Uncle, and me. White, the color of clouds, wispy vapors of water. White, the color of rice, essential sustenance of Nihonji. White, the color of paper on which we brush our poems, squeezing our emotions to leave only the essential purity of being.

White, the color of nothingness. I hated this color. I hated this kimono. I hated this day and the next and the next.

Father and Brother were being composed. Grandmother was very busy directing everything. She muttered on and on, "Why, why am I still here, the one left to do this? I should not be the one here to organize this funeral. It should be me in this jar." Every time she said the word *jar*, I jumped inside. Why did she keep going on about it?

Mother had already been cremated. It was her jar of ashes that we would bring to our ancestral graveyard tomorrow. We would walk behind the cart carrying her ashes to the temple for a blessing. Then later, we'd walk up the hill to our cemetery. That place had held wonderful memories for me, my cousins and I playing hide-and-seek around the old stones and bushes, laughing and carrying on. Or my romantic rendezvous with Haru—we'd come here, looking into each other's eyes and declaring our intentions. Or my cherished memory of coming here with my mother to place mochi cakes and fruit for the ancestors on their special days. Now, one day, I would bring my daughter here to place mochi for my ancestor, for my mother!

I awakened to the day. My obachan was very determined that we did not shed a tear. I felt so bottled up I might burst out with a wail in spite of myself. Thankfully, Ito managed to avoid my obachan and sneak upstairs for a quick visit in my room. I burst out in tears at seeing my dear friend's face.

"How will I be able to get through this day?" I asked her.

"Aagh, I cannot answer that. But just know that I am in the procession right behind your family. I will be here as much as I can. However, my family has another event I must attend in the late afternoon. I apologize for having to leave early." Ito gave me a warm hug and squeezed my hands until they hurt. Then she quickly disappeared down the stairs.

The family assembled for the procession. Obachan walked next to Otasan. Uncle, Auntie, and my cousins walked right behind Brother and me—all of us in white silk.

Father had hired the best horse and carriage to bring us back from the temple later on. Going toward the temple, walking the distance, he led us all while keeping his head held high. Many flowers decorated the carriage with my mother's ashes. I recognized the large bouquet and trailing ribbons from Ito's family. Before we had started to walk, Ito's mother came up to me and brushed my cheek gently with her hand and then returned to her position behind all of us. I dared not look up for fear of losing my composure. Obachan had been fierce in her instructions to Brother and me this morning.

We had returned from the temple. The carriages had let us off at the base of the path to the cemetery. We were trudging up the lane. Neighbors were walking behind us. Earlier, businessmen had been walking in the procession—all people connected with our store, and the suppliers, the silk merchant and his son. Now, only the closest family and friends accompanied us. At the top, we stopped. The priest was there. He was saying something. There was incense. There was bowing. Pieces of paper with good wishes and poems brushed on them had been let loose, the wind taking them to the sky.

It was finished. We turned around and walked back to the house. My legs were difficult to move, so filled with lead.

Ito came up behind me and grabbed my arm. Her eyes were filled with tears. "Saiko sends her best wishes. It was too difficult for her to journey back today, now that she lives with her husband's family." Ito waved goodbye and walked on up the alley to her house.

Jun and Madam had opened the storefront doors to all. The interior shoji doors that had previously divided the rooms into rear, middle, and front rooms were all completely folded back, making one large room with tables of food.

Everyone gathered around Father. They bowed and shook his hand or lightly grabbed his arm with affection. The silk merchant's son came to my side. We walked to the far edge of the veranda and stood gazing into the meditation garden. There was only a sliver left of the moon. "Soon, it will be a new moon," he said. I felt disconnected and floating.

Someone was sitting close to me, and I could feel the comfort and warmth of the person. Who was talking? Was the silk merchant's son talking to me? We were kneeling at the veranda's edge. I could hear Haru talking softly to me. However, I was having difficulty keeping the words in order. "Sadness, dear one, happiness comes again, future together, she was always kind ..."

Yes, that's it. My mother was always kind.

Oh, to feel her kindness now! Some tears fell on my cheek. Haru gently brushed them away with his kimono sleeve. *What? Why am I paying attention to his sleeve. Look at the material, a very expensive silk! Who taught me that, to look closely at fabrics?*

At that, I laughed. Haru was confused and felt insulted. Why was I laughing at him?

"No, no," I said to him. "It's just that I have been feeling so sad all these days, missing my mother."

"I do not understand you. Why do you laugh?"

"I felt your soft kimono on my cheek. Such a dear motion for you to make. I am sincere in that. But as I felt the cloth, I immediately recognized it as shantung from China, the finest weave. Do you see?"

Haru was turning red with confusion and embarrassment.

I continued, "My mother, the cloth merchant is here reminding me what she taught me. She would always say, 'Notice the kimonos people are wearing. Look at the styles. Feel the cloth. Do not be too obvious. We are merchants, and we must be ever watchful for the fabrics people will want to buy.' You see, she is here, here with me. She is like the water from that pond that evaporates to the sky becoming the cloud, an existence of a different composition than you and I today. But believe me, she is here!"

I rose to my feet and bowed to Haru. "Oh, Haru. Please understand. My mother is here. I can feel her."

Haru looked more confused than ever. I felt a compulsion to go to the kitchen. But shouldn't Haru be more important to me now?

Haru spoke. "Can we stay here together quietly? Let me comfort you."

I touched Haru's hand.

He responded by taking both my hands in his. "I want to comfort you, Ueme. But I do not know how. I feel you are so distant."

I was conflicted. What should I feel? Who should I respond to? I hadn't seen Haru all these months of mother's illness. I felt apart from him. But I did not want to insult him. Obligations to my immediate family were calling to me. "Excuse me, but I must go help my obachan now. She has been overwhelmed with her chores. It is only right that I should help her. I am glad for your company and the tenderness you have shown me."

Haru then stood and bowed, returning my pleasantries, "I only hope that, soon, we can plan to be together again on a much happier day."

I blushed, realizing he was referring to our betrothal. I put out my hand, and he took it in both of his and warmly pressed them with another quick bow.

Grandmother was surprised to see me so recovered. To her friends, she exclaimed, "Happiness gives me back my granddaughter, who has returned from her sadness to join us in women's work."

Obachan handed me a large tray of cups filled with sake. It was my job to deliver it to the guests without spilling. I felt completely up to the task.

Chapter 9

LIFE AFTER

A month after mother's funeral, grandmother instituted our weekly concerts. She said she was not going to stay in seclusion any longer. These events were for the public. She and I would play together at the schoolhouse for anyone to hear. We advertised. We talked to the printer and had him make up an invitation poster, which we hung outside the post office door.

Something let loose in Obachan. It was as if she had stayed with her strict rules of samurai status only for the benefit of teaching my mother. Now, she was going to do what she wanted. Only a few men ever came. Once they came and saw how many women were there, they never returned. So, gradually it became only a women's event. These music events were welcome to me because my contact with other people had been greatly reduced since Mother's sewing circle had disbanded. We played folk songs and some of the new popular tunes that my cousins would bring back from the governor's house. Everyone would join in the singing when they could.

Obachan and I were the principal musicians, but sometimes my cousins joined in. Here and there, one of the villagers brought an instrument to join us, with a drum or a flute. The villagers were happy to have the small distraction. The heavy rains had ruined much of the rice crop. The government had raised taxes, and people were having a hard time all around. These musicals brightened the mood for everyone.

I had taken over all the accounts and the serving of customers at the store. Brother would start out helping each morning. Somewhere in between that and the evening meal, he would disappear. He always said he was going to the warehouse, but I would check. He was never there. Father was not noticing, which was unusual for him. Father also never checked my figures for the accounts. His showing such confidence in my sums surprised me pleasantly. Since there had not been any secret meetings upstairs for months, the bolts of cloth had been returned to the storage room. Father had been refilling it with more cloth, silks and cottons from the warehouse.

Today I noticed Father looking grim as he returned with some bolts from the warehouse. There were fewer customers since my mother's death. My father seemed to have lost his genteel touch that had so entranced his customers. Suddenly, Father ran up the stairs, and I heard him throwing things around. He was agitated over something. He came back downstairs and had a wild look in his eye. Then he regained his composure and walked over to me, where I was kneeling at the accounting desk.

"Have you knowledge of Madam Kurasaro's order of five bolts of shantung silk?" He looked straight at me with his eyes full of hope. This was an important customer, and this was for a wedding to happen quite soon. I searched my memory.

"I remember when it arrived, Otasan. It was last week. We put it upstairs because we knew she was coming to collect it soon. Madam K has already paid for it. I know that. It is here in the accounts."

Father seemed agitated in spite of his outwardly calm demeanor. "I thought so. Yes, I do remember it. But … but it is not there. I cannot imagine that Jito has misplaced the bolt of silk. He has taken care of the warehouse since before you were born. He is meticulous and never makes a mistake. But I wonder, did Jito misplace it?"

"Oh, well, Father, I do not know that. I did not order it to be removed. Perhaps Brother knows."

Father looked devastated. "That is what I am afraid of. I think he does know."

Father knelt down on the tatami mat near me. He stared at the photo of Mother on the ancestor shelf. Then he continued, "We will have to contact the Chinese silk merchant immediately and see if we can procure more cloth."

"Father, that cloth is expensive. We will have to use the money Madam Kurasaro gave us to purchase more. I do not show much money in the accounts for this month."

Father bowed his head. His voice was thick as he said, "I do not know what is happening. I've lost control of things here. I cannot do this without your mother. Sumimasen, Ueme, I do appreciate all of your work."

"Oh, Father, we can. We can do it. We just need more customers. Perhaps Grandmother can help with her music."

Father brightened. "That is a great idea. We will have music to interest the passersby."

We tried using music to entice, but times were becoming hard. Ordinary people were not buying as much. Everyone was trying to save money. We had heard of families not having enough food. Fear of poverty was on everyone's mind.

We lost some of our more prominent customers due to the mix-up with Madam K's order. The new order of silk we procured for her arrived quite late. She was disappointed and told Father that his service was just not the same since his wife's death. She said everyone in town had noticed it.

Meanwhile, Grandmother encouraged me to do things with my friends. She berated me for spending so much time with the accounts and store. It seemed that she was after me to go to every event and fair that came to our part of town. Thus, I found myself dancing quite a lot with my friends. Roji, son of another merchant family, would seek me out to dance. He had always been the clown in school and made us all laugh so much. I found I needed the laughter and welcomed his entertaining wit and his gymnastic tricks.

Roji was quite the athlete. When not running in a race, he spent his time perfecting his somersaults and handstands, much to the delight of all of us young women. He knew some kabuki plays and would recite some difficult passages quite well. His grandfather had been a kabuki actor. He would pick me as his love interest to recite to. I was beginning to find him quite charming. Then I would remind myself to think about my engagement to Haru.

From time to time, I would ask Otasan about the silk merchant's son. When would the merchant be returning again? Wasn't he due sometime soon? Father or Obachan would change the subject and find a task for me to do that would take me out of the room. Something was wrong, and I could feel it. Perhaps I had been rejected. But why? What had happened? I no longer heard my mother in my ear. I felt I was losing her again. I was forgetting the sound of her voice. What did her eyes look like? Fear of the unknown started creeping over me. I looked forward to the escape the fairs held for me. I was especially looking forward to our most important fair that was coming soon.

I thought back to the day I had suggested to Obachan's friend, my music teacher, that I should like to honor my mother at the Obon festival this year with a song on my samisen. And then quickly, before I'd had time to rescind my suggestion, the songs were chosen and practiced. The musicians had welcomed my suggestion wholeheartedly. I would be doing a solo or two.

Chapter 10

SAYING GOODBYE

Ito's mother had offered to chaperone Ito and me to the summer Obon festival honoring the spirits of the dead. Father and Brother would join us later for the paper boats to be released into the river in the evening. However, Ito and I wanted to spend the whole day eating all the treats like we had as young girls with our obachans. We both were missing Saiko dearly, and we wanted to have a full day of fun.

My obachan loved the idea and wanted me to get away from the business, which had been consuming a great deal of my time. "You are not yet married. Go have a good time," she implored me.

My wedding had been postponed for another six months as I had wanted, but not because of my desires, rather, due to mother's death. I was not told who had decided the matter. It seemed it had been a mutual decision between the two families.

A decision had been made without my input. Was my life just a thing to be pushed this way and that for others' convenience? But there was no time for more thought about this.

As for Ito, her father, a merchant from a long line of merchants, had expanded his skills into accounting. This side business was growing, and he enlisted help from Ito, who had always been a good student in school. Ito wanted a day away from the abacus. Ito's father was a very serious person, and I had never seen him laugh. However, Ito assured me he was very lovable, and he wanted her to have a day of fun also. Saiko would not be joining us.

Saiko wrote us letters that informed us of her day-to-day life. She got along well with her mother-in-law, as they shared duties equally. Her husband was a shy, gentle soul. This was probably why it had taken him so long to marry. Saiko enjoyed living near the university, as she could attend lectures and plays there. She was quite sure that, eventually, she would find the passion of her purpose in life, given time, remembering our commitment at graduation to be modern, purposeful women. She never wrote harshly of her new circumstances but did lament her inability to visit her old village and friends. I realized that Saiko had adapted herself to her new life with complete grace.

After reading Saiko's letters to each other, Ito and I would acknowledge how we admired Saiko's character. We discussed our parents' characters and those of others we knew. We were very concerned with the character of men and women. We discussed different traits, analyzing and judging them. Was this person worthy of our attention or not? Wasn't this our job as modern women? How could we choose valid marriage partners without this information? And as the year had rolled on past my mother's funeral, I wondered about Haru's character.

How much did I really know about his character? I had only seen him on very short visits. Was it only physical attraction? And since I had not heard anything from him in all this time, I thought more and more about what I did not know. He appeared honorable. His family seemed honorable from all I had seen of his father. But other fears entered my mind. What hidden qualities that might not be visible did he harbor? Did he worry about me? Was that why he had not visited? My mind rolled these scary ideas over and over, and I begged them to stop bothering me.

But it was summer, and the fields were green, the sky was blue, and the mountains looked purple in the haze that fell over them. The birds flew from rice stalk to treetop, swooping down our alley filled with their songs. My mother's meditation garden was blooming with irises and lilies. I missed her. The garden brought me so many happy memories that it gave me joy.

Madam Iwata called me from the kitchen. "Madam Yokuri is here with the girls, Ueme."

I rushed down the steps past the tokonoma room and the rear office, noting how disheveled things had become in the last few months. My mother had been very careful to keep everything in its place. I had been so consumed with the store I hadn't "seen" the house. I made a mental note to pay attention to our home and straighten things as they should be.

Madam said to Madam Yokuri, "Ah, Ueme is here. May you all have a good time at the fair. I might see you later, as I will be there with my daughter and grandchildren. We will be sending boats out for my dear husband and other ancestors. The children and I have made beautiful paper boats with some origami touches."

With the mention of ancestors, I thought about my mother recently joining that illustrious group. I looked around, seeing her touch in everything of our household. My face must have betrayed my feelings because Madame Yokuri put her arm around my shoulders.

"Oh, how I miss your dear mother. She had such strong ideas about nature and balance and life. Let us go honor her with our best dancing and singing tonight. Ueme, do not forget your samisen. You are playing tonight."

I turned around to take the samisen wrapped in silk from Madam Iwata's arms.

Ito looked at my colorful yukata. "Ueme, how beautiful the material in your yukata! You are the picture of summer's glory."

"My obachan had this washed and repaired for me to wear today. This was the yukata my mother wore to meet my father for the first time." I smoothed the fabric with my free hand.

"How romantic and fitting for your first performance with the Obon musicians." Madam Yokuri turned toward the door, motioning for us to leave.

At the fair, we bought some treats for ourselves. Ito's mother took her younger children off to see the puppet show. Ito and I had decided it was not interesting to us. Now, we were on our own and strolled around looking at the crowd. We missed Saiko and were grateful we were not samurai born. We said to each other, "Wouldn't Saiko have loved this?"

When we were children, Saiko had not been allowed to accompany us to the festivals, as they were not considered proper places for her. This was one of many restrictions. Had it not been for the public school opening my mother and father sponsored in our village, Ito and I would never have met Saiko. Saiko's parents were not going to let her come to school. However, my mother was part of the "women's modernization movement, the WMM (for a time we had many a banner emblazoned with those letters in calligraphy flying at all the fairs). Mother had invited Saiko's parents to several teas with my very proper samurai grandmother present (to give a touch of samurai authority) and convinced them of the necessity for a young woman to be educated in Meiji Nihon. She explained that even those of samurai class were now choosing wives with education. Ah, my mother had her own talents for persuasion.

We passed by one of the five bridges for which our village was famous and had been named. The bridge was a high arch of beautiful proportions with a flowing weeping willow beside it. Ito and I both sighed. "What a romantic spot."

And just a few feet away, was a fishmonger frying up his delights to sell on a stick. We decided we were hungry and bought one each. These were quite messy to eat, and we had difficulty keeping the oily mess off our pretty yukatas. As we were leaning over in awkward positions to finish our treats away from our robes, Roji, our entertaining friend, approached us to wish us a good day. "Ohaiyo gozaimus, Ito and Ueme."

Roji bowed as we scurried away to another part of the fair. Our mouths were full, and we covered them with our hands in embarrassment. We entered an area of crafts work, beautiful wood carvings, calligraphy with original poems, and homemade eating treats. We searched for the music and followed the sound of the drums.

The ground rumbled with the vibrations, and we followed it, getting closer and closer to the heavy center of the earth beat. There we saw the crowd dancing in a circle around the bandstand.

I turned to Ito, "I am tired of carrying the samisen. Let me go ask one of the musicians to hold it for me until this evening's performance." I then maneuvered my way through the dancers to the center and climbed the steps to the stage. An older performer obliged me and assured me he would take good care of it.

Back down on the ground, I tried to part the dancers, searching their footsteps for an opening to get back to Ito. Someone bumped into me. I lost my balance, but this person grabbed my arm and rescued me. Looking up, I saw it was Roji. He was smiling wildly and laughing. "I have often wanted to speak to you but you are always surrounded by friends."

His bumping into me was so rude I was offended. "Well, this is quite an improper way to speak to me."

He instantly replied, "I do not care what is proper."

I said, "I have seen that at school many times. You play quite the joker."

"I like things to not be so serious. It is too serious at my home," Roji said.

I then remembered that his father had some business difficulties that had been widely discussed around town. Sympathetically, I said, "I can understand that."

"Let's get some mochi bean cakes and eat it together under the willow tree," suggested Roji.

"Oh, sumimasen. I first must ask Ito to see if she would like that." I turned to walk toward where I had left Ito.

Roji yelled after me, "Fine. I will buy mochi for all of us and meet you at the willow."

Ito was busy with another friend of ours, and they had decided to go inside a tent and watch one of the funny sideshows. They were looking for me to join them. They turned down the invitation from Roji and told me I should go by myself.

So, now this was an adventure on my own. I was sure he knew I was betrothed, so it was proper. I straightened my shoulders and held my head high, the exact opposite of a posture for a demure Nipponese young woman. I told myself, *Present your strong self, Ueme, and do not defer to any man.*

Later, Ito and I rejoined Madam Yokuri and the younger girls. We all were walking toward the direction of the music. In that direction, we met Mr. Toshita, a familiar local merchant whose hobby was composing poems and writing them on folds of origami he'd created.

"Ohaiyo gozaimas, Mr. Toshita!" greeted Madam Yokuri. "We haven't seen you for a while. My girls are so grown up, eh? And your children, they are fine, Mr. Toshita? Our dear Ueme, the Oyamas' daughter is playing the opening piece with her samisen at the Bon Dance in honor of her mother tonight. Her mother would be so proud. Will you and Madam Toshita be there to hear her?"

Mr. Toshita, a shy man, looked very nervous and bowed as a yes to all of her comments, backing away and apologizing that he must get back to his booth to sell his paper boats. Indeed, Mr. Toshita's poems were most beautiful. At mother's service at the Shinto shrine, my family had asked Mr. Toshita to recite one of his poems. He had composed a lovely verse for her.

The day passed by quickly. The sun had descended. The sky was becoming a purple blue. Down by the river, bonfires cast all the fairgoers in long shadows. Lanterns were strung between the trees, bobbing and swaying a bit in the breeze, making the whole landscape alive with a feeling of magic. Varying food smells wafted through the air, tugging our family of women to the food booths.

I spotted the bandstand just beyond the booths and left to join the musicians. People were laughing and some had started dancing and singing prematurely before the evening band had finished setting up. The bandstand had been constructed in the middle of the square. It was eight feet tall, covered with red and white banners, and supported the musicians far above the crowd.

I climbed the makeshift steps, more a ladder than steps, and retrieved my samisen from the friendly musician. Not knowing where I should be sitting, I stood quietly waiting for direction. Finally realizing there would be no direction coming, I grabbed an old stool that had been knocked over and squeezed in between two older musicians, hoping to not offend by smiling broadly at them and saying "onaigaishi masu" over and over again as I settled in.

I feared I would forget which fingers to use. Maybe I would drop the plectrum or forget the notes and words. Here I was again, in my own private world of nerves, my thoughts flying in and out, feeling I could keep nothing inside my brain, let alone the correct notes and words.

The drums started. Their steady booms vibrated, and the stand became alive with the rhythm. Looking down on the dancers, I could see the circle formation and the group motions following the song, sowing the seed, planting the shoots, down, up, down, up. Arms swung rhythmically, the drums controlling the beat.

I found my voice and fingers were moving on their own. Surprised I was already singing, I found the drums had overtaken my fear. My voice was clear and loud, carrying out over the crowd. Mixed feelings overtook me. Recognizing the fullness of my own voice, the clear sounds of my own samisen, my own music, I was filled with joy, an excitement, with the drums beating inside my head, in my heart, at the bottom of my stomach. I was inside and outside myself at the same time. The music released something in me. Was it my mother's voice singing or mine? Did it matter?

I started the next tune without waiting for the drums. I sang a song of autumn, my voice filled with the sadness of the dying season, followed by notes of spring and rebirth, followed by the fullness of summer, a tune full of the joy of life. I was only barely conscious of my own creation of the succession of these familiar tunes in my own order and symphony. There was no dancing. I began to realize that all eyes and ears were on me. Everyone was with me in the emotion and was singing with me.

As I finished the ballads, a contentment, a peace came over me from knowing who I am and where I should be. This was my village. These were the people who knew my family, who knew and loved my mother. I belonged here, and it was all good. Cheers from the crowd below rose up. The other musicians were bowing to me before starting their next dance number. I had made my public debut and was overfilled with joy and, shamefully, pride.

I climbed back down the stage ladder. Ito's mother was taking the children home and had offered to take my samisen with her. Ito and I decided to join the dance line, where many of our classmates were enjoying themselves. I saw Roji across the circle on the other side. He made a grand ninety-degree bow to me, and I laughed. The drumming hum was in the ground; it moved through my feet up into my body.

I stepped along with the line, bowing low and then lifting my hand high, feeling the motion. My whole body swayed forward and then back, singing about the rice harvesting. A number of movements later, Roji had somehow advanced in the line until he was right behind me. His exaggerated arm motions continually blocked my face for the forward motion. I was smiling and privately pleased at his forwardness. At the end of the dance, he dropped out of the line and disappeared.

I realized I had enjoyed his carefree way with jokes and laughter. I had been having fun dancing with him, and I missed having fun.

The dances started winding down. Ito and some other friends motioned me to join them to get some slices of watermelon. As we approached the food booths, fireworks cracked the sky. Red, blue, and yellow starbursts in the black sky announced the end of the three-day festival. It was just about midnight, and the full weight of the evening was coming to rest inside me. Exhaustion. I was being dragged by the energy of my friends. I could exert no energy to my own limbs.

A handsome young man, a nephew of the town fruit vendor who was visiting from a neighboring village, made a very big show of cutting a fresh new watermelon that he had pulled out of its storage in the shallows of the river for us. With a flourish, he brandished his short sword and deftly cut into the round, green-striped melon. Each piece was carefully wrapped origami style in waxed paper and handed to each of us with a slight bow. Cool juices dripped over our fingers, and the sweet pink flesh quenched our thirst. I felt quite revived after the treat.

The young "swordsman" asked our names and complimented each one of us on our dancing. He had been watching all of us that evening. How he entranced us with his attentions.

"And you," he said looking straight at me. "What an enchantress! Your singing has surely honored your ancestors tonight!"

I was only half aware of his compliment. With my face embedded in a slice of watermelon, I was looking across the road, where I saw two people linked arm in arm. Roji was escorting another young woman out of the square. There he was, the school flirt.

Lost in thought, I felt a tug at my arm.

"Come, let's go. It is time to release the paper boats." Ito pulled me back toward the bridge.

The crowds had been gathering at the edges of the river, lighting their candles and balancing them in the little paper boats. Those who had already released them were now crowded on the many bridges over the river to get a good view of the little vessels taking their cargo out to sea. The river was alight with all the candles floating on its current, taking messages and light to the ancestors in the afterworld.

I had made a boat carefully the day before while father and brother made theirs. We had made one for each of our ancestors and also one for mother. Brother and I had made haikus, brushing them in our best calligraphy onto specially colored rice paper.

Through the crowd, I spied Father and Brother coming across the bridge carrying our little boats.

Father looked kindly at me, "Ueme, we were so proud. Everyone was talking of your singing tonight." Father seemed genuinely happy as he said, "Let us light our candles and set the boats on the water."

Father recited a Buddhist prayer and, sitting on his knees, gently laid his boat on the water with a soft caress. This boat was truly for Mother, the one filled with the most emotion and care. Her spirit was embodied in the beauty of the folded paper design as well as in father's loving caress as he gently guided the boat toward the current.

As the fireworks crackled and boomed with the final starburst, Brother and I released our boats to the current.

My elderly music teacher walked toward us with her grandson in tow. Releasing the boy's hand, she took father's hand in hers and patted it with sympathy. Turning to me, she whispered, "The ancestors were surely with you tonight in your singing." She beamed at me as if she was praising her own daughter.

That's it, I thought. *I am confused with all the spirits dancing around me. I should feel gratefulness for having accomplished my goal to sing for Mother.*

Father, Brother, and I stood together until most of the crowd had dispersed, finding comfort in each other's presence while mourning the passing of a most important life.

Chapter 11

REVELATION

My father was falling apart. My brother often did not come home. Our bolts of cloth were disappearing. Often father neglected to open the store on time. He did not eat well. He would sit out on the second-floor veranda staring at the mountains in the distance, only talking to me when I brought his evening meal to him. He asked if I thought mother was there on top of those mountains. I remembered asking that question as a child. And my father would tell me, "No, the mountains where the ancestors live are different. They exist on another plane. We cannot see their mountains."

Now he was asking me? I trembled as I gave him the same answer, as if he were the child. I screamed in my head, *No. You are the parent. I am the child. What are you doing?*

Within months, all responsibilities had fallen on me. In the morning, I would sit and meditate. Who knew where my brother was? All the while, my father remained on the veranda. Father would sit on the veranda, eat on the veranda, sleep on the veranda. I guessed he was thinking that, in this way, he would be closer to my mother. I swept the floors. I gave the kitchen boy his orders. I bargained with the fishmonger. I opened the store. I welcomed the guests, who always asked for Father. I would stall and say he was getting the accounts in order, or he was doing inventory in the warehouse, or …

Then our customers were asking for bolts of cloth that had been put away for them. These bolts could not be found. Our warehouse steward, Jito, came to me with alarming news. He was sitting bowed before me in the formal middle room. I sat with my back to the tokonoma, which I had dutifully arranged with a scroll scene of winter to remind us during these hot days of the cool weather to come and a Korean pot with a dark muddy glaze.

"Mistress Oyama-san, the bolts of silk are mostly gone. All the indigo cotton is gone. There has been theft." He bowed his head.

"But who has access to the warehouse?" I replied. "Father, you, and I. Do you think the watchmen have been entering?" I was alarmed for many reasons.

"No, mistress, they do not have keys to the building itself, only to the gates."

"Who would deal us such a blow when we are in such a sad state of mourning? How cruel." I shook my head.

"Mistress, there is someone who has been to the warehouse regularly."

I looked up at him. "Jito-san, tell me what you are thinking."

"I am afraid it may be the young master, your brother." Jito was speaking very softly, with his head bowed.

"Why, why? What would he be doing with all those bolts of cloth?" I was afraid of the answer.

"Mistress Oyama-san, he is in great debt from the drinking houses. He has become involved with very bad people." Jito seemed to be crying.

He was old and had watched us grow and play all our lives in the alley. When Brother started practicing his kendo at age eight, Jito would often surprise him, jumping him in the alley, brandishing his own bamboo sword at Ushio. They would playfully duel together. My brother was the son Jito had never had, as his wife had died with their son in childbirth.

I had no idea what to do. After Father, Brother was head of household. I could hardly confront Brother about this. But the business could not survive these thefts. My head was aching as I remembered how people's attitudes had been changing lately. Thinking of the ladies in the sewing group now located at Obachan's, I remembered some odd looks. Now I knew what those bowed heads and silence meant. All the latest gossip up and down the road was about Brother becoming an irresponsible drunk and gambler.

I had refused to believe it until now. Jito's family had been trusted family employees for two generations. I had no reason to doubt him. However, I could not be direct in my instructions.

Thus, I said, "Jito-san, it appears that someone has access to the key to the warehouse. It is unfortunate that times are so desperate that people would even betray their own to feed a rat. I think that somehow we must ratproof the warehouse. Perhaps change the locks? Do you not think so?"

Jito stood up from his kneeling position and said, "Oh, mistress, yes. I am sure it is just rats. I will make some rat traps and, of course, change the locks."

This was not going to help my situation or prevent my brother from stealing, but it allowed dear Jito to save face and not insult his employer. And maybe I could just "forget" to inform my brother of the new locks.

Meanwhile, this was just too big for me. I ran up the alley, not carrying my samisen for a music lesson but to ask for serious help. Obachan was at the back of the ancestral home tending onions in her garden. She stood up, shook the dirt off her hands, and said, "Ah, I see you have heard some bad news. Now it's time to act like samurai!"

Obachan knew all the rumors. She had been mulling the situation over for some time. She also knew that the silk merchant's son was not coming back. She sat me down and said, "Haru will never come back. He will never marry you. Apparently, the ancestors have decided a new fate for us all."

I had not heard from Haru since their family's formal condolence gift after Mother died and my short visit with him at the funeral. It had pained me that it had been so long since that visit. Should I have spent more time with him, rather than playing the dutiful daughter? Perhaps my role was to be more the dutiful betrothed? I had questioned my actions over and over again. But with all my obligations in running the store, I had finally put these questions out of my mind.

In the last few months, I had asked Father repeatedly when the silk merchant was to arrive. We needed new shipments of silks. Father had said it was about payments. Now I was beginning to see. It was about our payments. We hadn't paid *our* bills for silk. I thought it was other people's payments. I kept looking through the books for overdue bills and hadn't found a customer lacking payment. It wasn't customers. We were the ones! Oh, how disgraceful.

I was kneeling on Obachan's polished kitchen floorboards and trying to light the fire to make some tea for us. My hands were trembling. The enormity of our family situation was crashing down on me within the beam of sunlight on my hands. I managed to fill the pot with water and put it on the brazier. I was fumbling with a teacup. I dropped it, and it rolled along the wood board and then fell to the dirt floor and broke. I put my hands into fists and brought them slowly to my sides and rested them on the wooden boards. Tears were streaming down my face.

I looked up at my grandmother. She spoke softly, "None of it will be like it should have been. Your mother kept the family together. Unfortunately, my son has a weak heart. He has not been able to present himself to life. And your brother has a similar weakness. He would have been a good man if hardship hadn't come in the form of his mother's death. Fortune may still bless him and make him a good man in the future."

"But we must deal with how things are now. A good samurai does not give up the fight. You are the true samurai in your family.

117

You have strength. You can do anything. You must envision it and then proceed, step by step, to your goal." Obachan was talking to me. I could not understand her words.

Tears were streaming down my face. "Why do you think Haru will not marry me? We have always been fond of each other, even from our time as little children. He asked me to be his wife. We had an elaborate dinner with you and his parents to celebrate our betrothal."

"Ah, ceremonies. They are wonderful social occasions. They are good for your family's business. People have to have new kimonos for ceremonies." Obachan was being very cold to me. She was forcing herself to have no feelings in what she had to say. Why wasn't Father the one to tell me all this? I could not believe Obachan was directing me to give up my life. I was her favorite. If only I could see one glance of pity in her eyes as she told me this. Her coldness made me feel so alone.

Grandmother continued, "I have heard some unpleasant gossip. Haru is engaged to another woman. They are to be married this summer."

I gasped. "How can that be? He never broke off the engagement to me! Did I not deserve to be told?"

Obachan continued, "Apparently, she will live with his family for the next year until he is finished with his studies. He has already been promised a government post in Kumamoto city for the following year."

My stomach was heaving. "But it has only been a few months since Mother crossed the Sanzu River. How could this happen so quickly?"

"My dear, it is all about honor. Your brother's gambling started even before your mother's death. We did not know, but others did. The silk merchant is a very shallow man. He was afraid to have his family's reputation spoiled by being linked to yours. Dishonorable man that he is, he arranged for a new betrothal immediately."

Obachan reached out for the pot of boiling water and poured it into the teapot. She prepared the tea as she continued to talk. "Because your father essentially disappeared after your mother's death, the head of household becomes the first son. And as we all know, Ushio is doing a terrible job."

I recoiled at this and with my head high said, "He isn't doing any job. I am running the store. I make up lies to cover for Father. I continue with everything. I run the household, pay the accounts, send out the bills. I just procured a new account for silks for the Namaki family, who has just moved into Five Bridges. I am doing a pretty good job."

Obachan looked very sad and shook her head. "Yes, but you are a woman. Nihonjin have yet to value its women. No one can even see you. I'm afraid that new account will be cancelled."

Obachan poured two cups of tea. "I am afraid there is more news for you. A marriage has been arranged for your brother. Your father thinks it is best to get him settled down quickly before everything is gone. A woman will settle him down."

At this, I felt relieved. "That will be most fortunate. I will have someone to help me with the running of the house and the accounts of the store."

Obachan said, "It is best that you leave."

"Leave?" I felt that I was losing my vision. Things were getting blurry, and I wasn't crying. I felt as if a piercing blade was entering behind my right eye.

"She will be mistress of the house now. You will be like a servant to her. She will treat you as a mother treats a daughter-in-law."

My back felt weak. Could I continue to kneel and remain upright to take a cup of tea? A daughter-in-law was about the lowest standing in the household a woman could have. If the woman had a jealous or mean streak, it would all come out toward her new slave, her daughter-in-law.

Grandmother added, "And you will not have the benefit of a new husband to comfort you."

"But who is she? She is probably one of my classmates. She will be my friend."

"It is Akeme Tadashi." Obachan looked at me with raised eyebrows.

This was not a friend of mine. Akeme! Akeme, who had cheated on exams in class a few years ago. She was not a woman of good character, although she was the daughter of a first-class merchant family equal to ours.

"Where am I to go?"

"A most fortuitous opportunity has appeared. The ancestors have smiled on you. You will go to Hawaii. The emperor has arranged such wonderful opportunities in this sister island country that many call paradise." Grandmother refused to look at me as she said this. She knew as well as I that there had been very mixed reports coming back from those Nihonjin who had made that leap in fortune.

"How can you send me there? Send me away from Five Bridges, my home?" I pleaded.

"Roji, your old childhood friend is going, and he needs a wife. It has been arranged for you to go with him." Obachan stated this as a matter of fact, as if this wasn't to be the biggest decision made about my life.

I was stunned. "When?" I stammered. "When … did you think … think of this plan?"

"Last week. It was at the quilting bee when we were discussing the young people of the village.

Madam Otahni had the idea. Roji's parents had asked her to find a wife for him."

"Oh, I cannot. I just cannot. My life is ruined. I just cannot. I will run away." Tears were streaming down my cheeks.

"You have samurai blood in you. You are samurai. You will not weep at misfortune. You will stab it in the eye."

"Oh, Grandmother. What does that mean?" I was sick to death of samurai talk.

"You will marry Roji and have a good life in Hawaii." Grandmother picked up her tea bowl, drank the thick green sludge, and put the bowl down very slowly and deliberately as she kept her eye on me. I did not like this stern, authoritarian side of Obachan. My stomach was hollow. I could not drink the tea.

Chapter 12

PREPARATIONS

Father now spent some of his time in the alley with people for whom he had previously had no time. It seemed he could not get enough of their stories. I was happy if that could cheer him up, for, surely, he was not productive with all his sadness.

Grandmother and Auntie had been preparing my trunk. Last week, I had woken up as I always had, a member of my household, looking forward to another year before my marriage.

Yes, the silk merchant's son was marrying someone else, and I was handling that shock. However, I could have had a full year before I needed to find other prospects for my future. But the elders had made other plans for me. How dared they do this? How different was this week.

Auntie and Obachan had come for lunch. Madam Iwata was doing her best to keep things running. She had prepared a formal lunch that we were eating sitting at small tables in front of the tokonoma. We three women made small talk and picked up our morsels daintily with our lacquered hashi. As soon as Madam served the tea, I stood up, bowed, and excused myself, leaving my dear elders to their own silly talk.

Father left the house every day in early afternoon now. I just saw him in the alley. He would not look at me. I, who had kept the family business going, kept the books, overseen the warehouse and workers, gone after new accounts when Brother ruined our old business connections, was to be married off and sent away to another country. I wondered how long these secret plans had been going on. All of it, all my hard work, was to benefit my brother and his soon-to-be new bride. I could hardly breathe. I was sure I heard the low wailing of the shakuhachi not in the woods but right here inside my head in our kitchen. I leaned against the broad side of our dear Madam Iwata.

"Ueme-san, we all have to bear parts of life that are not of our own making. Please be happy again. I miss your songs and your laughter in this kitchen," Madam begged. "Tomorrow, come to the kitchen early like you used to. We will get the fishmonger to cheat us royally with his prices, and we will make him laugh at his own self!" Madam Iwata put her arm around my shoulders, though I was now a bit taller than she.

"Can you see me with Roji? Roji as a husband?" I pleaded with her.

"Now, we have known him all his life, and he has been a very pleasant boy. A joker, that is true, but always well meaning. Perhaps he will turn out to be fine. I must say, I was surprised to see that he had that much adventure in him to be crossing the ocean! You, yes. I can see you as an adventurer. But Roji, for all his acrobatics and joking, has stayed pretty close to his family all these years." Madam was talking to herself. The only word I heard was *Roji*, and I would flinch each time I heard his name.

"But I am not in love with him!" I said quite resolutely as I swept the dirt floor back and forth, letting out my fury.

"Ah and look what happened with the man who you loved and who loved you also!" Madam Iwata was stern.

"Oh, I am sure that has all been dictated by his parents. Haru would not do this to me." Tears were flowing again. I remembered my obachan's directive on tears. How I hated samurai ways now!

Madam looked at me with pity. "Haru could have written you a note, sent you a message somehow. He is a grown man."

"Can you say anything crueler to me?" I was ready to run out to the alley when Auntie and Obachan entered the kitchen. I grabbed a towel, swished it into the water bucket, and covered my face with its cool wetness.

Madam covered for me. "We were just talking about Hawaii and how hot it gets there and how Ueme will be wanting to freshen her hot face with water every moment of the day!"

"Hmmm, soo, deska. It's time to do some work. Can you help us, Madam Iwata?" Auntie pulled one of the kitchen chests away from the wall. I left the room.

Auntie and Grandmother were dividing up kitchen utensils. They wanted to be sure to give me what I should need in this "frontier existence" and decide what should be left for the household, for the new mistress. My new existence was not to be a merchant's wife. I would be a farmer, an indentured one at that. How the ancestors had betrayed me.

I walked over to our shrine. The white paper that had covered it after mother's death had now been removed. I looked at the pictures of Mother and the scrolls with names of Grandmother and Grandfather. I wanted to pick them up and throw them out into the alley. But I thought of the Buddha. "Your strength is in your calmness."

I was to wait here. This was an important day. Roji was coming by for the formal proposal. Roji! Well, yes. I knew he was leaving. He had even asked if I was up for an adventure and to come with him. Phgh! Now Obachan and Auntie said I must accept his proposal.

After Obachan had revealed her secret plan to me, I felt sure it was a plan made by a woman in the dementia of old age. I'd determined I could get out of her plan. However, when Auntie and Obachan said this to me again over a cup of tea, I choked and made quite a distressing sound. I was scolded to behave. What had all this womanly behaving gotten me? I did not know what this new country was like, but I was going to always remember those final words. "Behave, you must behave." And I was going to ignore them.

Auntie had just reminded me to change into a formal kimono for the event. Upstairs I went to the preparation room with all the ready-made kimonos. I picked out the most beautiful kimono of pale pink rinzu silk with a trailing branch of wisteria down the sleeve and back. I would be most elegant now. It was my right as daughter of the one of the most prosperous fabric houses of outer Kumamoto province.

The silk in the kimono itself was worth the price of a trip on the train to Yokohama. But alas, Father had no money to spend on me. After the marriage, Roji and I would take a bullock cart to the train for Yokohama, where we would board a ship to Hawaii. A bullock cart! Father had no money for a carriage. But we did own this kimono, which was fit for an empress. Madam Iwata had helped me into the proper undergarments, positioning the red silk under kimono to just peek out over the back of my neck, just enough to entice any man. The brocade obi and string were tied around my waist. My hair had been oiled and shaped into the most fashionable bun of this season. I had borrowed hair ornaments from Ito, though she had no idea of this occasion as yet. Madam stood back to give a last discerning look.

"You may not love Roji, but you are certainly doing him proud with your dressing today, Ueme." Madam Iwata gazed at me with love.

Entering the middle room taking very small steps as only allowed with such a garment, I walked as regally as I could. Obachan gasped. You see, they were saving this kimono for Brother's bride. I knew this.

Roji stood up and bowed low. His face was flushed. I did not think it was from embarrassment. I was sure it was the sake! Most likely, he had decided to throw off any inhibitions to make this appearance. Father was sitting on a big cushion and staring at the table. I knelt down. Roji's father was opposite me. Father coughed a little and then made some introductions. How ridiculous, as if we did not know each other. All these little niceties, they were not for me. They did not serve me. I looked up and saw Auntie smiling at me. She knew about the silk, and she was proud of my boldness.

The two elder men made speeches about the bounties of the families being joined together and how this would benefit the next generation and honor the ancestors. Bounties! Roji's family was in a lower merchant class than ours. The bounties were not equal. A cup of tea was being offered to me. I took it and drank. I kept my eyes lowered. Sweets were sent around. I refused, and one was put before me anyway.

A voice said, "Ueme! Do you accept? Ueme!"

I looked up. All eyes are on me. Behave.

"Yes." I bowed my head very slightly.

The sake was brought out, and the two elder men said, "Kumpai!" I thought, *Ah, it is done.*

But no. Roji was motioning to me. He wanted me to leave the room with him. I got up, feeling very tangled in the excessive amounts of silk in the kimono.

We were walking on the road between the fields at the end of the alley. Roji was talking. What was he saying? The nerve he had to even speak to me. He stopped and turned and held me by the shoulders.

"This is not some Noh drama or Kabuki play, Ueme. We are in it!"

He was angry. I was stunned. What was going on?

"I do not want to go to Hawaii. I do not want to marry you." I blurted to him. It just came out.

"You must think I am stupid. I know all this. What do you think I want? I told you months ago I was being forced out of my life and family fortune as second son. I recalled you laughing. You said that, no matter what, as a man, I had more privileges than you. So here we are. Me loaded with privilege and you to be married to 'privilege.'"

There was a long silence. Thinking back on it now, Roji was

quite wise for the moment. But this was not fun. Where was the fun Roji? I wanted to be back at the fair, which seemed so long ago.

"We must make a go of it, you and I. We can do it. We've known each other our whole lives. We will work hard together, and somehow it will be a good future. We owe it to our parents to make a good future." He was so earnest.

"I will honor you as my future husband," was my cold reply. I'd always liked Roji. I'd never hated him before. Why did I hate him now?

"Ahh, I hope we can do better than this. It's going to be a long journey," replied Roji.

Chapter 13

HONOR

The next day, I sent Jun with a message to Roji to meet me at the Bridge of Lasting Happiness.

As I walked along the river, I saw Roji's form leaning on the railing far ahead of me. The sun was behind him. His broad shoulders and long limbs gave him an appealing air of grace. I remembered his words. *This is not a kabuki play.* I must not romanticize what was happening.

I walked to the middle of the bridge and stopped before him. He made no effort to approach me.

Roji spoke first. "What? You choose this bridge? Is this a joke on me?"

"I thought it would make for a more positive atmosphere." I continued, "I do not know what to say. Has it all been arranged? I feel sick to my stomach over this. I did not even know you were sure about going to Hawaii!" I looked over the railing at the water flowing beneath us. Who cared about proper behavior now? Who was I now?

"Whose idea was this?" I managed to look at him directly.

Roji seemed to soften. "Actually, it was mine and then others, too. My father said I had to get married before I left, and so I thought of you. I've always thought about you but figured you were above me. But with your father's turn in circumstances, I guess we are equals."

There was a long silence after this insult. Two merchant houses with recent reversals of fortune. But his merchant status had always been lower than the House of Oyama.

My mind was reeling. "If we are to have a good life together, you must never insult me with those words again!"

Roji looked ashamed and gave a slight bow. "Sumimasen, Ueme. Let us start with good feelings." Roji then said, "But you must remember, I did talk to you about this."

"Oh, that was to a whole group of us. We were all joking together. Do you not think I deserve a more direct question in person from you?" I was angry. I burst out with all my thoughts at once. "I have wanted so many things for my life. I have had so many dreams. And now, suddenly, other people have stepped in, and now I have no right to my dreams. I wanted to choose my husband and my style of life. I have no dreams of Hawaii. I have never wanted to leave Nihon."

Roji stood back at my outburst. He turned to the railing and held it looking at the water and then at me. "We can create dreams together. I do not want to trample on your dreams. If we do this together, maybe we can be stronger and make a really good life. We'll save our money and be able to buy a store for ourselves when we return to Nihon. Let's make a pact here today that we keep our dreams."

A long silence and then Roji spoke. "I think we would be really good together, maybe great together. I want you to know that I am extremely happy that you accepted my proposal. I feel very honored."

We stood there on the middle of the bridge looking at each other as if to see each other for the first time. It felt like the most serious moment of my life. I had all I could do to keep breathing.

Roji walked with me back across the main street, where we parted company. I continued up a block to the alley. He went to the right toward his home. I turned left down the alley to walk to Ito's house.

After a few blocks, I could see the familiar face of Inogi, Ito's kitchen maid, carrying a bucket. As soon as she spied me, she put down the bucket and beckoned me to come sit on the alley bench with her.

"Ito is out looking for you. We heard the news last evening from that old malicious gossiper, Bufuku. Ito is frantic. You must wait here for her." Inogi went inside with her bucket.

Inogi returned with a plate of rice balls freshly made. She offered, "Take one. You look starved. Come now, you can talk to me."

She put her arm around me and pulled me to her side. The familiar comfort of one who had known me all my life just seemed to open up my insides, and I started to cry. Great sobs issued from my mouth, ones that I did not feel free to let loose at my own home.

Ito came up to us running, her hakata flying in all directions. "What has happened? Is it true?"

She sat down on my other side now, filling the whole length of the bench.

I looked at her and had to smile. She, too, had been crying.

Ito spoke first. "Come let's go to our formal garden, where it is more private to talk of this."

We walked through the back gate past the laundry and bathhouse to the inner garden. Instead of large sitting rocks as in my family garden, there were two pleasant benches to sit on. Azalea bushes of various sizes and shapes lined the walls. They were neatly trimmed, having lost most of their blooms. There was a bamboo fountain splashing water in the corner making a trickling sound over some rocks.

Sitting down, we tried to encourage each other about my future with Roji. Surely good fortunes were smiling down on me. I had been a dutiful daughter, a good student, a kind person. I had honored the ancestors and dutifully honored Buddha with my meditations and prayers. We nodded positively at each other at these spoken thoughts.

However, I noticed Ito was clenching her hands into fists and digging them into her knees. Her cotton hakata was twisting and wrinkling under the pressure. I tried not to look at her hands, as it made my own heart clench.

Ito spoke again. "You know, this may be more about your brother than you think."

I looked at her. "What do you mean?"

"Akeme is expecting. She has grown big. They must marry soon." Ito said this while holding her breath.

I was stunned. Not stunned at this news so much as stunned that so many things had happened without my knowledge. Was I so stupid? All this time, I had been paying attention to the store but not to life!

"Don't worry. Most in the village haven't noticed. Her family keeps her inside. We are their accountants, so we see more than others."

"Ito, what was the point of me working so hard these last months? What is the point of being a good daughter?" I was feeling very betrayed by my family.

Ito replied, "How can we know anything? It is not just your family. It is life. Life is one thousand things, and it is not one thousand things. I wish Saiko were here to quote the poets. She would know what to say about the melancholy of life."

"Oh, yes, she would be able to tell us a story much more gruesome than mine with all those crazy magazine stories she reads!"

With this, Ito and I both burst out laughing, maybe more from missing Saiko than gaiety.

"Tell me one thing I can do, Ueme—one last thing I can do to help."

Then I explained to Ito the shame of Roji and I having to leave the village after our marriage in a cart rather than in a carriage, a clear vision that would show all the village how the fabric House of Oyama had fallen.

"Done," Ito exclaimed. "You shall leave in a carriage made of the finest wood, polished to bring out the soul of the tree from which it was hewn. I know just the one to rent. It has some beautiful designs on it. I shall see to it." And with that, Ito's final act of friendship would spare my family's honor.

Crossing the Pacific

Yokohama

Japan

to

Honolulu

Island of Oahu

Hawaii

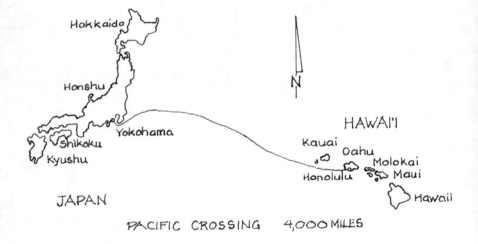

Hokkaido

Honshu

Yokohama

Shikoku

Kyushu

JAPAN

N

HAWAI'I

Kauai

Oahu

Molokai

Honolulu

Maui

Hawaii

PACIFIC CROSSING   4,000 MILES

Chapter 14

THE SEA

We had arrived at the harbor at Yokohama. The train ride was overnight, and we sat up rather than pay for a sleeping compartment. Roji and I had thought we could sleep as soon as we boarded the ship.

We were mistaken. It was a very full day, with no time for resting on the day we boarded. Once we'd shown our documents, all the men were led to the rear of the deck. The women were led to the ladder hatch. All the women were corralled into one side of the "tween" decks. As we walked down the steep, open steps to our quarters, the stale, putrid air hit us, causing sporadic coughs from our group.

At the bottom of the steps, an older Japanese woman approached us and bowed. Then she introduced herself as our matron. She would be in charge of us, to direct us and to give us whatever aid we might require during the voyage. Her eyes were kind, but her demeanor was stern. She immediately assigned beds to us.

Roji and I were to be in a room of six bunks that were secured to the floor and ceiling. The rooms were very small; the beds just narrow shelves. I tried to imagine both of us trying to sleep without falling out. I quickly claimed the bottom bunk for us. If we should fall, at least it would not be far to the floor. The middle-aged woman in charge, Matron Ando, called all the women out to the common area and assigned us chores.

Our group was to wash the floor there with buckets of seawater, to start at that very instant. I was hoping to be able to go above deck to watch the ship leave the dock. I washed the floor with energy but full of resentment in my heart. I was tired and already feeling the sadness of leaving Nihon.

I questioned the matron about going above deck. I could see her impatience with me as I explained the importance of the momentous occasion of leaving our homes. She replied that we would be allowed later to watch our homeland, from a distance, even to see Mount Fuji. However, for now, the crew requested the decks be cleared so they could organize the departure. We were to stay out of the way. Some of the women were to make the dinner meal. The importance of viewing our departure was not the most important item on her mind, she told me. I recognized the strained politeness in her words to me.

When the floor washing was completed, we were allowed on deck in the late afternoon to watch Mount Fuji disappear into the sunset. It was very breezy and cool. However, the sea life surrounding me took away all cares about my personal warmth. There were gulls, petrels, and some pelicans. One of the crew joined us at the rail, standing next to me. Being a very sea-wizened sort with tanned and wrinkled skin, he began pointing out all the birds, naming them and talking about their characteristics. We watched the porpoises jump out of the water as they swam in a mass of a hundred together, the water churning with dark mounds popping up in rhythmic waves. The late afternoon sun reflected off the water in a million tiny stars. The waves in the wake of the ship glinted with thousands of small golden fish catching the light with their scales. The men were oohing and ahhing over the happy prospect of fishing in such waters.

Mount Fuji, the home closest to the gods as it had been said in all our childhood tales, was visible. Mount Fuji inspired all the good within me. I had seen prints of the beautiful mountain of the gods, but its stature had to be experienced in person. Reflecting on my unexpected good fortune, I realized that, without this unexpected change in my life's future, I might have never experienced the white summit rising serenely through the clouds. Perhaps this was the start of some good fortune.

The sun disappeared in a glow of orange and purple. Lights on shore were starting to twinkle as the dark shapes that were our home receded into the distance, darker, smaller, and smaller.

The summit of Mount Fuji was now gone. It was our last view of our beloved homeland. Large dark birds were diving into the ship's wake for fish. The porpoises had swum off to the northeast, and the water was becoming dark and the air a biting cold. The white foam trailing our ship remained visible as all else darkened. The birds diving into its wake were now becoming dark shadows flitting down and up, finally blending with the night. Mesmerized by this new experience of the ocean, I stood with the breeze in my face, reflecting on the changes that had descended onto me in the last month.

There was some murmuring among the passengers, but most were silent. I think most of us were quite unbelieving of the journey we had chosen and what it was we were truly doing. I thought of the feeling back in school when raising your hand in class to answer teacher's question, and then, after being called upon, the fear rose within that you might not really know the answer after all.

I looked up and back to what was called the "bridge" and saw the captain. He had the stance of the samurai, rooted to his domain. He wore a sea captain's hat and a formal Western-style jacket with gold braids at the shoulders. Earlier when he had spoken to us, the passengers, in his welcome speech in the afternoon, he had seemed softer and gentler than his uniformed body conveyed. His demeanor seemed to brighten the farther we were into the great sea. He was a man obviously more at home on water than on land.

The horizon was so great I was having difficulty placing our ancestors anywhere within this landscape. I conjured up the vision of our ancestral mountain, and even so, it paled in comparison to the greatness of the ocean. The moon was low on the horizon and appeared that it would not rise very high in the sky tonight. The stars were bright but cast little light on the water. The darkness loomed in front of us as the ship moved into it.

The animals, the fish, the birds captured my inner being. I loved the smell, the salt, and the rush of wind on my face. What an adventure I was on. If I were not taking this voyage with Roji, I might never have experienced all of this. As if my thoughts had conjured him, Roji appeared at my side, tightly linking his arm through mine.

"Aren't you cold? Shall we go below? The matron is anxious for the women to get back to her. She has an opening information lecture she is anxious to give you." Roji was leaning his head to mine, our cheeks almost touching.

"Oh, I am enjoying it up here. I find I love the ocean! So, the women have a lecture. What about the men? Do you have anyone directing all of you?" I peered up at his eyes and smiled.

"Do not worry about us. We have a fearless leader in 'Old Socks.'" Roji started laughing.

"Old Socks? Who is that?"

"Ahh, that is our name for Kobayashi-san. He wears rather grim-looking socks with his sandals."

"He is not married then. He has no one to take care of him. You should not make fun of his misfortune."

"Misfortune? I rather think he makes his own *mis*-fortune. He is a pretty tough old guy. He has already made us wash the deck, clean and chop our vegetables, and organize what he calls the slop cans. I think he could very well wash his own socks."

The cold had reached my bones and I said, "I am ready to go down. The wind is picking up, and there is nothing more to see. It is so dark." I leaned into Roji, and we hugged each other tightly for warmth and strength before heading down below.

The waves had picked up, and the ship rocked back and forth ever more severely. Navigating the steep ladder stair was difficult, as I kept falling to one side and the other. Roji tried to help me, but we both found it better to hang onto the rope railing by ourselves with both hands.

Old Socks was at the bottom to make sure all had come down from the deck. Roji grabbed my hands as we reached the bottom and, pulling me close, whispered softly, "Our adventure has begun. I think it is good."

I breathed in the smell of him, remembering the warmth of his body next to mine. My hands reluctantly let go of his as my eyes searched his for comfort. He returned my gaze with such confidence all my fears melted away.

Old Socks spoke up, frowning, "Eeey, enough already, you two. Go now!"

I floated on Roji's words making my way over to Matron's group. Most of the women were kneeling around her listening intently. Someone motioned to me to come sit near her, and she handed me a bowl of warm rice and pickled vegetables.

"Well, I think we have all gotten our assigned sleeping spaces with trunks and cases stored safely away. You must be aware that organization on the ship is of paramount importance as it can be very dangerous in stormy weather if items are not securely stowed. I will be coming to check and instruct at each bunk to make sure we all understand this principle." Matron Ando turned her body and head slowly from east to west as she looked at each of our faces. We were all silent and obedient.

"May I ask a question?" A voice from the back of the group cut through the silence.

"Of course. Please ask." Matron strained to see who was talking.

"My husband and I have two trunks and two satchels, and there is not enough room under the bunk for them." The woman leaned forward as she spoke. The light from the swinging oil lamp hanging from the beam above shone on her face, off and then on again.

"Soo, deska. How many people have this problem?" Matron asked, leaning in the direction of the woman.

Suddenly, I realized I had two trunks also. I raised my hand as if in a school classroom. I felt sheepish. Were we allowed to have two trunks? I had seen the trunk storage room completely filled earlier in the day.

"Please come and see me after our meeting here, and we will figure out a solution."

The women began to stir and rise. However, Matron Ando was not finished. She remained upright with a stern mouth. The silence of her glare struck our eardrums. Then, all was quiet again.

"Now, tomorrow morning we are going to get organized into teams for work efficiency. I want everyone to think how their talents might help with all the tasks that will need to be performed in the next few weeks of our travel.

"The teams will be washing and chopping vegetables, cooking, cleanup, sewing, nursing, organizing, safety, and social." Matron looked slowly across the group of us and continued. "We have to run a very organized ship. I have been hired to do this for the passengers. I have been on three trips across the ocean. I understand what needs to be done. I am in charge of all of you. Thus, you will look to me for solution to any problems. Tonight, all we can do is stow our packages safely and get to sleep. We will rise early. The crew rings a very loud bell and expects everyone to get up and get busy with chores. We follow their times. So, for now, all of you must return to your bunks."

The other "two-trunk woman" and I approached the matron. Bowing to her, we both spoke. "My name is Ueme."

"And my name is Tameki."

Tameki and I looked at each other, sizing each other up. She was not a meek woman and, after bowing, stood very straight. She was a bit shorter than me, and she was wearing very good cloth. It was a heavy weave and of very good indigo dye.

Matron stood up. "Well, we shall see the size of these trunks and where we can store them safely. I do not mean just safely for the ship's rocking either. I want all our items in this location where we can keep a watch over them. There are gamblers on this ship. You cannot trust a gambler!"

We approached the tiny closet that was my bunk room. Our satchels and two trunks were in front of our bunk, blocking any passage into the space. Matron asked for my help as she pushed one of my trunks under the bed. There was already a trunk under it belonging to the bunk above me. There was room for the satchels and only one of my trunks. A narrow strip of metal screwed to the floor kept the trunks from sliding out from under the bed.

Matron spoke after a brief silence. "So, let me think. Perhaps we can get some rope and tie trunks to the bunk posts. First, make sure there is nothing you will want in that trunk during the voyage, as it will be bound completely to the post here and inaccessible." Matron looked at me questioningly.

I did a quick calculation and pulled the other trunk out from under the bunk and switched the trunks.

Tameki spoke. "I shall do the same with my trunks."

Matron was thinking, her brow furrowed. "We can find space, maybe under the next bed to yours. We will go look at your bunk room."

As they started to leave me, I asked, "Where shall I find some rope to bind the trunk?"

Matron replied, "Oh, no. The captain has certified only those knowledgeable in sailor's knots to tie anything. I shall speak to Kobayashi-san about that."

We had a crude washroom with some very little fresh water in a bucket allocated for washing. I was relieved that we had any water.

When I returned to my bunk, the trunk had already been secured with very beautiful knots. All the women had hung their day hakatas from the string above their bunks to make for some privacy. Mine was the last to be hung.

I fell asleep waiting for Roji to return from the men's group, thinking about how sweet Roji had been to me since we had left our village almost a week ago. We had talked to each other about our fears and our hopes. He had been very organized and responsible, taking care of all our papers and tickets. There was a growing warmth of affection between us. Knowing this, my shoulders relaxed a bit, realizing the future might be brighter than I had thought. Perhaps we had both matured a bit since the summer festival. My last thought before dreaming was of Roji smiling at me while we ate our lunch together yesterday, in the small noodle shop in Yokohama.

Roji came to our bunk. He slipped under the futon and put his arms around me. I woke to his touch. Realizing that this may be our first night together in our marriage, I was uncertain in my actions. Roji turned me around so we faced each other. He ran his fingers through my hair and said, "I like your hair when it is down, so soft." And he then held my head close to his.

I opened my mouth to kiss him, and then everything happened so suddenly I could not even relive it in my mind. Yes, we had come together, bodies comingling. It was forceful, if anything, but what struck me was the lack of feeling. It seemed there wasn't time for feeling. I thought my husband might need to learn how to do it better. Or did I not do it right, and I ruined it? Roji was asleep. I could not even talk to him about what had just happened. Where were the caresses and the warm feelings, the hearts beating together? Disappointed, I listened to the couple above us making love. It took quite a while, and there were quite a lot of whispering and expressions of excitement. I fell asleep hoping for improvement in our marital feeling in nights to come.

I was awake, but there was no light. I could feel the ship sway back and forth. But that was not what had awakened me. Agh! Then I heard it. Some women were sick. Roji was not in the bunk. I sat up.

I heard matron calling out orders. There were buckets hooked to each bunk. I had thought they were for washing, yet we weren't given enough water for that. I had mistakenly thought, looking at those buckets earlier, that someone was overly optimistic about our bathing. But now I could see the real use. I reluctantly left my warm futon.

Matron, with her supreme organizational skills, had created stations for this work. We women passed buckets, along a line of us, to the stair, where a crew member climbed to the deck and tossed it into the sea on a rope, cleaning it out with fresh seawater. The crew members expected our seasickness and never complained, just calling us all "landlubbers," probably the first English word many of us learned.

I had missed that part of the lecture about the bucket brigade. Those of us who were not sick handed the buckets up the line to finally land at the base of the ladder stair. Old Socks, was there with a couple of the men. I learned that, each night, we would take turns with these duties. The men carried larger buckets up to toss the contents overboard. I took my position at the front of the line near the ladder.

I could hear some crewmen from above us, yelling, "Toss leeward, away from the wind. Over here, this side."

I swung a bucket to Old Socks and said, "Here's another bucket, Kobayashi-san."

He smiled, showing some badly stained teeth, and said very

kindly, "Ah, hello. You must not worry. The first night is usually the worst because no one is used to the movement of the ship. Each night, there will be fewer and fewer people sick. Just keep your head up and your nose closed!" With that, he swung my bucket up, where it was quickly carried up the ladder steps to the deck above.

It actually was a rather good spot to have in the bucket brigade, as the cool, fresh ocean air came down those steps and relieved me of my gagging response. Someone poked me in the side. I turned, expecting the next bucket, and saw instead Tameki.

She was laughing and obviously not reacting to the rocking of the ship or the contents of the buckets at all. She said, "I just do not give in to this kind of thing. My brothers and I were trained not to care how things smell. My father made us sleep in the barn with the horses until we didn't mind the smell of manure."

My first thought was, Horses. Tameki grew up with horses! We all came from such different backgrounds.

I said, "Tameki, have you met Kobayashi-san?"

Another bucket came up the line. Grabbing it from Tameki and passing it to Kobayashi-san, I said, "Kobayashi-san, may I introduce Madam Ikeda to you?"

Kobayashi smiled and leaned past me to say, "Good evening, Madam Ikeda. It is a lovely evening!" as he passed the stinky bucket back to us. With that, he laughed and slapped his knee. He seemed like a very good-natured sort to me.

After that, the bucket brigade slowed down, and we were able to go back to our bunks. I fell into mine and curled up next to Roji, who was there fast asleep.

Chapter 15

TEAMWORK

Clanng!

No. No. No. My first thoughts on hearing the bells for morning. Night was too short.

Then the smell bothered me. I could recognize mold and mildew. It was bad for cloth. From my whole life training under my otasan, I knew the smell, and it signaled danger to me. That smell made me anxious. I tried to make myself not smell. There was so much happening, and I needed to pay attention to all of this newness. I pushed down those instincts so carefully honed as a merchant's daughter.

I quickly rose, washed, and dressed. Some women had already risen and were steaming the rice. Another was pouring hot tea into tin cups. The men had gone to the other side, busy with their chores.

Part of the morning chores was to make the rice balls and pickled vegetables for lunch so the cooking utensils could remain stowed during the day as the ship rolled over the waves. Everything needed to be tied down. The smell of seasickness was in the air, even though it was the beginning of a new day.

It seemed most everything was metal on this ship, even our dishes. We sat kneeling at three tables made of long boards. Ah, some wood for that at least. I was beginning to notice the metal. My whole youth, everything was made of wood. I was thinking about what had actually been metal—the ends of a shovel. Oh, yes, and Madam

Iwata had purchased a new soup strainer for our kitchen that had a metal mesh scoop. (Thinking of our kitchen, a pang of sadness hit me. I pushed it down.) Of course, swords were of steel, and weapons of all sorts had metal parts. But here, the boat was metal, our bunks were metal, the steps were metal, our dishes were metal. When the waves crashed into the sides of the ship, they made a boom sound, reminding me of the big drums at festivals.

My daydreaming was interrupted by a loud, "Ohayōgozaimasu." Matron Ando was holding court.

Matron was at the head of the middle table. She had poured tea and was passing the cups down to us. We ate our rice and pickled vegetables in quiet, not knowing at this time what was expected. Finishing our meal, we all washed our cups and hashi in the vat of boiling water and laid them on drying racks for later.

Clinking her hashi against her tin cup, Matron called our meeting to order. For the next hour, we volunteered our services for different teams, with Matron rearranging it all according to her specifications. I volunteered for two groups—social and sewing. I dreaded being appointed to the nursing crew. I feared my stomach would not be as good as Tameki's. Matron explained that everyone would take turns with the washing and cooking so there would not be specific teams for that. The rooms had numbers, and the "kitchen" crews would go as teams according to their room number.

I looked from time to time over to the men's side. It appeared they were having the same kind of meeting.

Someone asked why the couples were separated in work crews on this boat. Matron replied that they had found it made everything more egalitarian this way, as wives tended to spoil their husbands and stole extra food for them. We all laughed at this, knowing it was probably true.

Tameki was wearing a white kerchief around her neck today. This was the designation for nursing duty. I decided she must have volunteered for it. In our early morning meeting after our breakfast tea, Tameki spoke up with the thought that was on my mind. "Since the cleanup has been accomplished, may we, Matron Ando, go above deck to stroll around and breathe some fresh air?"

Matron looked up from her stitching. "I am afraid not. The crew has designated specific times when we can go above. We cannot interrupt their work." Matron looked at each of us as she said this, as an admonishment, as if all of us were lazy.

Matron continued, "But know this also. Most of the time, only part of our group may go. Kobayashi-san is very knowledgeable and will let us know how many can go up and when. Usually, we are allowed the hour before our noon meal." Matron bowed slightly from her kneeling position; calculating it in my head, a less than 10 percent bow.

Oh, how my otasan would enjoy analyzing the cast of all the people here by their bowing habits. And Mother was on my shoulder categorizing the fabrics and skill of the stitching. A pang of regret touched my heart. Oh, that I had spent so much of my getting-ready-to-go-away time in anger, rather than in just loving my family, who I might never see again. That was a most dangerous thought. *May the ancestors not hear that and take it for my wish! No, no, do not listen to me.*

Earlier that morning, Matron had talked to us very quietly. Matron frowned at us now. She began talking about wisdom. "You think you are going to a world where your money problems will be solved? How many of you have ever met anyone who returned from this land of milk and honey?"

No one raised her hand.

"Will you allow me to give you some advice?" Not waiting for an answer, she continued, "I have seen your arm muscles as we do our chores. You are the same as the women on my last ship. Very few of you have done heavy farmwork before. Your bodies are not equipped to do this hard labor. And the sun in Hawaii is fierce. Yes, there are ocean breezes, but not in the fields where the sugar cane is. And the cane rips your skin. You will have to wear heavy gloves and garments for protection, and this will be hot also.

"And heat can make you weak and sick. Do you know what else can make you weak and sick? Being with child! Take care not to get pregnant too quickly. Be careful with your husbands."

Matron clasped her hands under her kimono sleeves. She pushed back her sleeves, and then, seeming uncomfortable, her hands were out again. It was clear she did not relish telling us this information. She continued, "The pay is not adequate, and you have a contract to work for three years. Do not extend it by making foolish mistakes."

Someone giggled, but she was hushed by those next to her. We sat there with reality settling its unwelcome weight on us. Somehow, being on the ship on the great ocean had, at first, allowed us to forget the goal of the trip.

Matron Ando continued, "Some of us find strength in adversity. Some of us can be crushed by it. Others are made sick in the head with it. Ask yourself, What will I be?" Matron looked down and then ever so slowly, she looked each one of us in the eye, careful to grab our attention, one by one.

In a more hushed tone, as if telling us a secret, she added, "The plantation owners can be fair, and they can also be unfair. You must pay attention to your pay and keep track of it. You will be required to buy everything from the plantation. It will be difficult to save money."

There was some rustling among us as we shifted on our knees, uncomfortable hearing, for the first time, words about the true conditions waiting for us.

"How many of you think you are going to save money and return home in a ship like this after three or five years?"

About half of us raised our hands, mine included.

"Out of all of you, perhaps one or two of you will return."

After an uncomfortably silent moment, Matron spoke. "It is time to prepare for lunch. May the rest of you please go to your teams and organize yourselves for your work."

Across the way, the men were involved in a card game. I thought that, perhaps, each one of us was hoping her husband was not gambling for money.

I returned to my bunk before joining my work team. I realized I had not said my morning prayers. I did not want to lose my connection to the ancestors. Sitting with Buddha made me feel close to my mother. I took a few extra precious moments of silence, trying to feel the love of my mother in my heart. As my ancestor, was she able to protect me in this strange adventure? I concentrated on all my ancestors and their love of me. *May this love give me strength for this day. Remove all thoughts. Remove all thoughts!*

Joining the sewing circle, I saw everyone was busy with mending tasks. I sat down next to a pile of mending, which was probably Kobayashi-san's clothing, as it was so old and worn. There was some patching material provided, and I realized my job was to patch Kobayashi-san's well-worn jacket. I was beginning to have real sympathy for the man when Matron Ando sat next to me.

"Ahh, so you have been delegated that pile I see. That is what happens when one comes late to the task!"

At that, I resolved to get up earlier to allow for my time of silence to avoid more reprimands. I bowed my head and said, "I do not mind. It looks like poor Kobayashi-san has dire need of our help. His jacket has many holes."

Matron smiled to herself and then said, "Ah, so, do you think Mr. Kobayashi cannot afford to buy himself clothing?" Matron looked up at all of us, holding her own needle suspended between stitches.

The women looked toward her.

"Mr. Kobayashi has more money than the captain of this ship. In fact, he is part owner of this ship."

At that, I decided someone was either lying to us or telling us false tales.

"How so?" asked a woman, who I now could see was not sewing at all.

Matron continued, "Kobayashi-san likes these trips. He does not like to spend money. I think that is why he never married. He loves women, but he feels they are very expensive. But he is someone who loves the sea voyage and also loves young people. Since he never had any children, he has the opportunity to instruct all these young people as if he were their grand-uncle."

"But my husband says he is a bit of a grouch and yells at them all the time," volunteered one of the women from the far end of the circle.

Matron answered, "Oh, you wait. He is only getting them ready for a hard voyage. He has his methods. He toughens them up in the beginning so he has no trouble later."

"They call him Old Socks," one other woman ventured.

Matron chuckled. "He picked out that name for himself, you know. At every port, he goes out looking for a new pair of old socks. He buys them from men he sees on the street. He struts around until he sees just the right pair and then approaches the man with a deal the man cannot refuse. He makes trades all the time so he can keep his supply of old socks."

One of the women stood up and said, "I think it is time for tea. I shall go make some."

I thought about this new information—people playing roles for themselves, as if this life was a kabuki play. Perhaps life was a play. Ten thousand things and nothing, it was all the same.

Matron said, "I must go now and check on the other groups. Never tell Kobayashi-san that I told you his secret! He will rescind our order for fresh fish that we are supposed to have tomorrow noon!"

Before leaving, Matron Ando came over to look at my stitching.

"Very nice. It seems you are almost finished with this pile. But do you not know? I gave you the most mending to do because I knew you were an excellent seamstress. But that is not the point here."

I looked up, confused.

Matron continued, "The point I am trying to make is not for you or anyone here to excel at any task to show what a good background you come from. It is to make all of you understand that it is cooperation that will make you all succeed. I expected you to help those who cannot sew, to teach them, to share your skill."

With that admonishment, Matron left me with a very red face. I looked around to see who needed help and prepared some needle and thread for a lesson.

As soon as Matron left, the woman who was not sewing came over and sat kneeling next to me. She looked at me pleadingly, "Ueme, someone told me you know all about fabrics and sewing. I need to learn to sew. My family always paid for our sewing, so I know nothing. If you would grant me the honor of teaching me, I will be so grateful." She bowed quite low. I thought the bow had more to do with her lack of skill than her Nihongi status.

"Oh, pardon my ignorance," I apologized, returning the bow. "I should have realized you needed help when I first saw you in this group. Please allow me to show you how to thread a needle and make a running stitch."

And that was how I met Yumi, daughter of a business family connected with the governor. She had unfortunately been a third daughter, who had fallen in love with a third son. They'd married against parents' wishes, and so their plight was sealed—no money and Hawaii bound. Yumi proved to be a quick learner and full of good stories. The morning passed quickly with her tales of all the intrigues of the governor's entourage. I kept my head bowed as much as possible, as I felt my cheeks were still burning from Matron's scolding.

A familiar scent and warmth—Roji was kneeling at my side.

He had some of his own mending to give me. Taking the garment from him, I grabbed his arm and turned into his chest, pressing my forehead into his jacket, which already had the smell of the sea about it.

Roji asked, "What is wrong? Has something happened?"

I was ashamed of being so emotional. "No, I just have been having bad thoughts about not ever seeing Five Bridges again and pray that they may not come true!" I was also feeling shame at Matron's scolding of me, but I would not repeat her words to anyone.

"Oh, Ueme, you are so superstitious! Of course those thoughts will not come true. Just passing thoughts! I know you are stronger than that. You are one of the strongest and smartest girls in our village. You mustn't talk that way. You tempt fate." Roji talked to me while I put away my sewing.

Taking my arm, Roji spoke with a joy I had not seen until now. "I have been put on the fishing crew. I will be able to go above and fish with the crew on the few occasions when the captain allows a fishing expedition. I am so honored." Roji was beaming at me, his eyes filled with happiness.

He continued, "You know, Old Socks has given a few of us permission to go above for a short time before our midday meal. We are allowed to take our wives, too. Let us go look at the waves full of fish trailing behind the ship, our future dinners! Oh, Ueme, do not worry. Your Matron Ando has given permission." Roji was alight with enthusiasm.

Above deck, all seemed much brighter. The waves were calmer, and the air and sun were a relief to the cramped quarters below. The captain was walking among the few passengers allowed on deck. He was pointing out the whales in the distance—how you look for them by searching for their "blows" of steam spouting upward out of the water. Once we understood, we could see many blows off in the distance.

The whales were leaping out of the water—breaching was the

word the captain used—like giant fish in the distance. Sometimes, the whales turned on their sides, putting a large fin up, like an arm waving in the distance. The whales were swimming south for the winter. The captain apologized for not having time to sail nearer to them for viewing. But our schedule was very strict, he explained.

Roji had a look of complete happiness, as if the ocean had opened his mind to more possibilities in life.

"Ueme, know this. We will be sailing in the opposite direction three years from now with money in our hands. We will rent a small house near my family and use our savings to build a new house, with maybe even a teahouse and a garden."

I was amazed at such extravagant talk. Could work as farmhands bring us that much money? I decided not to worry about three years from now. The moment was all we had. Those whales in the distance were all we had, and that was most enjoyable. I decided that Mother had sent me the whales' visit as a gift to let me know that the ancestors had forgiven my awful thoughts. My shoulders relaxed with relief.

Roji and I climbed down the ladder steps to join others for our midday meal. I felt as if I was getting used to all the swaying, for I was handling the steps much more easily today than yesterday.

For lunch, we were allowed to cross over to the other side and eat with our husbands. The meal was simple, two rice balls covered with seaweed with an umeboshi plum inside. There was also miso soup and tea.

Some of the women were not eating their second rice balls. Thus, Matron invited the men to have an extra rice ball from our abundance. Roji availed himself of this treat and then bowed to me and then to matron. Matron and I returned to our side of the below deck. Our chores were beckoning.

That afternoon passed swiftly and the evening meal was already on the table. We served ourselves, dipping into large pots of stewed vegetable and noodles to spoon out our own servings into our tin bowls. We could see the men across the way eating their meal, apparently the same fare. Roji waved to me as he served himself from their pot, and then he sat down, disappearing behind the men's heads.

Chapter 16

SHIP LIVING

Now it was the seventh day of the journey. The noise of the steam engines was ever constant. The first night, I had tried to stuff my ears with cloth so I could not hear it. However, it was not really a thing of hearing. It was a drone, a vibration. The ship was metal. It vibrated, transferring the powerful energy of the engines to us. Once I got used to the rolling, rocking rhythm of the waves, I realized the vibration was in my bones. The boredom of our routine settled in. It was only every other day that Roji and I would get to go above deck, due to limits of numbers required by the captain and our team duties.

The women had started to gossip. They had been figuring out who was married to whom and where each of us came from and of what status we were.

Matron interrupted this talk one afternoon. "Hah, you talk as if you were going to Nihon! You are going to the island of Hawaii, which is run by businessmen from America. They care nothing for whatever class you have come from. They care only for how much sugar cane you can produce for them so they can stuff their own pockets with money. You will not see much of that money either."

A voice came out of the shadows. It was Yumi. "I have heard that they treat us Nihonji like animals."

Another voice retorted, "Well, if you knew that, why did you bother to sign up for this?"

One of the women was crying.

Matron spoke. "Listen to me. Do not turn on each other. You need each other. That is why I put you into teams. You will need to help each other survive. Only kindness to each other will get you through this trial."

Another voice spoke plaintively. "Why has the emperor encouraged us to leave our homes to live far away and do this work if it is so terrible?"

Matron was quiet. Then she spoke very slowly and carefully. "I do not want to insult anyone here. I believe all humans are wonderful people if given the chance. I see Hawaii as a different place, a place where maybe someone can thrive after all, even if of very low birth. Perhaps, although this is a difficult place, there may be opportunity there."

Then she continued, "Let us be honest with ourselves here. In Nihon in recent years, there has not been enough rice to go around. Second and third sons have no prospects. For some to remain in Nihon might be a life now worse than what we will find in Hawaii. The emperor has encouraged people to leave so fewer people will be starving in our lovely country."

A very stout woman stood up. "I am a farmer's daughter, and I can do manual labor. Thus, fate is good to me. I think it will not be so hard."

Matron rose from her spot. "Enough talk. It is time for our entertainment group to make some fun for us."

My team had been preparing for this very moment. Among us were two trained singers, two samisen players but only one samisen, two husbands who had been volunteered by their wives to drum on some empty oil bins, and one woman who had agreed to do a graceful dance with a fan. She was able to find her fan but refused to wear her silk kimono in the "dirty ship" and so would perform in her cotton hakata. So my hope for a little elegance went unanswered.

Roji and some of the men helped to hang some summer hakatas

from the beams to make a crude backdrop for the show. The table planks were moved aside to make a larger space for the audience. Matron had a short branch of pine. She said she always brought a pine branch on ocean trips, as we all needed to remind ourselves of nature's spirit. Matron admitted to us that being a "landlubber," she could not relate to the ocean spirit as well, and so she always brought a bit of land with her. We hung it to one side of the stage, careful to bind it to a post so it would not swing and hit someone on the head. I was pleased to see that Roji had learned some knots from the crew and was the one to tie the pine securely.

Because of my experience playing at the fair, I was made the director of the production. I motioned for the drummers to start. Then, with one pluck of my samisen, the group of us began to sing. We had chosen four songs, one for each of the seasons. After our songs, the drummers played again, but very slowly, while the other samisen player began to pluck a slow dance number, borrowing my instrument, for the fan dance. We finished with a group sing of some common folk songs, with most of the audience joining in.

Some of the ship's crew had assembled with us for the event. We had invited the captain, who was able to make a short appearance. At the finish, our musical program was deemed a huge success. Although some of the men managed to sneak some beer, most of us drank tea.

Roji started the clapping at the end. His enthusiasm for our show warmed my heart. He introduced me to several of the crew, who he had gotten to know, as his "charming and talented wife." I bowed and tried to be discreet, but I am afraid my pride in the show and in my new husband was showing all too much.

Cleaning up was rushed, as we wanted to get our evening meal and chores done. The afternoon had flown by. I scarcely noticed the drone of the vibration of the ship.

Kobayashi-san came over and bowed to me. "I appreciate your talent, Madam Ueme. May you always treasure it. But most of all, it will be most beneficial to share your talent when you are in the camps. Music soothes the spirit and elevates our hearts. May good fortune follow you always." Kobayashi-san bowed graciously, and as he exited, I noticed he was wearing very clean, very white socks.

He looked back at me. "For you!" Old Socks raised his foot up to the side with bent knee in a comical jest to show me.

As we bent over our brushes and buckets, we could hear the chopping of the vegetables and could smell the steam from the rice starting to fill the air. Matron was truly efficient. Across the way, on the other side of the ship, we could see the men doing the same thing—cleaning, organizing, and cooking. Our light came from the large open stairwell and from some oil lamps hanging from the low beams. It looked and smelled constricting to me. I had to remind myself that, in just over a week's time, we would be landing in Hawaii, with lots of space and fresh air.

Chapter 17

INTENTION

The sewing group had expanded our work; we had decided to make a quilt since the mending had mostly been finished. Madam donated some pieces of fabric. and the crew gave us some old shirts for it. The idea was inspired by one of Madam's stories about a young seaman who had perished in a storm on one of the last journeys across the Pacific. If we could finish the quilt, it would be given to the young man's mother, who lived in Yokohama, quite stricken with grief.

Happily, I was able to help erase my shame by igniting this idea in our group without taking credit for it. The quilt gave everyone an opportunity to sew more and contribute equally, no matter her skill level. A few of us more skilled sewers checked each square as it was completed and reinforced the stitching as necessary. Two women were working on embroidering the man's name in simple kanji script, including a good luck blessing for the family.

Roji had found much joy in the male companionship on our voyage. The fishing was a complete joy for him, though it was only every third or fourth day that the captain would allow the ship to slow down for this. He had gotten to know the crew members and the few other passengers who had been chosen for the fishing.

It was a little distressing that Roji was paying less attention to me. After all, we had tried to play our married roles properly, and it seemed like it had been working. But he kept disappearing, and I did grow a bit nervous with his secretiveness about his whereabouts.

However, one day after the evening meal, he surprised me with a recital of a few famous haikus of springtime. One of the other passengers had a book of haikus and had lent it to Roji. As he said the words, I was transported to my home in Five Bridges, listening to Otasan recite his favorite haikus to our customers. It transported me back—waiting for Otasan to finish his recitation, I felt myself kneeling at the shoji door, ready to enter, carrying a tray of tea and sweets for the customers. I could smell our house, our shop, the smell of freshly dyed indigo cotton; I was daydreaming.

"Ueme, Ueme, did you like the haiku? Did I recite it properly?" Roji's anxious voice brought me back to the present.

"Oh, Roji, it is wonderful. It is the best present ever." I wondered how this ocean voyage had seemed to open Roji up to new experiences.

One day, I found myself lamenting to Tameki about not being able to go above deck more, as I so loved seeing the birds and porpoises.

"What? I thought you just wanted to impress Madam with your industriousness! Many of us go up on deck for a few hours every day!" Tameki looked at me with her laughing, wide eyes.

"What do you mean? We are only allowed up every other day," I replied.

"Oh, just open your eyes and ears, Ueme. Don't try to be the teacher's pet all the time, and you will see what all of us are doing. My father always said rules are made for the man; man is not made for the rules!" Tameki was actually scolding me.

"You know, if you don't become more worldly wise, you may get crushed in this new land. I've heard it is pretty hard on us women." Tameki pulled my sleeve. "Come on, we are going up."

I found myself on the deck for the first time without Roji or permission from Madam. The air was clear; the sun was bright; and the sky was blue, with fluffy clouds interrupting its span.

I took a deep breath. "So you have been coming up on deck every day?

Tameki stretched out her arms wide and shouted into the wind, "Oh, yes, yes, yes!"

I laughed. "The crew will see us and think us improper."

Tameki laughed and said, "The crew feel sorry for us. They have told me so. One of them told me to cherish this fresh air as much as I could before we land in Hawaii. He told me the crew has to spend many days on the ocean out of the year for their work. But in the end, they go back to Nihon, to their families. But us, we are leaving Nihon, perhaps forever."

There it was again—words that loomed over us saying this adventure was going to be terrifying and never ending.

I yelled into the wind, "I will return to Nihon!" May the ocean and the ancestors hear me and feel my intention.

Chapter 18

DISCORD

Roji and I were clearly at odds. I thought he might be gambling every day. He disappeared all the time. I tried to take him aside and talk calmly to him. My calm was wearing thin. I was actually afraid. He seemed to have no goal beyond his bets for the day. He said I was taking away his manhood by questioning him every day. "The other men are watching me. They think I do not have control over you."

I thought, *Control! What is this?*

Roji and I never had an agreement about control. I was not some samurai's wife. I had not been prepared for that. All the rules about how a woman was to do this, how she was to do that, how to keep accounts, to make the household run smoothly, to entertain important business guests, to take care of the children, how to look, what language dialect to use correctly when dealing with each type of class in our store—these were things I knew. But Roji, the school joker and flirt, controlling me?

My thoughts were spinning. I had to think calmly. Think about my own life. Think about my family, the business. How I missed our store, the smell of the blue indigo cloth, the feel of the silk shantung, the colors of the Chinese silks. The sureness of how one earned money. The sureness of what time of day it was and what chore that time required, the sureness of numbers adding up on my abacus. There was no sureness now.

And this, this was like the nightmare that had become my

household after my mother had died. I felt my head go light but remembered Matron's warnings. This was no time to be weak-kneed. He was gambling away our money, and we would find it hard to save money in Hawaii. Somehow, I must make Roji understand this. No, I had already discussed with him the money issue at the plantation. I'd repeated Matron's warnings to him that first night on the ship. He'd laughed and said I was a worrier, and I needed to be a warrior. Yes, indeed, a warrior did what was required. I just did not know what that was.

One afternoon, I coaxed Roji up on deck with me to try to have some relaxing time together. We ended up watching the sunset together and had a good time counting the birds and the jumping fish. We made friends with one of the boatswains and traded stories of Nihon and Hawaii together. The moon was rising but not full yet. That night, I implored Roji to stay with me and not go gambling with those men. He agreed. But as we lay in the crowded bunk, I was not sure I could believe that he would not leave as soon as I fell asleep. I felt really lost and homesick. Somehow, the two of us were even farther apart than we had been back in Nihon on the Bridge of Lasting Happiness.

After a while, I fell into a dreamy, comfortable sleep thinking of Five Bridges and our alley. I could feel the sunlight on my shoulders as I looked down the alley.

Our fishmonger was traveling down the alley, stopping at each kitchen door with his wares. He had a long pole, which he balanced on his shoulders with a large basket hung by three chains at each end of the pole. Some of the fish hung from the end of the pole; some were laid flat across the baskets. His cotton jacket was quilted, light blue, and slightly stained; the sleeves were a bit worn on the edges. Mother had given him a new one as payment for extra good service. But we would never see him wear it, as he was saving it for a special occasion.

Inside our kitchen, Madame Iwata warned Mother of his arrival.

Mother stood in the middle of the kitchen, on the lower floor, level with the alley, made of pounded dirt. She took her power stand with her head held high. I marveled at her shining black hair perfectly wrapped in a stylish bun.

Mr. Watanabe entered. "Ohaiyo gozai mashto, Madam Oyama-san."

He bowed, and Mother returned the morning greeting with her one-degree bow. Her kimono sleeves were tied back, ready for the important examination of the fish. As mother looked each fish over, she touched the skin, peered into its eyes, and smelled it.

"Hmm, this is not so fresh, Mr. Watanabe. From where has this one come? Are we getting mullet now? How is its meat?"

Turning her head to see the other basket, she said, "Hmm, ooh, now this one is beautiful. Oh, what a beauty! However, I cannot afford it."

"What do you mean you cannot afford it? If the honorable House of Oyama cannot afford it, who can? Your establishment is the finest in Five Bridges."

I felt a warmth of security hearing of our family's success.

"Oh, such praise, Mr. Watanabe. We do not deserve that! No, things have not been going that well this week. Just yesterday, we lost some fabric to mold. Mold, Mr. Watanabe, mold! Do you have to deal with that? Oh no, I think we will have to get that smaller fish."

"Madam Oyama, I have not even mentioned the price of the larger fish. Perhaps you can afford it. Why, it is less than twelve sen."

"Ah, that is a very good price. I am surprised you can sell it for such a price. You must be doing very well, Mr. Watanabe! Perhaps you can spare me and sell me that fish for just a little less?"

"But Madam Oyama, I will go broke. My grandchild is not yet born!"

"My daughter, Ueme, is not yet married!" my mother replied.

Hearing my mother's voice say my name, a relaxation filled my body.

"Please, Madam, you pay that price for the big fish, and I will throw in five little ones for your breakfast tomorrow?"

"And this fine tako, squid, for our health, Mr. Watanabe."

"Done, Madam Oyama." He started pulling out the lines of the chosen fish and the squid.

Mother walked closer and smelled each of the smaller fish. "Mr. Watanabe, you are aware that the last time you sold me a very stinky fish, which we could not eat!"

Mr. Watanabe looked up with a most obliging smile. "Well, one small mistake. That happens in business!"

"Not my business, Mr. Watanabe. And if you cheat me this time, I shall send my son up and down the alley to spread the news. He would be happy for such an interesting task." Mother stiffened her back.

I thought about my brother. Where was he?

"My, my, such a horrible thing. I never intended to hurt you. You would make me lose face? Perhaps the fish was still good for pickling."

"No good, Mr. Watanabe, no good for anything."

"Aagh! So Sorry. Never happen again. May the Moon Princess strike me down if it ever happens again."

"The Moon Princess, Mr. Watanabe? How is she connected to your fish?" Mother looked quizzical now. She loved to hear about the different interpretations of Nihon's folktales.

"Well, she is only seen in the full moon, at night. And that's the best time to catch fish. Surely, you know that!"

"I really do not see how she has anything to do with fish." Mother was sticking to her point.

"Madam, she has a tragic love affair with a fisherman! That is the main theme of her story."

"Oh, really, Mr. Watanabe? Isn't it that she did not accept any of her suitors because they were cheats?" Mother emphasized the last word.

Mr. Watanabe explained, "It was a nobleman who had a special way of talking with fish. Some accounts say he was a fish who had transformed himself into a human!" The fishmonger was good at fabricating his own tale.

"That is an interesting viewpoint, Mr. Watanabe. But in any case, it is a sad tale, and she, the princess, was not of this earth and very much above the curious dishonesty of earthly men. Perhaps she had seen a need to elevate the fishmonger. I'm sure she must have seen many things on earth that needed to be made more pure. May she protect my daughter, and yours, Watanabe-san, from dishonest men."

I was trying to remember that tale of the Moon Princess. I felt so caught up with hearing the familiar tone of my mother's speech.

"Well, as you can see, any being who lives on the moon has much more control over earthly things than any of us. She definitely watches over the fishermen, and of course, she protects all young women, too." Mr. Watanabe had the last word while being exceedingly polite.

Mr. Watanabe deftly cut the strings holding the fish items and carefully laid them on our kitchen board, large to small, perfectly straight, caressing each fish lovingly as he laid it out.

"May your family be blessed with good health and fortune." Mother handed him the money with a slight bow.

I marveled at my mother's skill at bargaining. I found her presence so soothing. I walked toward her, but my feet were caught. The familiar feeling of comfort and warmth slipped out like rain off a petal.

I was awake. No, it could not be. The drone of the ship's vibrations filled by body. My feet were tangled in the futon. No, this was the nightmare, the ship, here. I closed my eyes to recapture the comfort of my dream, begging it to be the real time. Why couldn't that noise stop, those vibrations? I buried my face in the futon and tried to forget where I was.

Roji was not beside me.

Chapter 19

A VISION IN THE STORM

We were all below—the women on one side, the men on the other, except for those sick in their bunks. At first, the voyage had been new and exciting. However, we'd had bad weather for days. Now, though we feared the uncertainty of the work and life in Hawaii, we were anxious to get this voyage over and start our lives on the islands. We were crowded and dirty. Fear was as thick as the smell of vomit in the air. The ship rocked back and forth, up and down. There were people shouting; things were falling. Madam was urging everyone to be calm, to crouch together in our work groups or stay in the bunks.

I had all I could do to keep the contents of my stomach down. I sipped some miso soup offered by my top bunk neighbor. We were both sitting on my bunk, as she said she was afraid she would keep falling off the top bunk. It was late afternoon, but it was as dark as night due to the storm. The salty taste of miso helped a bit to ease my stomach.

I resolved to go above, to get some fresh air no matter what. Earlier, I had asked Roji to go on deck with me to get some fresh air. I had such a need for fresh air. He refused and warned me to "stay safe here below and to control your nerves." He returned to his newfound friends at the rear of the tween deck.

The desire for the air was completely overwhelming me. I pushed my way toward the ladder stairs. Kobayashi-san was guarding the steps and allowed no one to go above.

"Too dangerous," he said. "Captain has ordered."

Kobayashi-san smiled at me but shook his head no and pushed me back.

At that moment, the ship lurched. Everyone fell to the far side, tumbling over one another. I hit something hard. It was the ladder stairs. I took advantage of the confusion and scrambled up the steps before Kobayashi-san could grab my leg and pull me back down. I was driven by the need to survive by my konjo, my spirit self, not my head. If only I could feel one with the ocean spirit, I would be fine. I was just not in connection with spirit.

A sudden rush of cold damp air was filling my lungs. It was such a relief from the enclosed stale air below deck. It was dark as night, but there was a glow bouncing off the ocean. The waves were as big as small mountains. It was hard to see them, they were so big—a visionary landscape of froth and foam and constant movement, a slippery hill to be climbed by our ship, so tiny in comparison.

As frightening as the waves appeared, it was more calming to see with one's own eyes how well the little ship made the climb. It was better than to feel the swells against the sides of the ship from our cabins below with the only measuring tools being the time up one side and the time down the other side of the wave—imagining the drop down the other side to be the one time it just kept going down.

It was so dark that only by feeling did I reach the side rail of the ship. One of the crew was talking to me; was he telling me to go back down? We were awash in seawater with periodic crashing against the side, seawater licking over the gunwales, covering the deck, glistening, connecting us to the larger ocean. The generous air held me there, and I could not make my feet move back to the stair hatch.

Someone was pulling me away from the side, saying, "We need to tie this rope around your waist if you insist on staying up here. Otherwise, the waves will wash you overboard."

I could barely hear the voice. It was like a dream within my head, as if the words were actually coming from inside my head. I could not see him. But somehow, I was tied to a structure in the middle of the deck near some steel cases that were also lashed down.

A hearty laugh came from a sailor farther away. That seaman, with no note of fear in his voice, shouted, "Welcome on deck. You may have chosen the best spot to ride out the storm."

After a while, no one spoke. I sensed no one there.

Darkness, only feeling, hearing, and smelling. I felt as if in a cocoon by myself. I heard a constant roar, grander than that of the ship's sides being slapped. I smelled seaweed and fish. Sometimes, the seawater washed over my face, and I caught a gulp of its saltiness. As I gripped the rope, rolled with the swells, my mind wandered.

I heard my obachan. She was giving me advice. What was she saying? It really did sound like her. I memorized the words. "Listen and take care, Ueme."

There was light over the tops of the waves, above the clouds. At first, it was a small glow. I realized that, if this glow was the moon, it should rise to the top of the sky, for it was time for the full moon, gauging from where the moon had been when we'd started the trip. I stared at the glow. It started softly as an orange pink color. As the glow grew in strength and size, the fishy smell of the sea turned into a clean smell of mint and oranges.

The glow separated from the top of the wave. It grew Into the round full moon, but it did not stop expanding. The brightness of the moon created reflections on the giant waves. A few of these reflections grew lengthwise and, with the motion of the waves, reached up to the moon. The reflections seemed slippery and silky. with long fingerlike projections curving over the swells. An iridescence of blue and silver, then silver slipping into gold. The hues were constantly changing, the colors translucent. I could see through the slippery water to the undersea beyond, with large blurry images of seaweed, fish and dolphins swimming there.

The light dancing on the top of the water became stronger, and the images below the watery surface disappeared. The moon grew larger and touched the top of the wave. A figure then seemed to grow out of the center of the moon along the lines of the reflections. A rainbow of colors flashed in and out of the reflections, and a beautiful kimono rose from the swell. Long dark hair, like a shiny piece of satin, fell in graceful curves over the front of the elegant kimono. Long sleeves stretched down the length of the giant waves and were edged in light green foam. The bottom of the kimono flowed along the curved lines of the moving waves. The kimono itself was made of silky transparent fibers unintelligible to me. The bowed head with the black hair rose up, showing a face full of kindness and understanding.

The elegant woman emerged, walking down a path through the waves. The waves became a colorful glistening glass slide. Gliding in and out of view, the being approached me, gracefully navigating the huge glass mountains. Then she was standing before me. I could see through her. She told me she was the Moon Princess without opening her mouth. The princess, without talking, explained very carefully the journey before me. I was not sure who was speaking, the princess or the mountain wave. The words told of confusing trials ahead of me, of deep sadness, and of overwhelming joy.

I was hearing words while I saw visions. How confusing! The thought over and over was, *You are strong. You are blessed. You are good.*

I think I was being warned of danger ahead, but also, I felt a great comfort. My body relaxed back against the slippery wet deck and the roped boxes. The wave mountains turned into gray-purple dragon backs, with froth spewing from their mouths and then fire. The writhing bodies twisted into themselves and disappeared into their own flames.

My eyes opened. Torches had been lit on deck. The waves were gone. The storm had passed. Someone had put a blanket over me while I slept. I stayed in my blanket cocoon until the sun peaked over the horizon.

When the morning bells rang, the rest of the passengers rushed onto deck. I climbed down the stairs to prepare for the day. Roji was waiting for me at the bottom of the ladder. He was angry and would not speak to me. I tried to tell him of my dream. I wanted him to help me decipher its importance.

"Ueme, you disappoint me. Putting yourself in danger by staying on deck in the storm. The men say you are a difficult woman. You cause me shame." He proceeded to walk away from me up the steps to the deck.

I had so much to tell him, and now my thoughts totally escaped me. I was thrown emotionally back into my past, feeling the deep shame and embarrassment in my family's formal room sitting in front of the tokonoma. Madam Kumodo had scolded me for serving her improperly in front of Otasan, Mother, and Obachan. I had not served Father first. *Always the man first, dear. If you learn nothing else in this world, no matter where or when, the man comes first.* It had not been her place to reprimand me, so that, in itself, was embarrassing. However, the message had hit me hard. My heart had shrunk within my chest; I'd felt myself shrinking within my being. Oh, why feel this shame?

As I walked to my bunk, I felt deep confusion over the inner and outer messages that morning.

"Ooh, Ueme, do not tell anyone where you were last night." Tameki looked worried as she grabbed my sleeve in passing.

"Why? I am fine. Someone tied me to the middle of the deck, and I was safe," I explained.

"See this red kerchief about my neck here? I am on the safety committee. I saw you go up the ladder last night. You had such a look of desperation on your face, I felt I should let you get some air. But then you stayed! I could get into trouble with Madam if she found out that I knew. The safety committee is responsible for maintaining all rules of the captain. The captain's rules are called the Rules of Safety!" Tameki looked upset at my lack of knowledge of her team's efforts. She took my hand and felt me shaking.

Then Tameki stood in front of me. "Ueme, it is all right. I am your friend. I am just a little on edge from the storm. I think we all are. I am glad you are safe."

"Sumimasen." I bowed. Back to reality.

I'd had an incredible dream, but life marches on. No one had time for me to tell them about it. I made my way back to my bunk, weaving through women scrubbing the floor and straightening up items that had fallen during the night. I washed the saltwater off my face with some tea. There was no more fresh water for washing. That had been long gone, and I realized I would just remain with the sticky salt on my skin.

Chapter 20

CALM

The next morning, I opened my eyes because it was too quiet. The engines were off. I wondered, Was something wrong? Scrambling to get my clothes on and say my prayers to Buddha, I noticed that everyone else was up, above on deck.

I approached the ladder steps, where sun was streaming through the large hatch opening. I passed Matron Ando, who was busy scrubbing the table boards with seawater. Her brush slapped the water onto the wood; the bristles made a swishing sound. She looked up at me, motioning for me to go up. It seemed it was a day for all of us to go topside.

The sun was brilliant. But it wasn't just the sun. The white canvas sails had been let loose from their masts at either end of the ship. The crew was climbing the masts and walking along the horizontal spars, unfurling the canvas from its cocoons. The sun was reflecting off the sheets, illuminating the whole scene. Each mast had three sails, each of diminishing size above the other. I had hardly noticed the two giant masts at either end of the ship before today. This morning, the huge stretches of cloth filled taut with the power of the wind commanded the deck. It was a majestic sight. The sailors high above deck were seemingly weightless as they easily climbed around from spot to spot, adjusting ropes and horizontal spars, allowing the sails the best angle to catch the wind coming from behind. There was a stillness to the ship as it powerfully cut its way through the waves. Sailing the ship with only the wind and no vibrations from the steam engine was a perfect antidote for the fearsome darkness and violence of the storm the day before.

It had been decided that the passengers would create a banquet to honor the crew for the excellent work of keeping us safe during the storm. The 'tween decks were buzzing with activity. The captain had offered whatever assistance was needed. Thus, some crew brought more boards and food to the common space.

The women were busy in the kitchen area. I looked at the organization of the cooking utensils and the dishes and pots stowed. I saw there was a shelf only partially filled with a jumble of items. Food, dishes, pots, and utensils were all stored together, with no real order that I could see. I thought of our kitchen at home and how everything had a place, how everything was very neat and clean. The disorder stressed me, and I thought to myself, *This is not your kitchen. Leave it alone.* But my childhood Confucian learning of the proper order of things caused me stress. I'd started to rearrange some utensils when Matron barked at me, "There is much to do here. Do not waste time fussing."

Matron had requested some fresh fish from the crew, who had collected many fish from the storm waves that had washed over the ship's gunwales yesterday. She had begun to prepare it and was ordering some of the women about. There was such an abundance of fish that some of it was to be served cooked and some raw, as sashimi. Matron Ando had a reputation for her fried fish and kombu seaweed and noodle stew. She was busy with this.

The activity reminded me of preparing for large celebration meals for my father, uncle, brother, and all the cousins up at the ancestral home. Auntie and Mother would be ordering all the girls to help in the kitchen and telling the boys to clean up the paths and alleyway in preparation for guests. Lapsing into daydreaming, I was remembering how Madam Iwata had taught me how to cut the sashimi just so. I looked around for a very sharp knife to help with this chore. Matron Ando saw me searching.

"Ueme, what are you looking for?

"A very good knife for slicing the raw fish. I thought I could help," I replied, taking the cover off a box stowed beneath the shelves. I looked at the knives put out on the table for use.

Matron directed a woman to take a knife and start cutting the fish. In horror, I saw she did not inspect the knife or make a move to sharpen it.

Matron looked at me. "I am afraid that none of our knives will meet your standards. I have asked one of the other women to cut the sashimi. Perhaps you can help with washing the new boards needed to set up additional tables." Matron Ando dismissed me.

I felt as if I was being punished for my sewing crime all over again.

Tameki came up to me, "Do not pay attention. She is very busy and perhaps is overwhelmed with this impromptu banquet." Tameki continued, "Have you noticed that she favors the farmers over us merchants?" Tameki brought me a bucket and cloth to help her with the tables.

I was shocked. I hadn't thought to look at favoritism. I was so worried about my own shame, I had not paid much attention.

I pushed my wet cloth over the boards and leaned in to speak softly to Tameki. "Well, farmers are considered more valuable according to Confucian law."

"I think it is something else. Perhaps Matron is a farmer. Or it may have to do with merchant wealth. After all, you and I have the only two trunks. Some women have two satchels at the most. There are some samurai women, but they cannot do much and only brought one trunk each, lowly status." Tameki spoke softly while she wiped down the boards. I caught the reference to low samurai. That would have been my father's family had not Grandfather been so resourceful and open-minded.

Matron Ando came up to us. "I do hope you can be good role models for the other young women. Those who have advantages will be asked to do the same work as all the other women when you get to the plantation. But you two have skills that others do not have. You will need to share your skills."

Shocked that she had heard our conversation, we kept quiet until the tables were all set. In spite of our menial chores, I was happy to dwell in my childhood memories of working in our kitchen, grateful for such happy times.

The banquet was a success. Though, truly, we had run out of most food. We were lacking enough rice or pickled vegetables to satisfy a normal hunger. The crew was happy to be included. The abundance of fresh fish in the menu due to the recent storm had brightened everyone's spirits, as well as appetites.

The cleanup was still unfinished as the sun was setting. I volunteered to help dispose of the used washing water over the side rail just to be able to watch the setting sun and watch the foam in the wake as the ship moved closer and closer to our destinations. Staying to stare at the last glowing orb of sunlight in the direction of our families, I noticed Roji hunched over with other husbands and a few of the crew behind some barrels and coils of rope. I wondered how often he joined these people up here.

One of Matron Ando's talks had been about keeping track of our money—how men who had never had a bad habit could develop a bad habit when confronted with stressful situations. She had mentioned how advisable it was to hide money in clever places. I had taken some of our yen and buried it within my personal bag of mochi rice, a gift from uncle, which was in our trunk. Roji would not look there, as rice was women's work. I had sewed a few yen into the hem of my winter kimono. I had been using it as a blanket on our bunk. Matron had said hems would probably be the first place a gambler would look. She had advised us to not put all the money there. As I sewed it in, I remembered thinking that this was silly. Roji would not be dishonest with me.

Now I wondered. I hadn't even bothered to check the hem's

contents before this. Tonight, after preparing for sleep, I felt for the hem at the bottom of my kimono. Some stitches had been broken. I put in my fingers and counted the bills. Two bills were missing. Perhaps one of the other women was a thief. That I could believe. That was the only thought that allowed me sleep.

The next morning, I managed to do some of the morning cleanup next to Matron. I was torturing myself over the missing bills.

"Madam Ando, I have an embarrassing question to ask you. I would not bother you, but you have such knowledge. I am so limited in vision. If you have any spare time to give me, it would be much appreciated." I was bowing quite low, as I was feeling very humble and could not figure out the proper rankings between us.

"Ueme, you must learn to be more direct in your speech. I do not have time for this." Matron handed me a pot to dry.

"Oh, I am so sorry, sumimasen. Perhaps this is a bad time." I backed away, bowing.

Matron interrupted me. "Out with it. What is your problem?"

"Oh, it may not be a problem. It is probably my mistake. I could have counted wrong." I was turning very red with embarrassment about my private life."

"Oh, I doubt that, Ueme. I have noticed you are very exact with everything you do. If I needed something critical to be done that required no mistakes, as if our lives depended on it, I would give that job to you."

Matron Ando had stopped her washing and was drying her hands on a cloth, looking directly into my eyes. I had to look down.

"I am ashamed. I am not sure, but I think someone may have stolen yen from my bunk area, specifically from the hem of my winter kimono. Do you think one of the women may have done this?" I kept my gaze down.

Somehow, I felt dishonest trying to blame one of the women. A strange feeling in my stomach was telling me it was Roji. That was the reason I had desired to go on deck last night. The ancestors were helping to warn me and had put the idea into my head.

"Really!" Matron Ando had a look of disgust toward me. "This is why we separate the men and women in their chores. Women lie for their husbands. It is a known trait that is unworthy of a Nihonji."

I felt as if I had been struck across the face with her dishcloth. Trembling, I said, "But Roji and I have dreams for our money. We have talked about it. He wouldn't steal from our dreams!"

"If you want an investigation, I assure you, it will be an embarrassment to you." Matron receded to the drying line and pinned up the dishcloth.

"No, no, it is not necessary. It is only a few yen."

"It will be more before we get to Honolulu." She had untied her kimono sleeves from her back and was adjusting them on her arms for the proper length.

I looked at her in astonishment.

Matron shrugged, "It is not bad. It is good that he found some money to pay his debts. He would be angry if he lost face because you hid the money too well. I am sure he has calculated how much more he can lose without taking all the bills. When you question him, he will say you had miscounted your money and that it is not his problem. It will be fine." Matron then left to go to speak to another group of women.

My stomach was lurching. I poured myself some barely warm tea from the large kettle, which contained the only fresh water we had left. Matron had boiled all the water and made it into tea. The rule was now—washing of dishes or bodies was to be with seawater only. Because of that, I had taken to stealing tea water to wash my face. Sipping my cup of tea now, trying to keep the contents of my stomach down, I walked over to the sewing group and picked up a quilt square to work on.

Two days later, I decided to question Roji about the missing money. I woke early.

"Roji, please wake up." I squeezed his shoulder at first gently and then harder.

"Owee! Stop that, Ueme. What are you doing?" The tone of his voice was harsh.

"Roji, please keep your voice down. Our neighbors are sleeping."

"Well, that is what I would like to be doing!"

"I need to ask you something. Can you sit up so we can talk?"

Roji grunted in response.

I squeezed his shoulder again.

"All right, let go!" He sat up on the edge of the bunk next to me.

"Roji, I am missing some yen out of the hem of my kimono."

"So what, a few yen? Are you sure?"

"Yes, some are missing. I have calculated at least six yen are gone."

"Ueme, why do you bother me over six yen?"

"Roji, I am trying to keep track of all our money. We may not have any extra money in Hawaii, and each yen is important. It may mean a few bowls of rice for a month or medicine for sickness if we need it."

"There you go, inventing disasters for us. I cannot be bothered with the imaginations of your mind."

"But, Roji, there is money missing. Did you take it?"

"Ueme, why would I take your yen? What use would I have for it?"

"Roji, I saw you on deck with the other men gambling. Have you gotten into gambling debt?"

"Oh, now you do not trust me? That is too much. How can we have a good marriage if, right at the beginning, you accuse me of such ugliness?"

"Roji, if you have need of money, you could come and talk with me. We should discuss these things together. We should be working on problems together."

"Ueme, there is no problem, and I think this trip is having an effect on your mind. I never took any money. Moreover, just because you saw me sitting with the men on deck does not mean I was gambling. We trade stories. We have fun. It helps pass the time. You women are always jealous of how men are able to enjoy themselves, while all you can think of is what chore needs to be done next."

I could see that the conversation would be turning against me. And I could see that he had spent many an hour listening to the tales of the unhappy married men of how their wives were disappointing to them. I searched Roji's face. It was devoid of emotion. He was determined to stick with his answers. If I pushed, the conversation might take a bad turn. Roji needed to save face.

"Roji, I am glad you have made friends. I was worried. But now that we have discussed this, I need not ask you about it further. I will count the yen again. We were so rushed packing to make our train. It is very possible that I made a miscalculation."

Roji got up from the bunk and, without looking at me, left to go to the washroom. We prepared for the landing at Honolulu.

North Shore

Island of Oahu

Hawaii

Life in the Camp

Sugar Cane Plantation

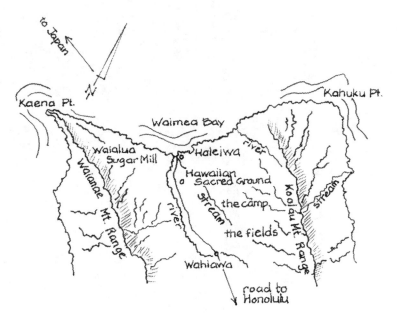

The North Shore of Oahu circa 1900

Chapter 21

ARRIVAL

In the morning, we were allowed on deck to watch as our ship came into Honolulu Harbor. The air was sweet with the scent of blossoms, and yet it was way past cherry blossom time. The new scents were all unfamiliar to us. Seeing the graceful palm trees on the beaches, the sights and new smells gave me hope.

The arrival itself was chaotic and humbling. We did not understand the language. An urgency was made evident by all the commotion, conveyed in hand movements with lots of shoving. Not understanding what was being said made it all very degrading to our personhood. There was a feeling of fear on both sides. Looking back, I understand the officials were fearful that we carried diseases and wanted us off to the quarantine barracks as soon as possible. However, there should have been a more welcome feeling shown to us on our arrival.

One thing we had not anticipated in everything we'd thought about this new journey was how difficult the language barrier would be. I had never met anyone who did not speak Nihonji, my language. Not only did I not understand them, they could not understand me. The importance of communication with other human beings had never been something I'd considered before, the very basic need of it.

We were made to stay in barracks-like buildings for many days to make sure we had no diseases. Time became distorted with the crowded conditions and the uncertainty of the future events. Yumi and Tameki and I became good friends in this period of time. Poor Yumi, she did not seem to have the strength to survive all these changes. She was more homesick than I was. Tameki was the adventurer. She relished all the strangeness, all the oddities thrust upon us.

One day, a representative of the emperor instructed us to take our chests and satchels and walk across the narrow bridge to the mainland. Hearing our language spoken so sweetly and correctly was music to my ears. Then we were packed into wagons to sit on crowded side benches, our luggage in the middle and on top of us while we were taken up a dusty road. The destination for our group was to be the north side of the island, far from bustling Honolulu. There was another group of us from our ship who were seen boarding another ship to go to another island. I saw Yumi being boarded onto that ship and tried to wave. But in the commotion, I am sure she never saw me.

I was grateful to at least be finally on the right piece of land. The road journey was made more difficult due to our uncertainty of what lay ahead. Our throats were dry, and our eyes were hurting from the dust. The wagon was rocking back and forth. The sun was hot, and I dozed off.

The wagon lurched over a rock in the road and woke me out of my daydream. Which was real? This day seemed more like the dream, a nightmare. Roji wasn't even in the same wagon with me. He had said it was fine; we would all arrive at the same spot. We didn't need to ride together. I thought he harbored anger at me for my independent ways on the ship.

It was late afternoon when we arrived at the camp located on a hillside below the sugar cane fields. It appeared to be a small very crude settlement. There were a couple of rows of wooden buildings on wood frames a few feet off the ground. It was surrounded by a high fence and locked gate. We unloaded our baggage from the wagons. A tall, very wrinkled American started talking to us in

English. I'd had a few lessons in that language in my upper school, but I could not make out what he said. When he was finished, a Nihonji man then explained that this was the foreman welcoming us to the camp. He explained that we were to come to the foreman with all our questions, not just work but food, clothing, housing. He was in charge of everything. *My goodness,* I thought to myself, *that American man really thinks he is something!*

The plantation owner would be coming later to introduce himself. In the meantime, we were to get settled in our quarters. We were to share a unit with another couple until more housing was built. No one knew how long that would be. The last night on the ship, the matron had explained to us that it was important to get settled as soon as possible, as the plantation usually expected you go to work at sunrise the next morning. We were given some plantation money and told where the company store was. Not trusting Roji to buy good food, I asked him to arrange our things inside while I went to the store to buy food. At the store, I met some of the Nihonji who were already working and living there. They gave me some tips on what to expect and how to deal with this new lifestyle. I was surprised at how much clothing I had to buy for our work clothes.

The heat was oppressive. We tried to ignore the heat. Honolulu had seemed mild, but this area was separated from the ocean by a small forest of thick scrub trees and brambles. No breeze came through. I got out our summer cotton clothing to wear for the meeting with the plantation owner. At that meeting, several well-meaning women came up to me and said we must be sure to wear our thickest, sturdiest pants and jackets for tomorrow's work to protect us from the sugar cane. Someone offered to inspect the clothing I had bought to make sure we had everything we needed.

The plantation owner knew no Japanese. The supervisor translated as best he could. An experienced worker then translated for our better understanding. The plantation owner seemed very elegant on his horse but, much like our Nihon government, distant and full of rules. One of the present workers told us he was a group leader and had been working here for ten years. Ten years! Why had he stayed for ten years?

The next morning, a loud whistle sounded, and there was a huge clamor before dawn. A man patrolled outside the cottages, yelling. It was difficult to wake Roji. He had gone out drinking with some of the other men from the ship. I had cooked rice and packed our lunches the night before. We ate cold rice and tea for breakfast. It took much longer than we had planned to put on our work outfits and attach our lunches and tea bottles to our waists. Every inch of our bodies was covered in at least two layers of dense broadcloth and treated canvas. We had thick boots and gloves that came to our elbows. In the early morning, the air was cooler. As the sun rose, the heat from the clothing was terrible. The women told me I would get used to it, that my body would adjust.

In the early morning before dawn, with the sun's light barely touching the dark sky, workers crowded the dirt road outside the cottage. Men and women in all their working gear were running and walking up toward the fields. At the top of the road, the women piled into a wagon to a more distant field. I waved goodbye to Roji, but he was already in intense conversation with two men. We had all been divided into groups called gangs. Each gang had a leader who was an experienced cane worker called the luna.

Today the women were to go to a field, where we would hoe and weed to prepare for a new planting. The men were to go to another field. I was disappointed to find we would be working in different fields. I had hoped to be able to join Roji for lunch at least. As we arrived over the top of the mountain, the saddle as it was called, we could see the plowed fields of red dirt stretched out before us. The sun was just rising over the mountain range in the distance. I was admiring the contrast of colors of the early dawn when something sharp struck my shoulder. In broken Nihonji, the luna yelled, "Hey you, number seven five two one, get going with these two women on this row. Move it." A hoe was shoved into my gloved hands.

At first, I reveled in the hard physical labor. I could feel my back muscles getting into the rhythm of the hoeing. I was singing one of the festival songs about planting to the rhythm of my hoe. But as the sun reached the middle of the sky, I felt only pain in my muscles. If I took too long to stretch in between my bouts of hoeing, that sharp pain revisited my shoulder with a nasty thump and a bark, "Hey you, number seven five two one, get going."

I hoed with fast, short strokes to get closer to one of my neighbor gang members. I asked her, while keeping up the rhythm of my hoeing, "Why do they call us numbers? Why don't they use our names? I hate this number thing. I thought it was only for our bills at the store, for accounting purposes."

She replied, "Can you think of a better way to deny someone his humanity? We are nothing but pack mules to them."

I said, "Well, you are not a pack mule to me. My name is Ueme. What is yours?"

She turned her head to the side and back to look at me. She was smiling. "My name is Aoki. I am from Kumamoto. Where are you from?"

"Why, I am from Kumamoto also."

As we exchanged names of schools, temples and stores, we realized that Kumamoto was a lot larger than we had realized. It was a district full of many little street villages, like mine and not like mine. This was probably one of the longest conversations I would ever have in the fields while hoeing. The ever-watchful luna must have been out doing his business for us not to be noticed.

The luna yelled something unintelligible, and we all sat down, gathering to a common spot to eat our boxed lunches of pickled vegetables, dried fish, and rice. The luna spoke Portuguese, and the women explained that, soon, I would understand most of his words. The women were exchanging all types of personal information. It was the most casual conversation between women I had ever heard. Some things were so intimate my ears burned. The break did not last long. I told myself I must learn to eat faster.

In the afternoon with the heat penetrating through my clothing through my skin to the innermost part of my body, I had no more liquid in my tea bottle. A man carrying water in two buckets balanced across his shoulders spooned water out to me with a ladle. Two days ago, I would have shunned drinking water from a common ladle, as this was a known way of passing sickness around. At that moment, with the sun high in the sky, with an ache so deep in my muscles and my tongue so dry I was choking on it, I gladly drank the ladled water.

My short walk down the dusty road to our cottage was filled with dread and anxiousness. Tomorrow was going to come very soon. I had to brush down all our clothing, make our dinner meal, pack the boxes for tomorrow's noon meal, and stand in line for water at the communal pump. I was so tired. Being so filthy and weighed down by my work clothes was an unfamiliar feeling. With the heat and the knowledge of how difficult it would be to get clean in this sort of community, I felt the contents of my stomach rise in my throat.

At the door to our communal cottage, our neighbors waved pleasantly at my approach. "Come here, we have a furo set up for you. Let my husband brush down your clothes while I help you wash off the dirt. We know what a shock the first day of work is."

At the back of the cottage was a small wooden tub with steaming hot water. My neighbor, Kikume, helped me out of my clothes and left to give them to her husband. I was left with a small bucket of soapy water, a brush, and a small cloth. Gratefully, I soaped and rinsed down and then relaxed in the hot water. It was not a deep furo such as I was used to but it was the first hot bathwater I had had since leaving Five Bridges. Then, with a start, I scrambled up, dried myself off and called to Kikume, "Where is Roji? I should be bathing him."

"Ahh, no worries, he came back earlier and left to do some errands. He said he needed to go buy some items at the store. You both should be careful about the 'store.' The company is not honest, and they try to cheat you."

Coming back into the cottage, I could see both Roji's and my work clothes, brushed and laid out neatly in the corner of the cottage. A length of cloth had been hung down the middle of the room to give some privacy. I started to prepare for dinner and tomorrow's meals. I could smell our neighbor's rice and hear their lowered voices discussing their day with each other. Kikume's husband was unusual for a man from Nihon, to help with cleaning the clothes! It made me wonder. It was not a manly thing to do.

I finally ate by myself. Roji had not returned. I was worried and asked Kikume's husband if I should be worried. They were about to go to sleep, and I did not want to bother them. Mori replied, "Ah, I'm sure everything is all right. He probably met someone from your old village and got involved talking about common friends. It happens all the time."

Having laid out the futons, I could not keep my eyes open any longer and drifted off to sleep.

Again, the shriek of the whistle awakened me. I felt like I had only slept a couple of hours. Surely, it was not the next morning already! Roji was asleep beside me. He was not moving. I forced myself to move and stand. Everything hurt—my muscles, my bones, even my hair. Then, realizing how little time before the luna would be ready to hit me between the shoulders, I dressed and assembled the breakfast for Roji.

I kept tapping Roji and then shoving him. He woke up with a wildness in his eyes. I could see the reality descend into his being. This life was only starting, and yet we were weary of it. I helped him dress and attach our lunches and tea bottles, while he tried to eat as much breakfast as possible. There was nothing dignified about our scramble. I determined that I needed to be more organized so my husband could have a more peaceful morning. Day after day, the routine would be the same, except that now I did not have help from my neighbors. However, with their guidance, I was able to establish a timelier routine, what chores needed to be done in what order.

In the fields, I learned how to sneak in a few moments of rest, to not move for just a wink of a moment, while the luna was preoccupied with other things. We worked with one eye on the luna and one eye on our hoeing or weeding or planting or cleaning the ditches, whatever it was that day.

And so, days went by; sometimes Roji would be present, sometimes not.

"Roji, I cannot think why you are not spending all your nights here at the cottage with me. If you are getting together with friends, surely, you will not be getting enough sleep. And not to spend every night with me, your wife, is very disconcerting. Where are you spending your nights?" I feared his answer, but I needed to ask.

"Really, a man does not have to answer to his wife. You need to get used to marriage. You have a very old-fashioned view of it. Things are different here in Hawaii. People are more independent. I cannot be tied down to spend all my free hours inside this cramped little cottage."

"But we are married. You are my husband. I ask you again how you can be getting enough sleep so you can rise to work on time?"

"Ueme, you are pestering me, and I do not think you have that right. Marriages are all different. You need to get used to our marriage. If I cannot have my freedom, I will not be able to bear this horrible life here. Don't you want the best for me?"

I became confused and could not find the right words to respond to his strange reply.

Roji looked at me and picked up his work clothes. "I find this atmosphere stifling. I am going to spend the night with my friends. I shall see you at the work wagon tomorrow morning.

"But I need help with keeping our food and the cottage and getting the water pail up the hill."

"Don't worry. I will help you. You have enough water now." He peered into the bucket as he said that.

I felt embarrassed. It was obvious there was no affection, so I could not beg him to stay on that account. I had been hoping we could develop affection as my parents had. On my part, I had been searching for Roji's qualities. He was passably handsome, and he could be funny in a crowd. Every once in a while, he was helpful and courteous. He could be an excellent worker when he wanted to be. He could be very generous to others. However, I noticed the things he shared usually belonged to me.

Lost in thought, I did not see him leave.

Chapter 22

SETTLING IN

One Sunday, a few weeks later, someone was knocking outside on our cottage wall.

"Aloha, you want some papaya? Very good fruit, ono. You will like it."

Hearing an unusual voice and words, I leaned my head out the door. There was a very brown woman, rather large and very brown, wearing a very flowing, flowery dress and carrying a basket of green fruit.

"Konnichiwa," I said, bowing to the fruit bearer.

"Aloha. I am aikane, a friend." The woman was walking up our steps carrying a woven reed basket filled with unusual fruit. At the top step, she stopped and cut open one of the smooth, green oblong fruits with a small knife she had retrieved from the bottom of her basket. Producing a slice of soft orange color with some tiny round black seeds, she held it up invitingly. She motioned for me to take and taste. "Ono, delicious, you like?"

I reached out and took the slice. It seemed a bit slippery and, biting into it, almost too sweet.

"Papaya," the woman said. "My name Malia. You malihini, new. My okurimono, my gift, to you."

She was speaking in broken Nihonjin. She gave me two of the fruits. I tried to pay her but was made to understand it was a gift. I bowed and smiled. She left saying, "All pau, finished, I go now."

I went down the stairs and around to the back, where Kikume was doing laundry.

"Look what someone gave me!" I showed her the two green fruits.

"Oh, you have met Malia! Isn't she wonderful? She will help you find anything. She lives in the *ohana*, the family compound, just down the hill from here. We can go visit her next Sunday, if we have time." Kikume talked as she pinned laundry on the line hanging over the vegetable garden.

"She lives near here? Does she work in the fields?" I asked.

"Oh, no. There is a small Hawaiian village further down the hill from here. That village has been here from ancient times, I am told. This valley once belonged to Hawaiian royalty."

I thought about that for a moment. There were people living nearby who did not work for the plantation. It seemed like a breath of fresh air, as if the world outside of the camp still did exist.

I went back into the cottage to prepare our clothes and food for tomorrow's workday. Kikume came through the door and went to her side of the cabin behind the curtain. There was much movement and rushing around.

Kikume poked her head around the cloth to my side. "We have to hurry, or we will be late for the sewing circle."

"Oh, I cannot go this Sunday. I have too much to do," I pleaded. I desperately wanted to find time to be still and think. The flow of this community was so steady, with no moment to slow down.

Kikume appeared, holding a big bundle in her arms and carrying a basket. "Let's go," she said.

"But I have work to do." I felt a bit embarrassed at my own whining.

"So? We always will have work to do. This is important. It's sort of our 'ladies guild.'" Kikume was firm.

She walked carefully down the steps, handing her basket to me. We started to walk up the hill. The sun was hot, and the road was covering our toes in red dust.

"You know, back home, we put oil on the roads for the dust." I was making small talk.

Kikume sighed. "I was like that."

"What?"

"Oh, always comparing to 'back in Nihon.'" Kikume was looking straight ahead.

"Is that wrong?" I did not take criticism well.

"Well, I do not think it helps one to adjust. After all, we are probably never going back." Kikume shrugged.

I gasped. "Well, I know everyone says that, but it's just that—" I stopped to think clearly. "It's where we belong, where we were born. We are the emperor's children. I think it natural that we go back after we finish our contracts." Now I had stopped walking and was turned toward her.

Kikume interrupted sharply. "Go back? Belong? Oh, forgive me. I am just a bit bitter, I think. Shame on me." Kikume was actually starting to laugh. "You know, we all start out thinking the same way. But then you begin to settle in. I do not intend to live in these cottages, in the camp my whole life, but maybe I will stay in Hawaii."

I had nothing to say. We arrived at the cottage second from the top of the road. The land had leveled out a bit, and there were fewer steps to enter. Inside, there were at least ten women all gathered, mostly all of a similar age. There was one older woman, quite stout.

The older woman spoke. "Welcome, aloha. I am so glad Kikume brought you, Ueme. My name is Hisako. This is our sewing circle, and we are in the process of sharing stories and cloth. We make quilts, muumuus, and whatever."

At that moment, Malia walked in the door. The room was crowded and felt very stuffy. I was still overtired from working in the fields. I could feel my head spinning.

Malia noticed immediately. "Oh, pilikia, trouble, kokua. Help; she's falling."

I felt a cold cloth on my forehead and realized I was lying down. Everyone had squeezed together against the walls to make room for me. They were all clucking over me and cooing at me to make me wake up. Looking up, I saw smiling face after smiling face.

"It will be all right. You're exhausted. Poor thing, she's not used to this," one of the women said as she looked up at everyone.

"Ah, she saw a room of all you ugly ladies, and it shocked her to her bones!" Hisako was laughing.

"Enough now, Ueme. Get up. We have work to do."

I forced myself to sit up. I asked to sit near the door to feel cooler.

Malia now spoke. "Well, I actually came to make big invitation to you wahinis to come to a luau. We just got two pigs from my cousin over in Haleiwa. The pigs are in the ground cooking now. Bring nothing, just come. Oh—yah! Bring the men!"

"Ha." Malia was laughing as she walked down the steps and up the road, disappearing over the ridge. On Sundays, the gate in the fence was left open.

I had no idea where Roji was. One of the other husbands went off to round up all the matching husbands. Roji came back just as all were walking back to our cottages. I helped him to clean up and explained our invitation to the luau.

Roji seemed to be in great spirits, talking animatedly with me all the way to the luau. He had made friends with some of the men and was enjoying their company. I felt a thrill in my heart that he was able to be so happy. We were able to find the Hawaiian camp by following the smoke coming off a great bonfire that had been set.

"Look, Roji, how green their little village is. So many plants and trees, not like the camp."

"Hai, such a pleasant atmosphere. These people know how to live." Roji was smiling broadly.

"We could plant a tree near our cottage. That would give us some shade for coolness," I said.

"We do not own that cottage, Ueme. It doesn't seem like there would be any point to that."

I felt deflated. Then I brightened as we joined the rest of the sewing group, who were all in great spirits.

Malia came toward us and with lots of alohas and welcome words. She draped fragrant necklaces, leis, of yellow and pink plumerias over our necks.

My sewing group kept saying mahalo over and over. Tameki answered my quizzical look. "It means thank you. You will be learning many Hawaiian words living here. Don't worry."

"Come here. Follow me." Malia beckoned us with her large brown arms. We helped her put some fruits and some flowers on a large woven mat on the ground.

The men had opened up the steaming ground, exposing the roasted vegetables and the pig meat under all the local ti and banana leaves. The Hawaiian men busied themselves tearing the meat off the bones and putting the meat in large wooden bowls. Our men were beckoned over to help remove the vegetables carefully from the pit. Tameki and I brought the bowls full of meat and vegetables over to the mat. What an impressive feast for our group. The flowers placed on the mat around the bowls created a setting like none I had ever seen before. After being in the poverty and scarcity of the camps, it was a surprise to be part of such abundance. Tameki looked at me. "It is hard to believe this exists just over the hill, eh?"

I laughed. "Thank goodness for the Hawaiians."

Malia made sure everyone had a full tin plate with meat, potatoes, rice, and taro. Someone was singing to a guitar, and children were running back and forth. It was overwhelming to be amid such joy and energy. Friendly faces came up to us over and over again, introducing their names. I felt I had met every single Hawaiian there. They seemed such friendly people and so generous.

As the afternoon faded, we Nihonjin started to say our grateful goodbyes. Food was packed up for each family to take back to the camp. We all needed to get back in time for lights out at camp. I had lost track of Roji during all the singing and commotion of the many food dishes and drinks being passed around. I spied him at the far end of the clearing behind some bushes with some other men, crouched over an old crate and playing some kind of drinking game. I asked one of the children to go get his attention for me. It was time to go. Roji turned and smiled. He was feeling satisfied with life and helped me carry our little bundle of food home.

Roji could not stop talking all the way back to camp. "These people are wonderful, Ueme. They are smart. hey do not work on the plantations. Next Sunday, I'm going fishing with these men. They know a good spot and will show it to me. We can get some good sashimi, Ueme. Such good fortune! Look, they gave us this wooden bowl made from koa wood, apparently very precious wood."

He had somehow bridged the language barrier with the Hawaiians more easily than I had. When we reached the top of the road, turning to our camp road, we could no longer see the smoke or the bonfire or hear the Hawaiians singing.

"Hoah, haha." Roji was laughing.

Sitting up on the futon, Roji had too much energy to sleep. He started telling me a story or joke he had learned at the party. One of the other husbands had translated the story for him. He started recounting it to me. He seemed to have missed the really funny part, but he was so happy in the telling of it that we both were laughing.

Kikume came over to our side of the curtain and said that she and her husband were so glad we had a good time, but it was necessary for all to sleep. She apologized and said she knew it was hard to share a house, but soon a few new cottages would be built and we could have our own spaces. I was ashamed. However, Roji just laughed into the futon. The lights out whistle blew.

Morning came too soon. Again, I had a hard time waking Roji. But when he did wake, he was resolute.

"No more thinking angry thoughts, Ueme. We will be happy

like everyone yesterday." He helped me with the work equipment and went to fill the water bucket, jumping down the steps and humming.

It was a beautiful morning. As the sun peaked over the mountains, the sky was filled with colors. I could hear the mynah birds cawing and the doves cooing. I breathed in the sweet perfumed air. Kikume walked with me up the road to the fields and said, "You look refreshed. Sunday was a good day, wasn't it?"

The luna was waiting for us at the wagon. "OK? We all here? Let's go!" And the horses pulled the wagon full of women weighted down by their water bottles, leather gloves that went to their elbows, and aprons over skirts over pantaloons over underclothes.

By noon, all of us women were a sweaty bunch. We all gathered together in one of the cane rows sitting down for our lunch break. I started to sit.

"Pilikia, watch out before you sit. There are dangerous centipedes here. Their bite can make you sick for a day or more," one of the women shouted to me.

I looked but saw nothing. I dared not sit down.

"Pau, enough, she is only kidding. Sit. It is all clear. Yes, there are bugs, but it is all clear here," another woman explained. "But see, some biting ants are just over there. It is wise to start being aware of the dangers big and little."

Laughing, I said, "How can any bugs get through all this clothing? I have never worn so many layers in all my life! If my mother could see me now! She was always concerned about my dressing properly to impress our customers!"

One of the other women said, "Well, there is someone who comes every once in a while to take pictures for a small fee. You can send her a picture of our charming outfits. It might make her sad, though, to see her daughter in such a circumstance."

"Ah, no. She died a while ago. Actually, her death is probably why I am here. Everything fell apart with my family and the business when she died." That sentence flowed out of me without thought and, once in the air, solidified. It was the first time I had said it.

Everyone was silent for a bit. Then one by one, the women told the circumstances of how they'd all ended up in "paradise." Hearing their stories, I could put the personalities and abilities of each worker together with the history. There were many of them who had never so much as planted a blade of rice, let alone sugar cane. No one had suspected the extreme heavy labor that was required. Nor had they expected that Nihon had made such a bad bargain for them in this slave-like labor. I also learned that many were not able to pay off their contract after three years.

The horn blew, and the luna started shouting at us. Rising quickly, we dispersed to the proper row each was working on. This week, some were weeding, and some were pruning extra stalks. While putting my hoe to the ground and pulling the weeds unearthed by it, I noticed that someone always came a few yards behind me. It seemed she would weed right after me, as if that spot hadn't already been weeded.

I remembered that I had noticed that last week, too. Was there a mistake? Perhaps someone was confused about my place on the line. Leaving to go find the extra water container to refill my bottle, I looked down the other rows to see how the workers were spread out. No one else had anyone following her like that.

I did not want to embarrass the woman who was following me. I would speak to Kikume about it later. The sun rose high in the sky, heating up—heating not just us women but also our tools and the dirt on which we were standing. Seeming always to be thirsty, I realized I could never carry enough water to satisfy my thirst. I must remind myself to drink more water before and after work to avoid dehydration.

I was thirsty. I must be smarter about water. I needed to drink more. Where could I get a sip of water? My mind was wandering. Where was I? Had I weeded this area yet?

The woman right behind me pushed a cup of water against my lips. "Sit, sit. It takes some getting used to, this heat."

"Oh, oh. Does the luna see me? Will he dock my pay?" I worried as I partially fell to the ground, catching my fall on one arm.

"Shhh! It's fine. He's on the other side of the field to check out where we will be working tomorrow. You picked a good time."

"Oh, you are the woman who follows me. Excuse me for asking, sumimasen, but why do you do that?"

I was recovering with the welcome liquid sliding down my throat. The sun glared into my eyes looking up at her; her face was in the dark. I could only make out her distinctive straw hat. I had to look down away from the glare.

"It's what we do to all the new girls. This work is tough. It's hard on the body, easy to get heat exhaustion. And also, until you get used to it, you really do not 'see' all the weeds. I just pull out the really tiny ones and sort of 'clean up' after you. We take turns taking care of the new workers. The luna sort of knows we do this and just stays out of our way. It's better for him. In essence, we are training you. He benefits!"

"Oh, I have not been pulling all the weeds? I am sorry for you to do extra work … Oh dear." I spoke slowly.

"Pau, enough of that. Every one of us was new once! We are all together. You will get your turn one day to help out."

That evening at the cottage, the water bucket was full, and there were some flowers floating in the koa bowl. Kikume pulled the curtain aside. "There is a plumeria tree at the end of the road not far from the water pump. I thought you would enjoy their fragrant blossoms. Not cherry blossoms but very lovely, no?"

I felt as if my heart would burst with joy. I was surrounded by unbounded kindness.

Roji returned from the community garden. He had brought a fish for our dinner, an unexpected elegant meal for tonight. The week had started well. I decided to tell Roji about the heat exhaustion and how we women looked out for one another. As I finished the tale, Roji became very quiet.

Then he said, "We must get a fish for that family, to thank them for their help. We owe them, Ueme. You must be more careful."

Was I to feel shame? What was I to feel? How was I to act? I was a kabuki player on a stage with no direction. The audience waited in anticipation for my voice, but nothing came out.

That evening before lights out, Roji and I sat outside on the steps until the moon showed a bit of itself in the still light sky.

The weeks had been following one after the other in a rhythm of exhausting relentlessness. The new friendships and obligations, the hard muscled labor were slowly crowding out the sweet memories of our lives in the village of Five Bridges.

Kikume and I had been able to work in the same row for a few weeks now. It felt good to develop a new friendship. Moving to this new land had affected our moods. Roji and I lived very separate lives, and Roji did not share his thoughts with me. I missed my walks with Ito and Saiko. I would rarely remember my times with them. But when I did, salty tears flowed down my cheeks. Loneliness had taken on a horrible reality, had become a new constant companion.

Sometimes, a memory would come while I was buying our supplies at the company store. The clerk, just another poor plantation worker, would mistake those tears for my old friends as tears over the elevated expenses at the plantation store. Then the clerk would slip an extra piece of dried tako, squid, into my bag and try to calm me down. "Now, now, wait until the festival," or "Wait and see. Things will be better soon."

I would leave thinking, *How kind. People are really kind.* And it would cheer me up.

Kikume and her husband had moved out a few weeks ago and

left us the one-room cottage to ourselves. Roji had sighed with relief. He is not a people person. I really had not noticed that quality when we were in school together. Now I can look back and see that his mischief making and flirting were all devices he used to keep people at a distance.

Emptiness had begun to envelop me in spite of my new friendships with my neighbors. Kikume and Mori were in the cottage next door, but it seemed to me like they were miles away. I was used to hearing their gentle talking with each other in the evenings and to having them look out for Roji and me. Their caring for us had softened the harshness of leaving Nihon. Staying close in the cane fields, Kikume and I could mull over the latest noontime gossip together.

The latest talk with the women at noon was the weather. It seemed to me Hawaiian weather was all the same. But others insisted I would notice differences after living in Hawaii for a while. Today it was about the end of the Kona winds and everyone looking forward to cooler weather. I really had not felt that the temperature this month had been any different than that of last month. I was assured that, after a while, I would notice the subtle changes in Hawaiian weather.

Kikume spoke up. "I for one will be grateful for even one degree of cooler weather. This baby is keeping me warm enough!" She patted the round ball that was now her stomach.

Tameki laughed and said, "Well, when is this little one due? I think she should be ready to greet us all any day!"

Kikume answered, "Oh, unfortunately, I still have more than one month left. And maybe it is a boy!"

One section of the fields was ready for harvest. Another field over the hill was burning. The ashes had been landing on us all morning, and the air was thick, making it hard to breathe. As the afternoon wore on, the air and heat became more and more oppressive.

The men were plowing up the last section that had just been harvested. We were in a neighboring field, though not so close we could see them. There was absolutely no wind. Kikume was very thirsty. I gave her some of my tea, as her bottle was empty. Her face looked pale, and her eyes looked strange.

"Kikume, maybe you should take the rest of the day off." I echoed what some of the other workers had said to her at lunchtime.

The luna screamed at us that we were too bunched up. "Separate. Spread out and cover more of the field."

To the luna, I said I wanted to stay near Kikume, as she looked sick. The luna hit me with his stick on my shoulders and then Kikume too. This was a new luna, a very nervous Portuguese man who did not understand our words. Kikume fell down.

I asked for the wagon to take us back to the camp. The luna said he could not let the wagon go, and we should get up and continue cutting the leaves off the stalks. I helped Kikume up and helped her to the end of the row of stalks. Our clothing kept getting caught on those nasty cane leaves. I called to the luna. "We need help for Kikume here."

We sat on the ground, but the dirt was hot, and the sun was hot. I went over to the water buckets sitting in the ground,where the water bearer had left them. There was no water left in them. Kikume was sinking. She seemed to not know where she was. Another woman nearby came over and gave me her tea bottle. I tried to get Kikume to drink, but she seemed unable to do so.

We started walking down the road to the camp. I had never walked it before and had no idea how much longer it would take compared to the wagon. Kikume hung on my arm, completely confused and delirious.

I lay Kikume down on the dirt and ran over to the men's field and yelled for help. "Tasukete! Tasukete!"

Two men came running. I yelled that Kikume was very sick, and we needed a ride to the cottages. "Someone get a wagon, and someone tell her husband to come."

They rushed off.

Minutes later, a wagon appeared over the saddle of the hill. The man driving it yelled to us, "Mori is at the far end of the field. He will come as soon as he can. Meanwhile, we'll get you back out of the heat. Here's some water for you both." He handed me a bottle and lifted Kikume into the wagon.

Then, as he took the reins of the horse, he turned to me and asked, "What is the matter with your luna today?"

I replied, "Agh! He is new and gets very upset whenever the owner comes by. This is what happens when he is in a bad mood. It is dangerous for us. All he can see is his numbers for the day." I settled into the back, cradling Kikume, trying to protect her from the rough bumps and rolling of the wagon.

Thinking of my limited knowledge of pregnancies, I asked him, "When we get back to the cottages, can you get Hisako-san to come to help?"

"Tashikani, certainly I can," he replied as he pulled on the reins to get the horse started.

"Kudasai. I thank you for getting this wagon to help us." I was pushing down fear and remembering politeness.

The wagon passed a vine-covered bush and, brushing against the vine, had released the smell of jasmine. Suddenly, I was back in my alley with my dear friends, holding my perfume box and discussing the characters of men and women and which traits made for a good marriage. The wagon hit a stone, and the jolt woke me from the daydream. Oh, the days when I had the time and freedom to ponder things. Here in this land, I was holding the head of a dear friend, worrying for her life. There was no luxury time to ponder anything.

Once at the cottage and out of the sun, Kikume seemed a bit more awake. However, Hisako-san was worried because Kikume's contractions had started. At her instructions, I went looking for a neighbor to fetch the doctor. The doctor came but seemed to be unable to help much.

By evening, Kikume had delivered a stillborn baby. She was

unaware, due to being delirious from the heat and lack of water. Later, while I was in back of the cottages doing some washing, I could hear Mori's muffled crying as he told Kikume what had happened to the baby.

Their cottage was filled with the ghosts of ancestors that night. The air was thick with sadness. Mori had asked the priest to come to bless the cottage. The incense, on top of the windless night, made the suffering more intense. At midnight, I brought the grieving couple offerings for their altar and prepared a short tea ceremony for their baby. As we passed the tea bowl from one to the other, I caught the looks of sadness and wrapped them in the tea cloth for burial.

Back in my own cottage, I wondered about Roji. Where was he? The news had spread rapidly in the fields. He must have known. I half expected him to show up with a fresh caught fish for our poor neighbors.

All I could think of was for Sunday to come quickly so we could all relax. I wanted sleep badly, but I also needed my wages. I spent a minute longer that morning at our altar to express gratitude that Kikume would be all right.

Our altar did not have pictures of our ancestors, but a local man had made beautiful calligraphy of our family names on pieces of rice paper. These were hung from a red cord over our little Buddha. Thinking of the altar back in Five Bridges, I was seeing my family home in my mind. I missed my family's meditation garden. I missed cleaning the pine needles off the gravel. I missed the carp in the pond. I missed looking at the moon from our garden rock. Ah, I was daydreaming again. Scolding myself, I rose, grabbed my lunch pail and tea bottle for another day in the cane fields.

Sunday finally came. Roji had been out again for the whole night. I could not dwell on this. I would think about this when I had more time. I needed to do the washing and prepare rice and tea for breakfast. With the washing hung out, I looked up at the sky. It was blue, with beautiful, fluffy clouds. There was a slight breeze. Perhaps we were at the end of the Kona weather now. I was aware of a small flicker of fear at the edges of my being.

Mori was outside doing Kikume's washing. I helped Mori with the laundry, wringing and hanging it on the line. When we finished, I offered my rice and fish breakfast to him for Kikume. Mori thanked me but said that they had been given so much food from the neighbors in the past few days that he would like to give me some food.

In a few hours, it would be time for the quilting bee. I set out to search for Roji. I walked down the road past the older cottages, where there were quite a number of children playing outside, running back and forth. A very scrappy-looking dog was running around. In the cottage doorways hung the typical split banners with silk-screened scenes depicting cherry trees, scraggy pine trees, and moonlit Mount Fuji. I felt a renewed spirit seeing these bits of familiar decoration and made a promise to myself that I would decorate our cottage— make it more of a home for our new life together.

At the bottom of the road before it turned toward the woods, I came to the barracks for the bachelors. The man who had driven the wagon for Kikume and me was there. He was busy tending a large vegetable garden, separate from the communal garden. I stopped to admire the eggplants that were ready for harvest.

"Would you like some for your noon meal?" the man called out to me.

Embarrassed that it looked like I was asking for something, I felt heat rising in my cheeks.

"Oh, I have plenty. But your vegetables are very healthy looking. I was just admiring them. That is all." I tried to save face.

"Please, let me give you a few. I have too many, and they must be eaten, or they will rot on the plant." The man walked toward me, smiling. His chest was tanned and sweaty, with streaks of dirt across it. Clean-shaven, his black hair was tied back from his face with a white cotton hachimaki headband across his forehead. He looked at me so earnestly I could not insult him.

"Well, I can take a few," I relented.

The man started filling up a newspaper with eggplants, daikon, green onions, and carrots. I wanted to say something, but awkwardness took over and my mouth wouldn't move.

"Please take these and eat well. It has been a hard week for you. You deserve some good." He put the folded newspaper bundle into my arms. He kept his hands on my arms for a minute while he looked into my eyes.

My eyes started to water. Was it the sun? Was it sadness?

Feeling confused, I finally looked down at my armload and spoke softly. "These are the most delicious vegetables I have seen."

He stood back from me. "Please come visit this garden whenever you want. The vegetables grow better with beauty near them."

I looked up and laughed at the flirt.

"Ah, that is better. Have a good day." The man turned back to his weeding.

I decided to forget looking for Roji and go back home with my vegetables.

Chapter 23

ANOTHER REVELATION

Our Sundays came, and our Sundays went. Our day of rest was the only way of marking time. There was too much to do to call it a day of rest. But it was the one day I could call truly mine. That was the day where we put our energies into making community. We needed each other, and we worked to make ourselves a community.

The camp had a small Buddhist temple, and all shared in its upkeep. There were communal gardens, where everyone shared the work. The more experienced laborers made sure we newcomers understood our duties and responsibility to the rest of the community. Growing vegetables helped us keep down our store expenses. Much like the women's sewing circle, the men had their governing group, where they discussed plantation policies while working in the garden.

I would spend an hour or so with the sewing circle while Roji worked in the communal garden. And just like my mother's group back in Nihon, the sewing circle was where I kept up with community news. I learned quickly that we call Hisako Hisako-san as an honor for her years of wisdom and all she shared of it with us. Being separated from our elders was a hardship, as most of us had yet to learn many things that came with age. There being very few elders, we appreciated those we did have greatly.

At the end of one of the Sundays, I realized that Roji and I had not spoken a single word to each other about our experiences in the sugar cane fields. Our routine was set—we washed up, we brushed the red dust from our clothes, we ate, we put out the futons, and we slept, ready to start the next day. It was a never-ending routine, with no time to think or to talk.

That day, as I put the rice bowl before Roji, I knelt down beside him and asked him what he thought about our time here in the camp.

"What do I think? I think this is a worst type of hell. Those supervisors, those lunas, treat us like animals, ah, even less."

"Oh, I agree with you. It is terrible. I have never been hit before, and now that luna often finds it necessary to remind us of his presence with his nasty tap. Shall we make a plan on how we are to survive this place together?"

"Together? You are the reason I even came to this stinking place! If it weren't for you, I would be back in Kumamoto working for my uncle."

"What do you mean? This was not my idea. You were already going to Hawaii, and my grandmother said you needed a wife."

"Hah! Your family is very tricky. You needed to get married and get out of your brother's house. I had several options before me. This was only one option. I was forced into saving you!"

"Did my grandmother give your family money to marry me?"

Silence. Oh, the shame of it. I'd thought he wanted to marry me. I bowed my head low to my knees. This was not a love match. I'd thought he had at least been attracted to me. Oh, I had thought I was such a modern woman. This was yet just another arranged marriage and not a happy one.

I tried to slide across the floor to the other side of our tiny room on my knees, keeping my head down in shame. However, the boards were not smooth like our floors at home, and a splinter of wood made its way through my cotton yukata to my shin. I turned my face away as the tears rolled down my cheeks.

I dared not move. What was I to do? How should I regard my life now? I was trying to figure out this misery with my partner.

But was this a partner? I did not know the correct attitude for this situation.

Was I to be grateful for being rescued? Or should I be miserable at this emotional desertion coming at the worst point in my life? A sudden noise woke me out of my dilemma. Roji had swept the bowl of rice off the table and left the cottage. The thump of the bowl on the floor brought me back to the chores at hand. With Roji and our cottage, I thought I had a small sanctuary from all the difficulties of this plantation life. Now that had been torn from me.

The week flew by. The following Sunday came soon. I traded some trinkets for a large fish to cook for a special dinner to try to please Roji. At least he could feel he was being well taken care of, even if he was not with the wife or occupation of his choice.

Roji thanked me for the fish dinner and then questioned the expense. He insisted he be in charge of all the money. I knew that would be dangerous and declared I worked as much as he did. I insisted on being in charge of household expenses like my mother had always been. I asked him if he wanted me to write to his mother to inquire about how his family ran that household. At that suggestion, he seemed to back down. I knew his mother was in charge of the money in his household.

The midday meal not being a success as I had hoped. I cleaned up our space and looked forward to hearing the happy chatter of my friends in the sewing circle later that day.

At Hisako-san's cottage, Kikume whispered to me that she was worried for me. She said she could feel a dead weight in me today. Was Roji sick?

Embarrassed that someone could sense our problems, I panicked. "No, no, everything is fine. But we are very tired. We are not used to such physical labor." I started to walk up the hill faster.

Kikume looked at me as if she could see through me. At Hisako-san's cottage, I avoided Kikume's gaze and began a conversation with the woman next to me, who was bursting with a pregnant belly.

Our current sewing project was making a new futon for a woman to welcome her baby. Hisako-san had bartered for the pieces of cloth with her produce from her vegetable patch. However, we did not always keep the quilts in the camp. Many of them were sold in Honolulu.

Hisako-san had developed a friendship with the plantation owner's wife, Elizabeth, over the last few years. Elizabeth had taken the quilts made in this camp to Honolulu to be sold. From this enterprise, we had been able to establish an emergency fund. Elizabeth also brought us many sewing scraps from all the American plantation ladies living this side of Honolulu.

Hisako-san started telling a tale of a couple who had lived in the camps over five years ago. We hungered for the stories of those who had come before us. The couple was no longer working the sugar cane and had moved away.

She continued, "The wife and husband worked in the fields. Unfortunately, the couple had ignored basic rules of right living, and their luck failed them over and over. The man was stung by a bee while working in the fields. He had been in the act of cutting cane and was holding one of those large cane knives. Because of the sudden bite of the bee, he fell against the blade, and the tendons in his arm were cut. He lost the use of his hand on one arm. He was no longer able to work in the cane.

"After that, they subsisted on her earnings alone. It wasn't enough, so the husband decided to earn some money, using their savings to gamble. Unfortunately, he cheated at the gambling and was beaten so badly by those he cheated that one of his eyes was no longer good.

"Meanwhile, the woman had been taking in laundry. However, she, too, stole from her clients and lost her business. The camp government asked them to be relocated to another camp. They live in Maui now."

"Ahh. What is the point of this depressing story?" questioned the very pregnant lady. "I do not want to hear depressing stories. I need stories that make me feel good so the baby is born happy."

Each one of us feared this story, and we all kept our eyes focused on our sewing. I immediately decided I would ask Roji how bad the bees were for him. And was he cautious when he used his cane knife? With this story, we all had new worries.

What could we talk about that was happy? We were so overloaded with survival. Then a woman who only came to our sewing sessions infrequently said she had heard an odd tale that might brighten the mood. Hisako-san encouraged her to tell it.

She started slowly, giving us many details and elaborate descriptions of the life of a friend of her grandmother. We listened intently, hoping for some happy wisdom to guide our dismal lives.

"In a village south of mine back in Kumamoto Province, the headman during my obasan's childhood was a rather pudgy, little gossipy fellow. He was a bit puffed up about his importance and prided himself on knowing everything. He always seemed to be in the vicinity of whatever was happening and would pronounce how he had done such and such a thing to save the day. However, in fact, he was lazy and never lifted a hand to help anyone. So, one of the older women of his village, Madam Uda, who had known the headman from his childhood, decided to play a trick on him.

"One day she let everyone know she had just purchased a carriage ride to visit her sister, who was sick and dying in Yokohama. She said she and her husband would be away for one week. She lamented that her very beautiful and magical garden would be missing her morning meditations. The garden had given her magical wisdom in all her life choices. How else could she be so lucky to have such a wonderful life?

"But she said that most people did not believe in its magic and actually feared it. Unless someone would offer to meditate in her garden every day, the garden might lose its magic by neglect. The bounties one would receive by contact with this magical garden couldn't be counted. Look at her life, she exclaimed. She had a good husband, successful children, many male grandchildren to carry on the family name, and a garden that produced more fruit and vegetables than anyone else's. Ah, it was too bad people fear magic so when it carried such riches!

"Upon hearing this, the headman wanted the bounties of the magic of that garden. He offered to meditate at least an hour in her garden every day while she was away. He said he knew it wasn't really magical and was not afraid. Madam Uda accepted his generous offer.

"The first morning he went to her garden, he settled himself on a rather nice flat rock in the middle of the garden. After a few minutes, he was disturbed in his meditations by some moans coming from the corner of the garden and the swaying of tree branches in that same corner. The headman stood up and walked over to the corner to see what was making the noise. It stopped as he neared it. As he returned to his seat, the moans started up again. He stood up on the rock to peer over the fence, but he could see nothing there. He decided to ignore the moans and continued to meditate.

"The second day, the moans became more audible and gave him instructions for a long and prosperous life. When he didn't respond, the tree branches shook quite violently. This disturbed the headman. Perhaps this was some evidence of the magic? The moans continued and insisted he promise to follow the instructions. If he did, this garden could make the headman as rich as the owner of the garden. Now, the headman had always envied Madam Uda's kimonos and her ability to ride in carriages whenever she desired. He wanted those luxuries for himself. He planned to follow the instructions.

"The moans continued with long instructions, telling him to meditate only in the nude for three straight days at that same rock. 'Well,' the headman said to himself, 'monks sometimes never need clothes. Maybe this is a spiritual edict.' He made a promise to do it, thinking this might make him a very rich man. The garden was enclosed on all four sides with a high wall. He felt secure in his decision.

On the following day, menacing clouds produced rain for at least twenty minutes, but he sat there fulfilling his promise. The rain poured down, and the wind blew, and he sat there obediently. Suddenly, the garden gate flew open. Looking up from his meditations, the headman expected to feel a gust of wind and see tree branches wildly bending. However, he saw nothing like that. It was just Madam Uda and her two friends laughing at the dripping naked headman."

"So! What was the purpose of that story?" asked Tameki, ever the practical one, expecting some more important end to the story.

Hisako-san, smiling broadly, spoke up. "Why, of course there is a purpose! Never meditate in the nude!"

We all laughed, and I think we were all the better for it.

Tameki walked with me back to my cottage and looked at me curiously. "I can see something is terribly wrong, Ueme. And it seems like it is not just the hard work here."

Oh, another friend noticing my situation. Why couldn't I hide my misery better? I felt like crying but held back my tears. After all, one's place in life is deserved. There is no point in arguing or crying about it. I tried to explain, "What it is, Tameki, is just same old Nihonji, Japanese life."

Tameki burst out laughing. "Ha! There is nothing typical Nihonji about this place. Where are the afternoon teas, silk kimonos, and the tofu woman coming down the alley? Where are the cherry blossoms and the moon festivals? Ueme, we live in barrack-type housing that does not belong to us. We are locked up in this compound every night as if we are prisoners. We have to buy everything from our employer's store, where the prices cheat us out of our meager wages. Our husbands are demeaned. We women are exhausted. We are in some backwater hell. Arranged marriages are worthless; people are divorcing like crazy. We cannot earn enough money to save to get out."

Hearing Tameki go on like this, I was encouraged to speak. "Speaking of arranged marriages, I found out that mine is one."

Tameki replied, "I never doubted it for a moment."

I was overcome. "How can you say that?"

"We all have arranged marriages. It is just the way. How is yours different from mine?" Tameki asked as she adjusted her basket to one side of her large belly.

We had arrived at my cottage. I did not want to speak about it there. "Let me put down my basket, and I will walk you to your cottage so we can talk."

Tameki put down her basket on my steps and settled herself on the bottom step. She was growing bigger by the day. The baby would be coming in a few months.

Finding Roji inside the cottage, I told him I was going to help Tameki for another half hour and then be back to make our evening meal.

Roji replied, "No need. I will get my meal with the men at the bachelors' quarters."

Surprised, I said, "Why would you do that? I will make our meal."

Roji shrugged his shoulders and said nothing. I left him inside and joined Tameki for our walk to her cottage. It was down a side road where there were some newer cottages given to the men who had families. As their child was due soon, they were allowed to have one of the newer cottages.

As we approached, Tameki's husband waved to us and put down his paintbrush to welcome Tameki. He was clearly happy to see her. He had been painting the trim around the windows. Theirs was a newer cottage, and their window trim colors made it very cheery looking. I was marveling at my own thoughts that had so changed in expectations since arriving in "paradise." A two-room cottage seemed elegant and desirable. How I had changed!

Aduki, Tameki's husband, had made tea and asked us to sit at their low table while he brought us two cups. Then he left, saying he had an errand to do and would be back later. Tameki explained that he knew we wanted to talk and knew he should leave for a bit.

"How considerate!" I was finding new kindnesses in men.

"Now, tell me, what is it about your marriage?" Tameki sipped from her cup, holding it with two hands. I noticed it was porcelain from China.

"Roji said my obasan paid his family money so he would marry me."

"Mmm, so if it was a really grand sum, he could have set himself up in business. So, it was basically nothing. He chose to accept the bargain." Tameki looked disgusted. "Is he holding this up to you as your fault he is here?"

"Yes."

"What a crying little boy he is. For shame. He has not insulted you. He has shown himself to be unworthy of a challenge. He is weak. My apologies to you. This, unfortunately, bodes poorly for you. A weak man is a dangerous man." Tameki seemed to dismiss and sum up my whole life.

"Tameki, what you have said is cruel," I admonished her.

"What? I am your friend. This is how it is. We are not some samurai who are going to be silent about the facts. We are merchant, and we can speak without politeness clamping our tongues."

"Dangerous? To me? To whom?" I was confused.

"Ah, who knows? But do not be stupid in this. He means to hurt you. Because he thinks somehow it is your fault. His misery is your fault. A strong person never blames another for his misery. He works his way out of it, knowing this challenge comes straight from the ancestors." Tameki spoke wise beyond her years. Perhaps her pregnancy gave her this wisdom. I was envious of her clarity.

I finished the cup of tea and rose from her little table. "Thank you for this talk, Tameki. Please keep these thoughts to yourself. They are helpful to me and no other."

"Of course. I am your friend." Tameki pushed herself to standing. "One thing about working in the fields like this—I am much stronger than my mother was in any of her pregnancies!"

I walked home pondering Tameki's words. They upset me so much I decided to immediately forget them. Kikume was outside sweeping the front steps of her cottage.

She looked up to see me. "Ueme, we have extra rice and vegetables and have made bowls for you and Roji. Please come and join us."

I answered, "Oh, I have some dried fish my auntie sent in her envelope with her letter to me. I shall bring it to share also."

The three of us ate, and no one mentioned that Roji was absent. I returned to my cottage and realized I was grateful to have made such close friends.

I sat down on the edge of the futon and read the letter from Auntie. I had been anxious to hear all of the news from home. Apparently, my cousins were all doing well in their respective positions. This was most likely true, as Auntie was always one to tell her troubles and not keep them secret.

However, Obasan had been having multiple health problems ever since my departure. Obasan was thrilled to get a letter from me and wanted Auntie to say that in this letter. The news of the alley was mundane, except that the fishmonger appeared to be wearing the new jacket Mother had given him years ago. He finally had found an occasion right for wearing it. When Auntie asked him about it, complimenting him on its beauty, tears streamed down his cheeks, and he asked to be pardoned for his new allergies that attacked him at odd moments. Madam Iwata said the fishmonger had gone soft since my mother died and that he missed the old kitchen ways. Madam Iwata said to put hello from her also in this letter.

Auntie said that Brother and Akeme had a very quiet wedding, and the baby was now crawling everywhere. Otasan spent many hours teaching both Brother and Akeme how to run the business.

Father now walked many evenings by himself down the road of Five Bridges, stopping at each bridge to say a Shinto blessing for mother.

Auntie said she saw Ito coming and going, always very busy. Ito's father was very proud of her. Oh, and grand news, Saiko was pregnant, expecting the baby in a few months.

Reading all the news made me have a rush of feelings, lost and lonely. How, how had my fates put me here?

I went outside to the back of the cottage to get some laundry off the line. The pale moon was rising in the evening sky.

Chapter 24

EXPECTATIONS

Our sewing circle had received a very large bundle of cloth and cotton stuffing from Elizabeth, the wife of the plantation owner. We had decided to invite her to our sewing circle for this Sunday. We were all crowded happily into Hisako-san's little room.

"Konnichiwa. Well, do you all like beautiful Hawaii?" was Elizabeth's opening sentence. She had learned some Japanese, and Madam Hisako translated the rest for us.

There was a silence. It was awkward, so I searched for words.

"Elizabeth-san, we all miss our beautiful Nihon. Nihon seems much more beautiful than where we live here in Hawaii. We do not mean to insult you, but we have come from very pretty places in our country. All we see here are scrubby trees and dusty roads."

Madam translated and kept bowing as if in apology. Seeing her bows, I knew she had translated correctly.

"Oh, you would not insult me. I am not from here, and I miss my home very much. Most of all, I miss snow. But Hawaii has its own kind of beauty, the waterfalls, the lush vegetation."

Madam kept the meanings passing back and forth. We were communicating our emotions past our word boundaries.

"I would not call this lush vegetation!" Tameki exclaimed.

Elizabeth was quiet for a moment. She started to stutter. Then she talked quietly to Madam, who translated, "Elizabeth has offered to take a few of you on a walk in the mountains and show you beautiful trees and flowers growing beside waterfalls. Would anyone be able to leave for half a day?"

"We could leave on a Sunday, but we would need to be back before the evening meal." Tameki seemed very interested.

"And we would have to have an excuse to leave our husbands for so much time!" said another woman.

No one else spoke up. We could not leave without our husband's permission, and that was not likely.

The plantation owner's wife then spoke to Madam.

Madam spoke. "It can be arranged that Elizabeth requires the help of a few sturdy women to help her choose and gather the appropriate plants for a Japanese garden at the big house. It can come as a request from the plantation."

Two women said they would like to go on this excursion. One said she planned to be a teacher, and she needed to learn about the local plants. The other said she needed a break from her demanding husband. We all laughed. Tameki said she would like to go, and though she was getting larger every day, no one should doubt her strength. Again, we all laughed.

Kikume spoke up. "Ueme would like to go. I can make sure her husband is fed all day. He won't complain."

My mouth dropped open. I was going to leave the camp for a few hours. I felt giddy with this unexpected gift.

As we walked back to our cottage, Kikume explained to me, "Your husband is hard on you because he cannot see beyond today. You deserve to see some beauty—especially since you are a musician. You need beauty more than some."

I squeezed her hand in gratitude. I was afraid I would owe Kikume more than I could ever repay her. I feared I was accumulating more obligations than I would ever be able to repay.

Chapter 25

BENDING

There were many things new and strange to Roji and me. We were in a new country. We had strange new jobs. The community was strange. It was a plantation camp, not a village. We did not have our village government. The owners controlled everything. The weather was different; the plants were different; the air was different; our marriage was different. That was the strangest. The friendship between Roji and me that had seemed so wonderful at first on the ship seemed to have disappeared. We were both different people in this new situation.

As a woman, I had always had to figure out where I would fit into the structure. At my parents' house, there had been many rules. The rules were supposed to help us in life. They did not seem to be always for my good. So, I figured out ways to live within and between the rules. In this way, I got to do many of the things I wanted to do without real permission for them—learning kendo, managing the accounts, going to the fairs without a chaperon, playing the samisen as much as I wanted. And as a daughter between the classes of samurai and merchant, it seemed my very existence was a "between."

But here, the heavy plantation structure weighed on all of us. I figured that I just needed to see where the cracks in the rules were to find my way.

For Roji, a merchant's second son, the rules did not really work as well for him. That was how he found himself in Hawaii, no inheritance for the second son. However, he had been raised as if he were a first son. A certain amount of respect had always been given to him. Until he had come of age, the rules had worked for him.

In Nihon at that time, merchants were beginning to be seen as a modern necessity, and the new modernization forces in Japan were waking up and recognizing the value and strength of the merchant class. In the past, it had been the lowest class but now was gaining more respect and power. We had reaped many of those benefits as children in the new era. Yet here we were, as plantation workers, doing hard physical labor for so little money we had to grow our own food to make ends meet. To go from expecting a certain level bow from your neighbor in the street to being called a number and whipped while at your job was close to a "screaming hell," the Nihonji way of saying our worst nightmare. The plantation meant to break our spirits, and it did. While I had learned to bend throughout my childhood, Roji had learned to stand erect, and now it was hurting him. He did not know how to bend. He was breaking.

It was the end of another hard day. Roji was at our cottage before I arrived. He was sitting just inside the doorway out of the sun, leaning against the wall. He was panting, and there was a trickle of blood running down his cheek. This was the second time Roji had come home with blood on his forehead from fighting with the luna.

I needed to help him somehow, but I was always unsure which words would help, which action would soothe.

"Roji, let me hold that cloth. Oh, it is too dirty. I will get a new clean wet cloth to hold on your forehead."

Roji held the new bandage to his head and went out the door. "Roji," I yelled after him. "Can you go to the pump? We need more water."

As was his usual manner now, he would not acknowledge me and turned at the bottom of the steps to go to the back.

I then yelled out the door, "Oh, well, all right then, if you are going in the back, the eggplants need weeding, and the cucumbers are ripening. Perhaps there is a good one there to bring in when you are done?" There was so much to do, and I desperately needed help with all of it. But Roji was so dispirited. He was not much help.

I heard someone on the steps. Hoping it was Roji bringing water, I leaned out the doorway to see.

"Please excuse me, Madam Kobata. Is your husband here?" One of the men from a neighboring cottage stepped into our little room.

I pointed to the back window.

"He is outside, weeding the eggplants," I said. "He got injured again today."

"Oh, I understand, so terrible." The man bowed his head before stepping out the door. He walked slowly down the steps and around the corner of the cottage to the back to talk with Roji.

I walked over to the window to listen.

"Ah, Roji-san, you trouble yourself so."

Roji grunted.

The man continued, "Ah, so, I understand. I feel it too. It is no good. Some of us are getting together tonight to talk about our troubles. Maybe you would like to join us?"

Roji replied sharply, "Aheeyah! All anyone does is talk and complain. I am sick of this place. I am sick of the face of that luna, Jona."

"Yes, Jona is quick with the whip. Too bad he doesn't know what it feels like, eh?" He stepped closer to Roji. "Oh, man, how is your cut? Let me take a look." He peeked under the cloth. "Whewtth!" He whistled under his breath. "But you know, you got him good. He is bleeding, too!"

They were silent a bit, both sitting on upturned buckets in the shadow of the cottage wall.

"Roji, you must come to our meeting. It is necessary. We know what is going on here with you." The man stood up and took his fist and swung it into his abdomen, beginning with a slow motion then speeding up to a hard thump in his belly, causing him to bend over. It was the infamous slow motion move of the samurai hara-kiri, stabbing the stomach with samurai sword, to save one's honor in face of defeat. With his fist hard against himself, the man stood up straight, pushed his stomach out, and smiled.

Taking a deep breath, he continued, "However, there is a plan. Before you and your wife arrived with this new group, we, who have been here longer, have been planning. You need to come and understand what we are doing."

Roji leaned over and groaned again. "What? You want me to behave? Now, I should bow to the luna, eh?" With that, Roji stood and made a fake deep bow due only to high government Nihon officials.

"No, no. You misunderstand me." The man put his hands out in a pleading gesture.

"I am tired. Not going anywhere, never anywhere!" Roji stood up and kicked his bucket, and it crashed into the cucumber vine, dislodging one very fat cucumber.

"Matter of fact, I have been sent here to bring you. I do not want to push you about this. You will be glad. You will see."

Astonished, Roji pushed his face into the man's. "So now, someone else wants to tell me what to do!?" This was clearly a reaction to my weeding request.

The man did not look away. After a long moment, Roji and he both looked down. Roji then sat in a cross-legged position on the ground, facing the garden now. The neighbor joined, and they both stared at the garden for a long time. I tried not to breathe as I listened to this exchange. For a very long time, both men sat there silently. It was obvious. The man was not going to leave.

Tired of watching this silence, I left the cottage with a bucket and went to go pump some water. Upon my return, I looked out the rear window. Both men had gone. I went out to get the cucumber.

Chapter 26

NEW PLANS

For the past month, Roji had been home every night. Things had seemed so much easier, as he helped with repairs, got the water, and tended to our little patch of vegetables. We had more money for our budget, as he was working regularly.

At first, I did not notice the strictures. But as time had passed, so much seemed inhuman. We were prisoners in these camps. We had to turn out lights at a certain time and be quiet. There was actually someone patrolling outside our bungalows who rapped on our walls if he heard a sound. We were not allowed off the campgrounds. There was a wire fence around all the camp, and someone was posted at the gates.

We'd signed contracts to work for a certain period of time, not to give our lives away. The abuses are hard for me to understand, except for pure greed, so I pushed it from my mind and continued on. All of this used to enrage Roji, but he seemed to be calmer since he'd joined the men's group. They met immediately after work, always in a different cottage. They'd worked diligently to compose a list of grievances to send to the managers of the plantation.

We had both internalized the morning gong, and we rose before it. We helped each other with the work gear every day. Roji's new sense of responsibility came at the same time as he started doing his community work.

Roji was in charge of bringing the extra buckets of water to the fields. He had a whole group of men working with him on this. Too often, the water bearer would run out of water when we needed it the most at the end of the day. The wagons had been commandeered for some more distant fields, and we now walked the whole way to the fields from the camp. It was more important than ever to have enough water on hand.

Some of the women have come up to me and complimented me on my husband's good work and organizing skills. Perhaps everything may become fine between us. With recognition from the other workers, Roji seemed to have regained his sense of self. Standing straight and tall, he had a strong bearing about him that made him attractive to everyone. But to the lunas, he was only our number, *bango* seven five two one.

Kikume was with child again and very happy. We demanded that pregnant women be given help in the field if it was needed. The luna said he would let us sit down if needed. This was fine, but he questioned us as to how much time we would need and when could we get back to our hoeing? He pestered us so much it was not really a rest. Of course, he always made his notes of each occurrence in his notebook, and time was docked. No one really was able to take advantage of it.

Tameki has been moved to a different gang. To keep in touch with each other, we would prepare our food sometimes in front of my cottage together while sharing our stories of the day. Then Aduki would come and carry the basket with the preparations back to their cottage. Once the baby was born, that time together would end.

Aoki, one of the first people I had met in the fields, decided to make a laundry business so she could stay home with her two children. Slowly, she built up a clientele. Some of the bachelors gave her their laundry and, also, several of the lunas. Hisako-san was checking with Elizabeth to see if there were some more clients around for her.

For Roji's birthday, I procured some sake and borrowed

Hisako-san's sake cups for the special occasion. I wore my kinsha silk kimono and put my hair up with decorative pins.

"Konnichiwa," I said, bowing formally to Roji as he came up the steps.

"How formal we are tonight! What is this for?"

"Your birthday!"

"Ah, how insignificant a day that is when we look at everything that has become of our lives." Roji was not in his usual good mood. I wondered what was bothering him.

"Still, we can celebrate." I motioned to him to sit at our small table. Then I brought over a steaming wet cloth and washed his hands for him. "Ooh, our hands are so rough, the cloth catches on our callouses. Well, fine sir, may I bring you sashimi?"

"Now, that's just fine. We don't need an excuse to have sashimi. I hope you sharpened the knife enough this time. It loses its appeal if the cuts are ragged." Roji had become quite the critic.

"Oh, no, look at you, worried for nothing." I placed the dish of the raw fish before him. I did not tell him that I'd had Tameki cut the sashimi with her excellent knife, as I wanted it to be perfect.

After a pleasant meal of fish stew and rice with pickled vegetables, we finished with the sake. There was actually a cool breeze that night. The warm sake created just the atmosphere a young couple needed for happiness.

Roji held up the pretty cups and commented on their beauty, with the gold painting on them.

"I borrowed them from Hisako-san for this occasion. It seems to improve the quality of the sake. Don't you think so, Roji?" I was trying to make small talk about frivolous details to make the evening atmosphere light.

"Oh, yes, I agree. These cups do indeed impart something to the sake." Roji continued to survey the porcelain set.

Roji asked for cup after cup until the sake bottle was nearly empty. I had hoped we could save it for yet another occasion. But he was so happy, I didn't mention my plans for it.

Then Roji said he had written a few haikus about our experiences in the camps. "Want to hear one, Ueme?"

"Of course. Pick out your favorite."

Roji straightened his shirt and put his shoulders back:

> Luna rules the camp
> A plan lives to redeem all
> Within hearts a secret

"Oh, that is not so pretty! It is about our troubles!"

"Listen to this one":

> She plays samisen
> Flowers children all around
> Music and promise

"Oh, that one is nice."

"It's about you. I have to admit that I had some help from some of the bachelors. They can be rather romantic." I wondered which one.

It was such an uncharacteristically sweet act for him, and it made me very happy. We both laughed more than we had since we had arrived here. I tried to always hold on to whatever good moments happened between us. We fell asleep feeling very relaxed with each other.

The next morning was Sunday, and Roji was off early to one of his group meetings. I gathered everything for the week's laundry and went out to the back to start my laundry. Kikume was already back there boiling water for the large tub that was our communal washing machine.

"Ah, Kikume, I think we may have appeased the ancestors.

Things seem to be going so well for us now. I am almost happy here, if it weren't for the work in the fields!"

"Hah, if it weren't for the work in the fields, you wouldn't be here!" We both laughed.

Tameki came ambling around the corner of the cottage. "You know what the men are planning?"

"A fish fry with lots of beer?" offered Kikume.

"No, this is serious. Come here." She looked around. "No. Can we go inside your cottage Kikume? I want to show you a gift my mother sent me."

Inside, she motioned for us to sit down. I was nervous about leaving the water boiling outside. Kikume spoke my concerns. "I can't stay long, Tameki. My water is boiling. I need to watch it."

"Aghyee, Kikume! There is no gift. This is important. That can wait. The men are planning a strike."

Stupidly, I say, "Well, what does that mean? What will happen?"

Tameki groaned. "We women must be politically astute. We must keep our eyes open. We are not stupid. They need our help in this, and they are not even talking to us about it!" Tameki's eyes were staring at us intently. "So, what do you think?"

"Think about a strike? What do we do for money? Will we strike, too?" I really had no experience with what a strike was.

"There you go. Now you are getting it. Yes, the men just assume we will do what they say."

Tameki finished telling us all she had heard from her husband. She made us vow to say nothing to our own husbands. I could have been intrigued by the news but instead had feelings of nausea come over me, wave after wave. I asked Kikume how she knew when she was pregnant.

"Oh, how exciting!" Kikume was already planning how our children would play together, and I wasn't even sure.

Chapter 27

MUSIC

The women were organizing a big communal dinner to celebrate the birthday of our emperor. The date was a Thursday, a workday. This was not the first year that the camp had celebrated this birthday. Though the plantation owners were not happy with a workday being taken for a holiday, they grudgingly allowed us the freedom for it. In years past, the workers had insisted we were still subjects of the emperor, as per our work contracts. There could be no disputing this. I was grateful to those camp workers who had come before us for insisting on this and gaining that little bit of respect for us.

Some of the men went fishing and brought back plenty to feed all of us. Kane, a local Hawaiian, had befriended some of the men and helped them find a good fishing spot. Roji was part of the planning and work on the men's side.

"Ueme, look what we brought you ladies!" A beaming Roji slung the string of fish onto a slab of wood next to our preparations.

"Hey, hey, Roji! Let's go clean these for the women and present them properly!" Kane laughed as he slung his fish into a bucket of seawater.

The two of them walked off singing some Hawaiian tune that was as yet unfamiliar to us.

We spread boards out on top of boxes to make a long banquet table. We had beer, and someone had produced some home-brewed sake. With the fish and all the vegetables and rice, we felt very grateful for the bounty.

Letting go of our cares for the day, the mood was light and cheerful. The children sensed our good moods and were running around, up and down the red road, making up tag games and running contests.

Once the men returned with the cleaned fish, they took charge of cooking it. The smells of all the cooking and the sounds of joy from the children transported us back to happier times. Looking up from our work into each other's faces, we women nodded to each other. It was if we were saying in those nods, *Yes, we can make this our new Nihon, and we can create some kind of good life here.*

As the day wore on, some of the more natural storytellers released their tales to us, one by one. We women kept the bowls of rice full and the beer flowing. There were many toasts to the emperor—lots of "Kumpais!" The children eventually tired and leaned against their elders. The stories got to be wilder and the laughing harder as the day drew to a close. We hurried to clean up before the sun started to set, as the next day was a workday.

As we prepared to pack up all the food and supplies, Kikume said to me, "It seems this is the kind of medicine that we all have needed. Look at your husband. I haven't ever seen him so happy and relaxed."

Someone yelled out that we needed music and grabbed an old oil can and started drumming on it with his hands.

Another said, "We need a flute. Anyone have a shakuhachi?"

"Ueme has a samisen, and she is good too. She can sing and play." Roji looked at me expectantly.

I was surprised. I hadn't even thought about music since we had arrived. Roji ran up the steps to our cottage and came back with the samisen. He took the pot of rice out of my hands and placed the samisen in them instead.

Some flutes came out of other cottages, and another oil can was turned upside down. We formed a little troupe of musicians and played our familiar folk songs. Some from the audience got up and formed a circle to dance.

Someone yelled, "Sing, sing."

I started to sing, and suddenly I was overwhelmed by joy. I was joined by other voices. Everything was flowing. My fingers were moving over the instrument on their own without my thoughts. Notes were coming out of my throat without fear. How could I have forgotten about music? Music! We did not leave music behind. We could all survive and survive well if we had music. The whole crowd was in unison with our joy. The air was soft. Hawaiian blossoms permeated the air with sweet fragrance. A gentle breeze blew in from the ocean. How my perception was changing about this new land.

I took a minute to survey us all with admiration for our spirits. I was proud of us, we Nihonji in this hardscrabble land. Roji was a short distance across from me. He was looking at me with the same eyes he used to back in our village when he'd spied me across the Bon Dance circle long ago. Music brought out the best in us. Perhaps at this moment, he felt a bit better about having married me?

As we were all cleaning up from our little festival, Roji came over to me and asked me to come to the cottage. Everyone else was busy; some were still singing and dancing. He led us off by ourselves, holding my hand.

Roji looked at me with sad eyes. "I am sorry, Ueme. You must forgive me. I am not myself. This country confuses me. I do not know who I am." Roji walked with me back to the cottage.

I felt a little beam of hope enter me. "Roji, I know we are all struggling to adapt to this place in our own way. Maybe we can help each other to do this." Would he think I was scolding him? I'd better not say more.

"Perhaps so. I have been feeling more positive lately. The men's community group has helped me."

"Can you tell me what you do there, when you meet together?"

"Ah, just men's stuff. How to adapt to the farmwork. What things to do to prevent the store from stealing from us."

"Stealing from us?"

"Well, their prices are inflated. We have someone who checks the prices of rice and soap in Honolulu. When we have evidence that they have raised the prices exorbitantly, we bring it to their attention."

"Oh, and do they lower the price because of that?"

"Only a little bit, but we do have some effect. It depends on who does the talking to the store manager."

"I bet Isamu Chikaru is a good one for that! He always has strong opinions and will not back down in an argument. His wife talks about him at the sewing circle. She is proud of his strength, but it does make it difficult for running their household."

"Hai, he can be effective. But we have found Toyo Nakayoku to be better at making someone see a new point of view. He is quite good at it. You know him; everyone calls him Yoku."

"Oh, yes, he is an agreeable person, always helping others. Roji, it seems you men are learning people skills in this new country. I admire this!"

"Ueme, I am glad you can see some of the positive things I am doing."

"Maybe we both need to do that more."

Hah, a new resolution together. And more insight into the men's group. I would mention this at the sewing circle.

Chapter 28

BEAUTY

The day for our outing with Elizabeth had arrived. Tameki came walking up to my cottage with her husband, Aduki. Roji was already out with his friends to fish. He was not happy I had been chosen to help the plantation owner's wife. He had such anger toward the plantation owner for all the poor treatment and financial cheating with the store.

"Ueme, I came to tell you that Elizabeth told Hisako-san that we need to wear our underclothes for work, the pants, lighter jackets, and our boots. The mountain trails can be muddy and overgrown." Tameki was beaming in her underwork clothes, ready for the forest.

Aduki spoke. "Ueme, please watch out for Tameki. She keeps forgetting she is pregnant! Make sure she doesn't try to uproot trees for that lady's garden!"

Laughing at my friend's singular personality, I agreed. "No worries, Aduki. She will only be allowed to walk—no picking up a shovel for her."

Then I continued, "Oh the clothing! That makes sense. I will change. Wait just a minute for me."

"One of the bachelors is driving the wagon," said Tameki. "Very ambitious one, apparently. He has made a name for himself. He has already requested a cottage, though he has no wife to keep it for him. He has said he is busy taking care of that problem." Tameki was laughing as she said this.

"My, he is very anxious to get a wife! But what makes you think he is ambitious beyond that?" I said as I grabbed my lunch box and tea bottle while closing the door.

We walked up the dusty road between the cottages, feeling rather carefree. It felt very dangerous to me, to escape from my life for a few hours.

"He has his own vegetable garden. He also fishes. And he sells everything to fatten his bank account. He also is knowledgeable about agriculture. He reads books and actually advises the lunas and bosses about the planting and fertilizing."

"Well, I don't know how he has the energy for all of that."

"Because he is not married!"

At that, we laughed and dodged some children running after a ball heading our way up the road.

At the top of the hill, the wagon was waiting for us. Elizabeth waved to us and introduced her teenage son, Robert, to us. He was sitting in the front talking to the "bachelor." Two women were already in the wagon waiting for us. The bachelor came around to help us up into the wagon. It was the man from Kikume's rescue and the vegetable garden. My surprise showed all over my face. He just smiled, saying, "Konnichiwa, ladies," and helped us into the wagon.

We arranged ourselves in our pants and boots, even Elizabeth, on the bottom of the wagon next to a lot of buckets and some shovels. These were for the plants we would bring back.

It was a rough ride, as the road to the mountain path was rutted out from rains and disrepair. Without a translator, we managed to teach each other some words in Nihojin to Elizabeth, and she in English to us. We learned the words for *bucket, shovel, blouse, collar, boots, face, eyes.* We did a lot of laughing and pointing. Somehow, we were able to understand that Elizabeth had four children—three girls and one boy and that another baby boy had died in childbirth. I learned that Tameki had also lost a baby at birth and that the other two women each had children at home with their husbands.

As we got closer to the mountain, the trees were denser and taller. Eventually, the breeze became a bit cooler, and we could see a mist in the air, probably from the waterfall that Elizabeth pantomimed was nearby. The wagon stopped.

The bachelor came around to the back to help us get out of the wagon. His eyes were so deep and dark. Embarrassed, I kept my head down and tried to regain composure. He asked our names as he helped us down. He introduced himself as Michiru. I was the last to be helped out of the wagon. As Michiru's hands touched my arms, an electric shock went through my shoulders. I looked at him, and he at me. He'd felt it too. Embarrassed, we both managed to get me promptly out of the wagon and not look at each other again.

Elizabeth started to organize our expedition. We each carried some tools. Tameki wanted to carry a shovel, and I grabbed it first and handed it to Robert to carry. I then took hold of some burlap bags and handed part of the pile to the ambitious Tameki. We each were carrying our lunch boxes and tea bottles like we did for our work outfits. We did not look especially dainty or womanly. I wondered how the bachelor viewed us. We started walking up the trail.

Michiru was very talkative and would change his position in the group so he had a chance to talk with each of us. He explained to us that he was especially happy to accompany us on this trip, as he hoped to bring back some tree mushrooms, which were great for cooking. This particular trail was known for its bounty of them. He also was pleased to accompany such adventurous women. I am ashamed to say that all of us married women giggled at his remark like we were schoolgirls. He was so very handsome. I scolded myself to stop noticing him.

Elizabeth and her son led us up the road to the trail. The sun was not yet overhead, and the trail seemed to disappear into the mist. There was a steep cliff to one side, where the delicate ferns grew out horizontally in lush abundance. We could smell the ripened fruits that had dropped from the trees onto the ground and had begun their fermenting. The two mothers went ahead of us into the misty trail. Elizabeth looked at us and motioned to a plant and questioned us with her eyes. "Good for garden?"

As the plant had some beautiful blossoms, as well as colorful leaves, we nodded yes. Her son Robert took out some colored string and tied it around the plant for digging up later. But then, Michiru came up from behind and said, "No good. It will die out in the sun. It needs shade. You have not much shade yet at the house." He was looking directly at the owner's wife.

Tameki and I looked at each other. What impudence! How dare he talk like that to the owner's wife! But there seemed to be no repercussions. That confused Tameki and me even more. We continued on up the red dirt trail, stopping here and there. Elizabeth would nod toward a plant, and the bachelor would either nod yes or no. Shortly, we saw our other two hikers sitting on some rocks next to a stream. "Look up there," they whispered.

Up and beyond us was a gentle waterfall that meandered down the rock cliff, bouncing off side to side, seeming to create tufts of greenery wherever it landed and then, with a long fall, landing into a small pool. Sunlight flickered here and there through the branches and leaves, creating little sparks off the falling water.

Wrapped in the cool mist of the pool, we sat and became quiet. After a while, the bachelor rose and walked off into the tangle of vines and ferns adjoining the stream. He seemed to know his way around the forest.

Elizabeth pointed to the trail going up to the left of the stream. We should walk further and eat our lunch at another place. We chose a spot completely covered with a low-growing, fernlike plant that made a soft bed for us to spread out and relax. The cliff edge shaded us from the sunlight here, along with trees that had sprouted out from crevices in the rock. The sounds of water splashing, birdsong trilling in the distance, and the coolness of the air had the effect of making me drift off. Was I dreaming? This was not the Hawaii we had experienced.

We did not want to leave, but time was running out. As we came back down the trail, we saw that the bachelor and the son had dug up all the plants and a few tree saplings (for shade, explained the bachelor) and had placed them in the buckets in the back of the wagon. The bachelor was trying his best to clean off the mud that had dropped from the buckets onto the floor of the wagon. He made us wait while he cleaned it. He dramatically dusted and wiped the floor with an old piece of canvas. Then with a broad grin, he lifted us each into the wagon. This man surely delighted himself with helping us women. On the way back, he slowed down the wagon at each large bump, turning his head to warn us.

By the end of the journey, his warmth had won over each of us. Sighing, we talked of how wonderful a husband he would make.

Before the wagon took off down the mountain road, Elizabeth had taken us aside. She said, "Utsekushi? Beautiful?"

We nodded yes and repeated, "Beautiful."

Chapter 29

THE CLIFF EDGE

Roji's attentions to keeping a regular schedule had ended. Once more, it was Sunday morning, and I was looking for him before the sewing bee. I decided to walk down past the company store, an area where all the gambling and other things were going on. I was half convinced I wouldn't find him there and half convinced I would. He would always tell me he was out fishing and drinking with Kane-that if I wanted to find him, I should go to the Hawaiian village.

Yesterday, I saw Malia and asked her about all the fish Kane and Roji had been catching lately. Malia looked at me strangely and then said, "Me no want pilikia, trouble. You sure it was Kane? Kane and I live same ohana. I care for his dog all month while he be away to Maui. His mother and sister are there."

Malia looked sad as she said this, probably guessing the lie.

I had hoped the fishing expeditions had really happened. I walked resolutely down the road. I stared straight ahead, preparing my heart for any type of surprise. Perhaps he was working in the communal garden. He did bring home a fresh vegetable now and then. I was prepared to see him in the garden with the other men. The garden was empty. It was too early for the communal work hours. Probably everyone was at home finishing a noon meal.

At the end of the cottages were the barracks for the bachelors and the company store. Past these was a sort of shantytown, some poorly constructed buildings that housed some bars and other types of entertainment. Everything seemed quiet. The store did not open until after midday.

I stood looking down the road past the buildings toward the cliff that overlooked the ocean. The men climbed down this cliff to fish off the rocks, but I had never had the time to venture down this narrow road. Could Roji have fallen asleep after a night of fishing? Maybe some of the men had gotten some beer and fished and drank a little too much?

I stood, looking and listening.

Scrape, scrape. The sound was coming from the other side of the barracks.

Walking toward it, I saw that Michiru was busy hoeing an additional garden he had carved out at the edge of the scrubby woods. He didn't see me and was leaning over intently picking up weeds and rocks and throwing them out of the garden. Suddenly one came at me and nearly hit me in the eye.

"Hey, watch out!! You almost hit my eye!" I yelled.

Michiru turned around and up in a start. "Whoa, I didn't know anybody was around. What are you doing here?"

"Oh, hello again! Those eggplants are ready for picking, I think." I said this as I was surveying his crop. Then I explained, "Oh, I am looking for Roji, my husband. He must have gotten up very early this morning and left without eating any breakfast." It wasn't the first lie I'd told regarding Roji.

The bachelor looked at me strangely and said nothing. I refused to acknowledge the fact that everyone seemed to "know" but not say out loud that Roji was keeping company with a woman in the drinking houses. My reputation as a proper wife was resting on a thin veneer of respectability.

"Well, that's all right. If you haven't seen him, I will just go on down this road and keep looking. He may have gone fishing off the cliff. Perhaps, I will try there."

"Have you gone to the cliffs before? It's a very narrow path and not to be traveled in a summer yukata." The bachelor seemed to think I needed education.

"Oh, well, I wasn't going to climb down it—just look over the edge."

I could make out a muffled snort from his direction.

I started walking, and suddenly, he leaped over his little fence and was right beside me.

"OK, then. I needed to take a walk this morning, so I might as well join you."

The road went past the bachelors' barracks and the store, turning into the little shantytown. We were coming up to some of the "establishments." Michiru developed the unusual habit of running ahead at each little building, closing the front doors to, as he said, "Just make sure no unworthy bums are about."

I laughed to myself. Surely these doors would be opened again as soon as we passed, as these places were always open for "business." And most likely, Roji was behind one of those doors. I half hoped he would see me walking by, looking for him. I wanted him to be embarrassed, but that would only happen if he cared.

After the little buildings, the path became rough. But the bachelor tore off branches before me and made it easier.

"I guess you wish you had your 'hiking' pants on today," he said, making reference to our mountain outing.

Suddenly, we were at the edge. I caught my breath, saying, "Oh, oh, oh," and wishing I had time to come here regularly. The view was beautiful, and there was a cooling breeze. The ocean stretched before us in a blue-green so clear you could see the coral beneath it.

We sat down. Michiru pulled out a papaya and knife and proceeded to cut slices up for us to taste. He said nothing but offered the fruit to me. I took it and thought how strange it was to sit here with a man other than my husband, but how enjoyable. We stayed there silently until I noticed that the position of the sun had gone from overhead to now descending in the west.

Then the bachelor moved a bit so he could face me and asked about Kikume. He said he was very sad that she'd lost the baby. To cheer him up, I told him that Hisako-san had said that Michiru bringing her down from the fields in the wagon had probably saved her life.

"Yes," he said, "but not the baby's."

"Oh, yes, but it was not the baby's fate to come here at this time. Perhaps another time." I stood up and said, "It is time for me to go back. I must hurry to get to the sewing circle." Obviously, I am not going to find Roji here." I pointed across the cliff rocks and down to the sea, where there was a single fisherman, very old and wrinkled, carrying a bucket walking far down the beach.

We walked back up the old road and bypassed all the other buildings. I recognized that we seemed to be carrying the same load of sadness, sharing it between our shoulders somehow. Michiru walked me to the water pump and filled his bucket with water. Then he walked me back to my cottage and handed me the bucket.

He bowed and said, "Take this water as my appreciation for a lovely unexpected walk today." He turned and walked down the hill. Something in my chest leaped.

Chapter 30

EMPTINESS

Lost in thought, I scolded myself for looking to the past. I was sure Roji and I had been happy once, hadn't we?

When I tried to talk over my marriage troubles with Tameki, the response was always, "Oh, marriage! It is best not to think too hard about it!"

But I felt such a need to talk about it. It was clear there was more to life than an absent husband who only had unkind words for me. My little friendship with Michiru was showing me how different men could be. Was there an answer? Obachan was in my thoughts. Whenever I felt life's rules were not right, she came to mind because she was the one to remind me of rules and propriety. One doesn't question one's husband. But if she could see my situation?

Remembering the first feeling, I recalled it wasn't a fullness like I had expected. It was an emptiness, as if my insides were being carved out to make space, I guess. And my breasts, that was the real clue. They swelled and became so sore. At first, I was sad because Matron had told us that it was economically impossible to return to Nihon once you had a child. There were too many expenses. Basically, the company owned the child. We would be deeply in debt. I entertained a slight hope at that point that my brother would have rebuilt the fabric business by then and would be able to send us money. Ha, I had written a letter to him and never received a reply.

I had been feeling more homesick, as the camp routine had now been drummed into me. I seemed to have more space in my brain to think about my home and family. Whenever I felt homesick, I would go to my chest in the corner of the room and kneel in front of it. Rubbing my hand over the wood, I pictured the kitchen and the meditation garden. Imagining myself kneeling on the veranda, I would try to see my parents sitting on their rock together. Then I would unlatch the chest and carefully lift off the rice paper protecting my fabrics that my auntie and obachan had packed for me to use when Roji and I got settled—silks for more kimonos, heavy indigo for a new jacket for Roji, red silk for a baby girl's first kimono. Putting my hand between the layers of each type of cloth, recognizing the differences only a cloth merchant would know by feel, I marveled at the education I had been given and how little use I had for it now. Tears would usually follow, thinking of the life of my dreams as I carefully replaced the fabrics with the protective rice paper on top of each layer.

I had written to Ito in care of her parents to ask her about my family. I was sure by this point that she was married, and I did not know her address or name. She replied quickly and described her upcoming marriage to the son of the awful village headsman! She explained he was very different from his father and had been sent to university when we were still in school. They would live in town, as he had a position in charge of roadbuilding, which had a favorable future, as the emperor has put much tax money into paving roads with macadam.

To hear Ito talk of the emperor and roadbuilding filled me with some anger, when all we had here was dirt and dust. Ito had also written about Saiko's news. She had become a schoolteacher and was much revered for her talent with the children's learning. I was actually jealous of my dear friend, rather than feeling joy for her.

The emperor seemed so far away. Did he even care about his subjects over here in Hawaii being treated like untouchables? Ito never said a word about my brother. I remembered our obachans' words to us when we had been children. "To say something bad about another will bring the winds of misfortune to your own roof." We would giggle and say we didn't have a roof! Ito's letter with no words about brother said everything I needed to know. Ito always refused to say anything about those whom she did not respect.

I marveled at our one room with a door in the front wall and a window in the back wall. To have simple privacy was wonderful. The garden was doing well and expanding in the back. We had carved out a bit of scrub brush to make more space for it. I looked longingly out the window at the red rows of dirt for every ripe vegetable I could find. I was so hungry. This baby was very demanding. I did not want to do it, but I cooked the last handful of rice in the bag. I had a bit of pickled vegetables left and made a meal of it, saving half for Roji. Hungry still, I lay down to sleep and tried not to think of my hunger or of Roji. I was fearful of the coming week. I could not ask for help, such shame. Besides, everyone here struggled. How could I take food from people who had so little themselves? I scolded myself for needing so much to eat and decided to dream of plum blossoms. If she is a girl, I shall name her Blossom. If he is a boy …

The gong struck. I was barely able to get up. Seeing Roji had not returned, I again ate his portion of the night's meal. It was a mixed blessing. If Roji were here, there would not be a morning meal for me. But if he were here, he would be working, and there would be so much more money. I was trying to think only good thoughts for the baby's sake. However, I felt angry that my household was missing the man's wages, which were twice the woman's. I could buy rice. I could buy vegetables. I could buy fish! Oh, this rice and pickles was just not enough. This baby was so greedy! I walked down to the water pump with my bucket. I could see no happiness or good feeling ever again in my future. Hunger and tiredness filled my days. Could I stand another whack on my shoulder from the luna? I understood he had his quotas. But human life was human life. We were human beings. I was a human being carrying another human being.

Where was the mercy of our ancestors? I realized I had forgotten my offerings and prayers for weeks. I must remember to kneel before our little altar tonight when I get back. I used to be so strong, but this baby was sapping my energy.

At the water pump, one of the other women saw my distress and said, "Oh, Ueme, do not worry. The first few months are the worst. Next month, you will see how much better you will feel!" She walked off cheerily with her full bucket of water.

I put my bucket down and rested a bit. Hisako-san stood over me. "What has happened to Roji? I haven't seen him for a while. Is he sick?"

I looked up at her. I was embarrassed. To have a husband leave you is most disgraceful. So I lied, "Oh yes, he has been laid up for a while. He is gathering his strength to return to work soon."

"Ha!" One of the more experienced older women from farther up the road burst in upon our conversation. "No need to feel ashamed about him and lie for him! He spends all his time and your money down at the 'establishments'!"

"What do you mean my money?" I suddenly had a body full of energy and stood up.

"Well, aren't you the one with the family fortune in fabrics?"

I turned and ran up the hill to my cottage and unlocked my chest. I saw that the folded silks were now inches below the rim of the chest. Layers of fabric were missing. Roji had been stealing my cloth to pay his debts at the beer hall. "My silks, my fabrics, all that I have left of my family. And here I am starving, and he is spending my family's gift to me." I suddenly realized I was yelling. How shameful. I broke down. I was splayed across the top of the chest as if trying to protect it from the unknown. It was the first time I had cried in this place.

Hisako-san had followed me home and was standing in my doorway. "Ueme, you must get ready for work. Do not think of him now or your sadness. I have brought you some rice balls for your lunch. Do not worry. You will receive some rice from the community funds. I am in charge."

I looked at her. "He will steal more until it is all gone! What shall I do?"

Hisako-san smiled. "I will have one of the men remove it to my quarters immediately, and we will figure it out later." She left the doorway and I heard her yelling. Hisako-san had no time for niceties in this place she'd once told me.

One of the men on his way to the wagons responded to her. Immediately, this man appeared in the doorway.

"Which case am I to carry to Hisako-san's cottage?"

I pointed, and it was gone.

That evening, there was a fresh fish, some newly picked vegetables, a huge bag of rice and a note of well wishes for my baby sewn into the top of the bag. I was not to worry again.

I looked out the door and saw the normal goings on of the camp. I noticed Michiru down at the pump with a number of buckets he was filling. A few moments later, he was at the door with them. "I have been 'hired' by Madam Hisako to bring you enough water for your furo tonight. Shall I fill it and start the fire under it?" Of course, our furo was just a large bucket. There were plans for a community bath to be built soon.

I just looked and could not say a word. I knew Hisako-san never hired anyone. She ordered, and everyone complied. This was women's work. Roji and I shared a furo with the neighbors, and I knew they would be pleased. I walked down the steps and around to the back to see the fire going and the water heating. My neighbor was outside, and she was motioning for me to use it first. I had never used the furo first. But in this new land, I saw things were changing.

She helped me soap up and wipe down before entering the steaming water. She spoke softly saying, "You must always ask for help. It is no shame here. We have to help each other. It is so hard. Healthy babies come first. Not husbands. Remember that."

The steam enveloped me, and I closed my eyes to see my mother in our garden, sitting on the meditation rock.

A few days later, Roji appeared as if nothing had happened.

"Ueme, we worked hard at a new section of land today. The clay was hard and like a rock to break open. One of the men on our row injured his shoulder wielding the pickax on it. You should have seen the luna. He hit Umegi twice on the back because he had fallen to the ground in pain." Roji had expected my sympathy for the men's troubles and yet made no mention of any sympathy for me having no food or being pregnant and alone all this time.

I would pretend that nothing had happened. I had seen men be shamed and how violent a husband could get with it. I did not need that. "That is a horrible thing. I hope Umegi doesn't lose too many days of work with that injury. I know he needs the money with two babies at home." I looked to see if Roji would recognize the hidden rebuke.

Nothing registered on his face. So we were to continue like this. He did not leave again for many months, and with his wages, we had enough food.

In the fields, I had time to reflect while I worked. I had always worried about my future and Roji's future—being intricately linked. What intruded on me now was a third future—my child, our child. Oh, I couldn't bear it. What kind of future was there here? A slow dread came over me. There was an ache; it seemed not to be located anywhere specifically. I should drink more tea, flush out the dread. I was sure it was in my stomach. But then my shoulders ached. I put hot compresses on my shoulders. My fingers felt weak. I soaked them in the rice water before I slept. Roji said I was going "strange" on him. I should keep a lookout. He was ready to be out the door again.

How could I have gotten to this place? I looked up and saw

a beautiful blue sky with shapely white clouds floating in it. In the distance, the mountains lifted jagged peaks of the half-eaten rim of the volcano. So much was similar, old volcano mountains at the horizon and beautiful blue sky. So much was different. We Nipponese were low here. We were not respected. How could that be? We were children of the gods! We were first in the universe.

I was a merchant woman, daughter of a samurai. I was educated and could run an establishment. I had run an establishment. But my brother was a weak man, prone to gambling and drinking and getting into debt. And stealing. He'd stolen my father's fabric, and he'd ruined the business, and I'd had to come here. And I was married to someone just like my brother! Obachan! Was she still alive? I should write her another letter.

I bent lower to pull the rake over the remains of burnt cane stalks. The small of my back was hurting, so I stooped at different angles to see what felt better. The luna yelled his lunch call, and we gathered to sit in groups to eat our lunch. The women were gossiping about one of the prostitutes in the "establishments."

I was quiet and just looked at everything. Our hoes and rakes lay at our sides. We were all sitting at different angles; some were squatting, whatever felt best. Red dirt was crusted on our boots. Red dust covered all our clothing. Even the smallest woman of us looked large in this protective gear. With our gloves off, the little hands seemed disconnected to the dusty, dirty beings attached to them. I looked at all these remarkable women who came from families similar to mine, women who did not have to work in the fields, some who had never done any work with their hands at all. At least I was familiar with working in dirt. And yet, here we were, all of us not complaining, working harder than a worker in a rice paddy and earning only enough money to live for the next week.

Suddenly, they were quiet. I thought back to what they were saying and then remembered the last was about a woman bringing some silk to Hisako-san to be sewn into a kimono. Hisako-san had told her she didn't work on stolen fabric. Apparently, there was quite a bit of a verbal fight, but Hisako did not relent. The woman had to take the fabric to Honolulu to be sewn. I then realized why the silence. It was my fabric. I looked up.

What could I say?

The luna broke the silence. Lunch was over. I would like a pocket watch. I was sure he didn't give us our full time for lunch. I should mention this to Hisako-san and find out how to purchase one.

Evening came, and I spent the evening working to prepare for the next day as usual. Roji had arrived before me, removed his muddy clothes, and left them to be brushed clean. Swallowing my resentment of his expectations of me, I dutifully brushed both our sets of clothing. The smell of fish from our neighbor's cottage made me gag. I made some tea and had rice and tea for my dinner. Just before lights out, Roji returned from wherever and rolled into his futon. I sat up and questioned him about the fabric.

"You ask me about fabric? What do I know? There are thieves all over this place. It is no news that you come from the fancy House of Oyama, best fabrics in Five Bridges." Roji was angry. What was he angry about?

I stated, "I have never talked about my family business. Why would I? No one here has heard of it. It is not famous past Five Bridges."

"It was probably your friend Tameki. She knows all about your life." Roji rolled, over feigning disinterest.

That was so untrue that immediately I knew. "It is you, Roji. You are the only one who would boast about it. You are the one who took the fabric. Do not disrespect me with your lying about it."

There was silence. Then I remembered something else.

"Roji, I want you to return Hisako-san's porcelain sake cups. I borrowed them for your birthday dinner, and you took them. I know you did. They were missing the morning after. You had left early that morning. Where did you go before working in the fields that day? People say that you have gambling debts and use my possessions to pay for them. We have lost respect in this community. We are shamed."

I felt it. I knew this was the end. There was no more pretending. We had crossed a bridge and the bridge had dissolved. There was no going back. The silence that followed my accusations was the dissolution.

Now I felt the aloneness. It surrounded me everywhere I went. It followed me up the steps to the cottage. It hung at my elbows as I put the rice over the fire. It was there when I looked into Roji's eyes.

Chapter 31

END OF THE STORM

A strange new feeling permeated the camp. There was an electric charge to the air. There was some danger, unseen but felt, as when some unknown danger causes a flock of birds suddenly to take flight straight up into the air.

Tameki had been warning us repeatedly. "Something is happening soon. Ask your husbands. Maybe one of them will break the secret. The strike has been scheduled. Who can find out when?"

I decided to ask Roji. It was not possible to alienate him more, so why not?

"Roji, can you tell me what you men are talking about at your meetings?" I was anxious to understand what the men were planning. We women knew something was about to happen through sensing our men's nervousness.

"Why do you want to know?" He was annoyed, and I was sure he felt I had no right to ask him anything.

"Well, a woman likes to know and appreciate all the things her husband does." This felt hollow even as I said it.

Roji looked at me suspiciously. "It is nothing important. You would not be interested, and you would not understand." Roji was near the door. He seemed like he was ready to leave the cottage.

"I think I am interested. Go ahead. Tell me, please." I hoped he would respond.

"We have not heard back from the managers about our list of grievances. So we are planning a strike. You must not tell anyone."

"Could the women help with planning the strike?"

"No, you would be of no use."

"But this strike involves us, too, doesn't it?"

"It does not involve you. The men are striking."

"But if the men are striking, won't the women be striking, too?"

"Well, of course, you won't be going to work."

"Then we are striking."

"This is between the men. The managers are not going to listen to you women."

"But if we go to work, they will still have workers for their fields. If we don't work, then those fields will not be productive. So, we will have an effect on them."

"Fine. Fine. You are striking, and you will have an effect."

"Yes, that is fine. Now, what about planning for the time when we are not working?"

"We will have signs and meetings, and we will notify the newspapers."

"No, no. I mean what about how we will survive without wages for all that time."

"We have figured out that we have enough money in the community chest for two weeks of food and necessities."

"But what about the third or fourth week?"

"The strike will not last that long. We are quite sure they cannot do without us for longer."

"Tameki said the managers will bring in outside workers and drag this out to punish us."

"What does Tameki know? How can she know anything of value?"

"She said that's what they did on Maui last year."

"How does she know that?" Roji then got up and walked out of the cottage. It seemed I had angered him.

253

The next day, Tameki said she was in trouble with her husband for "talking too much."

"It doesn't matter," she said. "What is important is that we be prepared. We cannot do this in a halfway measure. We must slow down the men and wait until we have more money saved for this."

"How can we slow them down? They do not listen to us." Kikume seemed distressed. She constantly feared for this pregnancy and, only naturally, for the safety of this baby.

I could feel my own insatiable hunger rising within me. These babies demanded a lot from their mothers.

By that Saturday, it was determined we would strike the next work week. Roji came home that night with a very proud smile on his face. "We have figured it out. We will not make it easy for the scabs to come here and work."

I wondered what he meant. That Sunday, we had a union meeting. Everyone was required to sign a piece of paper, and we were given instructions. We had to make some signs that we would carry as we marched around the fields. Tameki's husband would somehow sneak word out to the Japanese newspaper in Honolulu.

The men were all jubilant, but the women were worried. Sunday was a heavy day. There was much praying to the ancestors. We asked our Buddhist priest to bless us. Even the priest looked worried.

Monday was strange. We got up at the usual time. We put on our work clothes. The gong sounded, the whistle blew, and we ate our breakfast and tied our tea bottles to our waists. Then we walked solemnly to the fields. The sun was taking longer to rise in the sky.

Tameki's husband had unusual theories about the sun and moon and earth. When times were especially momentous, the earth slowed down its rotations about the sun. We had always laughed at his cosmic theories. Today, Tameki and I looked at each other as we walked up the hill, and we both said, "Late sunrise."

Gloom settled over our group. My feet felt leaden. We all were walking more slowly due to the excessive weight of our feet. The lunas knew something was up.

At our designated fields, we took out our signs and started marching on the road, up and around and down, the men and women together.

The lunas were screaming at us and took out their whips. But when they saw the reporters walking up the hill, they put the whips down. The owners and managers came on their horses and rode around and around, yelling at the lunas and at us. It was frightening. Someone started singing a work song. The singing felt good, and we drowned out the rest of the confusion in our heads. Our union president stopped the march and brought out the list of demands and presented it to the owners. The reporters asked what was on the paper.

"It is a list of stupid demands and make-believe issues. This is all about nothing," yelled the owner. At this, the owner turned his horse around and rode off with a couple of the managers in the direction of Honolulu.

The rest of the day dragged on. We women found this marching almost as hard on us as our field labor. The union president said the women could go back to the camps after lunch, and the men should stay the rest of the day.

The days continued like this for weeks. But the marching did not stop the owner from bringing in other workers. Police came on the second day and every day after that. They were there not to protect us but to protect the scab workers. Every day, the lunas yelled at us. They took particular delight in screaming directly into the women's faces.

We women got together to see how to handle this. "Never look back at them. Keep your eyes down. Remind yourself that this is only a screaming hell, which is not real. Think of Buddha and his trials."

We women instituted a ration system from the very first day. We were eating half of what we normally would eat. The men did not like this and were cranky. However, we hid the food and the trust money. We did not believe this strike would be over in a month.

In the first month. Roji was proud and defiant and seemed to exude excess strength of mind that enabled some of the weaker men to gather their own strength. Roji was becoming one of the leaders in this trial. One time. as I walked past a gathering of men, I heard Roji directing a few of the men on their position within the strike line and explaining in detail some strategy. The tone of his voice reminded me of how he was back in our school days, full of confidence.

The baby was moving more now. We women would often talk to each other of the imagined physical and mental characteristics the coming baby might have. Someone had mentioned Roji's confidence and his ability to do a somersault at parties to amuse the children. Would these be abilities the new baby would have? Most often, I would not join in. But lately, I was nodding yes to some of these comments. My feelings toward Roji were possibly softening, as I wanted a good father for my baby and was more willing to believe that Roji could change.

There was a lot of camaraderie in the evenings, as we did not let the night watchmen come into the camp. We now had our own guards at the gates. We had transformed our little community, strengthening our bonds to each other. To my own amazement, I started to feel at home here.

The second month became a trial for all of us. Victory no longer seemed sure. Tempers flared. We were hearing disagreements up and down the cottages. Some of the women tried to steal extra food from our community food bank for their husbands. We held meetings to remind everyone of our purpose and how to behave and how to think.

The strike was on for nearly three months. Roji was becoming surly and mean. People stayed away from him. He never would speak to me and would not help with the chores. He reasoned that, as I was home every afternoon, "You can very well do all the things that need to be done." He barely acknowledged my pregnancy.

Carrying the water from the pump became very difficult. Mori started bringing my water bucket to me every day. I felt such shame with this obligation I was incurring. When Roji was at home, I told him of the obligations we incurred by his not helping me. This only served to anger him more and resulted in his absence that night.

During the second month, the president of the union had asked me to organize music events to take place twice a week. We found another samisen, and I gave lessons to a woman who seemed to have talent. One woman played the shakuhachi. We asked for women to volunteer to do some of the drumming, since the men were occupied with strategy and marching. The women were reluctant, but Madam volunteered someone and herself. Soon, we had an almost professional music group. The events softened the air around us for a while. But at the third month, people were calling for meetings to call the strike off.

We had put on little entertainment skits and games for the children to play. Everything was created around the theme of duty to one's community and the benefits of steadfastness and silence. Children recited poems about caterpillars staying in their dark cocoons for months in order to be rewarded and emerge as butterflies. Other stories exalted famous samurai warriors who were kept captive on desert islands for years, only to return home eventually to a festive parade. We exalted the monks who silently prayed in their lonely mountain shrines in Nihon for the well-being of all Nihonji. We did all this as we secretly wondered if anyone truly cared about us out there in the broader world.

After each performance, Michiru made a special point of commending our music committee about the good work we were doing and how much it helped everyone. He always bowed deeply. He brought us flowers of wild hibiscus. Some of the husbands were also very appreciative and would clap very loudly, especially for the children's performances. It helped us to know that the men appreciated our efforts. The strike was a lonely business for all of us. Fear gripped our minds and hearts.

Some of the community thought that we were just silly women, and therefore, they did not need to attend our performances, in spite of the urgings of our camp leader. However, overall, the music and poetry events engendered more community feeling, to the betterment of all our spirits.

There was a brightness to my days, in spite of all the turmoil. Roji was mostly living somewhere else, and I only needed to make meals for myself. Mori had not been able to bring me water due to his increased duties with the strike. But fate had intervened. A bucket of water appeared every morning at my steps. I emptied it into my bucket and left the empty bucket out on my steps each night. Every morning, there was a fresh bucket of water. I then started leaving a vegetable from my garden in the bucket. The morning bucket would have a flower tucked into the handle. Each day, a different vegetable, a different flower. I had such fun with it all and wondered, Who was my benefactor?

Then one Sunday, Michiru appeared at my doorstep carrying some horse manure in a large burlap bag.

"I have been privileged to come by some fertilizer for your garden. It is contraband, so do not ask how I got it!" He smiled and left the bag behind the cottage.

Ah, of course, he knew I had a garden! I smiled to myself, and we never spoke of our game to anyone.

As the fourth month approached, we depended on help from the Nipponese community in Honolulu. We were running out of food and money. And we were running out of patience and hope. Some days, the men returned bloodied from fights that they'd picked with the scab workers or from fights with the lunas.

It was almost four months long before it ended.

The owners were about to evict us from the cottages. With help from the Honolulu Nipponese community and their newspaper that had covered all the details of our actions, with pressure from public opinion, a settlement had been made.

We returned to the fields with a small raise in pay and a guarantee that we would not work more than ten hours a day. Only two demands of the twenty were granted. And the pay raise was still not enough to live on. It seemed like so little for such hardship. But the limit for the ten-hour days was very appreciated in the end, and we did notice the pay raise, spare as it was.

At first, the men were surly about the results. But soon, everything was back to normal. We had more food to eat, which seemed to calm everyone down. Roji, however, did not recover. He'd had very high hopes for the bargaining, and the poor settlement put a final end to any hope he had of a better life. He returned home only to spend a night or two, followed by another absence. He reappeared again for a few days. It was difficult knowing how much food to prepare. It was difficult to create space for him in my heart.

I tried to talk to Roji about the future. "Roji, what name would you want for the baby if it is a boy or what name for a girl? Maybe your grandmother's name? You once told me you had a special bond with her."

"A girl, why would you think it would be a girl? My family is all boys."

"Yes, that is true. So, what for a boy's name? Tell me several, and we can mull them over together until the birth."

"Oh, Ueme, quit pestering me about the baby. I am so tired of you saying this cucumber will be good for the baby, and this fish will make the baby smart. Can't we eat a meal without such stupid ideas?"

"I am concerned to eat proper foods so the baby will be healthy." I had no idea the level of disgust he felt toward me.

"I think you just want the extra attention!" At that, Roji got up and left the cottage.

I no longer looked for him when he was gone. I knew where he was. He was not fishing on the beach but behind one of those closed doors past the bachelors' barracks and the store. He missed many days at work. I questioned him because his pay was so low, sometimes lower than mine. He never answered me. He barely acknowledged me except to vent his anger.

"I don't have to put up with you questioning me!" And he was out and down the steps.

The baby was kicking, and the thought of greeting this little person was keeping me somewhat cheerful.

One evening, when Roji was sleeping next to me, I said, "Oh, Roji, this baby is quite a samurai. Feel my stomach to see how he is kicking."

Roji answered with a grunt and turn of his head. He was not interested.

That night, I had a hard time sleeping, and when I fell asleep, the Moon Princess was gliding across my floor. The door was open, and light from the full moon spilled across to the foot of my futon. She was smiling and turned around and around in a sort of graceful dance. But what was astonishing was that, each time she turned, her face became the face of my mother, and then back to the Moon Princess again. I wanted to get up and touch my mother, but I could not move. My arms laid at my sides as if not connected to me.

I awakened with the start of the birth. Kikume, Hisako-san, and Tameki all had come to help. Mori was constantly at the door, asking for another way to help us. Madam made me walk around every few hours, although I really needed help to even stand. But soon, our beautiful baby was born. At some point, Roji appeared and everyone congratulated him on his new daughter. The neighbor men took him away to have some congratulatory drinks.

I told Hisako-san about my dream.

"Oh, that is a very good sign. It means your baby will always be protected, no matter what trials come for her. Your mother has joined with the Moon Princess to make the contract for her." Hisako-san smiled.

Roji was cheerful after the birth. Perhaps in some way, he was anxious about the baby coming, and now that it was here, he was able to relax. He was home every evening and held the baby while I made the rice and vegetables for dinner. I was very tired and worked more slowly in the fields while carrying little Hatsura on my back. We decided on the name Hatsura after the Nipponese word *hatsu*, which means "first" or "beginning." One of the older women suggested it would be perfect because, depending on how it was written, it could also mean "love."

After a few months, taking care of the baby became easier, and my strength was returning. Roji enjoyed bouncing the baby up and down and holding her little finger in his. I often saw him smile while cooing at her. But now he had started to disappear again. He came in each night to hold the baby for a while. He would talk to her and tell her about our beautiful life in Five Bridges. Talking about Five Bridges would make him melancholy, and then he would disappear after those tales. He was missing more work due to his drinking. He was fined for missing work, and his pay was docked.

The days and nights were long. My only joy was holding Hatsura in my arms. Her cheeks were so chubby, and she smiled at everything. Babies are a trial. One needs so much for them. Hatsura was growing so quickly I had a hard time keeping up with clothing for her. Luckily, my friends all shared their baby things, and Hatsura never went without anything. I was feeling the strain of caring for her on my own. I wanted a father for her and a partner to plan a future for her.

I suppose my sadness was showing, much to my shame.

Hisako-san stopped me on my way back down the road after work one day. "How are you doing, Ueme?"

I was so determined to get all my evening chores done before I collapsed that I did not hear her.

She stepped in front of me and repeated her question. "Ueme, how are you?"

"Fine, fine. It is so good of you to ask." I did not stop walking.

"Ueme, slow down. I want to speak with you," commanded Hisako.

What? Was someone holding my arm? I was confused. As long as my routine went without interruption, I could do it. Interruptions confused me, as I must stop and think. I was annoyed.

I stopped walking and bowed my head slightly, saying, "Hisako-san, is there something you need from me?" I spoke with great annoyance in my voice. I felt shame at being disrespectful, but everything was caving in on me.

"Yes. Come into my cottage. I have arranged for Roji to eat with Mori and Kikume tonight. You can eat with me and spend some time here with your baby, relaxing. We can have a visit."

Hisako-san guided me into her cottage. Thankfully, there were only two steps up into her cottage. I did not have the energy for more. Hisako-san took the baby off my back and cradled her, giving her a moist cloth to suck on while I settled myself.

"What a good baby she is!"

"She is my joy for living," I replied.

"Good. Now tell me what is wrong." Hisako-san was very serious.

We drank tea, and I was not able to voice what was wrong. I started telling stories of my family in Nippon as a distraction. I actually did not understand what was wrong. I thanked Hisako-san profusely for the tea. I bowed and hoped I had satisfied something. She demanded I stay for some food, but I could not eat anything there. I needed to return to my routine.

Hatsura and I returned to our cottage. The evening felt strange, and I put the visit out of my mind.

Roji returned a few minutes later after Hatsura and I had already settled in for the night.

We said nothing at first. Then I said, "I had a nice visit with Hisako-san today."

"It is late. I need to sleep," was Roji's reply.

Hatsura was starting to crawl. I was frantic about keeping the cottage clean. Hatsura was not doing well on my back in the fields. I could feel her wriggling and trying to escape the little sack of material she was tied into until she fell asleep. I had to have help from my neighbor to bundle her onto my back every morning. At times, I would untie her and nurse her sitting down in the middle of a row of young cane. However, the heat was too much, and she was getting dehydrated. The other mothers warned me of this and said I must keep track of how many diapers she was using. If the count was lessening, then it meant dehydration, and that was dangerous. I was sweating so much and that was normal for me, but she had stopped sweating. It was too hot for her. At the end of the day, she would be purple with the heat.

Moreover, my back was beginning to bother me, as she was getting heavier.

I decided I needed to pay for her care at one of the mother's cottages. I sewed quilting squares in the evenings for a few minutes every night before sleep. I was able to make a game of it for Hatsura with squares and triangles of color. She held up her chubby fists to grab the squares of quilting. I marveled at her little fingers and how quickly she grasped our game of putting the squares in a pile. She would take the pile apart and then put it together again before I finished the next square. *Oh, she is smart!*

"What a smart little girl you are!"

Hatsura would look at me with a broad smile. Her eyes sparkling at her new skill. Her face was now framed with beautiful black hair shaped into bangs with a few snips of my scissors. With the extra money making a few quilts, I believed I would be able to pay for her care.

The love I felt for Hatsura was powerful. I had never experienced anything so strong. Nor had I received any love so strong. I felt I ought to talk to Roji about this. However, the stronger I felt love for Hatsura, our child, the more distant he became to me and to our existence as a family.

Thinking this was all in my head, I kept arranging words in my mind to say to Roji that would draw him into our lives. He was the father, and this was important. But the opportunity to speak seemed to evaporate after the first few words I floated out to him. He had no patience with me trying to formulate my ideas to him. His storming off down our steps was becoming the norm.

Finally, I inquired about working in the camp store on Sundays for a few hours. My need for money for food and supplies had increased, as Roji's salary and interest had decreased. Luckily, my application was accepted, and the job became mine due to my experience working with accounting at my family's business. I was figuring out how to survive. I also felt like I was running nonstop.

Chapter 32

BREAK

I do not know where the impulse came to me. But one Sunday as Roji had stopped in merely to collect some clean clothes, I grabbed his arm just as he was leaving.

"Roji, you are never here." I looked straight into his eyes.

He immediately averted his.

"So, do not tell me you wish to spend more time with me!" Roji laughed.

"Roji, what about your baby, Hatsura? Don't you care to spend time with her? We have a family now. We must discuss this." I was still holding onto his sleeve. I could feel him tugging away.

"There is nothing to discuss. You are doing a fine job. Hatsura seems healthy enough to me."

"But you are her father. You do not really act like it." I let go of his sleeve.

Roji pulled his arm back, looking at me with a sneer. "I do not need any more criticism from you. I do not need this talk." He shook his head as if to be rid of me.

"Do you want a divorce?" My words surprised me. Shame engulfed me for saying it.

"Ha, no! Hatsura is my child. This is my house. What do I want with a divorce?"

"I don't want a divorce either, I just—"

Roji cut me off. "No divorce, and that is the end of it."

The last Sunday before I was tostart working at the store, I had an unexpected visitor. Aooki, who had helped me with dehydration those first days in the field so long ago, had sought me out. "How are you doing?" she wanted to know.

I told her about my joy in motherhood and how I was managing with childcare and expenses and my upcoming job in the store.

"That is why I wanted to talk to you." She gave a slight bow. "I think you and I may have a similar problem, but I think you need help in seeing it. Since I have taken steps to help myself, I thought maybe I should be the one to help you."

My first thought was, *Is this a riddle?*

I did not understand her. Well, no wonder. We were not really close friends. I invited her to come sit and have something to eat. It was afternoon, and I had not planned on going to the sewing circle, as I had too much personal work to accomplish.

Aoki kneeled across my little table from me and flipped her hands back and forth on the table. It was an uncommon thing for someone to state something very directly. I thought to distract her by talking about how fast Hatsu was growing. Hatsura was sleeping on her futon in the corner.

"Ueme, sumi-masen, please." Aoki was insistent that I listen to her.

I clasped Aoki's hands in mine to assure her I was listening. I asked Aoki, "Please, just tell me what is bothering you."

She informed me that she had left her husband even though they had two children together. She said she had moved in with another man and was planning to divorce her husband. She'd had papers prepared for it.

I pulled my hands away from hers as if they were on fire. I started to shake. To leave Roji would be the act of a disloyal wife. A samurai's duty is always to loyalty first. Unhappy wives would commit hara-kiri before bringing such disgrace upon a family. And what—had Roji said something about our "talk" to others in the camp?

But then, was I a samurai? No. My mother had stressed how important being a merchant was. I was married to a merchant. I was more merchant. But a wife's duty was to family. And family meant husband. Roji didn't act like a husband, but that didn't allow me to be disloyal. But surely something was wrong. I remembered my mother saying a woman had a right to be treated well—and my obachan saying loyalty above everything else. A wife must remember a man had hardships. It was a wife's duty to understand.

But me. I had hardships. I was trying to think what my mother would have said in this situation. I wanted to see her face, but the more I thought about this, the more I could only see a blur in front of me.

Aoki shook my hands, stirring me from my thoughts. "Ueme, are you hearing me?

"Now, this is important. The husband is the only one who can file for divorce. It is important that you can get Roji to agree to it. I had to threaten embarrassment to my husband, to shame him about his behavior to the rest of the camp for him to sign the papers." Aoki released her hands from mine.

"Your hands are shaking!" She said this as she put her hands firmly on top of mine.

I pulled away.

"See, this is it. It strikes a chord in you, doesn't it? Roji is horrible to you. He is not in the marriage or the family. He spends all his time away. He makes things harder for you because he is in debt and does not give enough money for you and the baby to live." She took a deep breath as she stared into my eyes.

Then she continued, "I know this is true. We all know this is true. Leave him. He has already left you. When was he here last? Weeks ago? You have a right to a good man. You are a good woman." She grabbed my hands, which were balled into little fists in my lap. She squeezed my hands and then stood up.

"He refused to talk about divorce. He will not do it." I looked up at her with tears streaking down my cheeks.

At the door to my cottage, she stood with the sunlight shining all around her so her face was in shadow to me. "Please think about this. There must be some way to make him agree to this. He can be shamed into it. Ask the union president. He has power over the men."

"You know there is someone else in the camp here who does love you." She smiled with warmth toward me. Could everybody see how Michiru helped me often, bringing me water? How we smile at each other? I thought my feelings were secret. Oh, feelings would have a way out!

She stood silently for a while and then said, "You know all this complication about divorce is due to us being subjects of the emperor. We are still Nipponese under the law. The law is old-fashioned. Here in the camps we are changing out of necessity."

She turned and walked down the steps. My short curtain hanging at top of my door painted with images of Mount Fuji waved in the wind as she left. I started to cry, and I couldn't stop. Then Hatsura woke up and started to cry. It was the worst Sunday I had ever spent in Hawaii paradise.

That night, I could not sleep. Ito's last letter to me had implored me to be strong. I was being strong. I was about to hold two jobs. I was raising my daughter with no help from Roji. How else to be strong?

I walked to the doorway. I opened the door and let the moonlight in. Where was my Moon Princess now? Could she help me figure out the riddle of life? What were my desires as an emerging woman?

Did I even have the right to think of myself as an emerging woman in this hard place? This place where the sun beat down, where the red soil colored everything? Where I had a husband but did not have a husband?

Were things so bad that all saw it but not me? Why did Aoki feel the need to speak to me? My mother's words from long ago came to me. *Sometimes we have to stand aside to see the truth.*

I walked down the steps and into the dirt road. I turned to look back at the cottage. I looked at the cottage next to mine up the hill, and I looked to the cottage next to mine down the hill. My cottage was clean and neat. My cottage was—

And then it hit me. I was saying *my cottage*. But that was the clue. I was saying *my*, not *our*. I wanted my future to have an *our*. I wanted there to be *true feeling* in my life. Turmoil distilled into a stillness within me, turning yet into a flow of warmth surrounding me. The edges of my being softened. A decision made itself known from somewhere outside my own self. I felt the moonlight cover me. The heaviness of the future with Roji released itself. Just as the worm having transformed itself leaves the cocoon, I left the marriage. Calmly, entering my cottage, I lay back on my futon and slept.

Midweek, I brought Hatsura to her new daycare. She could now walk with support from me holding her hand and, in fact, insisted on walking everywhere. We walked together up the hill. Hatsu's hair was long and shone silky black in the sun. Her cheeks were rosy and so big I had to protect her from the unwanted tweaks from all her admirers. After getting her settled with distractions of a new toy, I left her, with mixed feelings of sadness and gratitude that I had somewhere safe to leave her.

I walked up the road to the wagon that took us to the field. I looked at no one, and I spoke to no one all day. At lunch, I was quiet. It seemed everyone was quieter.

After the work cart delivered us back to our dirt road and I had picked up Hatsura, I walked back to the cottage. With Hatsura in my arms, I entered the door with purpose. I took off my work clothes and brushed them down in the backyard. I washed the red dirt off my body. I washed my hair and combed it dry and fastened it into a chignon of the style we used to admire in Five Bridges.

I washed and dressed Hatsura in a little cotton kimono. Hatsura was gurgling and playing with my hairpins. I had earlier pulled out my kinsha silk kimono from my chest now residing at Hisako's, and now I put it on. Carefully wrapping it around me, I secured it with my brocade obi. As I was doing this, I remembered how, just a few years ago, my mother and Madam Iwata had helped me to dress quickly for Haru's unexpected betrothal visit. No tears. I was a modern woman living in a new land. I would never have dreamed back then that I would be the woman I was now.

With Hatsura strapped onto my back crumpling the precious silk of my last kimono, I stepped out of my cottage and walked down the road. Wearing clean white tabis with my sandals, I was aware that my tabi socks were fast becoming stained red with the dust of the road. I kept telling myself to concentrate on the larger, more important issue. Concentration, one point concentration. There in front of me was the barracks that housed the bachelors' quarters. I looked straight ahead. I was afraid to talk to anyone.

Gratefully, no one even noticed me. I walked around to the side near the Eucalyptus woods that edged Michiru's garden. He was there bent over, hoeing a line of red dirt. I prayed, *Thank you ancestors for making him be here at this time.*

I walked over to the edge of the garden nearest him. I stood before him. I could feel Hatsu's hands clutching my chignon and pulling it down and undoing the bun. *No worries. My hair is not important.*

Maintain your concentration. My shadow covered Michiru's hoe and arms. He looked up. His face made me want to cry, but I held firm.

"Michiru, I need a new husband. I would be honored to have you as my husband," I said firmly.

Astonished, he straightened himself carefully. Slowly, he picked out his words. "Ueme, I have been waiting for the proper moment to ask you. But now, you have asked me!"

There was silence. He dusted off his shirt and placed his feet squarely in front of me. He cleared his throat. With a voice as gentle as the little lapping waves of the ocean, he spoke. "I am honored to be your new husband. My cottage is almost ready for you and Hatsura to move in."

I replied, barely able to stand with all my emotion, "That is fine. Until it is ready, we will live in mine."

I turned and walked back up the road. Hisako-san met me at my cottage. She said, "I will stay here with you until Michiru moves in."

Apparently, I was wrong in thinking that no one noticed me.

That evening, Michiru came and knocked on my door carrying a box of his belongings. I opened the door and pulled him inside. We hugged and cried together for a long time, forgetting the presence of Hisako and Hatsura.

Then Hisako-san said, "I am taking the baby for overnight, and I will see you both in the morning."

I made us tea and served it in my porcelain cups on my little table covered with a piece of silk from my trunk. Michiru and I talked, laughed, cried, held each other tightly, and finally fell asleep.

I slept like I had not slept in a year. It was amazing how one's whole body and mind can relax when in the presence of someone with whom you hold a sacred trust, with someone who shares your true feelings. In the morning, realizing how much sleep I'd had, I felt the presence of my ancestor's protection.

The next morning, I dealt with the divorce and marriage issues. I did not go to the field. I talked with the union president, Mr. Sato, about my circumstance. He said he would make sure Roji caused no problems. His drunkenness had brought shame to the whole community. Mr. Sato said he would send someone over as soon as possible to collect Roji's futon and his meager belongings.

There was no money to be divided. The one problem was that Roji's debts might be entailed to me. I decided we would deal with those legalities later. The president advised me what forms I needed to fill out for the divorce.

Michi would take care of the marriage. We planned to go to the Buddhist priest together that afternoon. By evening, all was accomplished. Michi and I were unceremoniously but happily married.

Roji came by later and just stood in the road staring at the cottage. I came out of the door and asked if he wanted to talk. He continued to stare. He was good at not speaking.

I explained that we would be moving into Michi's cottage by the end of the week. That weekend, I witnessed another woman carrying a satchel into my old cottage. Roji was not overly sentimental.

Chapter 33

NEW BEGINNINGS

We were in our new cottage. This cottage was two doors away from Tameki and Aduki and their little boy, Riku. Riku treated Hatsura as if she were his baby sister. They were very charming together. It was convenient to have babies able to play with each other.

The new cottage was full of happiness and joy. I felt I had never known such joy and thanked the ancestors daily in my prayers. Michi was very industrious, earning money with small carpentry jobs for the plantation, as well as for any of the workers and their families. He made friends in the new Filipino camp on the road below us on the mountain. Everywhere we walked together, people stopped and asked his advice and help. This made me so proud. He was a good stepfather to Hatsura. He spoiled her with love, attention, and little toys he made for her.

Michi created a little heaven in our cottage. With his knowledge of plants, he created a meditation garden for us, with special trees, a fragrant plumeria, a luscious tree fern, an ohia's with its red needle flowers. None were like those in Nippon, but they had their own beauty. We had a kitchen area with a worktable and shelves and cupboards. Michi said we would recreate our Nipponese lives as much as possible. He was making the kitchen like what his mother had back in Kumamoto. I did not know if that was accurate, as our kitchen here was only a corner of the room. His mother's farmhouse kitchen had been quite large to fit at least four women working at once.

Michi smiled and hummed tunes while he worked. There had always been a new flower for me atop the bucket of water each morning. It had become our tradition. That flower every morning opened my heart and filled it to bursting.

Some Sundays, I took Hatsu to spend time with Roji. He now lived in our old cottage with the woman who had been his prostitute. They did not take good care of the cottage, and it pained me to see how they neglected the garden behind it. Roji always waited on the steps just after the noon meal for our approach. The woman never came out of the cottage when I arrived.

Hatsu was always happy to see her otasan. He often had a piece of sugar cane for her to suck on. I asked him to give her more healthy treats, such as dried nori seaweed. But he would turn away and take Hatsu into the cottage whenever I spoke. I worried about the cleanliness of their cottage, but there was nothing to be done about it.

Sometimes when the sewing circle was finished at Hisako-san's cottage, I would walk back down the road to collect Hatsu from the old cottage. Then we would visit awhile next door with Kikume, Mori, and their new baby to catch up with each other. Kikume now took in mending and laundry for the bachelors instead of working in the fields. She was still quite weak from the pregnancy, but her new job seemed to agree with her. We usually found her in the back with a large tub of water boiling away, ready for her next batch of laundry. Mori would take over while we sat and had a chat together. Sometimes, she had a new little cloth doll for Hatsu. Hatsu now had a whole family made by Kikume. They sat on top of Hatsu's rolled futon every day when not actively in play.

I protested at all the gifts. But Kikume said, "What, you refuse gifts from her auntie?"

I'd had to stay home myself due to an accident in the fields. I tripped over a bundle of cane stalks during the last Kona winds. I had been so dehydrated I was dizzy and did not see the bundle lying there. Falling on my shoulder, I heard something tear inside it. I'd had to wear my arm in a sling for a few months. The doctor insisted I not carry Hatsu, or I may have permanent damage. Luckily, this happened after Hatsu had already taken her first steps.

Hatsu was on Michi's lap while he was reciting an old tale about the Moon Princess. I was in the garden collecting some vegetables for a nice pot of kombu stew when I spied an especially long, beautiful purple eggplant. I put a small piece of cloth over the eggplant and danced her around Hatsu pretending to be the Moon Princess. Hatsu reached up to grab the makeshift "doll" and just naturally stood up from her comfortable seat and grabbed the doll, clasping it to her heart, cooing to it. She was truly the child of the moon!

In the fields and now at the store, I was paying attention to all the "women talk," while sipping water, while eating, while riding the wagon to and from the fields. How were parents raising their babies? What were the hopes and dreams? There was a one-room schoolhouse, but was it quality education? And what about university? I thought back to my mother and how insistent she was that all the girls to go to school to learn as much as possible. What chance would my Hatsu have here?

"We are sending Teru to the missionary school. It is very expensive to get all the clothing together that he will need." It was at lunch, and I was overhearing some women talk about their children. The conversation put me on high alert. They were talking about education.

"My son cried all the time he was there. We had to bring him home."

"How can you do this? Your husband is so sick he falls behind his team in the fields every day. How much longer will he last?"

"We are doing this precisely because my husband is sick. We do not want this life for Teru. My son will not work in the fields."

"But if your child gets so homesick that you have to bring him home?" The sadness in the voice seeped into my heart.

"We have been preparing Teru for this day since he was born. He knows he is of a prominent Kumamoto family, and it is his duty to study at the boarding school in Honolulu. He must carry on our proud name. He knows his duty." The firmness of tone indicated a strength of supreme will. May the son carry that will with him.

I was listening to a conversation in a group of women next to me as we ate our lunch. I finished my rice and pickled vegetables and planned to sit near these women in the wagon on the way back to the camp so I might learn more of how people could educate their children in this foreign land.

In the evening, Michi was about to leave our cottage to help with the community garden. I had to talk about my fears. I'd been having nightmares about the future for us. We'd accumulated debt at the store even though we both worked two or three jobs. I hated debt. It was the ruin of my family in Five Bridges. I hated to do this, but I planned to sell more of my fabric from my chest to pay off some of the debt. It was a sacrifice I wanted to make. I needed to talk to Michi. Thankfully, Michi did not shy away from talking about hard things. He always took on whatever troubles came his way and never blamed anyone. Maybe it was his farmer background and connection to nature that gave him such a strong spirit.

"Michi, I must have some time to talk with you. I have many worries. Can you stay home this evening?" My voice carried a plaintive tone. I wished I could always be sweet, as a wife should be. The rules for behavior in good Confucian marriages were very difficult to uphold in this crude land.

"Ueme, I know something is bothering you. But tonight the men are discussing some future issues with the sanitation of this camp. It is important. Perhaps we will have time this Sunday." Michi bowed low in apology and exited our cottage.

Hatsu had been asleep for a while. I bent over her sleeping face and leaned closer to feel her breath on my cheek. My heart softened, and tears rolled down my cheeks. "My dear child, I want you to know how beautiful life can be, how it once was for me in my childhood." Truly, the ancestors had a plan for her that was better than this sugar plantation.

"Can I speak about my worries here?" I was desperate to get some advice to guide my life and secure a good future for Hatsu.

"Where else can any woman speak so freely?" Tameki answered me and gestured with her hand, circling the room where we were all working on quilt squares.

"I have been trying to have a discussion about Hatsu's future, and my husband finds excuses to avoid talking with me." I felt embarrassed to say something unflattering about Michi.

"Oh, he is so handsome. Do not bother talking. Just get on with it!" another woman said as a few giggles escaped from others in the room.

"Pay no attention to those giggles. Just jealousy and envy, the burden of all good fortune," Hisako-san counseled me. "Now what do you have that worries you so, Ueme?"

"Hatsu is my worry. What future does she have? What education will she be able to get?" I noticed the silence.

"She will be like all our children. She will learn to read and write in our schoolhouse. Perhaps she will be able to work in Honolulu instead of in the fields," another woman offered.

How could I say that is not good enough? To be a woman who carried airs here was to break the bonds of community.

I continued, "I hear that some families send their sons to the missionary school in Honolulu for an education. Some boys are able to go to university on the mainland on missionary scholarships. I wonder what are the opportunities for our girls?" I tried to phrase it so as not to offend.

"I do not think the missionary school gives scholarships for girls," Hisako-san replied. "You may have to pay for her tuition there."

"That is a cruel hardship for a child, especially a daughter to go away to school," a woman sewing with her head down during this discussion offered.

"Oh, perhaps we would be able to send her to secondary school when she is older. Maybe by that time, we will have saved up enough money." I now felt as if I was pleading with the forces of fate.

"Ha. At the rate our wages go up, she will be a married woman before you save any money for her education." A woman in the far corner had the final word.

"Well, the plantation owners all send their children to schools in Honolulu, even the girls. That is where they make their good marriages." This woman sat up straight from her sewing, looking at all of us as if we could make things more equal by pointing out the injustices.

"May we talk about something else? What about sanitation? The men have been talking about pressuring the company to install a drainage field and sewage pipes," one of the women said. She was new to the camp and had come from Honolulu, where they had a sewer system with toilets, and all buildings were connected. I agreed it would be great to get rid of all the outhouses.

"Ueme, are you planning the music for our next festival? You must sing again this time. My daughter enjoys singing with you at those events. Perhaps you can teach her a little folk tune on the samisen?" The woman wanted her daughter to have music lessons. When had we had the time for these things? No time or energy.

We continued our sewing until time the time had gone, and we returned to our cottages having completed another quilt for our community hardship chest.

⟶ ✾ ⟵

Michi looked at me with delight. He had some secret. His eyes were dancing, but his mouth was straight and severe.

I asked him to go get some water for our family bathing, but he just stood there.

"Oh, you mock me with such a stare! Agh, you tempt fate by being so mysterious! What is this prize?" I wanted him to show his secret.

He said, "Ueme, you must take the bucket."

He stretched out his arm holding the bucket just a little too high for me.

"All right. I can do that!" And I jumped to take hold of its handle. The bucket tipped, and something red fell out.

"What is this? It is silk. It is shantung from China! How did you get this?"

Michi smiled. "Pick it up and look at it."

I did so and saw that I was holding a little red kimono sized for a three-year-old girl. Tears came to my eyes. "Hatsu will not fit this for another two years, Michi." I smiled at his merry eyes.

"I know you were worried about Hatsu, and I have a friend who goes to Honolulu often to make trades. He made a trade for me. The same person who has a little girl who is now too tall for the kimono wanted toys for her. I made a few toys in exchange." Michi was looking at me with a little smile. "Is it good? Will she be able to wear it?"

"Oh, it is beautiful, and she will be able to wear it. Such good fortune comes in many different ways. You bring us good fortune, Michi." I reached over to hold onto him as his arm encircled me.

I thought to myself, *Just take things day by day. Goodness always comes seeking those who are receptive.*

Michi was making tea for us while I examined all the stitches and the lovely design of chrysanthemums on the silk. Hatsu cooed in her sleep as if she knew she had just received her very first silk kimono, an important day for any proper Nihonjin, Japanese, girl.

Chapter 34

A SINGLE STEP

The Kona winds were over. We had suffered so in the heat. The lunas did not make allowances for bad weather, as if we were just machines that worked in rain, in heat, in sickness. However, we said nothing to each other about it. The misery of the strike was too close in our memories, so we just carried on.

Now with the trade winds blowing again, we could feel a bit of comfort when we took off our thick work clothing. For the last month, the heat and humidity had been so unbearable, we'd only felt relief when soaking in the community bathing pool.

We had our Obon Moon festival during the awful weather days. I was proud of all the activities and music and drama displays created from all our local talent. Michi and I sent out boats in the ocean current toward the moon with our parents' names on them. Both my obachan and otasan had died in the last year. Knowing I would never see a letter from my obachan again, I felt the occasion more somber this year. However, with our little Hatsu, we made a great fuss with all the treats and games and music. Even Roji seemed happy, joining us for some of the activities.

The first I heard of the terrible news was at the sewing circle.

"Ueme, take care about your Roji. I have heard that he is talking with the headman of your old village," the bold one said to me while everyone was getting settled in their places with needle and thread.

"Whatever do you mean?" I had never been close to this woman, but she had never done me harm.

"Your village is Five Bridges, am I not correct?" She looked at me and lowered her voice. "He has received a large piece of mail from an official of the village."

"How can that concern me? We are divorced. He has no power over me now." I felt confident this was gossip that had no meaning for me.

The next morning as we were being carried by the wagon to the field, I had more time to think about Roji and Five Bridges. I remembered that Ito had said Roji's father was furious I had divorced his son. Ito said she let it be known in the village that Roji had become a drunk and an absentee father. However, Roji's father still felt it was all my fault. There was much gossip in the village. I dismissed all that news as being so far from me; what did it matter?

As we walked to our respective rows in the field, Aoki came up to me. "Ueme, I am worried for you."

"What do you mean?"

"Come talk to me at lunch," she said as she departed for a more distant row of cane stalks.

There was a huge rainfall at lunch. We were all scattered, looking for shelter. I forgot about finding her.

That evening, Michi looked at me and asked me to put Hatsu down on the futon. I tucked her in and sang her an autumn song about little birds.

Michi seemed impatient. I took delight in singing to my little girl. I would not be rushed.

"Michi, why are you looking so impatient tonight?" I stood up to walk over to him.

Suddenly, Michi grabbed hold of me encircling me in his arms. I struggled to get away from this furious hold. "Listen to me, Ueme.

Something terrible has happened. I must tell you now. I have verified the facts of it with our community elders." He was holding me tightly and crying.

"Whatever can be the matter that you are so emotional over it?" I tried to free my hands from his arms.

"Ueme, Roji has gotten permission from your village headman and the elders of Five Bridges to take Hatsura away from you."

"What? That is impossible. I will go talk to him. He doesn't really want the care of her. He is too lazy and unfeeling."

"He has purchased a ticket to send Hatsura back to Nippon to be raised by his sister." Michi's grasp on me loosened a little so he could look at my face.

"It cannot be true! It cannot be true." I pushed Michi away. "Who says this? What mean gossip is this?"

"I verified the facts. Someone is coming tonight to give you the papers from the headman." Michi's voice was cracking now.

"But I am her mother. He cannot take her away from her mother!" I slumped to the floor.

Michi's face contorted into tears. "It is about me. I am so sorry, Ueme. Roji's family argues that the child cannot be safe in the house of a stepparent. A stepparent cannot be trusted to be kind to the child."

"Oooh, that is old dogma. And I am her mother—what about me? I am here! How can anybody be better than her own mother?"

"Ueme, you are a woman. In Nihon, the man is everything. The father owns the children. The mother has few rights. Even here, where the Americans rule rather ambiguously, the father has all the legal rights."

It was then that I remembered those old men arguing about the constitution in my parents' house. One man was trying to represent his wife's view that the women should be given more rights. The other men ignored his statement as trivial.

Hisako-san had entered our cottage. She went over to Hatsu, who was sleeping soundly.

Madam spoke very quietly to me. "Ueme, Michi asked me to come here to be with you when Roji's representative comes to deliver the legal papers. I will help you in any way I can."

I stood up straight and collected my thoughts. "I must not let Roji see any weakness on my part. I must put on my silk kimono to receive this document. Michi, please make some tea for the guests who are coming."

Michi looked at me aghast. "We need do nothing for these people!"

Hisako-san added, "Roji will not be coming. He has not shown his face during this whole affair. He has representatives. He is too much of a coward."

Michi spoke. "I do not understand this. Surely, men have more rights, but you rarely see them exercised in this manner. As much as a marriage dissolves, the father wants his children to have their mother. There is compassion for the child. Perhaps there is an issue with money? If so, we will give up everything to keep our Hatsu!"

Hisako-san replied, "I think it is a matter of honor. Ueme divorced him. She has taken his honor. In Roji's mind, and maybe even for the family in Five Bridges, she must pay. It is not about the child. It is not about money. It is about revenge." Hisako did a slight bow with this pronouncement.

"They will be here soon." Michi put some coal into the hibachi for the tea.

"So, we will act with dignity and politeness." I opened my chest and unfolded my silk kimono. "Hisako-san, will you please help me with my hair? I shall put it into a stylish chignon."

"Certainly, Ueme. We will make you look your best. Michi bring me a cloth and a bowl of water so I can help Ueme."

Michi fumbled with the water ladle but managed to splash out some water into a bowl and some into the bronze kettle. He stoked the fire with nervous jabs of a stick while Madam and I combed my unwilling hair into a chignon.

"Madam, I fear my eyes have water in them and I cannot see well. Please look in my trunk for a hair trim to pin into my chignon."

Hisako-san cast about through items in the chest and finally pulled out the ornament. It was fastened to my hair. Madam adjusted my obi. Sadly, I was remembering a much happier time when I hastened to get ready for an impromptu important event. Women helped each other in joy, and we helped each other in despair. I felt a tug at my heart knowing that Madam Iwata would be heartbroken to see me in these circumstances. Which life was real? My life in Five Bridges was the dream.

There was a knock at the door. I looked to see the tea items assembled properly on our little table. Michi had found some sweets my friend Ito had sent from Nippon last month. He placed them in a pretty dish on the table. He knew me so well.

Michi opened the door. Three men stood at the door and asked for me. I stood back from the door and welcomed them to my home. I bowed very slightly making sure that they did not receive any undue honor from me.

"Honorable sirs, I understand you have come to see me on business. Please come in and sit to have tea with us. We can discuss your business after tea."

The camp headman, who only last month had stood at my door pleading for help with another music event for our community, now stood here about to steal my child. He spoke. "Madam, we do not need to take tea with you. We only came to deliver this document."

He bowed and extended his hand, holding a packet of papers.

I refused to lift my hand. "I insist on a civility here, gentlemen. You owe me that," I said, glaring at each one of them who had benefitted from my music, my sewing, or my music lessons for a child. I thought to myself how quickly one can sink to the bottom in status. I refused this status.

The men looked at Madam and Michi questioningly. Michi and Madam did not return looks but sat at the head corners of the table.

I waited until the men were seated, each one to a side. Then I sat at the head between my two supports. I could hear Michi's breathing, a nervous rhythm. I decided to not hear it. Madam at my other side was as calm as a stone. She sat rigidly, coldly staring at each man, slowly, one after the other. Michi put the bronze teapot on the table. I wanted to stretch this moment out forever. As long as I did not have those papers, Hatsu was safe with me.

"Honorable sirs, please take a few sweets. They are from my town of Five Bridges. They make the best rice sweets there. Fumigato sweets are famous in the area. Included with the package is always a poem from Basho or one of the ancient poets. I would like one of you to read the poem for all of us to ponder." I handed the small paper to the headman.

"Mono ieba, Kuchibiru samushi, Aki no kaze." The headman turned red with shame and bowed his head at those biting words.

I wondered at the perfect words that only happened to be in this box from Ito. Surely the ancestors had a hand in this message! I willed this moment to stretch out longer.

"How profound, gentlemen. Shall we think a moment on these words? And I wonder to whom do the words of the poem refer? *When a thing is said, The lips become very cold, Like the autumn wind.*"

I then picked up the plate of sweets and passed it to the men. "Take a sweet and then choose a word to say to me." I was ordering the men. Looking at them, I saw them stiffen. Ah, to be ordered by a mere woman.

Michi picked up the cue. "Ueme is not asking much here, considering your dirty task. Think of a kind word!"

Each man then picked up a sweet and, holding it with both hands, looked down and one after the other said, "To good fortune."

The headman started to rise.

"You come here to insult my hospitality?" I was shaking, fear and anger bubbling up.

Madam reached over to hold my hand. Madam spoke.

"Gentlemen, please have some tea." She held the teapot and poured out the steaming liquid.

We all had our cups in front of us. Michi picked up his cup and, holding it with both hands, bowed. "May the fates bestow only good upon us."

I drank my cup first, and everyone followed. All cups were then settled on the table.

"Gentlemen, you may put your package on the table and do leave quietly. There is a baby sleeping here." I spoke slowly and with a voice as cold and hard as I could muster.

As the door opened for their exit, we saw my dear friends, Tameki, Kikume, and Aoki lined up frowning at the men as they left and the chorus of them saying, "Shame, may you feel shame."

Tameki entered as the door closed. "Ueme, I will not stay. I just want to let you know we think Roji and these men are wrong. Terrible men!" She came over to me and knelt down to hold my hands.

She looked around the room and then stood to leave. The emotion weighed heavily in the air. I could see she was discomforted. She stood to leave, and as she closed the door behind her, said, "May this little cottage never again see such a sad day!"

Hisako-san picked up Hatsu and brought her to me. Dear little Hatsu, she knew little how this day changed her life.

Hisako-san said, "Think not of tomorrow. Enjoy your baby right now."

I held Hatsu, trying not to wake her. Tears rolled down my cheeks. What was this fate that had befallen Hatsu and me? I got up and walked outside, holding my daughter tightly. The sky was dark blue, the stars were out, and the moon was just a sliver. Within minutes, the darkness increased and swamped my baby and me.

I could not get out of my bed the next day. I slept all morning, trying to hold Hatsu near me. She walked around, stopping here and there to look and touch things. She brought me little gifts offered in her little chubby hands to cheer me up. Hisako-san returned and encouraged me to drink tea. The day passed slowly. I walked with Hatsu down to the cliff edge to stare at the ocean, to imagine Five Bridges just on the other side of the vast ocean. How could its power stretch here, to this distant island?

Michi returned from the fields. Hisako-san made our evening meal. When the meal was done, Michi asked me if I would allow him to see the papers. I nodded a yes. I could not bear to read them. He carefully unfolded them and spread them on the table. He picked up the first sheet and turned his body away from me so I could not see his reaction to the words.

I recited some bedtime stories for Hatsu and laid her down on my futon. I sat over near Hisako-san and leaned into her for strength. I stared at Michi's back and started to shiver. I could not stop shivering.

Madam said, "I know it is hard to eat, but you must. You must eat in order to steady your nerves. You will need to have more strength than usual to get through this trial that the ancestors have sent you."

I replied, "I fear that I will not be able to hold anything in my stomach. It is not my desire to be weak."

Hisako spoke, "Michi, when you have read the important parts. Please summarize what the papers say. We need to hear what is in the documents. Ueme needs to hear it as soon as possible."

I thought to myself how much Hisako sounded like my obachan, giving orders and creating timelines for events. I watched as Madam heated more water in the kettle and poured it into the teapot. She poured each of us a cup. She tapped Michi on the shoulder. He put his sleeve to his face in a wiping motion and turned to face the table. I wished I had not understood that movement. I was trying to contain my emotions.

Michi gestured for us all to drink our tea. He was composing himself in order to be able to speak. I picked up my cup, but somehow it fell and spilled onto my kimono. Madam reached for a cloth and handed it to me. I replaced the cup on the table and said, "Michi, please talk to us."

"Ahh, well, the document is very wordy, actually quite pompous," Michi explained.

"I expected that. The headman of my village is like that. I think he has finally found a way to rise in status over the Oyama family."

Madam looked at me.

Michi continued, "They list numerous citations of Nippon family law that bolster Roji's claim to the child. There is a timeline for the transfer of Hatsu to Roji's family. Hatsu is to be raised by Roji's older sister in a neighboring village close to Five Bridges. She has two other children, both boys, and they welcome a daughter."

I gasped. "Hatsu really is to go away from here?"

Madam put her hand over my mouth and her arm around my shoulders. "Ueme, you must be calm in front of your child. Her memories cannot be of screams and emotions."

Ah, Obachan again.

One month, we had one month. How to live?

Oh, Nihon! How I have loved you, my homeland. And yet you have reached out to me only to betray me. We were supposedly under the emperor's law here. But the reality was we were in two lands and not wholly in one or the other. And now my loyalty to Nihon and its laws for women were not working for me. We obeyed plantation law for our working lives, and marriages were outside of this jurisdiction.

I went out and walked up the hill. What was I to do with my arms and legs, my hands and feet, my head, my face? I felt a blackness inside me that enveloped my world. When I looked around me, the blackness edged my view, crept in, threatened to extinguish all vision. I slumped to the red dust of the road. My hands folded themselves, and I sat there as a Buddha looking down at the camp, imagining the sea just beyond. We beings had such little control in this world.

The sun set, and dusk became night. I followed the lights in the cottages back to the center of the camp. The guard blew his whistle for lights out. I hurried back to our cottage.

"Michi, do you think I could hire a lawyer?" We were lying down and I was still awake. I slept very little and had had trouble working in the fields with the lack of rest. My shoulder had healed, but with this new news, I felt it hurting again.

Michi rolled over and mumbled an answer. "What defense would you give that would help, Ueme?"

"I am a good mother and provider. Roji isn't," I said firmly.

Michi sighed. "I didn't want to tell you, but Roji charges you with infidelity in the marriage."

I was incensed. "But he was the one who was unfaithful. You and I did nothing until he had left Hatsu and me."

Sighing, he continued. "Ueme, he states he has witnesses in the camp who saw us together many times."

"But we only talked." I was feeling cornered. A wife's position was completely defined. The husband could do anything.

Hatsu had started talking. I told her many times a day how much her mother loves her. I pointed to myself and said, "Remember, I am your mother."

Hisako-san heard me one day and scolded me. "Ueme, you are making it harder for Hatsu. She is about to be adopted into another family. The more insistent you are, the larger the wall you make for her to break down to accept her new family."

I started to sob inside. I was being asked to give up my daughter even while I still had her with me. Where did my pleas to the ancestors go? I had visited our little temple daily and burned incense in devotion. I had meditated every morning before I dropped off Hatsu at her caregivers. I had chosen my thoughts carefully, careful to be positive and kind, to create the honorable person who deserved to keep her daughter. What had I done to deserve this cruelty?

Kikume walked up to me in the field. "Ueme, are you eating? You have gotten so thin. I do not think you are healthy! Come share my lunch with me. I made some rice balls with umeboshi and some eel. I brought extra just to feed you. Please share with me." Kikume's pleas hit me in my heart. People did care for me. I couldn't be all bad. I said as much to Kikume.

"What? Hatsu is not being taken from you because you are bad. Roji is bad. He is a sorry excuse for a man. He wants to think he is better than you. But we all know what kind of man he is. He carries the weight of our disgust on his shoulders. Do you see how he walks with hunched shoulders now? He makes his own burden."

I sent a letter to Ito as soon as I could compose myself to think of words to say. I told her of the situation and asked her to help me, to see if she had any way to sway the headman's judgment. As soon as I had mailed the letter, I received one from her, too soon for her to have received my letter. Of course, it was a small village; everyone in Five Bridges knew about Hatsu's adoption before I did.

Ito had made pleas to the headman. But unfortunately, she did not get along with her father-in-law. He barely let Ito talk about my case at all with him. He did not like independent women. He was a very backward person, and Ito had no good words for him. Ito promised to try to go visit Roji's sister. She sent her love and care. (She knew not to send pity, as we three always said we never wanted to be a woman anyone pitied. We were strong women.)

There were only a few days left. My heart was so heavy my feet moved ever more slowly. Hatsu was happy. She liked to play with the little doll I'd made her out of scraps of cloth. I packed a chest with items for her to use as she grew up. Her futon would be packed on top the morning of her departure. I worried about her safety on the journey across the Pacific.

Tameki and Kikume came over for tea and to comfort me on a Sunday afternoon. I had not gone to the quilting bee for this last month. They brought some gifts from the women. They had collected money for me. I was shocked I had been considered a charity case. I had incurred more obligations. Tameki said I was not to think about it. This money was for Hatsu, that she would not arrive penniless to her new home.

"If I could afford it, I would pay for someone to care for Hatsu on the journey, someone beside the guardian—someone who would play with her, keep her clean and well fed." I was wringing my hands as Kikume poured the tea in our cups.

Tameki looked at my hands and exclaimed, "You will rub the skin off your hands with your worrying."

"Mama." Hatsu came over to me and patted my cheek.

"She knows something is bothering you," Tameki said.

"I am trying to hide it. I am not very good at it," I replied.

"Oh, that is foolish. How can you hide a burden so great? She is the child of your heart!" Tameki exclaimed.

"Tameki, I see you keep glancing at my chest in the corner. What are you looking at?" I questioned my friend.

"Well, I see the elaborate seal in that bronze plate at the base, that round piece of metal. It is quite elaborate."

"It is the crest for our business. This chest had been used in our family store," I replied.

"You know, it looks very old."

"It is. It belonged to my mother's mother. She traveled with it from her home village to join my grandfather's family in Five Bridges when she married. The chest was a gift from her husband." I reflected on her circumstances so long ago.

"Sometimes those old chests had secret compartments in them. Let's look at the chest more carefully." Tameki was getting excited.

Tameki pulled the chest to the middle of the floor. Hatsu toddled over to watch us. Tameki opened the chest. She stretched her arm into the chest through to the bottom.

"Oh, Ueme, come her and feel this." My friend looked like she had won a prize.

I felt in the chest where she had her hand.

"See the height of the outside and the height of the side inside?" Tameki showed me with her hands. "It's different, Ueme."

She pulled the chest over on its side. "I think these decorative pieces are the key to a secret space in the bottom."

Looking at the chest with a new perspective, I thought, Why had I not seen this before? With all the turmoil of coming to this new country and trying to get along with a difficult man, I just never had any time for contemplation. I never really looked at the trunk.

I brought over a knife to poke at the edges of the metal. "You may be right; the knife goes right past the edge of the bronze as if there is a cavity beneath it. We need to figure out how to get the medallion off."

I looked through Michi's tools and brought over a small blunt metal tool.

"Look at the design. It has some ridges in it that we can push against. Maybe it screws out." Tameki had put her eyes up close to the crest.

Using the tool, we pushed against one of the ridges at the edges and the crest appeared to turn. We kept pushing, and the crest kept rotating around and around and eventually fell out. Inside, we could see some cloth. Then Tameki poked her fingers into the hole and found a small dowel attached to the back side.

She pushed on it, and a narrow panel at the rear of the chest fell out.

We both screamed. Kikume came over to see. Hatsu ran to me. I hugged her and let her sit in my lap as I turned the chest around. I carefully pulled on the cloth that could now be seen in the rear panel. There was some thin paper covering the cloth, and as I pulled on the cloth, the paper tore.

"I am afraid to pull the cloth out further. It might tear like the paper!" I said fearfully.

"The cloth will do you no good in there. Just keep pulling slowly. The paper is doing its job protecting it," Tameki said. Kikume put Hatsu in her lap so I could have my hands free.

Very gently, I pulled on the cloth, and little by little, the fabric revealed itself. It was of the finest pink rinzu silk, a beautiful kimono, which I recognized immediately. It was the kimono, the one I had worn that afternoon before I left, the one meant as a bridal kimono for my sister-in-law, Akemi. Remembering the incident, I felt shame about my brazen actions but, at same time, happiness at my brazen actions.

"Tameki and Kikume, I recognize this. I must tell you about this kimono. There is a story here!"

"Oh, do. I cannot wait to hear it. This is the most beautiful kimono I have ever seen!" Kikume exclaimed.

I told them the story, and they looked at me with wide eyes. Tameki had a bit of an evil glint in hers. "What a devil you were!"

"I do not think your obachan packed that kimono for you," Kikume said. "She seemed rather upset with you for putting that kimono on. Who do you think packed it?"

Tameki chimed in, "Who knew about the secret compartment? Who had access to the kimono that night while everyone was asleep?

I sat down on the floor and started to cry. Hatsu walked over to me again and patted my cheek.

"What is it?" Kikume was concerned.

"My otasan, my father, must have packed this. Oh, my father did love me! He could barely speak to me while all the preparations for my leaving were going on. Oh, if only I could run and put my arms about him now."

"This is quite a gift! The more I look at this silk, the more I see the delicate design of the flowers is so beautiful." Tameki was admiring my father's gift.

"Those are wisteria blossoms," I said as I pulled the silk to my cheek, saying a silent prayer to Otasan, asking for forgiveness. Then I remembered.

"Ayeah, my sister-in-law, Akemi, did not receive her wedding kimono. I can just see all the accusations flying around that day! I must explain about Akemi. She is not a good person. I cannot say I am unhappy about her not getting this."

"Put it on!" Tameki was impatient with my emotions.

I stood up, "Well, it needs to hang out. It is quite wrinkled." I put one arm through a sleeve and then another.

Tameki grabbed the front edge and wrapped it around me. I wrapped my arms around to hold it. There had been no room in the compartment for an obi to tie the garment closed.

"The ancestors are looking down on me! You know what I am going to do with this beauty?"

Tameki smiled and said, "Yes!"

"I now have the money for a caretaker for Hatsu!" My mind was working fast.

Tameki said, "You know who would love to help you with this?"

"I will ask Hisako-san to get a buyer in Honolulu for it. This is an uncommon kimono and will bring a good price."

"No, not for just selling the kimono. She might want to go back to Kumamoto!" Kikume stretched her hands out in a gesture of wonderment!

"Oh, my heart is full. I can provide for my Hatsu." I picked up little Hatsu and twirled around and around, clasping my little moon child to my heart.

"Hatsu, we will be fine, you and I!"

That evening, I sat on the steps looking out at the fading sky. My otasan had risked great shame in hiding this kimono in the trunk for me. Our finest silks had all been spoken for at the shop. Due to the selfishness of my brother in paying his debts with our cloth, our store was on the brink of fiscal disaster. There was no other elegant silk left in our warehouse to make another such prize kimono for Brother's bride, Akeme. The House of Oyama being the foremost provider of elegant silks in Five Bridges, it would be assumed this would be our family's gift to the bride's family.

Her kimono would be missed just days after my departure, and fingers would be pointing. It would not make for an auspicious start to the marriage. The in-laws would have demanded some retribution on Father's part to save face. This one act would have surely set off a cascade effect not beneficial to the House of Oyama. But Ushio was now the head of our establishment, so the shame would be brought on him! Had Father planned that also as a teaching lesson for his son? Would Brother even understand the lesson? He did not seem to be one to honor family ties or reputation.

And where had "honor" and loyalty gotten me? I'd worked hard to save our shop. I'd worked hard to save my marriage—all in the name of honor and loyalty. Hadn't we been taught from our earliest years, we were part samurai and we needed to honor our family's name, our family's reputation? And as part merchant, we were to uphold the honor of our business, to always be honest in our dealings? If we were forthright in our business dealings, our good fortune would be certain.

Then I thought how carelessly I had treated the news of my father's death in that letter last year. I'd felt he had thrown me away and, so, had tamped down my true feelings for him, making light of his passing. We could never truly know another's trials. The gift of this kimono was his final way to show his love for me. If I could only bring him one more tray with teapot and cups to sit with him and listen to his recitation of his favorite poems or to help him trim his azaleas. We just never recognized the precious moments when we were in the midst of living them. *Oh my otasan, I wish you could know how your gift would help your grandchild, how this deed provides for her good future, for the future of one who is part Oyama.* I prayed Roji's sister would treat that family name with more honor than Roji ever had.

The day arrived for Hatsu's departure from me. She would stay for two nights in Honolulu with the guardian and the caretaker. Again, my ancestors had pulled strings for me. Hisako-san had decided she needed to go back to Nihon for a visit. She needed money for her return trip, and my kimono provided it. Hatsu went willingly with Hisako-san, who she knew so well. My fears of my baby feeling deserted were somewhat allayed. Roji sneered at what he called my maneuverings and showed no emotion on saying goodbye to his daughter. Roji had buried his heart in anger at me so deeply he was not able to feel with his heart for his own child.

The day for the ship's departure was here. We were in the fields. I knew the hour, as I had borrowed a timepiece to take with me. I dropped my spade to the ground and stood up right. Tameki yelled, "Time!"

All the women in my row and the two adjacent rows all stood and looked west toward the ocean, which we could not really see from this point. I removed my heavy straw hat and stared to the west.

Silent tears rolled down my face. I heard Kikume quietly crying. She had always had the softest heart. The luna came over to us and started to yell but saw me with my hat off and tears streaming. He knew. Everyone knew. It was the tragedy of the month in the camp. After a few minutes, we all turned back to work. I put my hat back on. Life went on. And so did the cane.

That evening, I went to the cliff edge to stare at the ocean. Michi followed me. He watched me closely now. He feared I might do something awful. He knew not what. But I'd had a plan all along. I would earn passage to Nihon. With one less mouth to feed and with my quilting and extra work part time at the mill, I would be able to get the money together in maybe a year or two. I would go back. My life was now here with Michi in Hawaii, but I would arrange to visit her as often as I could. Perhaps Roji's sister would have a soft heart on one of those visits and let my daughter return with me to live once again with Michi and me. I would not let my baby forget me. Yes, those were my thoughts until this afternoon.

This afternoon in the field, when I put my hat back on, I had been seized with a feeling of nausea. And now, standing here in my cotton hakata, which was very soft with age and many washings, my nipples hurt. I had to face it. I was pregnant. I would never go back to Nihon. As we all knew, a baby kept you in the camp.

The ocean looked blue-green with a hint of orange forming a line at the horizon. I could see the pale moon beginning to glow as the sun was sinking. It was full. The moon maiden would be vigilant over my baby tonight. I silently said my goodbye to Hatsu. In my heart, though, I knew that it would not be my final goodbye.

Michi stood behind me waiting patiently. Michi's loyalty gave me new meaning for the word, a new perspective on loyalty and honor. It had to be tempered with knowledge of facts, of character. Here in this new country, we Nihonji women were boldly changing our lives, not following traditions blindly that were perhaps detrimental to us. Perhaps the old ways from Five Bridges still reached their tentacles to us, but I had a new life with a brighter future. My daughter would be raised by a good woman, not Roji's prostitute. I could be grateful for that. And I had a good husband of sound character with an uncertain but most likely prosperous future ahead.

Michi smiled as I turned to him, this someone with whom I could lay my trust, this someone who had stature in our little camp community, this someone who loved me without payment. His arms opened wide, and I folded myself into his embrace. Leaning into his warmth, I whispered, "Michi, I have some good news for us."

He stood back away from me in surprise at good news on such a sad day. "Oh, we could use some good news. I assume it is something more than that the eggplants are ripe?" His eyes were twinkling with the joke.

"It's much better and grander. We are going to have a baby."

Michi's eyes squinted with droplets of water at the corners. "I have always dreamed of this."

We started to walk back up the hill. Silently, we prayed for good fortune for both our children.

We could make out our cottage from a distance, as it was the one with the trees tall from Michi's gardening skills, growing high above all the roofs. Our garden was prospering.

As Lao Tzu said, "A journey of a thousand miles begins with a single step."

Epilogue

Ueme, not her real name, went on to have a very full life with four more children, three boys and a girl. She had her own musical radio show. Records were made of her singing accompanied by her samisen. Several of her progeny became musicians carrying the musical gene forward. How Ueme and her daughter were separated is unknown to me. I used material from research to create a totally fictional story. She did stay in close contact with her daughter through the years.

During WWII, the Japanese cities had no food and people were starving. Her daughter's family lived in Kumamoto city and needed help. Ueme was able to get the family of her second husband, Michi in the story, to help. His family was in the countryside of Kumamoto prefecture in the agriculture business. They were able to keep her daughter's family fed through this alliance. Much later in 1989, in Japan, two descendants of the two husbands' separate families announced their betrothal- finally uniting the two families, (fictional name) Roji's family with (fictional name) Michi's, in marriage.

Ueme was able to educate her children in schools in Honolulu with scholarships provided through the missionaries. Through the sugar workers' union negotiations, along with their peers, Ueme and her husband were able to own a three-bedroom house. She lived with her son and grandchildren in that house and lived to see all her grandchildren grow to adulthood.

Unfortunately, she did endure more sadness. One of her sons, working on the west coast of the mainland, newly married, was interred in the Japanese camps during WWII. Her eldest son died serving as an American soldier in that war and her daughter's son died in the Viet Nam war.

Ueme completed her final wish and went back to Japan. She was able to spend the last year of her life finally reunited with her daughter.

Acknowledgements

I have a number of people to thank for helping me bring this book to fruition. First, I thank my daughters for they are the inspiration and the motivation. I owe much gratitude to family member, Eiko, who encouraged me decades ago to learn about the importance of the Meiji era and to Marilyn who provided me with details for the epilogue. In the beginning, when this was only a few chapters, I read pages over the phone to Bonnie Blanchard who always listened enthusiastically saying, "What happens next?" My fellow colleague, Lawanna Dixon, an English professor, kindly read a few versions of this story asking key questions and slashing through whole pages of unessential material. My writing buddy, Karen Marshall, encouraged me to treat the writing process as a job and provided emotional support throughout the editing and publishing process. My book designer, Rachel Sten read the story enthusiastically and ended up being a talented partner in the cover and book design. Caroline Leavitt, an editor found through the Reedsy website, provided excellent and thoughtful questions that were critical to the flow of the story. Archway Publishing has provided me the expert help needed for self-publishing.

Appendix

Cast of Characters

Japanese and Hawaiian Words

Cultural Glossary

Lao Tzu Quotes

Cast of Characters
Kumamoto Prefecture, Village of Five Bridges

Akeme	brother's girlfriend
Bufuku	village headman
Haru	silk merchant's son
Hachi	male cousin
Ito	friend, family of merchant class
Jintaro	uncle, father's older brother
Jito	manager of warehouse
Jun	kitchen boy
Madam Iwata	kitchen maid
Madam Kumodo	elder woman of samurai heritage
Masumo Oyama (Otasan)	father
Meme	female cousin
Miki	female cousin
Obachan Oyama	grandmother, father's mother
Roji Kobata	second son of local merchant
Saiko	friend, family of samurai class
Ueme Oyama	main character, Ueme (oo emm ay)
Ushio Oyama	brother
Watanabe	fishmonger
Yuki Oyama	mother

Journey across the Pacific

Akeme	passenger from merchant family
Kobayashi-san, "Old Socks"	man in charge of male passengers
Matron Ando	woman in charge of female passengers
Tameki	passenger on ship from wealthy merchant family

Hawaii, sugar plantation camp, North Shore, Oahu

Aduki	Tameki's husband
Aoki	friend from the cane fields
Elizabeth	wife of plantation owner
Hatsura, "Hatsu"	Ueme and Roji's baby
Hisako-san	elder woman with years of experience living on the plantation
Jona	Portuguese field supervisor, a luna
Kane	Hawaiian friend of Roji
Kikume	neighbor
Malia	Hawaiian woman from nearby village
Michiru "Michi"	bachelor worker on plantation
Mori	Kikume's husband
Tameki	friend from the ship

Japanese words

bango	number, used by plantation authorities instead of names to undermine spirits
Bushi	another term for samurai, Bushido

furo	deep small tub for soaking in very hot bath; one soaps down and rinses first
futon	thick quilt used as bedding, folded to fit in a closet during daytime
hai	yes
haiku	unrhymed verse with odd number of syllables, only three lines
hakama	traditional male trousers, very full
hashi	chopsticks
kimono	formal outerwear robe, often silk
kinshu	fine light silk crepe material—very smooth texture, popular in summer wear, dyed after weaving, decorated with hand painting
kombu	type of seaweed commonly used in fish stew
konjo	one's own inner spirit
kurumatsu	black pine, the seminal tree of a Japanese garden
meiji	enlightened rule, (may-jee)
mochi	short grain rice, pounded into thick sweet paste to make little cakes for special occasions
obachan	grandmother
otasan	father
raku	type of pottery using naturally occurring materials and dyes for glaze
rinzu	silk satin damask fabric; threads are dyed before weaving and form the design
sashimi	raw fish, fresh and sliced very thin on an angle
sen	one hundredth of a yen, the Japanese dollar
shakuhachi	Japanese bamboo flute, held vertically when played

shogun	military head of Tokugawa government that preceded the Meiji era
shogunate	referring to officers of the head of the Tokugawa government
tabi	cotton sock with separate part for big toe to be used with sandals
tako	squid
tenugui	thin cotton cloth used for small kitchen towels
yukata	cotton floor-length robe, summer kimono

Japanese Phrases

Konnichiwa	Good day
Konbanwa	Good evening
Kudasai	Please give me *"something"*
Ohayu gozai masu	Good morning
Onegaishimasu	Please, please give me (interchangeable with *kudasai*)
Sumimasen	I'm sorry; excuse me; thank you—as in, "I'm sorry for bothering you, but thank you for putting up with me." A humbling phrase.

Hawaiian Words

aikane	friend
aloha	hello, goodbye, love, with my love
koa	Hawaiian tree has beautiful wood used for decorative wood in household items and more
kokua	help

luau	feast where pig is roasted inground with ti leaves, banana leaves, and vegetables
luna	plantation field supervisor, many times a Portuguese man
muumuu	floor-length dress that has no waist
ohana	family group, community
pilikia	trouble
ti plant	Hawaiian plant with long, pointed red and green leaves
wahine	woman

Cultural Glossary

Basho. The poet who crystallized the telegram-like or stenography-like haiku style, considered the greatest master of haiku poetry. Basho lived from 1644 to 1694 and was the most famous poet of the Edo period in Japan.

> The old pond
> A frog leaps in.
> Splash!

Buddhism. One of two main religions in Japan. The religion's founder, Buddha, is considered an extraordinary man but not a god. The word *Buddha* means "enlightened." The path to enlightenment is attained by utilizing morality, meditation and wisdom. Buddhists often meditate because they believe it helps awaken truth. There are many philosophies and interpretations within Buddhism, making it a tolerant and evolving religion. Buddhism encourages its people to avoid self-indulgence but also to avoid self-denial.

Bushido, Bushi. "Way of the warrior," referring to samurai class code of behavior. Everything was bound to this code. It regulated how the samurai lived, worked, moved, and more. The "Bushido" demanded many aspects of the warriors, such as self-sacrifice, absolute loyalty, vigor, exceedingly superior weapon skills, and much more.

Buson, 1716–1784. A Japanese poet and painter of the Edo period. Along with Matsuo Bashō and Kobayashi Issa, Buson is considered among the greatest poets of the Edo period.

> In nooks and corners
> Cold remains
> Flowers of the plum

Confucianism. Stresses the importance of correct behavior, loyalty, and obedience to hierarchy. Confucianism is a system of ethics devised by the Chinese scholar Confucius in sixth century BC China. An itinerant teacher, Confucius essentially systematized elements of ancient Chinese philosophy. He emphasized the importance of the family and social harmony, creating a system of ritual norms and propriety that determined how a person should properly act in everyday life. According to the Confucian structure of society, women at every level were to occupy a position lower than men. Most Confucians accepted the subservience of women to men as natural and proper.

Koseki, 1867–1916. "Modern" poet of the Meiji era.

> Now gathering,
> Now scattering,
> Fireflies over the river.

Meiji era, 1868–1912. The Meiji era began as a political revolution that brought Japan from a feudal land system with a military government that had been isolated from the world for two hundred years to a modern era with a representative government within a short period of time. It caused dramatic economic, social, and cultural changes in the lives of the people. It was considered the era of enlightenment and was brought on by the country's need to strengthen itself to stand up to the Western powers that were colonizing Asian countries. The new emperor took the name Meiji as it meant "enlightened peace."

Moon Princess. A Japanese fairy tale. A fairy child is found by a lowly bamboo woodcutter and is adopted by him and his wife, who raise her as their own child. She grows up to be a great beauty. However, after many suitors ask unsuccessfully for her hand in marriage, she returns to her real home in the moon.

Raku Pottery. A type of Japanese pottery traditionally used in Japanese tea ceremonies, most often in the form of hand-shaped tea bowls made in a low fired kiln. It is highly valued for its naturalness.

Shintoism. One of two main religions in Japan. Human beings are basically good; there is no concept of original sin or of humanity as "fallen." Everything, including the spiritual, is experienced as part of this world. Shrines draw visitors from across the country, the Shinto rituals being an integral part of Japanese life. Shrine visiting and taking part in festivals play a great part in binding local communities together. It coexists with Buddhism with no conflicts.

Taoism. Philosophy of the Lao-tzu way of life. Lao-tzu was a Chinese philosopher of the sixth century. Taoism emphasizes the importance of nonaction, nonresistance, "going with the flow" to live an elevated and transformative life. The four base principles are *simplicity, patience, compassion,* and *harmony.* The focus of Taoism is the individual in nature, rather than the individual in society. It holds that the goal of life for each individual is to find one's own personal adjustment to the rhythm of the natural (and supernatural) world and to follow the Way (Tao) of the universe. In many ways, it is the opposite of rigid Confucian moralism. The phrase "ten thousand things" reflects the principle of the one is the many and the many is the one; might as well "go with the flow." "Water is fluid, soft, and yielding. But water will wear away rock, which is rigid and cannot yield. As a rule, whatever is fluid, soft, and yielding will overcome whatever is rigid and hard. This is another paradox: "What is soft is strong."

Zen. Exalting simplicity and mindfulness in the daily chaos of life. The samurai code exemplified Zen.

Lao Tzu Quotes from the Tao Te Ching

"Simplicity, patience, compassion.
These three are your greatest treasures.
Simple in actions and thoughts, you return to the source of being."

"Knowing others is intelligence;
knowing yourself is true wisdom.
Mastering others is strength;
mastering yourself is true power."

"The journey of a thousand miles begins with a single step."

"Be content with what you have;
rejoice in the way things are.
When you realize there is nothing lacking,
the whole world belongs to you."

"The Tao begot one.
One begot two.
Two begot three.
And three begot the ten thousand things."

(*The "Ten Thousand Things" refer to the distractions of daily life.*)

Printed in the United States
by Baker & Taylor Publisher Services